KITTY PECK AND THE PARLIAMENT OF SHADOWS

Kate Griffin was born within the sound of Bow bells, making her a true-born cockney. She has worked as an assistant to an antiques dealer, a journalist for local newspapers and most recently for the Society for the Protection of Ancient Buildings.

Kitty Peck and the Music Hall Murders, Kate's first book, won the *Stylist* / Faber crime-writing competition. Kate's maternal family lived in Victorian Limehouse and one of the inspirations for this series came from tales of life around the London docks told by her grandmother. Kate lives in St Albans.

Kitty Peck
and the
Parliament of Shadows

KATE GRIFFIN

FABER & FABER

First published in 2019
by Faber & Faber Limited
Bloomsbury House
74–77 Great Russell Street
London WC1B 3DA

Typeset by Faber & Faber Limited
Printed and bound by CPI Group (UK) Ltd, Croydon, CRO 4YY

A CIP record for this book
is available from the British Library

ISBN 978-0-571-32560-3

MIX
Paper from
responsible sources
FSC® C020471

2 4 6 8 10 9 7 5 3 1

For Oliver **Geoffrey** Cain, June Griffin and Joan Hewitt

Prologue

By hand
Sam

    My fingers are black. You should know that first off. I reckon I've drained a well of ink trying to write this. A hundred crumpled versions of what I want to tell you are lying on the boards round my feet. Seeing as how there's only four sheets of paper left now, I haven't got much choice in the matter.

    I didn't know how to begin, how to address you, I mean. In polite circles I suppose they write 'dear' or 'dearest', but it seemed a liberty.

    Thing is, Sam, I wonder why it is that I haven't heard from you? I know you're not dead. I've seen your name often enough in my newspaper these last two weeks to prove that you're very much alive.

    (I'm sure it hasn't escaped your notice that I'm paying your salary too – yours and all the others at The London Pictorial News. *Looking back, I should have realised it was more than a fancy to keep Mr Peters in tea leaves that made me buy it.)*

    I didn't know I had feelings for you until I thought you might be lost to me. Then, after what happened to you and Lucca, I didn't think I had a chance. I know he told you all about me when you were held prisoner together. Now you've had fair time to consider the matter at a distance, perhaps you've washed your hands? I wouldn't blame you, truly. Most men would put a desert between themselves and the trouble I carry around.

    But you're not most men, are you, Sam?

Don't get me wrong, I've seen through you. For a start, I've always thought that twitching and bumbling was a show. I'm in the trade, remember? I know a good act when I see one. You're sharp as a bailiff's nark, and sly with it. But what you did for Lucca was a fine thing, a brave thing. There's not many who'd do that. Even if I never hear from you again – and like I said, I wouldn't blame you – I'll always be grateful.

No. More than that. Much more.

When I read that note you left for me I went straight to my Bible and looked up the reference. I won't deny it, I was wound up tight as a lace maker's bobbin thinking you were taunting me, having a last clever word like you always do. But I was wrong. At least I think I was wrong.

Is that right?

I'm going round in circles here avoiding the target and I'm running out of paper.

I need to know, Sam, if you meant what you said about love.

There. I've written it down and it cost me. You'll notice the ink blot where my hand trembled on the word. If I had the paper I'd start again. It would be a blessing to know for a certainty one way or the other. I've got enough on my plate to keep me occupied without you taking up valuable room in my head.

Lucca said I should write to you. He says a lot of things. As you spent so much time cooped up with him, I imagine you know that already? If he wasn't an artist he'd make a good vicar – or a father 'fessor. That would be more his line, given he's a Roman. Thing is, he's usually right. I trust his judgement. These days Lucca Fratelli is the nearest thing I have to a brother.

He thinks I should be straight with you, shine up the past so we know exactly where we stand. He reckons you're waiting for me to show my hand. That's easier said than done, partly on account of the fact that I've not got the paper left, and partly because the past leads to the future.

I don't know if that's somewhere you'll want to join me. Not after you've read this.

You asked me once what I'd done to make Lady Ginger so partial that she passed her three halls and the bulk of her estate to me. You made it sound like a dirty thing, and you were right, but not in the way you sinuated.

In the end it was a matter of family.

Lady Ginger was my grandmother. It all begins there – and most likely it will end there too, but I'm getting ahead of myself.

She didn't just leave me her house in Salmon Lane or her scrag-end music halls or even her money. My own grandmother left me caught like a fly in the middle of a web. Sometimes when I try to imagine the threads of it, I can't see it whole – not the starting nor the finishing of it. It loops back into the past and it winds into the future, twisting itself into so many dark places that I'm frightened to move in case the shivering of the strings causes a spider to come scuttling from the shadows.

I reckon you understand by now who the spiders are? It's a funny thing, but I was never frightened of them as a child. Joey, now, that's another matter. Our rooms were festered with them, especially in the autumn when they trooped inside to find a nice dry hole. It was always me who caught them in a cup and carried them to the window.

I told you once about Joey. I loved my brother fierce. There was a time when I would have done anything for him, and I did, but it turns out he wasn't worth the effort. I don't know where he is now and I don't much care. That's a thing I never *thought to write, but I learned it the hardest way.*

I've only got one sheet left and I'm not getting to the meat.

The Barons are creatures to be feared, Sam. That's something you need to know whether or not you decide to answer this.

Most of them you wouldn't notice. There are a thousand black-backs in the City, sitting in silent offices behind great mahogany desks and spinning their threads. They buy the world cheap, wrap it up tight and parcel it off to the highest bidder on behalf of Her Majesty. Very respectable they are, with their plush little wives and pink-cheeked children; a house in the town, a place in the country and a plate on the family pew.

The Barons are just the same, except when they sit at the mahogany desks in their silent offices, they're waiting for a jangle on a web that hooks up every foul trade and noxious game you can imagine. And some, I'm glad for your sake, you probably can't. I wouldn't be surprised if the fog that rolls regular from the river isn't the steam off their labours. They've got it all portioned and weighed. They all have their place in the scheme of filthy things and a territory to call their own.

Like I said, you're a clever man, Sam. You knew she was a Baron all along, didn't you? Lady Ginger, I mean. And now you know about me.

A year back when my grandmother knew she was dying she passed everything to me – her territory, Paradise, included. She told me it was named for plenty; the spices and the silks, the furs and the ivory, the tobacco and the opium – everything that washes up right here on the banks of the dirty grey river. Everything that washes up in my lap.

At first I was flattered, I won't deny it, and I won't insult you by pretending I didn't understand what I was entering into when

4

I agreed to take it from her, even though Lucca warned me.

It was like a game at the beginning. My head was so turned by the crowd that called out my name night after night in the halls when I was singing seventy foot up in that cage that I wanted to hear them shout for me again. The joke of it is that you gave me the name they was hollering. It was you who called me The Limehouse Linnet when you first saw me perform in my cage at The Gaudy. You wrote it in your newspaper and the name stuck.

Even though Paradise was riddled with rot like the canker eating my grandmother from the inside out, I thought I could deal with it in my own way. I reckoned I could brush it up, make it a cleaner place for the poor types who came with the dirty trades. I could make them all love me, I thought.

I was wrong about that. I've been wrong about so much.

'We have fallen, but the wonders and riches of the world are crammed into the warehouses that huddle by the Thames.' That's what my grandmother said the night I took her place as a Baron. She made it sound like a second Garden of Eden.

Well, I've fallen right enough. Like I said, my fingers are black, but not just with ink.

Bad luck follows me around like a starving dog. It sniffs at my skirts and snaps at the heels of everyone I care about. You need to mark that, Sam, because the Barons will have marked you. They have a particular interest in my family and anyone close.

The very first time I spoke to my grandmother she said my brother was a murderer. I didn't believe her, but she was telling the truth. Joey Peck murdered one of the Barons and the man he killed was the brother of Lord Kite, the most powerful among their number.

I fear him. I fear them all, but Kite the most. His real name

*– the name he goes by in his business – is Anthony Carstone.
The Barons dress their cant with secret names and ceremonies
that would turn a cardinal green. They treat it very serious and
that's the greatest joke of all. I suppose it takes a girl from the halls
to see through to the bone.*

*Carstone's a legal, a judge, and he's got the reins of the law
tight in his hands. I'm telling you this because in your line of
work you might come across him, and because you'll need to know
it if he comes for you.*

*Soon he'll come for me. Not Kite personally, you understand –
he's too grand to dirty his hands. Most likely it will be his man of
trade, Matthias Schalk.*

*You already know him, Sam. He took your eye in place of
Lucca's.*

*There's less than half a side of paper left. I've been scratching
away all night and it's light outside. Lok is standing at the door
now. I asked him to come to me sharp at six to collect this letter.
He's to put it into your hand only. He won't wait around for an
answer and I don't expect one immediate. You'll need to think
hard before you come to a certainty.*

*I've not got the space to tell you more, except to say I'm not a
Baron, not any more. I'm Kitty Peck, proprietor, female, of three
dog-kennel music halls in the arse end of London. But it's not
over with the Barons. There's only one way out of their number
and it don't come with a pat on the back and a golden fob.*

*I'm going to make them pay for what they are and for what
they've done. I swear it on my mother's grave. Turns out Lady
Ginger left me what you might call a family obligation there.
It's the one thing I've been happy to take from her hands.*

I wasn't straight with you from the beginning and I should have been. I've caused you pain and a loss I cannot repay. I've led you into danger and I regret that more than I can say. But even if you never want to see me again you'll be walking in my shadow and that's a dark place.

I'd be a liar if I said I didn't want you walking beside me, Sam Collins.

Yours in truth,
Kitty

Chapter One

The limes were spitting like cats and burning fit for Guy Fawkes. I could hardly make out the body slumped in a chair in the middle of the stage on account of the light.

I shielded my eyes, but it didn't do no good. I still couldn't see him clear. He was just a shadow beyond the flickering wall. I wasn't sure I wanted to, not after what Fitzy said about the way he'd found him.

Three tables and six chairs were set out in a neat row just below the apron of The Carnival's stage. That was when he knew something was up, Fitzy said. The night before, see, he'd piled the furniture up against the sides to get to the floorboards. There'd been complaints about the smell fugging up the hall and it was most likely rats, dead ones, a rotten nest of them. As manager of The Carnival, he'd come in early with a crowbar to take up the floor and deal with it.

Fitzy had found a corpse right enough, but it wasn't a rat and it wasn't buried under The Carnival's greasy boards.

He pointed to the table in the centre of the row. Two figures showed up black against the blinding light from the stage.

'You want to take a look at them first.' He fished a silver flask from a pocket in his chequered jacket. I noted the tremor in his hands as he unscrewed the cap. For once I gave him the benefit. I didn't think it was the liquor that made him fumble.

From behind, it looked like there were two children, a boy and a girl, sitting there meek as a Sunday school in front of the stage. The girl's long black hair was twisted into a plait that trailed over the back of the chair, and the red mop on the boy caught the flare from the cups dancing dangerously high along the apron. I went forward until I was almost level with them.

I could feel the heat off the limes licking my face. The brass cups jittered with the force of it. I turned to Lucca and Tan Seng, who were standing behind me. Tan Seng's unlined, oval face was blank as usual, he never gave anything away, but the skin around Lucca's one good eye pulled tight as he stared up at the stage.

I pointed back down the hall to the fringed curtain drawn across the doorway leading out to the street.

'Tan Seng, will you stand out front and make sure no one comes in, please? It's early, but you never know. The hands need to go through the hall to the workshops.'

'Lady.'

He bowed and slipped silently back to the entrance. His long grey plait, still black at the tip, swished down the back of his sober tunic as he walked. I rarely went anywhere these days without one of the Chinese brothers who'd come to me with my grandmother's house. Tan Seng and Lok had been Lady Ginger's servants, but I was glad to call them my friends.

I turned to Lucca. 'Can you go behind and turn the cylinders down? Firing like this, they'll take The Carnival and everything in it.' He nodded and went to the stairs at the right of the stage, disappearing behind the painted flaps that screened off the sides.

I shouted after him. 'Turn them low, but don't turn them off.'

A moment later the hissing grew faint and the brass stopped chinking. The limes dimmed, but there was still a glint in the black glass eyes of Signor Marcelli's red-haired boy. Which was more than I could say for Lena.

Deep scratches slanted across the marionette's painted face and there were two ragged black holes where someone had gouged out her eyes. The shadowy pits gave her the look of a skull.

To be straight, I never liked Lena and her brother Milo, them being the names Signor Marcelli gave his darlings. To my mind there was something sinister about their hard, pointed little faces. In the act they were supposed to be his children, but their rouged cheeks, dark arched brows and pouting lips gave the impression that they were adults shrunk in the wash.

Lena was the worst. I'd seen tuppenny bangtails north of forty who looked a deal more innocent than she did. Signor Marcelli was a regular slave to her paintwork on account of the harshness of the limelight.

'My little one has to look her best.' That's what he used to tell us as he dabbed at her lips and brought a rosy glow to her wooden cheeks. Lucca said it was like he was in love with her and I reckoned he was right. Thing is, I didn't think Signor Marcelli loved Lena like a child and that's why I was wary of her. And I didn't go much on him, neither, even though the punters liked him well enough. He was a peculiar, scrawny-limbed little man, with a painted face like his marionettes. God rest his soul.

It was unnerving the way that bleedin' puppet sat there now with her wooden hands cupped in the lap of her white smock. As I grew customed to the light, I saw there was something in her upturned palm. I reached down, but she was finely balanced on the seat and the movement disturbed her. She slipped to the left. One arm dislodged from its pose to swing loose at the side.

Something, *things* more rightly, fell to the floor. One skittered over the boards towards Fitzy. The other span round and came to a rest next to my foot. I bent to take it up and turned the small twisted lump around in my fingers, trying to make sense of what I was looking at.

'I think it is an ear, Fannella.'

Lucca had come down from the stage. As he stared at the shell-like object, the scars tightened round his mouth.

'And here's its mate.' Fitzy held out a similar curled nubble. The hairs on the back of his fat freckled hand showed up ginger in the limelight.

'From the boy.' He nodded at the other puppet, blew out his cheeks and added, unnecessarily, 'Some bastard's cut off his ears.'

He delivered that in a tone of mournful disgust as if it was genuine meat and gristle he was clutching, not a bit of pink-painted plaster. I almost laughed out loud, but I buttoned it on account of what was on the stage behind me. It didn't seem respectful.

I turned to Milo and pushed back his thick red hair. It was just the same as the girl. Ugly grooves and deep score marks across the side of the puppet's head showed where the ear had been hacked away. The knife, or whatever it was that had been used to do this, had cut through the plaster to the wood beneath. Frayed splinters fringed the plaster wound. Even though this wasn't a child of flesh and blood, the butchery was still uncomfortable to look at. This hadn't been a delicate, careful job; the jagged furrows bore witness to a savage attack.

Of an instant, I caught a scent, or thought I did. Just recently I'd been waking in the early hours convinced there was someone with me in the dark, someone standing so close to my bed

12

I could smell the leather and spice of their cologne.

I glanced at Lucca.

'Do you recognise it?'

He frowned. 'Recognise what?'

'The stink of cologne. I thought . . .' I stopped myself. Even as I put it into words, I knew I was mistaken.

Lucca shook his head slowly. 'There is a . . . scent here, Fannella, but it is not cologne.' He looked to the shadowy figure on the stage and crossed himself. I took a sharp breath and caught his meaning. Signor Marcelli must have loosened his bowels and pissed himself, poor sod.

I stroked Milo's hair back into place, but he slid towards his sister. Someone had cut the strings off both puppets in order to make them more amenable to arrangement. Now they were slumped at the table together like a pair of drunken half-pint punters, their heads angled close to take in the view.

Fitzy held out the flask. 'You might need a drop of this before you go up there.' He jerked his fat head towards the stage. 'A terrible sight, so he is.'

I ignored the offer. 'You told anyone else about this?'

I heard the wet glug of Fitzy's swallow as he tipped back the flask and drank deep. He wiped the neck on his cuff and offered it to Lucca, who stepped back sharp, surprised and, given his notable fastidious nature, most probably repelled.

'I sent the boy to The Palace, straight after I found him.' Fitzy moved the flask from hand to hand as he spoke, the silver glinting greenish in the limelight. 'Then I was reacquainted with my breakfast.'

Fitzy's little eyes slid to the stage. I saw a shudder roll across his broad shoulders. He crossed himself, which was most unlike him, and Lucca – being of the same persuasion, but a more regular kneeler – did the same, again.

What was up there?

Two months back, when Netta Swift lit up like a Roman candle on the night of her first solo outing at The Carnival, it had been Fitzy who had doused the flames with buckets of sand. But not before we all got an eyeful of the pitiful, blackened wreck of her. I thought I'd never get the rancid pork-chop stench of melted human flesh out of my nose, but Fitzy, now, he took it in his stride.

If the sight and smell of Netta didn't turn his gin-lined guts, then Signor Marcelli must have been a ripe eye-poker. I looked up at the stage. Now the limes were burning lower it was mostly in shadow, only the sloping boards showed clear. From where I was standing all I could see was the back of a chair.

Fitzy cleared his throat and pointed at the steps. 'I think you'd best go up and have a look before I clear him away.' He rolled Milo's ear around in his palm. 'If you think these two are . . . Well, like I said, take a look for yourself.'

I couldn't put it off any longer. I put Milo's right ear on the table and wiped my hands on my skirt like it was real. I turned to the stage.

'You two follow me up.'

*

Nanny Peck, the woman I thought to be my true grandmother until I knew different, used to let me play with her wool box. We'd sit together in front of the hearth and she'd show me how to wrap yarn round and round my hands, changing the pattern with a single movement of the wrist or a twist of a finger. I thought about the old girl and her yarn game now.

Signor Marcelli was caught in a cat's cradle. The limes flickering in a semicircle behind him cast his shadow to the back of the stage, but I could see a tangle of criss-cross strings rising above him.

We'd gone up the side stairs and now we were standing to the right of the stage. It was plain as the boil on Fitzy's nose that none of us wanted to go any closer. I glanced at Lucca; the scars down the right side of his face pulled tight round his mouth and jaw.

'Like I said, you'd best take a look.' Fitzy motioned me forward in the way you might usher a guest into a parlour. Apart from that fussy flap of the hand, he didn't shift himself. I went three steps nearer before the stench of blood stopped me short. My feet turned to lead. The boards squeaked as Lucca came to stand next to me. He took my hand and I gripped tight.

'Courage, Fannella,' he whispered. We went forward together.

I could see Signor Marcelli quite clear now. A thick black, flat-headed nail had been driven into the old man's upturned hand. It split his palm and bored straight through to the wooden arm of the chair. His other hand was nailed to the opposite arm and his bare feet were skewered to the boards. One of his toes was pulped and crushed where the hammer blow had missed its mark.

The head of another nail protruded from his breeches. There was a wet dark mess in his lap.

'Jesus Christ!' I tore my eyes away and stared up into the flights where the strings attached to the nails in his body disappeared into

15

the gantry walks far overhead. Signor Marcelli had been strung up like one of his own puppets.

'*È l'opera del diavolo.*'

I heard Lucca whispering a prayer in the Roman. If I'd been a Bible type I might have joined him. My stomach pitched like a herring smack. No wonder Fitzy saw his breakfast again. I swiped at the tears running down my face.

'It doesn't get any better the second time, so it doesn't.' I heard the whistle of air through the thicket in Fitzy's nostrils as he breathed deep. 'I thought you should see it for yourself. His face, now . . .' The metallic rasp of the flask cap came again and the cut of cheap gin in the air was a relief. 'The mouth. I haven't touched it. I left it for you.'

I couldn't see what he meant at first.

The limes were burning low now and Signor Marcelli had his back to them, his chin buried on his chest. The boot black he used to paint hair on his balding crown was melting onto his collar. I didn't want to touch him.

Lucca squeezed my hand as I reached out to tip back the old man's head.

I couldn't hold down the yelp of horror.

His cheeks had been slit from the corners of his mouth to his ears, and then the gaping bloody wreck of his face had been crudely sewn together again. Wide black stitches sealed his puckered lips together into a permanent, hideous, lop-sided grin. The effect of it, with all the strings rising around him, made poor Signor Marcelli look even more like one of his own marionettes.

Fitz cleared his throat. 'What kind of a bastard would do that to a man?'

'Schalk.' Lucca whispered the name that had been slicing through my mind like the swish of a blade since Fitzy's smudge-faced messenger boy had arrived breathless at The Palace. The scent of leather and spice came to me again, tart as the image of the hawk-headed cane that Matthias Schalk carried in his left hand. He wasn't lame and he wasn't a man of fashion. That bleedin' cane of his was a weapon.

As I stood there, looking down at the wreck of Signor Marcelli's face, I thought about what Schalk had done to Lucca. What he'd done to all of them – Danny, Old Peter, Netta, little Edie, Swami Jonah, Brigid . . . Sam.

God forgive me, but at that moment I found myself think-ing most especially about Sam. If Lok had done as I'd asked, he'd have read my letter by now. I felt the shift of the hairs on the back of my neck. Maybe writing it out like that had twisted the key and now all the clockwork cogs and gears were turning to a conclusion?

I heard Fitzy mutter something under his faded whiskers and turned to face him.

'I didn't catch that.'

I waited for him to repeat himself, although I knew full well what he'd said.

'Jonah.' That's what he'd called me from the day I inherited three halls, The Carnival, The Comet and The Gaudy, from my grandmother. He had a point. The Gaudy had burned to the ground, The Comet was still being repaired after I'd fallen from the ceiling in my cage, taking half the ceiling with it, and The Carnival reeked of Netta's death. Even if it wasn't the actual roast-meat stench that lingered, it was the membrance. And now Signor Marcelli.

'You'll have to do something about that mumbling, Fitzpatrick. A person might suppose your wits have gone for a ramble.' I stared at him, trying to master the fear stroking a feather down my spine. 'The boy you sent, did he see any of this?'

Fitzy shook his head. 'After I found the poor bugger, I needed some air. I went out front to the street. The coal drays were about early. I gave the carrier's lad a penny to fetch you and a sixpence to his master for the use of him. I'm the only one who knows about this.'

He paused and seemed to examine the reflection of his face in the flask in his hands. 'It's not like we want the law to come knocking, is it, Ma'am?'

He gave that last courtesy a garnish of insolence and took another swig. I caught Lucca's eye before I answered, slowly.

'You did well, Fitzpatrick. Your discretion is noted. And now I want you to deal with the body. Treat it decent, with proper respect, but take it away somewhere and lose it.' I felt Lena's sightless eyes on me from the hall as I went on. 'It's not as if he had family, so there's not likely to be anyone asking questions.'

'But what about the other acts? Even if he didn't have family, they . . .' Lucca faltered as I turned to him.

'Are you telling me he'll be missed?' I felt bad putting it so spare without dressing it up, but it was the truth and we all knew it. I wouldn't wish ill on Signor Marcelli, but I wouldn't wish him luck either and I knew the turns he shared the bottom end of the bill with felt the same. I'd seen the way they avoided him backstage and out in the workshops. He wasn't what you'd call popular, which was a sort of relief under the circumstances.

'Of course, people will be curious as to where he's gone.' I looked straight into Fitzy's bloodshot eyes. He had a mouth on him slack as a sandboy's pouch, so I spoke slowly to be certain we understood each other. 'I reckon he's moved north, to Leeds, say, or maybe Edinburgh, don't you? They still like the old stuff up there. From what I hear The Panopticon in Glasgow's a regular rest home for sentimentals. So, if anyone enquires after Signor Marcelli's whereabouts you'll say he's taken up an offer he couldn't refuse.'

'Well, that's true enough, so it is.' Fitzy wiped the back of a hand across his mouth. 'You'll be knowing the story of the three wise monkeys, Ma'am?'

Of course I did. It was one of Nanny Peck's particulars. I quizzed at him. 'What's that got to do with Signor Marcelli?'

Even as I asked the question, I had a clarity. As did Lucca.

'*Non vedere il male. Non sentire il male. Non parlare male.*'

He turned to the darkened hall where the puppets slumped together. 'Lena's eyes, Milo's ears and . . .' He crossed himself again.

I forced myself to look again at the stitches sealing Marcelli's slashed and bloodied mouth. For all his faults – and God knows there were enough of them to keep him jawing in a 'fessional until a fortnight after the second coming – Fitzy knew a theatrical tableau when he saw one.

See no evil. Hear no evil. Speak no evil.

It was a message.

Since that time at the cemetery when I'd taken my grandmother's bitter little corpse on its last outing, I'd been waiting for them. When nothing happened for what seemed a very long time I even wondered, of occasion, if they'd forgotten me.

I barked out a laugh and just as quick I smacked a hand over my mouth to force it back and seal the noise inside. Lucca and Fitzy stared at me like I was a Bedlam.

I might have finished with the Barons, but the Barons hadn't finished with me.

Chapter Two

The steps of the hack clattered down to the cobbles. Tan Seng went out first. He stood for a moment, turning his head slowly from left to right. When he was certain of safety, he offered up a hand to help me down. The light blinded me for an instant as I stepped through the narrow door. A gust of wind caught the ribbons from my bonnet and whips of dark blue satin stung my cheeks. Lucca clamped a hand to his own broad-brimmed hat as he joined us in the road. He always wore that hat when we went about. Conscious of his scars, he hid them in the shadow.

It wasn't far from The Carnival to Salmon Lane, less than a mile, but we'd kept the blinds drawn close all the way back. We didn't talk as we sat there in the gloom, breathing in fusty leather and listening to the clip of the hooves, the squeak of the springs and the rumble of the wheels.

Once I'd squared it with the driver, we set off in a tight huddle down Salmon Lane, turning sharp into the alley leading to The Palace. There was a time when I thought the house my grandmother had left to me was a fine thing. She'd ruled Paradise from here, sitting in her nest of cushions on the second floor, coiled about with the noxious fug from her opium pipe. French jet eyes glinting through the smoke, she'd tap her ringed bony fingers on the boards, give orders in that peculiar voice – my grandmother spoke like a child who'd swallowed a mouthful of fine dinner crystal – and the world turned. The sheer force of her will made everyone see both her and her house as something great and terrible.

Years back when we lived in two rooms off Church Row, Nanny Peck had told me and Joey stories from her old country. As a consequence, I knew all about the danger of the glamour. The little folk could blind the unwary, she warned us. Their spells could make a mortal believe the impossible.

I should have paid more attention to those tales.

Now The Palace was mine. It was a good deal cleaner and more fragrant inside than it had been in half a century, but without Lady Ginger clicking her fingers and rattling her jewels it had lost the glamour. These days, all I saw when I looked up at its soot-stained bricks, peeling paint and rows of narrow windows was another sort of cage.

Peggy was waiting in the hall. She was sitting barefoot on the stairs in her wrapper. Sunlight slanted from the fan over the doors, shining up the red in her dark hair.

She stood, put her hands to her waist and arched her back. The rounded bump of her unborn baby showed clear against the cotton.

'You were up at the crack. I thought you'd all deserted me. What was it that took you out so urgent?' She waited for a reply. Lucca removed his hat and started to fumble with the rim and Tan Seng found a smut on the brass of the door handle that needed attention.

We were an odd collation, I won't deny it.

Lucca and Peggy lived with me at The Palace now. I'd insisted on it. I told them both it was for my sake. I dressed it up and said I felt safer having them around, but the truth was quite the opposite. I wanted them where I could protect them.

For once, Lucca hadn't argued. Tell truth, I'd expected him to put up more of a fight about it, him being so independent and having . . . well, let's just say he had a particular life of his own to attend to. Then again, after what happened with Matthias Schalk, I wasn't surprised.

Lucca needed friends nearby when the nightmares came. These days they came often. I was no lay abed, but it didn't matter what time I roused myself, of a generality I'd find him sitting alone in the parlour, dressed for the day with a book open on his lap.

I'd arranged for all his gear – his paints, canvases, sketches, brushes and that – to be brought to The Palace from his lodgings by the river. Now he had a room for his art at the top of the house just below the attics, where the tall arched windows gave a view over the roofs of Limehouse to the masts of the ships riding on the river.

The light was good for painting, he said, but I noted he never went up there.

Point of fact, he never went anywhere much. We didn't talk about it, but I knew Lucca couldn't go back to the workshops. After Matthias Schalk forced him to paint those vile pictures of me at The Comet and at The Carnival he couldn't face the memory of what he'd done.

Fitzy wasn't pleased to lose his best painter. These days the old knuckler's ample backside was lodged most firmly in the chair behind the desk at The Carnival. He was revelling in his role as titular manager of my halls, lording over the hands and the acts as if he was the actual proprietor.

To be fair to him, which is something I never thought I'd say, he was making a good fist of the job. The Carnival was actually turning a mouse-spit profit again, and I knew he was itching to make an impression with The Comet when it re-opened.

Part of that impression was his plan for a grand mural of the 'muses at play' above the arch. What he had in mind, he told Lucca, was 'something artistic'.

This turned out to be a group of ample beauties disporting themselves in a field with only the faintest suggestion of drapery minding the view of their arts. When Lucca refused, Fitzy took it as a personal slight on his taste. He asked me to force him to take the job, but I never mentioned it.

I knew why Lucca never wanted to paint a mural at The Comet again.

'Has Lok come home yet, Peg?' I pulled a pin from the crown of my bonnet.

She shook her head. 'He went off early too. He brought me tea before he went.'

Like his brother Tan Seng, Lok was old. I didn't know which of them was the senior and I couldn't put a figure to either of them. They didn't look much alike. Tan Seng was around my height with a face smooth and gold as a harvest moon. Lok was tiny with skin crumpled up like morning bed sheets.

Tan Seng had a curious grace to him and something I might describe as presence. He was more serious than Lok and given to still moments of distant thoughtfulness. In contrast, his wiry brother was wound tight as a clockwork mouse. Rest wasn't something that came natural to Lok and, as a consequence, The Palace was a shining tribute to his skills with a duster and a tin of beeswax. Where Tan Seng liked to keep his thoughts private, Lok was a gossip and, on account of that and a natural affinity between them, Peggy was his friend.

If I ever tried to quiz the brothers about their past, they had a neat way of changing the subject or slipping away to attend

24

to something more urgent. The things I knew for a certainty were that Lady Ginger had come across them in the halls and taken them into her service; that they were utterly loyal to her. And that now they were loyal to me.

Peggy yawned and covered her pretty mouth with her hand. These days there was a ripeness to her I was glad to see. There was a glow to her skin that suggested somewhere deep inside there was a lamp burning bright.

'Before he went off, Lok said Fitzy wanted to see you. What brought him out of his kennel so early, Kit? He's no lark.' She looked from Lucca to Tan Seng and then at me. The set of our faces must have told her this hadn't been a regular bit of business.

'Something's happened, hasn't it?' Her hand clutched the wrapper, wrinkling the fabric tight across her body. 'It's not . . . it's not Danny, is it? Have you . . . heard something?'

The question was almost a whisper.

Danny! Always Danny with her. Every day Peggy Worrow lived in hope of hearing that her man, Danny Tewson, was coming back. He wasn't, not unless he was a second Lazarus.

I was about to say something tart, but I buttoned it. Peggy was a good soul. I'd known her since we worked together back-stage in the halls. Apart from Lucca she was my oldest friend. There was a time when I could tell her everything, but I could never tell her the truth about Danny. She deserved better from me, and certainly not the lash of my tongue.

I shook my head. 'No, Peg. It was nothing to do with Dan.'

She sighed. It was a sound of a relief watered with disappointment.

I turned the hat pin between my fingers, wondering how

25

much to say. The light from the fan caught the facets of the blue glass stone set at the blunt end. It didn't seem right to describe what we'd seen at The Carnival to a woman in her condition. Peggy didn't need to know the detail.

I decided to keep it simple, but close to the truth.

'Signor Marcelli is dead. Fitzy found him at The Carnival this morning. That's why he sent word.'

'What happened?' Peggy's hand loosened on the wrapper. She came down the last few stairs to stand on the black and white marble tiles of the hall. I twiddled the pin and didn't look at her direct.

'When Fitzy went to open up, Signor Marcelli was on stage with his puppets. He . . .'

I cast around for a way to finish that and I was grateful when Lucca carried on.

'He used to practise . . . at night after everyone had gone, do you remember, Peggy? How he liked to be alone there with Milo . . . and with Lena.' He placed an emphasis on the girl puppet's name that opened a box of meanings, none of them pleasant.

I saw a sort of understanding flower in Peggy's eyes.

'Is that it?' She grimaced. 'He must have been well past sixty, maybe near seventy. It was hard to tell under all that paint he used on himself. It was his heart I suppose.'

It was a statement rather than a question. When none of us spoke she took our silence for agreement.

'Well, I never liked him much, or them puppets of his, especially that Lena. Horrible lively thing she was. I know it's wrong to speak ill of the dead, but if you want my opinion, I don't reckon he'll be missed.'

A part of me was glad to hear her say that. It's what I was banking on. I pulled off my bonnet and placed it on the hall table next to a vase of roses. As I did so a scatter of yellow petals fell to the floor. The roses were Lok's doing; he liked to have fresh flowers around the place.

I wondered about that letter. Lok would have put it direct into Sam's hand by now. I felt a quick sharp jab beneath the ribs at the thought of him reading it.

Peggy brought me back.

'What's going to happen then? Is he going to be buried decent? I don't mind telling you, Kit, there's not many who'll follow his coffin.' Her bare feet slapped on the tiles as she went to gather up the fallen petals. She straightened up and faced me. 'It's a shame, but there it is.'

I glanced at Lucca. 'There's not going be a funeral. To be straight with you, Peg, I don't want word getting around that he died on stage. The Carnival's had its share of bad luck recently and that's not good for trade. I've asked Fitzy to deal with it. He'll put it about that Signor Marcelli's gone north. An offer from Leeds.'

As I lied, the small silk bird sewn to the brim of the bonnet regarded me with glittering black-bead eyes. There was a loud metallic rattle and a precise, cold voice called out from somewhere above.

'*Deal with it. Deal with it.*'

There were times when it was as if that bleedin' bird could read my thoughts. Jacobin, my grandmother's mangy grey parrot, had come to me along with The Palace. He lived in a big gilt cage in the corner of the parlour. The worst of it was that he'd picked up Lady Ginger's voice – along with her malice – to perfection. Half the time you could almost believe it was her hunched up in the shadows, watching and listening.

Peggy wrinkled her nose and turned to look up the stairs. She didn't like Jacobin, and neither did I.

'There's another early riser.' She pushed the petals into the pocket of her wrapper. 'So that's the story, is it? He's gone to Leeds?' She nodded. 'I can see the sense of that, I won't deny it, especially after what happened to Netta. But what about his landlord, Old Steddings? Signor Marcelli's been lodged with him down Maize Row for as long as I can remember. He'll likely miss him, although he'll be about the only one who does.'

I'd already thought of that. I carried on twirling the pin. If I let my eyes roam into the glass, I could see tiny versions of my face, pale and pointed, reflected over and over in the facets. I didn't look up.

'I imagine he'll miss the rent, Peg, but not much else. I've asked Fitzy to make a visit to his rooms, pay his bills and collect his belongings. He'll tell Steddings the same story – that Marcelli's had a smart offer and gone north. Before he went – in a terrible hurry he was – he asked for his things to be sent on.'

'But what about a funeral? Even if you're not telling folk he's dead, you've got to bury him somewhere. It's only decent, even under the circumstances.' Peggy turned to Lucca. 'He was one of your lot, I should think?'

'*Sì*.' Lucca shuffled uncertainly. 'It's been some time since I last went to mass, but I think Signor Marcelli . . . he . . .'

He was about to be wrapped in an oilcloth and dumped in the Thames estuary east of Gravesend; I knew that's what Lucca was thinking. It was all decided before we left The Carnival. I cut in to save his guilty conscience.

'I've asked Fitzy to deal with that too. It will be quiet, nothing fancy.' I looked at her now. 'On the parish.'

'Well, it sounds like you've got it all worked out then, Kit.' Peggy stared at me for a moment longer than was comfortable. 'You're being straight with me, aren't you?'

'Of course I am.' It came out too quick. I dropped the pin to the marble floor. It spun around in a lazy circle and came to a rest with the sharp end pointing at me.

Peggy bent to retrieve it. 'Is that right?'

I nodded as she straightened up and handed it to me.

'Only when you came in through that door just now, your face was paler than a sheet of Bible tripe. And there's blood on the hem of your dress, Kit.'

Chapter Three

The faded Turkey rug was still covered with my half-finished letters, every one different, every one wrong. There was a disorderly mound of papers covered with my scrawl spread across the desk too.

I wondered if he'd read my letter yet. Or perhaps he'd thrown it away without bothering to open it? Christ! I'd just spent half the morning staring at a corpse and all I could think about was whether or not Sam Collins still cared for me.

'You need to get a grip on yourself, girl.' I spoke aloud and tried to concentrate on Signor Marcelli.

See no evil. Hear no evil. Speak no evil.

I reckoned Fitzy was right about the three wise monkeys. It was never simple with the Barons. There was a message tangled up in them strings tied to the old man's body, but what did it mean?

'Think!'

Somewhere outside, a bell chimed the hour. Depending on the wind and the season, the bells that sounded in Salmon Lane were either swung in the tower at St Dunstan's over Stepney way, or closer to home at St Anne's, Limehouse. This was a flat, dull, broken sound. According to Lucca, there was a crack as wide as a fist in the skirt of the single bell in the tall square tower at St Anne's. I counted twelve leaden strokes.

He'd had that bleedin' letter for at least four hours.

'Tell truth', now that was a neat little phrase that always came easy to my lips, but it was a very difficult thing to put down on paper. What would Sam think of me now?

When Peggy saw the blood, I couldn't get away from the hallway fast enough. I cantered up the stairs to my room without giving her the answer she wanted.

At that moment all I wanted was to get out of that dress and wash away the stench of Signor Marcelli. Tell truth, I wanted to get away from Peggy too, from the accusing look on her face.

I planted my elbows on the desk top, rested my forehead in the heels of my hands and shut my eyes.

There was a soft tap. I ignored it, but whoever it was tried again. I heard the rattle of the handle and a creak as the door swung open. I looked up to see Lucca out on the landing. He bent to retrieve the tray at his feet. Straightening up, he stared at the papers strewn across the table, the rug and the boards. There was a crumpled ball near the door. He kicked it as he entered the room and it skittered towards the hearth.

'You'll need to clear a space for this, Fannella.'

He crossed to the desk and waited while I moved the mess to one side. In the confusion earlier, I'd left the pen lying open. Black ink had seeped into the worktop, leaving a bruise in the leather. I started to rub at the stain with the tip of a finger, but it spread the mark. I balled my hand into a fist and thumped it down hard.

'Useless.'

I wasn't talking about the desk.

'I'll bring some turpentine from the attic – it might help.'

I looked up. Lucca's brown eye was round and knowing as an owl's. He'd taken to wearing his thick dark hair combed forward to hide the scarred half of his face. It suited him. He was still thin from the illness, but then again, he never had much meat on his frame. It was only the purple-grey hollow slung beneath his left eye that told a tale.

'Tea – just as you like it, Fannella. Just tea, no milk.'

Fannella was his special name for me. It came from a time when I was no more than a slop girl clearing out the halls. Lucca was on stage late one evening, fixing up a bit of damaged scenery, and I was up in the gallery thinking that all I had in the way of company was a frowsy mop. I was singing, as was usual, and when I stopped to rinse out God knows what, I heard someone clapping on the stage. I leaned over the rail and there he was at the front of the apron, lit up like a demon in the flares.

On account of his face – all puckered and scarred on one side – all the girls in the halls were wary of Lucca. And I was too back then. I ducked down quick, thinking he hadn't seen me. Limelight is a dangerous thing. Word put about was that Lucca Fratelli had got himself badly burned up west. Why else would a talented scenery painter hide himself away in a thruppenny hall?

As I hid there behind the rail, choking on the rank coming off the mop, I heard him start clapping again.

'Bravo, *Fannella,* bravo.' That's what he called out. Back in Naples where he came from originally, Fannella means 'little bird'. The name stuck, and so did we. After that night we was close as two halves of a walnut.

Lucca rested the tray on the desk. I noted that there were two cups and saucers set out beside the pot. He pulled out the chair opposite and sat down.

'It was a terrible thing to see. Signor Marcelli was a strange man, but to die like that . . .' He shook his head, crossed himself and muttered something in the way of a prayer.

'I think we both need this.' Lifting the china pot from the tray, he poured a stream of hot amber liquid into a cup and handed it to me. As steam wound into the air between us I caught the tang of smoke and spice. Truly, I never understood all the fuss about a decent cup of tea until I came to live at The Palace. Lok and Tan Seng had taught me a lot. I don't think I'd ever swallow a sour mouthful of London dish rag again, not after the tea the brothers brewed up. Lucca filled his own cup and stirred in a spoonful of sugar and then another. I was glad to see it.

As I sat opposite him now, sipping my tea from a fine china cup like a lady, not slurping from the dish like the slop girl I was, I knew that the nutshell bond between us had nearly been the death of him. And another. The tea burned my throat as I thought about Sam and swallowed hard. I was a dangerous person to know.

Lucca put his cup down and looked at the balls of paper on the rug.

'You have written at last.'

I nodded. 'It went off first thing this morning. I set it all out, just like you said I should. I told him everything, nearly everything . . .' I took another mouthful of tea. There were some things I couldn't write down in case it made them true.

I felt Lucca's eye on me and rattled on sharp. 'Lok took the letter to Holborn this morning. I told him not to leave it with anyone else, but to put it direct into Sam's hand. I want to be sure.'

Lucca nodded slowly. Don't get the thought in your head that he might be jealous. With us being so tight, there were plenty in Paradise who thought we might be a pair. They were wrong. I wasn't Lucca's type.

I stood up abrupt and went to the window with my cup. The leaves on the trees in the walled garden behind The Palace were tinged with the same colour as the tea. Autumn was coming early this year. I watched a black tom cat slink along the far wall. He stopped dead and flattened himself down on the bricks behind a hummock of ivy. There was a small dark bird, a starling most like, perched on the wall six foot ahead of him. At first the cat didn't move a muscle, but then very slowly the tip of his tail began to flick back and forth. At the same time his rear end started to rise and sway.

It was over in a moment. The starling never stood a chance. I saw wings and feet moving in the cat's mouth before he dropped from the wall and disappeared from view on the far side. Soot had moved delicately and precisely like one of them fancy French dancers Fitzy was so keen to book for the ankle-grabbers. I wondered at the terrible grace of such a deadly creature, and then I thought of Matthias Schalk.

I turned back to face Lucca.

'And now I wish I hadn't written. What we found this morning at The Carnival, Signor Marcelli left like that for us to see. If I was a superstitious type, I might think that letter had prodded at something that should have been left sleeping.'

'It was always going to begin again, Fannella. You knew that.'

I shook my head. 'Of course I did. But you have to admit it was a ripe coincidence? Poor old sod. None of us cared for him or his act – or his ways, come to it. But Marcelli didn't die because he wasn't popular, did he? He died because of me.'

34

God forgive me, but at that moment I wasn't thinking of Signor Marcelli at all; it was Sam's face I kept seeing in my head. I shouldn't have sent that letter. I didn't want Sam hurt again.

I looked down at the china cup in my hands. The ink had caught in the whorls and loops of my fingertips. It put me in mind of the Scottish play. A year or so back, when I was still a slop girl, we'd had a touring party in for three nights of Shakespeare. The punters weren't impressed – it wasn't lively enough for their tastes. For a start, there wasn't a single song in two hours and there wasn't much flesh on show, neither – but I'd enjoyed it and so had Lucca. We'd sat together at the back of the gallery.

I raised my blackened fingers.

'Not all the perfumes of Arabia, eh? It would be better for Sam if he kept himself at a distance.'

Lucca nodded. 'Perhaps. However, I think it might be too late for that. Lok returned from Holborn ten minutes ago. He made the tea and asked me to take it to you, and he asked me to give you this.'

He reached into the cuff of his shirt and produced a small buff envelope. Putting it on the desk, he rose from his chair.

'I will leave you alone to read it, Fannella.'

Once he'd shut the door behind him, I flew across the room and snatched up the envelope. I tore it open and pulled out a single sheet of paper. No, not even that, to be straight. I don't know what I was expecting to see, but I certainly didn't reckon on a torn scrap.

It wasn't neat and it wasn't much, just a crudely ripped corner from Sam's paper, *The London Pictorial News*. To be accurate, it was from *my* paper seeing as I'd bought *The Pictorial* to save his bleedin' job, his and the rest of them all in that flea pit office.

I flattened it out on the desk. Half of the top of page ten from yesterday's paper, it was, and not even a proper story, just an advertisement of sorts, all hemmed about with scrolls and columns of a noble type.

A FIRST General Meeting Against
～◎ the MENACE of the MUSIC HALLS ◎～

The Reverend WILLIAM AUCHLYNE-DOUNE calls upon the GODLY, the RIGHTEOUS and the ABSTINENT to stand with him against the CORRUPTING foulness of this CITY. All that speaks of goodness and virtue has been swept from our streets on a tide of PUTRID FILTH, that great swell of INCONTINENCE and CHAOS rising from the meanest establishments masking their VICE as entertainment. Be in no doubt, it is the DEVIL who is at work here. He has guised himself in MOTLEY and leads poor FOOLS on a merry dance to HELL. If you would JOIN this CRUSADE against the apostate temples of PROFANITY, commonly known as MUSIC HALLS, a first meeting of the CHILDREN of PURITY will be held tomorrow evening at the Martingate Mission Hall, Raven Street, Whitechapel, eight o'clock. All who are in sympathy with this enterprise of COURAGE are commanded to attend.

With so many words picked out in capitals, I fancied I could almost hear the Reverend Auchlyne-Doune bawling his sermon at me. There was a note scratched in pencil across the bottom of the advertisement. I recognised Sam's bold untidy scrawl.

Care to join me?

Chapter Four

I pulled down the veil of my hat to cover my face and smoothed out the skirts of my drab brown street coat. Even though this was the last place people would expect to see me, I didn't want to take the risk of being recognised. Lucca was more bundled about than usual. His black coat swept the tops of his boots and the dark woollen scarf round his neck was wound about so many times it almost reached the brim of his hat.

No one quizzed our gear. They were all tight-buttoned and muffled up themselves. The swelter of summer had been washed away in a great storm weeks back. We hadn't seen much sun since the back end of July, but there'd been plenty of rain. It rinsed all the colour from the streets, leaving behind a stodgy greyness that threatened to gather itself into a fog earlier than you might expect.

These early days of autumn held more than a promise of winter, a hard one.

I'd told Tan Seng and Lok to stay at The Palace with Peggy. They weren't too happy about it, but as there weren't many young women in Limehouse who went about regular with a couple of Chinamen in tow, I thought it best, for once, to go without their protection. Besides, I knew of a certainty that these days Lucca never ventured anywhere without that delicate ivory-handled pistol of his. It's an odd thing, but I'd never asked where it came from, I just accepted that he had it. Christ knows, there were enough dark corners in his own past to tell me all I needed to know.

I peered through the net of the veil, hoping to catch a sight of Sam. As I scanned the people walking with us up Raven Street towards the hall, a sparrow shivered its wings beneath my coat. After a moment I realised I was holding my breath.

A fair-sized crowd was making its way up the steps of the Martingate Mission Hall. The sickly light from globe gas lamps hanging either side of the doorway showed that a variety of types had answered the Reverend's summons. Some were the pinch-faced, purse-clutching parabolists I expected. They'd swallowed a Bible whole and now great chunks of it rose like bile on a regular basis. You could tell from their crimped lips and scuttling eyes that saintly disapproval brought as much fire and delight to their shrivelled lights as ever a jug of gin could stoke in a regular punter. They were here for entertainment, just the same.

There were a few ragged men and women gathered together in the shadows beyond the steps, waiting for their moment. They'd done their best to look decent, but when you live on the streets, or good as, it's hard to hide the wear; of your clothes, your skin and your soul. To be fair, I didn't think they had much against the halls. They were most likely at the Martingate Mission on the promise of a warm room and a free cup of tea. I wondered if the Reverend would let them in.

Others were more difficult to give an exact place to, but I knew their game. From their gear you could tell they were comfortably stationed in life. Quality stuff it was, but plain as their big, bland faces. If it wasn't for their dress you'd have trouble sorting the men from the women in this mob. Lofty – that was a word for them, although I could think of more. These poker-backed, horse-toothed temperance types had made their peace with their family fortunes by making war on those they considered to be beneath them.

To my mind, they were the most dangerous people who'd answered the Reverend's call.

I searched among the faces slicked yellow by the gas lamps. Halfway up the steps I turned just once to look down at the crowd still waiting in the street, but I couldn't see Sam.

Once we were through the door at the top, we were herded into a narrow panelled hallway. I'll tell you this for nothing about the GODLY, RIGHTEOUS and ABSTINENT pressing close around us: they stank as much as the MOTLEY in the halls without the taint of liquor to cut the frowse. It occurred to me that the postulant CHILDREN of PURITY might benefit more from a regular appointment with a bar of Pears' finest than an evening with the Reverend Auchlyne-Doune.

The queue was flowing like river mud. I turned to make sure Lucca was tucked behind me and then I stood on tiptoe to see what was holding us up. I couldn't make out anything above the greasy heads and sober bonnets, but there was certainly a clump of bodies blocking the doorway leading through, I supposed, to the mission hall itself.

We shuffled forward with the crowd. I was surprised so many had turned out for the Reverend's patter act. Once we were almost level with the door it became clear why we were moving so slow. Just inside the hall there was a table set to the side of the entrance and people were bending over to sign their name in a book laid open for the purpose. I could see a pile of printed papers on the edge of the table too. I tugged Lucca's sleeve, pointed to the book and rose to whisper in his ear.

'Mr and Miss Smith. You sign for us both.'

He nodded and we moved a few steps forward. As Lucca scrawled our names in the book, I clocked the hall. If Sam was here, he was keeping himself private. Twenty rows of collapsible slatted chairs set out in front of a plain wooden stage were nearly full. The air was thick with polish and carbolic, which was preferable to the meat stew of the hallway. There was a deal of rustling and a murmur of conversation. I won't deny it, there was a spark of something else there too, something expectant like the nights at the halls when a new turn takes the limes.

I found myself thinking of Netta Swift. Her first night as a solo at The Carnival had been her last. Matthias Schalk had seen to that. I bit my lip. What was I doing here, chasing after Sam Collins, when I should have been concerning myself with other things? Despite the street coat, I felt a sudden chill. I pushed my fingers under the veil to secure the ivory button at the neck of my coat.

'Please take a seat, Mr and Mrs . . . ah, forgive me, *Miss* Smith.'

The soft voice had a pleasant musical lilt to it. I turned from the hall to take in the young woman sitting behind the table trying to read the register upside down. She was around my age, skinny and fine-boned with a knot of dun-coloured hair pinned to the top of her head. From the look of her rig she was in mourning. Her plain black blouse was buttoned tight and high at the neck and there was a single black ribbon tied in a loop around her wrist – the only bit of her flesh, if you could call it that, on show.

'The address will begin at eight fifteen prompt. If you'd care to take some literature to read while we wait. You'll find everything you need here.'

The young woman's features were small and tidily placed. If she'd had more in the way of colour about her you might almost have thought her pretty, but as it was, she was the sort you'd pass in the street without tossing a second thought at. It was only her eyes, which were a very clear blue, that had what you might call a quality to them.

She held out two sheets. 'I think there are still some seats towards the front on the left side, Mr Smith. And as you can see, the last two rows on the right are also free. If you and your . . . sister, is it?'

She glanced at me and I nodded. I recognised the particular tone in her soft voice now: she was Scottish.

'Well, if you would both like to seat yourselves, as I said, my father will commence at eight fifteen. There is no charge for this evening, but we are grateful for donations, however small.' She pushed a slotted wooden box towards us and waited expectantly.

I fumbled in my pocket and found a couple of coins. Lucca did the same.

The young woman watched us feed the box without a word of thanks or a flicker of a smile.

'As I said, everything you need is in your hand.' She turned her blue eyes to the man behind me in the queue. 'Good evening. If you could just sign here, sir.'

We went to the end of the back row and perched uncomfortably on the small wooden seats. Lucca started to read the sheet, but I kept twisting about to look at the door to see if Sam came in. He didn't, but plenty of others did. Soon it was standing room only at the back.

Lucca nudged me. 'You should read this, Fannella. It is almost *uno scherzo –*' he chased the right word around his tongue – 'a jest, a joke. But I don't think you will find it funny.'

'Why, what is it then?'

'It is a declaration of war.'

I took a printed sheet from his hand and began to read. At the same moment a big brass-bound clock on the wall over the door struck the quarter. The gas lamps dimmed and organ music started somewhere up front. A proper dirge it was, nicely played, mind, but not the sort of thing you'd catch yourself humming on the way out.

There was a commotion from behind. A deal of scuffling, then silence. I turned again to see that the people standing around the door had parted like the Red Sea.

Moses, well, his twin brother good as, stood there framed in the doorway under the clock. His eyes caught the low light from the lamps as he took in the room, then, satisfied with the size of his audience, he strode up the aisle to the stage.

That bleedin' organ strained to a pitch of perfect piety as the Reverend Auchlyne-Doune positioned himself at the centre of the platform and raised his hands. The jets hissed and dimmed again, leaving the hall in darkness except for the one lamp positioned directly above the stage.

The Reverend was tall, above six foot I reckoned, and built like a brewer's stack. I was wrong when I compared him to Moses. He was the mountain. The light falling straight on his thick grey hair, craggy forehead, prominent nose and full beard made it look, for an instant, like there was a lion standing up there, not a man of the cloth.

He made a circling motion with his right hand and the organ music stopped.

43

For a long moment, the Reverend stood still. Under a pair of tangled brows his eyes glinted fierce in the lamplight. Little points of fire they was, raking the depths of the hall. I knew he couldn't see us on account of the dark, but it didn't feel like that.

Even though I knew better, I could swear he was taking us all in, eating us up like little lambs.

*

'. . . A great reckoning will come. A price must be paid. I tell you all, the Seven Plagues of Egypt are as nothing compared to the vengeance He will cast down upon upon this city if we do not scour the filth from our streets. For London is become a new Sodom where every perversion, every vice and everything that is unnatural and unclean is allowed to thrive. This is the Devil's work and Lord Lucifer is the great deceiver. He has sweetened the rotten fruit so that their tongues know it not for what it truly is. We must be as Adam before the Fall. We must clothe ourselves again in the innocence and modesty that sinful Eve bartered away. Knowledge of decadence is the weed that chokes the God-given flowers of our garden. We must cut it out so that we can thrive in the Light. We must pluck it from the very soil where it has spread its fibres deep. We must kill the root.'

Here the Reverend William paused. He came forward and linked his large hands together. The knuckles showed bone white as he tightened his grip like he was throttling the life from his words. He threw back his head, careful again to catch the lamplight in his eyes. He'd positioned himself in just the right place to snatch the glare.

At The Gaudy a couple of years back, we'd had a travelling mesmerist in for a fortnight. Monsieur D'Aiment was French – he told us – but he could have said anywhere and we'd have believed him. He had this way of looking straight at you and speaking in a very deliberate way that clouded up your mind. Most of the girls gave him a wide berth, on account of the fact that after spending any time in his company you could never quite remember what he'd said, or, more precisely, what he'd done.

I had a clear membrance of Monsieur D'Aiment now as I sat there watching the Reverend work the hall. It was an act weighted and rehearsed to bring the audience to just the place he wanted them.

He took a breath so deep and loud you could almost imagine him to have emptied the air from the Martingate Mission. He stared up at the rafters arching somewhere above and then he let his great shaggy head roll down to his chest again. As he glowered into the hall I got the keen impression you could light a match from his eyes.

'Where is that root?'

It came out as a whisper, the sort that carries to the back of a room. He raised his clasped hands, which had the look of a fist rather than a prayer, and asked again.

'Where? Where do Satan's deceivers walk among us? Where are we tempted, like our grandsire Adam, to fall again and again?'

The room was silent for a long moment, then someone – a woman's voice it was – shouted out: 'The halls, that's where. All them painted women flaunting themselves. Dancing about with their breakfast on show. My Charlie – he's fallen all right.'

Another voice – a man's this time – chimed in. 'There's the liquor too, even on Sundays. Diabolical, that is.'

Someone else took up the chorus to that. 'It is an abomination. The halls should not be open on the Sabbath.'

A new singer provided another verse. 'Or any day, come to that. What about the songs? A Christian shouldn't hear such indecency.'

And suddenly it seemed like the Martingate was on fire with voices coming from every corner, words spitting into the air like sparks off a Catherine wheel.

'Places of low repute.'

'. . . corrupted my poor son.'

'. . . sinful perversion.'

'Drink!'

'Lechery!'

'Lewdness!'

'Obscenity!'

'Flesh!'

'Whores!'

The shouting grew so loud it became impossible to winkle out meaning from the sound. There was a pulse to the wooden boards beneath my feet. People were standing up now to stamp out their disapproval.

If the punters hollering around us thought a well-turned ankle and a salty chorus were an 'abomination', what would they have made of the old man nailed to that chair at the centre of the stage at The Carnival? Christ! If they knew!

Up on the platform the Reverend nodded his head, unclenched his hands and started to clap. It was a signal. The lights brightened enough to shine up the hall and that only made them bolder. I shifted in my seat. Just along from Lucca a man was bellowing and smashing a balled fist into the palm of his hand. Little flecks of spittle spurted from his lips as he shouted and rocked to and fro. In the row directly in front of us a woman pounded the air with a roll of paper, the sheet given out on the door most probably. Her thin face was a twist of spite as she worked her arm like a piston.

Lucca bent his head close to my ear. 'We should leave, Fannella.'

I nodded and looked to the doorway behind us. It was blocked by the latecomers who couldn't find a seat, all of them calling and thumping. I wasn't sure how we'd push our way through, but Lucca stood and took my hand. We managed to slide out of the row, but our way was blocked by a woman with a beam as broad as a coal barge. She leaned in close to my face. Through the spotted net of the veil I saw her fat lips curl.

'Leaving so soon, are we, when there's God's work to be done?'

The reek of her last meal – cabbage, onion and boiled bacon – breathed hot and damp into my face. I was grateful at that moment to hear the Reverend's deep voice toll above the uproar.

'Cease, cease, cease.'

I clutched Lucca's hand and turned to face the platform again.

The Reverend raised his hands and the noise stopped dead. You could have heard a roach fart in the sudden silence.

'Praise the Lord.'

Auchlyne-Doune let that hang there for a moment and then he repeated himself.

'Praise the Lord. I did not think to find so many righteous souls in this city. I must . . . I must . . .' He faltered. A tremor shuddered through him. He stepped to the edge of the platform and seemed to be on the verge of continuing, but the words didn't come. Instead, shaking his head, he reached into the lining of his jacket and pulled out an oversized 'kerchief. The pristine whiteness of it showed up clear in the light as it furled from the pocket. Given the size of the thing, it looked like he was dabbing at his eyes with a dead swan. The audience was left in no doubt as to the strength of his feelings as he wept openly and loudly. Several women and a couple of the men started crying too. I could hear the sound of noses and throats clearing all around me.

Up on the stage the Reverend appeared to be grappling with the most powerful emotions along with that bleedin' 'kerchief. Eventually he stopped wiping and weeping and brought the 'kerchief, clenched in his fist, down to his chest. He beat against his heart several times and I heard that practised stage whisper again.

'Thank you. Thank you all.'

He straightened up, careful to let the light swim free in his watery eyes, and slowly extended a hand like he wanted to catch hold of everyone there.

'I apologise for my frailty but these are tears of the purest joy.' His cracked voice deepened. 'I am a sinner too. I have betrayed His trust and yours, for I dared not to believe it possible that you would listen to me. Tonight He has shown me the error of my ways. Your fire has humbled me and revealed the weakness of my faith. I weep before you, because I have been tested and found wanting. But you, *you* are my joy. Today, my children, you have lit a lamp in this city that shall never be extinguished.'

Very touching it was. 'Calculated' is another word that came to mind.

I knew it was part of the act, but he was good. He'd boiled them up into a stew of anger and now he was cooling them down again. The genius of it, if you could see it like that, was the fact he was sinuating that they had a power over him, when in fact, quite the opposite was the truth.

The Reverend nodded to the left of the platform and the organ started up again. This time the tune was almost a lament as he came down the steps and started to walk up the aisle towards the door.

A man called out, 'Tell us what to do.'

Auchlyne-Doune stopped, his big head sunk low between his shoulders. He seemed to consider the question for a moment, but then he started off again.

He was almost level with our row at the back when a woman shouted, 'Don't leave us, please.'

The Reverend halted once more and this time he looked up. He turned slowly, taking in the crowd, before he answered in that deep sad baritone.

'I am not worthy of your trust.'

I noted that despite all that vigorous dabbing with the 'kerchief, his cheeks were still wet with tears. The hall was quiet for a moment, then a new female voice called out high and clear.

'Lead us.'

I couldn't be certain, but the words seemed to have a Scottish lilt. There was a ripple of agreement that grew quickly to a chant accompanied by more stamping and clapping.

'Lead us! Lead us!'

The organ started up again. The anthem – it was definitely something victorious this time – thrummed through my body and I knew that everyone else in the hall could feel the power of it too. A man stepped into the aisle. He took Auchlyne-Doune's hand and worked it up and down like the handle of a street pump. People started to queue behind him, waiting for their turn.

All the while, 'Lead us, lead us' hammered the air. I glanced up at Lucca. His face was buried in the coils of his scarf, but I could see the twitch of the muscles around his eye. His attention was fixed on the Reverend and the crowd now pressing around him. I gripped his hand tighter and he squeezed back.

Auchlyne-Doune reached out over a sea of heads to grasp more hands, all the while smiling and nodding. Through his grey beard, I caught sight of teeth – a fine strong set – and I was reminded again of a lion.

Lambs to the slaughter.

At last, satisfied with his conquest, he turned and made his way back to the stage. Me and Lucca stayed put, but most of them surged forward to be as close to him as possible. As he climbed the steps the music whipped itself to a howl of glory, stopping the instant he took up that place beneath the lamp again. Almost like he'd planned it.

'Are you with me, children?'

The Reverend stretched out his arms as if to hold back the torrent of sound that answered his question.

*

We waited until the hall was almost deserted. I stood against the wall and watched out for Sam, but I never saw him in the crowd. Once the Reverend had removed himself from the stage – he disappeared through a curtain at the side this time, not down the aisle – the audience he'd churned to a good thick butter didn't know what to do with itself. The punters shouted out for a while. Then they stamped their feet and clapped their hands, hoping to tempt him back, but he didn't come.

When it was finally clear that he'd shut up his shop for the night, they fell quiet and shuffled about, uncertain what to do next. He'd wound them up like cheap tin toys and now their clockwork was running low. Of an instant, the lights came up bright and a welcome gust of cold air moved the skirt of my coat. The doors to Raven Street at the end of the passage must have been opened wide.

The evening was over.

As people headed to the door, the skinny girl who'd taken our names started to collect up some papers left behind on the chairs. She walked briskly down each row, snatching up the discarded sheets, tutting and gathering them to her prim black blouse. She looked across at me as she reached the end of the row where we'd been sitting.

'My father will be resting now. He'll not be coming back again, if that's what you're waiting for.'

I shook my head. 'No. We're going. I . . . I felt a little faint. Your father is a most powerful per—' I stopped myself from saying performer, ' . . . a most powerful person. A great speaker.'

She straightened up, clutching the papers tight against her breast. Now she was standing, I realised she was taller than I'd thought her to be. She took after her father in that, but there was little else of him in her pallid delicate features. Those clear blue eyes of hers flicked to Lucca and then back to me. There was something guarded in that look.

'The Lord speaks through him.'

I was glad she couldn't see my face clear through the veil. I didn't think it was the voice of God I'd been hearing this evening. She glanced at the clock over the doorway where the last stragglers from the Reverend's audience were filing out to the street.

'We have to clear the premises by ten o'clock. If you are feeling better, Miss . . .'

'Smith,' I said.

'Of course. I remember. If you're feeling able to leave now, Miss Smith, then I'd appreciate it if you and . . . and your brother could—'

She was interrupted by a sudden piercing howl. The sound, coming from somewhere up near the stage, was like the cry of an animal in pain.

'Donny!' The girl twisted about, her drab skirt swirling around her. 'I'm here. I'm coming.'

She moved quickly back along the row and then ran up the central aisle. The howling came again as she flew up the wooden steps to the platform and darted off to the left behind the curtain. The noise stopped, but the girl didn't reappear.

Lucca tapped my shoulder. 'It is late.'

Beneath the veil I bit my lip. 'He wasn't here.'

Lucca shook his head. 'But you must be grateful to him. If Sam had not alerted you to this –' he gestured at the hall – 'then I do not think you would have come here tonight. It is good to know your enemies.'

I nodded. Something was misting up my eyes, the dust most like. 'I'm not sure that grateful is what I'm feeling at the moment. Calls himself a reverend, does he? That's a ripe one. If he's a regular man of the cloth then I'm the bleedin' Pope. And the worst of it was he took them all in.' I swiped a cheek through the net. 'By the time he finished up tonight he could have told them black was white, night was day, water was wine and shit was gold, and they would have believed him.'

I saw Lucca wince. It fired me again, although I wasn't angry at him, or perhaps, at that moment, even the Reverend.

'Don't give me a face on it, Lucca Fratelli. I won't apologise for telling the truth of it. He had them in the palm of his hand, that's what I mean.'

Lucca stared at me. 'I know what you mean, Fannella.'

The lights flickered and dimmed. The ones at the front of the hall above the platform went out with a soft phutt. There was still no sign of the mourning girl.

'We must go. Come.' He took my hand and we went to the doorway. We passed the table where the Reverend's daughter had signed us in and walked along the passage to the wide open doors leading out to the street. We were the last to leave the Martingate Misson Hall.

Once we were on the steps, the gas lamps sputtered, and then the yellow light died in those big dirty globes, leaving us standing there blinking in the dark. It was cold. I freed my hand from Lucca's and pulled my coat tight around me.

'We should take a cab. It's too dark and too far to the Commercial. If we go left up to Whitechapel Road there'll be plenty of hack trade running west at this time. I'll give them double to take us east.'

I heard the scrape of a Lucifer. A match flared below. Seconds later a glowing red dot moved in the night. The scent of tobacco smoke came to me. It was a familiar smell, a brand I recognised. Cheap. That fluttering started up again beneath my coat. I knew exactly who it was standing there in the dark on Raven Street.

'Well then, Kitty, what did you make of all that?' There was a pause as Sam took a drag on his smoke. The red dot burned bright and moved again. 'If you ask me, I'd say that you have another battle on your hands.'

Chapter Five

The world seemed to stop. As I stood there at the top of the steps, eyes fixed on the red dot of his smoke, it was a good long moment before I remembered to breathe. I gulped down a lungful of London's thickest, tasting the tar and the soot. Being near Sam made me feel weak. I didn't like it. And once I got an eyeful of his rig I didn't like that neither.

At first he was just a shadow at the bottom of the steps, a patch of night that had thickened itself to the size and shape of a man. We agreed to trek up to the Whitechapel Road together to look for a hack, like I'd suggested to Lucca. It was when we came to the first lamp, about sixty foot along the street from the mission hall, that I got a good look at him.

For a moment I was confused. The man walking alongside Lucca wasn't Sam Collins at all. For a start there was a beard, lodging round his collar like a badly built nest. Then there was a limp-brimmed hat that covered most of his face, and last there was the general state of him. His dark shapeless coat was ragged, patched and mottled with stains.

It was only when he spoke that I knew him; that and the cheap tobacco. He didn't offer an explanation and I couldn't trust myself to ask for one. I couldn't help wondering if his reduced circumstances were directly due to me. Perhaps he couldn't work with just one eye? As we clipped along Raven Street I chewed my lip, thinking about how I could make it right for him. I noted the way he talked to Lucca, enquiring after his health, his work and his plans. Considering what the pair of them had been through together, it was natural, I supposed, that they should share an affinity. But I won't deny it, I was hoping for something more.

Sam told us he'd been waiting outside the hall. He was with the poor types huddled near the steps, hiding himself among the threadbare men and women. It was as good a place as any to watch from without being noticed, he said, adding that he'd dialled us going in.

Just before the meeting started up, the Reverend's daughter had come out to the steps and handed out food – a currant bun each – and then she allowed them all to enter the hall, although they had to stand at the back behind the regular punters.

We passed the gated entrance to a side alley. A ball of yapping grey fur flung itself against the bars. Sam's grimy coat flapped as he turned to look at it.

'They called out the loudest when the Reverend threatened to leave, you know – the ragged ones, I mean. Perhaps it was the charity?' He delved into a pocket and produced a sorry spotted lump.

'Here, boy.' He ripped a chunk off the bun and tossed it into the alley. The animal fell on it.

'Do you think Auchlyne-Doune keeps a dog?' Sam asked. 'That noise from the stage at the end? I wouldn't have supposed him to be an animal lover. In fact, I'm certain the only thing he truly loves is the sound of his own voice . . . and the jangle of coins in his collection box.'

I looked back at the mutt in the alley. The light from the street lamps shone up its teeth and glowed in its eyes in a way that minded of the Reverend.

The Whitechapel Road was never at rest. At night carters

carried loads into the City from the docks. Their wide heavy wagons weren't popular during the day as they slowed down the regular traffic. Although it was late, a fair number of cabs were rattling west. There was always brass to be made from taking gentlemen punters back to their high-set wives at the end of an evening in low company. Lucca stepped out to flag down a hack and the man up top agreed to a Limehouse run.

It was only once we was all inside in the dark – sitting uncomfortably close because it was designed for the carriage of two persons rather than three – that Sam turned his attention to me.

'We need to talk, Kitty.'

The hack bumped over a rut and I pitched into his flank. Beneath the rough tobacco and that ridiculous gear I recognised the soap he used and the particular scent of his skin. Warm and clean it was, sharpened by the musk of the day in a way that made me want to keep breathing it down. I dug my nails into the palms of my hands to make sure my mind was set on what he was about to say. The tang of Lady Ginger's opium sticks never affected me like this.

Sam shifted himself and peered through the window. It was raining now.

'First we need to talk about that meeting, Kitty. Is there a tavern, an inn, where we can speak? Somewhere you trust? I need to see real people to convince myself that for every fool who swallowed Auchlyne-Doune's hellfire cant whole this evening, there are a hundred free-thinking souls more inclined to test God's patience, which, of course, as the Bible tells us, is infinite.'

Through the net of the veil, I stared past Sam at the rain

trickling down the small square pane. Just for a moment back there I'd thought he meant something else.

'The Town of Ramsgate on Narrow Street is one of mine.' My voice came out like the bleat of a lamb. I straightened on the leather bench seat all the while aware of his knee jammed close against mine.

'And there's The Britannia on the Commercial, or The Colet.'

Sam delved into a pocket for his box of smokes. 'The Town of Ramsgate? How appropriate. Judge Jeffreys – he of the infamous Bloody Assizes – was captured outside that very establishment as he tried to escape the Glorious Revolution. I'm sure Jeffreys and the good Reverend would have had much in common.'

I felt a prickle of something like anger. I'd put my heart into that bleedin' letter and all he could do now we were face to face – or knee to knee, to be more accurate – was prattle on about some old-time judge.

'I didn't pick it for historical interest.' My voice came stronger now. 'There are booths at the back end where a person can sit private. The landlord there, Poulter, he's under my . . . protection. Well, he *has* been. Like I told you, I'm not intending to carry on running Paradise. Not in the old way like she . . . like my grandmother . . . I wrote it all down.'

I clutched the handle of my bag so tight I heard the bones of my knuckles crack. I hated myself for mentioning the letter. Surely that was up to him?

'The Town of Ramsgate it is then.' Sam pushed at the slat behind us and called up to the driver. I folded back the veil to get a good look at his face, to see if I could read anything there, but it was too dim in the cab to see anything clear. There was a long silence. The three of us sat listening to the clopping of the horse's hooves, the rumble of the wheels on the cobbles and the drumming of the rain on the roof.

Lucca cleared his throat. 'It has been a long and tiring evening. I would be happy to continue alone to The Palace after we have reached Wapping Old Stairs. If . . . if . . .' He found it hard to finish that off, but I knew what he was driving at. I was grateful to him, and sorry too. He must have felt like a plum growing on a peach tree sitting there with us in the dark, knowing . . .

Knowing what exactly?

If I was a romantic type, I might have imagined choirs of angels going off like it was Christmas in St Paul's when I met up with Sam Collins again. I might have imagined him holding me close and stroking my hair. I might have imagined the wiry strength of him pressed close to me as he whispered into my ear. Like I said, I might have imagined a lot of things, but luckily I'm not the romantic type. And neither, as it turned out, was he.

Sam struck up a light and took a drag on a new smoke. A tiny red dot bobbed in the dark. 'I'd be grateful if you came along too, Lucca. There's a lot we need to discuss.'

We?

*

Sam peeled off the beard that had clambered up the lower half of his face like ivy on a wall. The rip of it sounded painful. I sidled at him as he rubbed his jaw. His skin glowed in the lamplight where that bleedin' thing had been attached. Little flecks of gum rolled beneath his fingers.

'That's better. Blasted nuisance. It's a useful disguise, but I haven't yet found a way to keep it on that doesn't take a layer of skin away when I remove it.' He rubbed again and then he stuffed the beard into a pocket of his shabby street coat, at the same time retrieving a silver strike case.

'You say we're safe to talk?'

'Like I said, it's one of mine – we're private here. No one can see us or hear us. That's right, isn't it?'

I looked at Lucca, who was spinning a little brass tray set on the table between us.

'*Sì*.' He span the tray again with the tip of a finger. It came to me that there might be reasons other than a natural embarrassment at sitting there sour as a gooseberry that made him feel uncomfortable tonight. Sam Collins was a reminder of everything that had happened to the pair of them. I reached across and laid my hand over his. 'We're safe here.'

He looked up now and shot a glance across the table. He could see Sam's face clear from where he was perched. If Sam had any delicacy for the way Lucca was feeling, he didn't show it.

'Good. I'll get rid of this too.' Sam pulled off the crumpled hat and his thick brown fringe fell across his face. 'You warned me about being noticed, Kitty.' He scraped at his chin and I wondered if he was about to say more about the letter.

We were snug in a curtained booth at the back end of the long, low bar of The Town of Ramsgate by Wapping Old Stairs. It was private here, like I said, and no one had cast a second look at us as we came in through the side entrance. Behind

Lucca, through the steamy panes of the window, I could make out little points of light from the ships moored across the river. The lights moved in the bumpy glass as the boats rocked on the tide.

Sam had settled himself next to me. Tell truth, I was grateful for that. It meant I didn't have to look direct at him. Don't misunderstand me. All I wanted to do was drink him down. I liked a gin rinser as much as the next girl, but of a rule I knew when I'd had enough. Sam was different. I wasn't sure I could trust myself to stop when it came to him.

Now I could see the side of his face, without the beard and the hat, I was aware of a heat rising from my neck to my cheeks – a warmth that didn't come from a bottle.

I concentrated on the battered silver case in his hand. Sam had long fingers that put me in mind of Professor Ruben, the pianist at The Carnival. As usual, those fingers were smudged with ink. There was a smatter of freckles across the knuckles that matched the scatter across the bridge of his strong nose. I slid a look at his profile, noting the way the oil lamp overhead burnished up the red in the dark stubble of his jaw. Now it was out in the open, I wanted to run the tip of a finger over his cheek and down to the jut of his chin to feel the prickle of it.

And then I wanted to give him a good hard slap.

I dragged my eyes away and stared at a knot in the wood of the table top. Somewhere a piano – one that hadn't been tuned in a good while – started up and a woman began to sing.

> *Your Polly has never been faithless she swears,*
> *Since last year you parted on Wapping Old Stairs.*

'Can I offer a smoke?' Sam delved into yet another pocket of his baggy coat and took out a square brass case. He pressed the catch in the side to open it. 'Blast. I appear to have exhausted supplies. No matter, I'll make some more.'

He busied himself with the rolling of one of his scrawny cigarettes. He flicked his fringe away from his eyes as he worked at the paper and I caught a first sight of the thin leather strip that crossed his forehead. From where I was sitting, I couldn't see the patch covering his left eye. I reckoned it was deliberate. Sam had waited until me and Lucca had taken our seats in the booth and then he'd chosen his place, opposite Lucca and next to me.

I remembered what he said the last time I sat this close to him.

We'll make a matching pair for you now, Lucca and me. We could be bookends.

If it hadn't been for me, he'd be sitting here now with perfect vision and two eyes in his head. Sam's elbow nudged against my arm as he licked his thumb to seal the edge of the smoke. Under the cotton, my skin burned where he'd caught me. I reached for my glass and took a mouthful of gin. A big one.

He offered the roll-up, but me and Lucca both shook our heads.

'No takers? Can't say I blame you.' He clicked open the silver strike case. 'Thing is I've rather got used to them. Thanks to your patronage of *The Pictorial*, Kitty, I can buy myself better tobacco, but it doesn't do the trick. Not like this stuff.'

He scraped a Lucifer along the top of the case and held the little flame to the scrag end of his newly screwed smoke.

It was like nothing had happened. As if nothing had ever been said or sent between us.

The woman came to the end of her song and the punters packing the bar clapped and yelped for more. The piano jangled again, a lively tune it was – or would have been if more of the notes were in the right place – and she started up afresh. Her voice was raw, but powerful.

> *Don't bring me roses when it's violets I adore.*
> *If you've got an itch you want to scratch you'll have*
>   *to give me more.*
> *If it's tickle and not prickle that you want before*
>   *the dawn,*
> *Then you'd better choose a flower that comes without*
>   *a thorn.*

I had enough thorns in my garden to flay a man alive. If Sam was paying any attention, he'd have done well to take her advice. That knot in the wood on the table minded me of a single eye. No wonder he was distant. Since we'd met outside the Martingate Mission Hall, the closest he'd come to sinuating anything in the way of a connection between us was that casual remark about business.

His cheap tobacco filled my nose now as I fixed on the knot and tried to see it all from his point of view. He'd made a mistake, that was it. What with the pain and the laudanum, no wonder he hadn't been able to think straight. He'd been under a delusion when he left that note for me. And now the easiest way to deal with it was to pretend he'd never said anything about having feelings or that I'd sent him that letter saying much the same thing, over four bleedin' pages.

Trouble was, seeing as how I was his employer, he couldn't ignore me, could he? And that was why he'd arranged the meeting this evening. I was in the trade the Reverend Auchlyne-Doune was all for setting his dogs on and because of that I was useful. Sam Collins was on the scent of a story and I was a part of his research.

It came to me with a clarity that he was trying to prove that he was a professional and that there were no hard feelings – or any feelings at all, come to it. The knot in the wood seemed to water up and blink.

Sam reached forward to flick ash into the brass tray. He drummed the fingers of his free hand on the table. After a moment he spoke.

'I owe you an apology, Kitty. You too, Lucca. I had no idea that Auchlyne-Doune would turn out to be such a . . . persuasive speaker.' He shook his head. 'I actually thought it might be amusing, but now I see how idiotic I was. If anyone there tonight had recognised you . . .'

That thought lingered as he turned the smoke between ink-stained fingers.

'It was ugly in there. Violent. The way he worked them into a baying mob. I'm not sure that even the Reverend could have called them off if they'd turned on you, for all his oratorical skills.'

'You mean his way with words?' I sat up straight on the bench now. The thought of Sam worrying about me was like throwing a bone to a starving dog. I watched the side of his face; his cheekbone showed up clear as he took another pull.

'Perhaps it's more than a way with words. You had a lucky

escape tonight, no thanks to me. At his command they would have marched out of there and taken fire brands to every hall in the east of London. As it was, he planted a dangerous seed. There was something odd about the meeting. Did you feel it, Kitty?'

I felt something all right. I breathed deep and considered the question.

'It was like he had a power over them. One minute he had them blowing hot, then cold. It was like he was conducting a bleedin' orchestra up there. It was . . . practised. I thought it was more in the way of an act than a gathering of religious types.'

'An act? Yes, that's it exactly.' Sam nodded. He still didn't look at me direct, mind. Lucca leaned across the table. 'There was a man at The Gaudy, a Frenchman, he called himself, but I do not think he was from France. He was very skilful. His name was . . . was—'

'Monsieur D'Aiment!' I broke in. 'Mesmerist, that's what he called himself. He made people do things they didn't want to do on stage – and behind it as well from what I heard. Mrs Conway was stone-blind to a lot of things, but even she warned us girls never to be alone with him. I thought of him tonight too, Lucca. The Reverend had something of his talent.'

'If he really is a reverend.' Sam drummed his fingers again. He stubbed out his smoke, reached into the pocket of his coat and took out a small black notebook and a pencil.

Lucca turned his glass slowly. 'But what does this Reverend want? I do not think it is money – no one would go to such trouble for so little. There is more, there must be.' He unwound the scarf from his neck and plucked at the bottle-green wool.

'For me the meeting was like an opera. It rose and fell, but always you could feel it building towards something. Then it ended . . . *improvvisamente*. There was no finale. They called on him to lead them and—'

'And he agreed to that, sharp as a broadsman pockets a lady,' I put in, 'for all his talk of being unworthy.'

Sam looked up from his notebook.

'What the Reverend actually said was this . . .' He flicked through the pages and then he began to read aloud, following the lines of his shorthand with the tip of the pencil. *"I am a sinner too. I have betrayed His trust and yours, for I dared not to believe it possible that you would listen to me. Tonight He has shown me the error of my ways. Your fire has humbled me and revealed the weakness of my faith. I weep before you, because I have been tested and found wanting."* And then later he said, *"I am not worthy of your trust."'*

He tapped the end of the pencil on the table and sat back.

'I think you'll find that's exact.'

I folded my arms. 'Well, I'm glad you were taking notes – after all, it's what I pay you for, Sam Collins.'

He turned to look at me straight for the first time and then he smiled. The skin creased up round his sharp brown eye. The patch didn't make him look any less handsome, quite the opposite in fact. If anything, it added something to what had been taken from him. He caught me staring and turned away.

'Let's see if you were taking notes too, Kitty. The call to lead them. Where did that come from?'

'From the girl on the door, I reckon. His daughter. It was a woman's voice. Scottish. She was his monkey?'

Sam nodded. 'Or to continue Lucca's rather accurate opera

analogy, she was his claque. She and the bun-fed rabble. She was standing at the back just along from me. No one was looking at her – they were all hanging off the Reverend's every word. But I was watching her, and she was watching her father, waiting for the moment, waiting for the signal.'

'*Sì*, but lead them how?' Lucca frowned. 'Lead them where? It was not ended, not finished. One moment he was there, and then –' he clicked his fingers – '*scomparso!*'

I dragged my eyes away from Sam's face. 'If you mean he did a disappearing act, he definitely left them calling for more. I'd offer him a place on the bill at The Carnival if he was amenable. There's not many who can work a hall like that.'

'Precisely!' Sam pulled a fold of paper from his notebook. 'Actually, Lucca is quite right, and so are you, Kitty. This evening was merely the warm-up. Look at this.'

He pushed the paper towards me. I recognised it as one of the sheets handed out on the door by Auchlyne-Doune's daughter.

'It's on the back.' Sam flipped the page and pointed the pencil at a line printed along the bottom in bold black capitals. 'Here.'

**THE CHILDREN OF PURITY WILL GATHER
AGAIN. ATTEND THE CALL OF THE LORD'S
TRUE SERVANT, FOR HE SHALL SUMMON
YOU TO GREAT WORK.
BE READY.**

I stared at the paper. 'What does that mean?'

Sam reached for his glass. 'It means I should keep a close eye on the advertisements accepted by *The Pictorial*, and all our rivals for that matter. You should keep watch on the streets too, for posters, fly sheets, bills pasted to walls.'

He took a mouthful of porter. 'The Reverend is a dangerous man. All things considered, it's a stroke of luck we attended that meeting.'

Luck?

Sam rested his glass on the table. 'If I may appropriate one of your charming sayings, Kitty, tell truth, I didn't come here tonight to see Auchlyne-Doune. It was a ruse. Oh, I thought he might be an interesting diversion, but I came to see you. Or at least, I *hoped* to see you. I suppose you could call it a test. To be honest, I wondered whether you'd come.'

'But you read my letter. How could you doubt it?' That question came out a pitch higher than I was aiming for. He pushed at that fringe of his. I noticed the careful way he moved it to cover the patch and I regretted the fact that I'd ever taken the liberty of imagining myself at work on him with a pair of sewing scissors.

'In my line of business it's always better to expect the worst. Cynicism is the armour of a journalist.' He looked up at the yellowed, smoke-stained ceiling above the booth. 'I often find that once people have . . . unburdened themselves, they have second thoughts about what they've actually said. Writing it all down like that might have been a sort of catharsis.' He took up his glass again and swilled the darkness around.

I watched the frill of white froth on the top begin to spin. I couldn't believe what I was hearing. Words. It was always words with him, that was his real armour. I picked out a nugget from his little speech.

'An arse what?'

Sam choked, sputtering a mouthful of porter across the table. Then he started to laugh. I stood up.

'Are you making fun of me? Because if you are, you can stick *The London Pictorial News* up your own catharsis and look for another job, Sam Collins.'

I turned away so he couldn't see the tears pricking in my eyes. I grabbed my hat from the bench end and snatched up my bag. 'It's late and I've got better things to do than sit here drinking the last of my profits. Thank you for alerting me to the Reverend. I'll deal with it, like I deal with everything else.' I threw some loose coins on the table. 'And I'll pay my own way.'

'No, please, Kitty.' Sam caught my hand. I felt my fingers burn as they curled in his palm. He looked up, his lean face serious for once. 'I meant that after you'd told me everything, as you did in your letter, you might feel different, cleansed – that's what catharsis means. I've seen it happen before.' He looked across at Lucca. 'In your faith I believe that confession to a priest has much the same effect? It's a wiping of the slate, a new beginning?'

I saw Lucca swallow, hot as a chestnut on a griddle at being caught between us. He nodded and reached for his own glass as Sam continued. 'After writing it all down I thought you might feel . . . well, to be more precise, that you might *not* feel . . .'

He paused and started again.

'Listen, if you want to know the truth, I thought that you might not come tonight because you'd changed your mind about me. If you hadn't come to the Martingate Mission this evening, I could have pretended to myself that I was there for the sake of *The Pictorial,* but it wouldn't have been true. I was there for one reason only.' He gripped harder. 'And I put that reason in danger. Forgive me.'

I tried to answer him, but for once I couldn't find the words. I sat down again, still holding tight to his hand. The pair of us stared at each other. As it turned out, instead of choirs of angels going off like it was Christmas in St Paul's, I got a knackered piano and woman with a voice like a coster-boy touting a tray of cabbage.

Lucca fiddled with the brim of his hat, pulling it down low. He stood and took up his scarf.

'It's late. I must return to The Palace. Peggy, she . . .' There was an awkward pause and he tried again. 'I promised to make a tisane for her, for the baby. To ease her.' He looked down at Sam. 'Perhaps you will escort Kitty . . . to make sure she is safe?'

Sam pulled his hand free from mine.

'Stay, Lucca, please. As I said in the hack, there's something we have to talk about, the three of us. Dangerous as he is, Auchlyne-Doune is the least of our worries. Even if you hadn't come tonight – and what a stupid, thoughtless game that was – I would have had to swallow my pride and come to you. What I have to say next is far more important than the Children of Purity.'

Chapter Six

It took a moment before Sam found a place to begin. He didn't play with his smokes or fiddle with the pages of his notebook. When he finally started, the edge to his voice that always gave the impression he was on the point of delivering a punchline was blunt.

'Your letter, Kitty. I read it a dozen times over. First because it was . . . well, it was . . .'

Lost for words, for once, he looked away, but not before I caught the look on his face. The wings beat so hard under the cotton of my blouse it was a wonder to me that I didn't fly up from the bench.

He didn't find the rest of what he was going to say 'first'.

'But then I read it again because I recognised a name – Carstone. You described him as the most powerful of the Barons of London. That's right, isn't it? You said he calls himself Lord Kite?'

I nodded, trying to concentrate.

'There's not a journalist in London who is unaware of Anthony Carstone, the great blind judge, famous for the harshness of his decisions and for the brilliance of his mind. He is consulted on the most obscure and ancient laws, statutes and precedents –' he tapped at his right temple – 'because it is locked in his head. Blindness has sharpened his memory. There is a saying of him: Carstone *is* the Law.'

I managed to pay attention. 'And he's also beyond the law?'

'Exactly!' Sam flicked through his notebook, starting from

the end. 'It's a wonderful story. The scoop of the century if I could prove it. Where better for a master criminal to hide himself than at the heart of the legal profession?'

He looked up. 'The thing is, Kitty, *The Pictorial* has received some rather unwelcome *legal* advances. The sort of advances that could close us down. And now I think I know exactly where they came from. I'll keep it short, but the nub of the matter relates to our premises in Holborn. Hundreds of years ago, a chapel connected to the Inns of Court stood exactly on the site of our office today. According to a letter received three days ago – one might more correctly call it a threat – that chapel was never deconsecrated. The deeds of title were never revoked.'

I quizzed at him. 'What does that mean?'

'It means that in the eyes of the law – a very singular one at that – *The London Pictorial* is written and printed in the House of the Lord. Which, in turn, means that every salacious story I write, every slightly suggestive print block produced by the boys in the basement, every profanity that escapes my lips and every drop of alcohol consumed on the premises by our esteemed editor Mr McPherson, is an act of blasphemy. The Reverend Auchlyne-Doune might have used the word "abomination".'

I pushed one of the coins I'd thrown on the table to the centre of the knot in the wood. 'I still can't see it. If every person who used a salty turn of phrase or took a skinful of an evening could be turned out on their ear, London would empty overnight.'

Sam shook his head. 'It's not as simple as that. The law is very specific when it comes to buildings under the jurisdiction of the Church and what may or may *not*, more to the point, take place within them. According to the letter from

Messrs Pagett and Drage, Proctors to the Bishop of London, blasphemy incurs some very stiff penalties. Heavy fines, perhaps even imprisonment. When I read your letter again and recognised that name, I asked myself who might know about such an obscure law – and who might use it against us?'

Of course! Now I knew exactly where Sam was taking this story. I moved all the coins into a line as he went on.

'In your letter you said you were telling me about Carstone – Lord Kite as he styles himself – because I'd need to know him if he came for me. Well, it seems that he might already be on the move.' Sam flicked through his notebook again. 'This morning, I made some enquiries about Anthony Carstone—'

'No!' The thought flew out as a word. The last time Sam had gone digging on my behalf he ended up trapped along with Lucca on a paddle ship in the middle of the Thames.

I looked up from the coins. 'I mean, you shouldn't have done that, Sam. Not on my account.'

'Don't worry, I was very discreet.' He grinned at me, and I saw a fox on the scent. Sam was excited. 'Actually, it was quite normal, run-of-the-mill stuff and easy to come by without attracting attention if you know where to look.'

The deal planks of the table juddered as he tapped his foot on the boards. He worked the pencil under the thin strip of leather above his right ear and returned to the notebook.

'And it wasn't entirely on your account, Kitty. You might say that I too have . . . unfinished business with Justice Carstone.' The way he said 'Justice' made it sound like a profanity.

'Here.' He pointed at the page of shorthand. 'I now know that Carstone's chambers are in Middle Temple Lane, his country estate is in Buckinghamshire – a place called Staple Hall, near Medmenham – and his London address, when in town, is the Angevin Club in St James's. And that's rather interesting.'

He sat back, clearly pleased with himself. I recognised a feed line when I heard one.

'Interesting in what way, Sam?'

'Well, I'm glad you asked that.' He pulled the pencil clear, brandishing it like a stubby conjuror's wand. 'The Angevin Club is one of London's oldest and finest establishments. Its members are drawn exclusively from the highest ranks of society. A gentleman unable to trace his pedigree back to the Conqueror would be regarded as an upstart by the board of the Angevin. It has a reputation for absolute discretion, so naturally –' he rapped the pencil sharp on the table just the once – 'I have a connection there.'

He flipped over the page and turned the notebook about so that we could both see it. 'Take a look at the names listed here. I wrote them out in full to show you. My friend at the Angevin was good enough to supply me with a complete list of the current members. The one you'll be interested in is just there.'

He pointed the tip of the pencil at a name midway down the page.

General Arthur George Denderholm, Baron Denderholm.

I pulled the notebook towards me. 'But that's . . .' I looked up.

'The man I lost my eye for, Kitty.' Sam ran the ink-stained tips of the fingers of his left hand over the small leather patch. 'It was when I made enquiries about the good general there, partly on your behalf, that I found myself in a spot of trouble. This is the original article you asked about. I kept it.'

He took a folded scrap of newsprint from the back of his

notebook. It was torn and creased, but I recognised the block print of the notably whiskered gents wreathed around a larger image of the General himself.

ESTABLISHMENT OF
LONDON IMPERIAL AGENCY

On Tuesday last, the first meeting of Her Britannic Majesty's newly established London Imperial Agency was held at Windsor Castle in the presence of the Queen. These good men, under the guidance of General Lord Denderholm, stand ready to guide and advise Her Majesty in all matters related to the Empire when their consequence is manifest at home.

I stared at the paper. Strictly speaking, it wasn't the General I'd been interested in when I asked Sam to make those enquiries. The man I'd wanted to know about was clean-shaven and at least thirty years younger than the General and his mutton-chopped mates. His likeness was there at the bottom right of the article. High forehead, long nose, neat hair. I still had his card in my desk at The Palace:

33 LITTLE SANCTUARY

That was all. No name, just the briefest address. A sharp pain jabbed at my right temple.

'According to my friend,' Sam continued, 'Denderholm has been a member of the club for less than four months. Do you recall me telling you that he was recently returned from India?'

I looked up from the print. 'At the time you said he was nothing remarkable. Her Majesty was creating a nice little job for him to keep him comfortable in retirement, that's what you reckoned.'

'What a memory you have, Kitty.' Sam smiled. The lines round his mouth sharpened his cheekbones, and his eye glinted in the lamplight.

'Perhaps . . .' I forced myself to concentrate. Sam's face seemed to be shifting and fraying at the edges. 'Perhaps it's just a coincidence that he shares a London address with Carstone?'

'Perhaps.' The gleam in Sam's eye struck fire. 'But given that it was when I made enquiries about General Lord Denderholm that I became . . . acquainted with Carstone's dog Matthias Schalk, what do you really think?'

I thought about Signor Marcelli. He came to me like one of Nanny Peck's clarities. That was Schalk's work – the cruelty of it was unmistakable. The old man was no saint, but he didn't deserve to die like that. And he was just the beginning.

Kite and the Barons were coming for me on my own ground. They'd already started on Sam.

Now the pain sharpened. It scraped against the bone like someone was stirring the contents of my skull with a spoon. I gasped, sat forward and forced the heels of my hands against my eyes. Lights started to explode in the darkness. Twisting, flickering lines moved against my closed lids. Then, just as soon as it had come on, it vanished.

I spread my hands flat on the table and opened my eyes. The yellow glow of the lamp shone up the concern on the faces of the two men I cared most about in all the world. If anything was to happen to either of them . . .

'Fannella?' Lucca stared at me. Sam rested his hand on mine for a second before moving it away sharp.

'It's nothing. It's the heat in here, that's all.' I took a deep breath. 'Listen, Sam, you just asked me what I thought about old whiskers there.' I nodded at the scrap of newsprint. 'Well, this is what I think. I reckon I'm going to have to see a man about a dog.'

*

On the way back to The Palace I told Sam about Signor Marcelli, how we found him at The Carnival. I noted he went quiet when I described what Schalk had done. Point of fact, we all did.

The growler was a deal more spacious than the hack we'd taken earlier on the Whitechapel Road. The size of it and the gap between us made the silence seem like a fourth person sitting there eavesdropping in the dark. I was surprised Lucca managed to find a ride at all at such an hour, let alone a four-seater.

There was a sharp rap on the roof as we jolted to a halt. The driver thumped up top and shouted something, but I couldn't make him out above the sound of the rain. It could have been Barney Knuckle up there dancing in his Lancashire clogs.

I peered through the trails of water sliding down the window. On account of the dark, the rain and the fugging of the glass, I didn't know where we were. Lucca gripped a strap set into the roof. The growler rocked and grated on its springs as he stood and pushed the slat to call up to the driver. A moment later I heard him jabbering away in his own tongue. The cabman was obviously one of his own; no wonder he'd managed to persuade him to take us. There was a jangle of coin. Lucca pushed his hand up through the slat to pay the fare, then he reached across me to open the door.

'He says it is as far as he can take us, Fannella. It is late and the roads in the City are flooding.'

'Where are we?' I rubbed the window. All I could see was shadow and rain.

'The end of Salmon Lane is just down there.' Lucca pointed. 'Not far.'

The carriage bounced and dipped to the left as he stepped down to the street. I gathered myself together and tried to make out Sam's face opposite. The brass candle lamp set into the back wall of the growler had burned out long before we'd even got in. I wasn't sure what to say, what the right thing to say might be. My mouth was dry as the bottom of Jacobin's cage.

'You . . . you'd be most welcome if . . .'

If what?

What was I expecting? I heard the little jet beads sewn into the lip of my bag rustle as I held it tight against me. I tried again.

'Do you . . . are you . . .'

'I'm going on.' Sam's voice was low. I heard the rusty creak of the seat springs and then I felt his warm breath on my face.

'It's best that we don't see each other, Kitty.'

He took my hand in the dark. 'It was a risk being seen with you this evening, but I had to come, just to reassure myself.'

'Reassure yourself of what?'

There was a silence, then he made a noise that was something between a snort and a laugh. 'For a man who makes a living from words, it's ironic that I can't seem to say the ones that really matter. Listen. I'll help you fight them, Kitty. I'll use every contact, every favour and every skill I possess to find a way to bring Kite and the rest of the Barons to justice.' He tightened his grip. 'Promise me you'll be on your guard. Use everything and everyone you know. I wouldn't do this unless I knew you'd be protected.'

Do what?

His voice came again. 'You know there was a time when I would have given my right eye for a story like this. But now . . .'

'Now what, Sam?'

The rain hammered overhead.

'Now it seems I'm a part of the story. I'm going to have to disappear. It's too dangerous otherwise, mainly for me. Look at what happened in your own theatre to the puppet man . . . Marcelli?'

I sat forward, trying to convince myself that I could see his face.

'What do you mean by *disappear*? You can't just vanish like Swami Jonah used to.'

As soon as I said the name, I felt cold lips brush the back of my neck. 'A corpse kiss', that's what Nanny Peck would have called it. Michael McCarthy, that poor wretch, was the last man I needed to be reminded of now.

'Actually, I can, Kitty, and it's what I'm going to do. You need someone who knows his way around every corner of this grimy city to help you. You need someone who can navigate a path from the highest places to the very lowest. You need a sharp-witted, sharp-eyed – of course I mean that in the singular – ally who knows how things tick along. In short, you need me. Now you must go, Lucca's waiting.'

'But—'

'Go, Kitty.' He released my hand.

'But I don't see . . .'

I was in such a coil that I didn't know what I was saying. I snatched at something that made a sort of sense. 'What about your job? What about *The Pictorial*?'

I was about to add something more, but I couldn't on account of the fact that Sam had gripped my hand again so tight I yelped out loud. I was aware of his face very close to mine in the darkness of the hack. I could feel his warmth on my skin. He was so near I could taste the smoke and porter on his breath. A fire caught me like kindling, spreading its heat to the pit of my belly. My bag slipped to the floor of the cab as I reached for him, but he drew back.

'You have to go now, Kitty. Lucca will be soaked to the skin.' I heard the crackle of dry leather, the grating of the springs then the rattle of beads. A moment later my bag was thrust roughly into my lap. I stretched out my hand, but the old leather protested again as he pulled himself back into the darkness.

'Sam, I—'

'If you don't go now, we'll argue, properly, for the first time. I mean it. Go!'

His voice was hard, angry almost. Confused, I gathered myself together and shifted along the seat to the door. My head was a tangle. In the light from the growler's lamps I could see poor Lucca hunched below on the cobbles, rain streaming from the brim of his hat. I took hold of the strap to steady myself and turned back. 'Sam, I—'

'Go!'

'Fannella, take my hand, please.'

Lucca, who must have heard quite a lot of that, helped me down. When I was standing on the street with little rivers running over my boots, Sam's voice came again, deepened to an echo from the empty darkness.

'Use everything and everyone. And don't worry about *The Pictorial* – I'll sort something out with Peters. We'll arrange it between us. Just make sure you buy every copy as long as it runs and keep a close eye on the announcements column at the back. My mother's maiden name was Simpson, Esther Simpson. Remember that.'

The door slammed shut. The driver, a mound of oilcloth, waved at Lucca and flicked his whip over the horse's glistening back. The growler lurched, jerked back and then it rumbled away into the night and the rain.

Chapter Seven

The street name was fixed to the pale stone wall beneath a row of tall windows. Lucca held his hat as he craned up at the sign.

'It is not the right place, Fannella. This is Broad Sanctuary.'

'It must be here somewhere.' I shook out the street map again, trying to make sense of it. The tissue-thin paper flapped in the wind, folding itself over the dark sleeve of my velvet jacket. I'd dressed myself sober and smart for the meeting I'd imagined, but at this rate my reunion with Lord Vellum was likely to stay that way.

I turned the map around and peered close at the tiny writing scuttling sideways along roads that looked like scratches on the paper. It was so fine the shadow of my gloved fingers showed clear through the sheet.

'It stands to reason that if there's a Broad Sanctuary, there has to be a little one too. According to the directories there's no other street in London with "Sanctuary" in its name. This has to be right. It's here, I know it.'

Tell truth, I wasn't as confident about that as I gave out. Behind us, Big Ben, the great bell in St Stephen's Tower, started to toll the quarter. A moment later the chimes from Westminster Abbey joined in. The sound echoed off the buildings, falling about us like iron rain.

It wouldn't be long, I reckoned, before we were soaked by the real thing. I turned to look up at the tower. The spire on top looked likely to prick the belly of the grey cloud massing overhead, but the gold on the clock and the fancy work above it glinted in the sun. It was the kind of day that couldn't make up its mind.

Lok and Hari stood in silence. Tan Seng had insisted that if we were travelling up west, we needed an escort. The pair of them, Hari most particular, had caused quite a stir on the streets of Westminster. Then again, I reckoned the sight of a young woman out for a constitutional with a doll-sized Chinaman and a lascar built like a camel was worth a second, third, or even a fourth glance.

Lucca had that ivory-handled gun hidden about his person somewhere, but Lok and Hari were always the best protection. I'd got used to Hari's silence now. It wasn't that he couldn't talk, it was just that he weighed his words like diamonds. As for Lok, I'd never again think of him as an old man after seeing him at work on the paddle ship the night we went to save Sam and Lucca.

I folded the map into a more amenable square to get a better view of our bearings.

'Look, we're on the corner of Broad Sanctuary and this road just here, aren't we?' I tapped the paper. Lucca moved closer.

'*Sì*, but it is Little *George* Street. I cannot see the road you want. We must be mistaken.'

He used the word 'we', but I knew he really meant 'you'.

'Hold this.' I handed him the map and opened my bag to fish out the stiff white square. I could tell by the weight and the sheen that the card was quality. The address was stark and spare, printed in neat black capitals.

33 LITTLE SANCTUARY

I flipped it about and stared at the back in case I'd missed a trick. I knew I hadn't – I'd examined it a dozen times since making my mind up – but I wanted to reassure myself. Now it was out in the light I could see a thin line of gold running round the sharp-cut edges, but that was all that was fresh. It gave nothing away. That card was a blank, just like the man who'd handed it to me.

Another bleedin' mystery, as if I needed one.

I ran the tip of a finger over the bold black letters, feeling the raising of the ink. Perhaps I was wrong, like Lucca said, and this wasn't the place after all. What if Lord Vellum was sending me to shoe a goose? I looked up to the metal street plate above Lucca's head and then back at the card.

'A fat lot of good this is. How am I supposed to find him when he hasn't given me a proper address?'

'My question is, why are you seeking him at all, Fannella? He is one of the Barons. This does not seem . . . *Questo è sciocco.*'

Lucca muttered that last bit into his collar. Something in the tone of it riled me.

'And what does that mean then, when it's in London?'

He pretended to study the map. 'I think you would call it the quest of a madman . . . a fool's errand.'

'Well, it's all I have. And if that's what you think, you might as well go back east because you're about as much help here as a violet in a tannery.'

I was sharp with him. Partly because I could see the sense of what he said and partly because it was Sam I wanted to argue with, not Lucca. It was him who'd abandoned me.

I'd had a night and the best part of a morning to think about it all now. How could he leave me like that? I was furious with

Sam, but, tell truth, I was stirring myself into a stew for allowing him to play me like a kitten. The Kitty Peck who'd sat there
pining for a kind word was a girl I didn't recognise. More than
that, I'd come to realise she was a girl I didn't much like.

Use everything and everyone.

That was what Sam had said while I stood there fretting and
dripping on the cobbles. Easier said than done, wasn't it? Especially when one of those 'everyones' had deliberately removed
himself. It came to me then, on the corner of Little George
Street and Broad Sanctuary, that it was a good deal more convenient to slip away into the dark than to stand at my side.

I touched Lucca's arm. 'I'm sorry. I spoke out of turn. Don't
go, please. It's not you I'm angry with.'

He stared at me, his head angled to the side, and tilted back
the brim of his hat for a better view. In the sunlight I could see
a network of fine lines in the skin around his eye that I hadn't
noticed before. The illness and the sleepless nights had cost
him. I got the impression he was seeing more than my face.

'I know, Fannella.' He smiled and shrugged. 'But what if
this is a trap? Have you considered that?'

I squeezed his arm. 'If it's a trap then I need you near me.
That's all I know.'

I pushed the card back into my bag and my fingers brushed
the folded scrap of print from *The Pictorial;* it was the story
that linked the man I was trying to find to the man who shared
Lord Kite's London address. I snapped the bag shut.

'Let's have another look at the map. The writing's so small
we must be missing something.'

As we bent our heads over the paper I wondered if Lucca
was right. Putting myself in the lap of one of the Barons was

the last thing that made sense. I couldn't blame him for being wary. Then again, he hadn't been there on the train when me and Lord Vellum – or whatever his real name was – had sat tight as shillings in a purse.

I'd had a lot to deal with on the day of Lady Ginger's funeral. There were parts of what I'd heard about the past that I couldn't – no, that's not right, that I *wouldn't* – allow myself to think about. At the end of that bleak summer day, when the Necropolis train had stopped abrupt and Lord Vellum had climbed into the carriage, I thought he'd come to finish the job the Barons had started when they gathered round my grandmother's box in the chapel of rest. But I was wrong.

Will you work with me, Miss Peck, to destroy them? You need not give me your answer now. Vellum had handed me the card. *If your answer is yes, seek me out.*

That's what I was trying to do.

I looked up as a plush black carriage rolled past. Its lacquer had such a sheen to it I could see us all reflected in the paint. The curve of the woodwork gave the effect of a fairground mirror, pulling us into strange, unnatural shapes. Of an instant, I saw very clear how we must have appeared to the world.

We made an odd group, there was no point in denying it. We looked like a carnival sideshow standing there.

As the carriage rounded the corner its big wide wheels churned a fountain of mud and rainwater from the gutter that sprayed up across my skirt and jacket. I took the brunt of it. I heard the driver laugh. It was no accident; he knew what he'd done, all right. I could feel the wet freckling of dirt on my face and taste the foulness of earth, metal and muck on my lips. The velvet was ruined and the sodden tissue of the map fell apart in my hands.

'Thanks for nothing!' I whipped about and shouted, not that the driver bothered to look back. I wasn't worth a second glance.

I saw the truth of it. It didn't matter if the map turned to mush because it was useless anyway. If Little Sanctuary was here we would have found it by now. Point of fact, it could be anywhere from here to bleedin' Timbuktu. It was like searching for a thimble in a sewer.

The carriage came to a halt some twenty yards away, stuck in a queue of similar highly polished and highly private conveyances. I screwed the remnants of the map into a soggy ball and started off up the street. Lucca called me back, but I was in a mood for a fight. I drew level and shouted up at the driver.

'Oi! You up there . . .'

The man scratched his chin and didn't look down.

'Are you deaf as well as blind?'

He affected not to hear me, although everyone else within fifty foot of us did.

'Yes, I'm talking to you – you up there on your perch. Look at me.'

I don't know what I expected, but an apology or at least an acknowledgement would have been something. He kept his eyes fixed on the broad shiny rumps of the two bay horses in the traces. Weak sunlight glinted off the brass buttons on his coat and the forked ribbon of his tall hat fluttered in the wind.

'If you don't want to talk to me, perhaps whoever you've got tucked up inside will.' I stepped back and rapped on the door of the carriage. 'Anyone home?'

Now the driver took account of me. I dodged back as he raised his whip, but instead of lashing out, his arm froze. In the black-lacquered sheen of the carriage's paintwork I could see Hari standing just behind me. A moment later, Lok was at my side, taut as a cat on the scent of a rat.

The driver's eyes flicked between us. A muscle worked his jaw and his thick lips curled into a sneer, revealing a tooth that matched the buttons of his coat. I've no doubt he was on the verge of making a vinegar comment, but it died in his throat because the carriage door opened and an old gent leaned out.

'What is this? Why have we stopped, Jenkins?' He stared at me, his eyes sharp beneath a pair of brows that could nest a wren.

'Who are you? What do you want?' You could slice a vein with his voice.

I stepped forward. Lok and Hari followed close. Lucca had now joined us too.

'Your driver just ruined my skirt and jacket. It was deliberate. Look at this.' I thrust an arm up at the carriage. 'It's velvet. I can never wear it again.'

I tuned my voice to a quality pitch. I could always speak like a lady when the occasion presented itself. Unfortunately, given that I must have looked like a soap-starved mumper and that I was keeping what you might call irregular company, this was not one of those occasions.

'Street beggars!' The old gent snorted and pulled back. 'Drive on, Jenkins. Talk to Weston when we reach the mews. We cannot have this sort of thing in the Sanctuaries.'

He made to close the carriage door, but I leapt from the kerbstone onto the metal step and put myself in the way of it.

'Fannella!' I heard Lucca gasp and was aware of the driver shifting up top. I leaned into the carriage and took down a lungful of leather and cigar. 'You just said "Sanctuaries". There's more than one, then? I'm looking for Little Sanctuary.'

The old man's eyes hardened beneath the thatch. 'I do not know what you mean.'

'Oh, but I think you do.' Careful to keep my balance, I dug into the bag hooked over my arm and took out the card.

'I was given this by a . . . gentleman. Here . . .' I forced the card under the passenger's long, high-bridged nose. He frowned and tried to take it from my hand, but I was too smart for him, swiping it away and dandling it out of his reach.

The door on the far side of the carriage opened, framing the broad shoulders and flat, angry face of the driver. A gust of wind snatched the ribbon of his hat and slapped it across his mouth. He pushed it away. 'Sir, are you . . .? Is everything . . .?' Jenkins scowled at me. 'I can call an officer if—'

'That will not be necessary.' The old man raised his hand. I noted that there was a gold ring on his smallest finger. 'Leave us for a moment. I will deal with your carelessness.'

Jenkins lingered in the doorway, his lips working at words that couldn't find their way out of his trap.

'I said leave us.' The old man swotted the air lazily. It was a dismissal. Jenkins huffed, closed the door and clambered back on his box. I steadied myself on the step as the carriage lurched. I heard a light pattering sound as raindrops began a jig on the straw of my bonnet.

'Where did you get that card?' The man sat forward. His dark coat was trimmed with sleek black fur at the collar and his breath smelt of cloves and good tobacco.

'Like I said, I was given it. "Seek me out." That's what he said.'

The old gent took me in. His gaze ran from the muddy tips

of my boots and lingered on the smuts on my face. His eyes were surprisingly dark given his age, which must have been near seventy. It came to me then that he might be one of them, one of the Barons of London, I mean. They all looked so bleedin' similar – with one or two notable exceptions – but perhaps this was one I'd overlooked?

My heart thumped under the soiled velvet. I glanced back down at Lucca, Hari and Lok as the old man spoke again.

'And you are?' There wasn't a trace of interest in the question.

'That's none of your business –' I tried to keep my voice steady – 'but if you know where I can find this Little Sanctuary, I'd take it in payment for the jacket.'

The man sat there still and silent as one of them marble statues Lucca used to be so fond of drawing when he took himself off to a museum for an afternoon. Under his stony consideration I felt the hairs stir on the back of my neck.

He drawled again. 'You say a gentleman gave you that card. Under what circumstances?'

This was going too deep. I swallowed. 'I . . . I'd rather not say. It's a private matter, between me and him.'

'Describe him.'

I stared at the man and wondered what to say. It was raining heavily now. The half of me poking out of the carriage door was already soaked.

'Come now, that is a simple question, surely? What was this man like?'

'He . . .' Why did he want to know? What was it to him?

It came to me then, with a clarity, that the old man knew exactly who I was talking about. Was that good or bad? I took a breath.

'He was young. He had dark hair, grey eyes and a good rig. Well spoken too – a regular toff, he was.'

I'd given up playing the lady. Something told me the old man sitting in front of me had smoked me on that one, as Sam might have said. If he was here.

There was a long silence.

'You have described a thousand men in this city. Think again.'

I went back to that meeting on the train. I saw my man of law Marcus Telferman, the Beetle as I called him, being marched from the train across a field by Vellum's men. I saw Vellum remove his grey kid gloves and fold them neat. I saw his long fingers trace a pattern on the flat silk crown of his hat. I saw the rain trickling down the window.

And I remembered something Vellum said.

'*But when the melancholy fit shall fall*
Sudden from heaven like a weeping cloud . . .'

'Poems! He likes poetry. He quoted Keats to me.' Tell truth, until that day I'd never heard of Keats, but I'd lodged it away.

The old man blinked and breathed out long and loud like he'd been holding his breath. 'I will take you to Little Sanctuary. Ride with me.' His gaze strayed over my shoulder. 'You will come alone, your . . . companions will not be necessary.'

'No.' I shook my head so hard that drops of water flew from the brim of my bonnet and spattered across his face. He didn't move to wipe them away.

'I can't leave them. What if . . .'

The man's brows tangled together over eyes like chips of polished jet. Now he shifted forward.

'It is a simple choice. If you would like me to take you

into the Sanctuaries, you will come alone or not at all.'

'Fannella!' Lucca tugged the hem of my jacket. 'You cannot.' I turned to look down at the three of them. The rain was coming so hard that the long loose tunics worn by Lok and Hari were plastered to their skin. Lok, whose tiny, bony form showed clear through the sodden cloth, shook his head.

Lucca reached up to catch my hand. 'You do not know this man.' He hissed the words, but the old gent caught them. That tight-bred voice came again.

'You will be quite safe, I assure you. I give you the word of the Crown, Miss Peck.'

Chapter Eight

After I climbed in, the old man asked me – ordered is more like – to pull the blinds down. I did as I was told and then, when I was perching there in the dark, wrapped in the scent of good leather, sweet cloves and fine cigars, I spoke.

'How come you know my name?'

He didn't answer. The only sound for the next five minutes was the grind of the carriage wheels on the cobbles. I sat on the edge of the seat, keenly aware of him opposite me. It's a funny thing, but the old gent seemed bigger in the dark. The sense of him filled the little space. When we came to a halt he spoke again.

'This is as far as I can take you. Go straight ahead into the passage. Knock four times on the black door you will find on the right towards the end. You cannot mistake your way. You will find Little Sanctuary there.'

He rapped on the roof with his cane.

'Good day to you, Miss Peck.'

The door opened to reveal Jenkins dripping outside. I gathered myself together and reached for the strap to steady myself before I went down. I paused. It was worth another go.

'You might as well tell me now we're here. How do you know me? What am I to you?'

The old gent busied himself with the ring on his smallest finger; it was clear he wasn't going to answer that. I tried again.

'What made you bring me here? You can tell me that at least.'

He looked up. 'Ah, I almost forgot. When the door is opened you will be asked who you wish to see. The answer is Endymion.'

*

I found the black door easy enough, just as the old gent had said I would. It was the only one on either side of the blank brick walls. I looked up at the chink of slate-grey sky overhead and back to the entrance of the passage. The carriage had gone. I was alone.

I don't know what I'd been expecting Little Sanctuary to look like, but it hadn't been a back street in Limehouse. I'll admit it for free, I was surprised when the carriage stopped dead and Jenkins opened the door to reveal a passage rutted with puddles.

I knew what Lucca would have to say about this, mind. I deliberately didn't look at him when I closed the lacquered door behind me and sat down opposite the old gent for fear of seeing the face on him. But what else could I do?

The card in my bag was all I had.

Will you work with me, Miss Peck, to destroy them?

That's what Vellum had said on the train. And something else came back too. He'd promised me that Telferman wouldn't be hurt. I wasn't sure about that as I'd watched the Beetle, suddenly small and old to my eyes, being led across the field through the steam, but then Vellum had given me his word on it – *the word of the Crown.*

Now, wasn't that just what the old clove-sucker had said too? *What are you getting yourself into, girl?* The thought went off in my head loud and clear as the Grand Surrey shift bell.

Of an instant, I had the strongest wish to have Lucca standing there in the passage with me. I stared at the scuffed, mud-spattered door. It was an ordinary door, a poor sort of door, the kind of door no one would cast a second glance at.

Beneath the knocker I could just make out the number 33. It had been painted over numerous times. Only the way the trickles of rainwater slid around the raised metal plate showed that the number was there at all. It was almost invisible, a ghost.

Number 33 Little Sanctuary wasn't a place a person was supposed to notice.

I took a breath, reached up for the ring of the knocker and rapped four times. The sound echoed off the walls of the passage. I waited and was about to try again when the door opened. A small bald man, whose large, round, gold-rimmed glasses gave him the look of an owl, considered me and found me wanting.

'No hawkers.'

He made to shut the door, but I stopped him with my foot.

'I'm not selling anything. I . . . I have an appointment.'

'I find that hard to believe, Miss.' He shook his head. 'You must be mistaken. If you'd stand aside, please.' We wrestled with the door.

'Endymion. I'm here to see Mr Endymion.'

The owl man stopped trying to force my foot from the jamb and peered at me again. He was quite still now, his eyes sharp as pins in their vast glass pools.

'Could you repeat that, Miss?'

'Endymion.'

He frowned, but stepped back. 'In that case follow me,

please, and shut the door behind you, if you would. We don't like draughts in the Sanctuaries.'

The little man led me along a low dim passage that hadn't seen a lick of paint for the last fifty years. At the end he stood aside to let me go first through another very ordinary door.

That's when I realised the faded entrance to 33 Little Sanctuary was as much a bit of scenery as anything Lucca might have painted in the workshops.

I stepped through the plain wooden door into the grandest hall I'd ever seen. The size of it stopped me at the threshold. You could fit The Carnival in here twice over and still have room for The Comet. Fifty pairs of eyes turned to take me in.

Whey-faced clerks sat at desks arranged in four rows beneath chandeliers the size of madeira casks. There was a long, uncomfortable silence broken by a couple of coughs and the rustle of papers as the men in their mahogany rows pretended to return to whatever it was they was doing.

The Owl led me between the desks to a broad archway opposite the door where we'd come in. The tapping of my heels echoed on the marble tiles as we crossed the hall. Some of the clerks tutted and shuffled their pages in protest at this female intrusion.

We went beneath the arch and I found myself in another long room with a fancy gilded ceiling. The wall in front of me was covered in an enormous painting stretching from corner to corner.

A map of the world it was, with all the countries named and clearly bounded. There were several full-sized figures dotted about the painting, all of them most exotic and all of them presenting armfuls of fruits, cloth, jewels, fur and ivory tusks to the viewer. Some of them were kneeling and one was riding on something like a very large and dirty goose. There was a quantity of blue water as well, in which a school of buxom mermaids bobbed lazily about without giving too much thought to their modesty.

I didn't go on it much. And I reckoned Lucca wouldn't have liked it neither. It was a brash, bold thing, full of swagger and show but not much else.

The Owl went towards it and grasped a mermaid's nipple, which I took for a liberty until it turned out to be a handle. Half the wall swung inwards.

'There's another door just through there.' He nodded into the shady space behind the painting. 'Go out across the courtyard, enter the building directly opposite by the central steps. Straight up the stairs, you can't miss them, and then through the double doors at the first landing. The room is at the end of the corridor. He knows you are here.'

He dipped his head once, turned and headed back to the hall of clerks. I almost wished he'd come with me.

*

The panelled double doors whispered to a close behind me. A faded red carpet that put me in mind of a tongue rolled away to another set of polished doors some twenty yards ahead. There were no windows, but the empty corridor was brightly lit by rows of gas lamps burning fierce as little suns. The flames were set so high I could hear the jigging of the glass shades in the brass fittings. The lamps were placed at intervals between more doors, four on either side, set along the walls.

I wondered if I'd done the right thing. Perhaps there was still time to go back down the wide marble stairs beyond the panelled doors, out across the courtyard with the dolphin fountain in the middle, back into the building that appeared to be a perfect mirror of the one I was standing in now, cross the echoing hallway where fifty clerks worked in silence and out again through the narrow peeling door to the dingy alleyway where I'd come in.

The gas lamps hissed and rattled. My shadow danced on the walls. It looked ragged, unfinished. I remembered the way the Owl had mistaken me for a hawker or perhaps even a beggar outside on the step. I swiped at my face with the back of my hand, hoping to clear away the smuts. Judging from the state of my gloves, it probably made matters worse. I tore them off and pushed them into my bag. Then I twisted the limp strands of hair that had come free from their pins back up beneath my bonnet. As I pushed my hair under the straw, I caught sight of the sleeves of my jacket, the black velvet blotched and grey where the scum and the rain had spoiled it. I tried to smooth it down, but it only spread the marks in the grain. My skirt was crusted with mud.

I fumbled with the top two collar buttons of the jacket that had worked loose and pulled at the stiff cotton neck of my dress to neaten the line. There was nothing else I could do to make myself a lady.

I gripped the handle of my bag. He already knew I was here, that's what the Owl had said. But what did I know? Was Lord Vellum – or whatever he called himself – a Baron? If he was, this was a trap and I'd walked right into it. One of the gas-lights popped and flared, sending my shadow to the ceiling.

A moment later, as the flame dimmed, it shrank back to the wall where it quivered on the red scrolling flock.

I stared at the doors at the end of the corridor. Vellum had had ample opportunity to do me a mischief when he'd cornered me on that train. It would have been an easy thing to take me, despite the gun in my hand. He'd had a dozen men with him waiting beside the track and a carriage parked up in the lane beyond the field.

Why didn't he make a move then?

There was only one way to answer that. I hooked my bag over the crook of my arm and started off up the red carpet. At the door I raised my hand and saw it was trembling like my shadow. I balled it tight into a fist and knocked once.

'Enter.'

I reached for the handle. Despite the fact that every bone and muscle was pulling in the other direction, I walked into the room. It was smaller, more intimate you might say, than the halls I'd already seen, but it was still fine. A row of arched windows opposite the door allowed grey-blue light to slant across a figured rug. Over to the right a fire crackled in the hearth beneath a carved marble surround. There were two tall-backed chairs set before it. One of them had its back to me. I wondered if . . .

'Miss Peck.'

I turned at the voice. Cultured it was and there was a particular tone to it. I remembered the time we met on the train when I thought there was something in the way he spoke that suggested he had better things to do.

At the other end of the room Vellum sat behind a wide desk. He raised a hand in greeting.

'I've been waiting.'

I nodded. 'Your man downstairs, he said you knew I was here.'

He smiled. 'I mean that I have been waiting a long time. Indeed, I was beginning to wonder if you would ever come.'

Of an instant, it wasn't fear I felt, it was anger. The blood rushed to my tongue.

'And whose fault is that then? All I had was that card you gave me on the train.' I marched up to his desk. 'You didn't make it bleedin' easy, did you?'

There was a moment of silence during which we took the measure of each other like cats spoiling for a scrap. He stared up at me, his cool grey eyes amused, but alert.

'That was rather the point.' He steepled his fingers together. Gold studs gleamed in the cuffs of a shirt that was at least three shades whiter than anything fresh from a Limehouse wash shop. There was a sheen to him that didn't come cheap. Now I was close I got the scent of him again. Lavender and something I couldn't quite place, although I could tell it was quality. In the light from the window there was almost a gleam of blue in his smooth dark hair.

Sleek as a thirty-guinea horse, Vellum was a looker. I remembered dialling that before, and just like before I hated myself for noting it. I dragged my eyes from his and fumbled with the clasp of my bag, thinking to throw the card in his long pale face.

'That will not be necessary. You are quite safe with me, I assure you.'

I quizzed at him, confused. He gestured at the bag.

'The gun, Miss Peck. That moment of theatre on the train

when last we met? I assume you are about to produce it again.'

I shook my head, although the thought occurred that it might have been useful to have Lucca's pistol tucked away.

Vellum stood. 'Good. That would have been most . . . unwise. Now, I have asked for tea.'

He rounded the desk and walked past me to the hearth. I turned; from here I could see a low table set between the chairs. He bent to lift a china pot.

'Will you join me?'

Chapter Nine

'The north range is always cold. Even at the height of summer I keep a fire burning here.'

He lifted his tea cup and saucer. I copied him, uncertain what to do. Sitting there close to the hearth, I was aware of the stench of the streets rising from the hem of my skirt. The difference between us couldn't have been clearer. I'd brought the gutter in with me.

The china was so fine I could see my fingers through it. I wasn't trembling now, and I was glad of it because the cup and saucer would rattle together like buttons in a tin. I didn't want Vellum to know how I felt. Sitting here, I didn't rightly know that myself. The tea tasted of flowers and smoke. It wasn't quite like the blend Tan Seng used at The Palace, but it was near. The warmth and familiarity of it made me bold.

'Your man at the door – the one who looks like an owl – he said you didn't like draughts in the Sanctuaries.'

'An owl!' I thought Vellum smiled, but he raised the cup to his lips. 'Yes, you are quite right about that. And so is he. The building is nearly three hundred years old. As you would expect, after such a very long time, it has developed some troubling . . . fissures.'

'Troubling what?' I sipped again.

'Fissures, Miss Peck. Gaps, chinks, cracks.'

'You mean you can't keep the heat in?'

I watched Vellum stare into his tea. He nodded slowly. 'In a manner of speaking, yes.'

I looked at the fire. A pile of papers burned in the grate; the pages blackened and curled and little fiery scraps rose into the throat of the chimney. The papers had been covered in close-packed script. As I watched, a page on the top of the pile unfurled and shifted as flames snatched at the edges. It scorched from the corners, spreading a smudge of darkening brown that ate up the words. At the bottom of the sheet, the last portion visible, was a name written out bold, but upside down.

VICTORIA

As I watched it burn, it came to me what it meant when Vellum and the old man in the coach had given me *the word of the Crown.*

'I don't think you mean draughts, not in the ordinary way.'

Vellum didn't answer. Now we were sitting tight I could see fine lines around his eyes and mouth that gave the lie to his easy manner. He wasn't much older than me, or Lucca and Sam come to that, but despite his general sheen, there was something worn about him. There were threads of silver in the black at his temples and shadows beneath his eyes that suggested sleep wasn't his natural bedfellow.

Despite my frowsy gear, I felt more like an equal. And the thought went through my head that the reason I was sitting here was that he might need me as much as I needed him. I sat up straight in the chair.

'Things get out through chinks and cracks, don't they? You didn't ask me here to take tea and talk about keeping house. This place is hidden away behind a peeling black door that looks like a thousand other doors in London, but on the other side it's something very different.'

I couldn't read the expression on his face as I went on.

'See, what I reckon is this. When you try to keep something close it's a hard thing. Secrets get out, don't they? And by the looks of things, this is a place with a lot to hide. Let's get to the meat in the shell, otherwise there's no point in me being here. Where am I? If this is Sanctuary, what's it keeping safe? And for that matter who, most exactly, are you? When we were on that train you talked about the Barons. You asked me to work with you to destroy them. That's the only reason I came here to find you. I've got good reason to hate them, but you . . . you're bleedin' one of them!'

Vellum's neat black hair fell across his face. He swept it back and the firelight sparked in the golden studs of his cuffs. He looked as if he was about to say something, but then he thought better of it and busied himself with the pot. After a moment he spoke.

'You are quite mistaken in that, Miss Peck, although your observations are . . . correct in some other matters. Would you like more tea?'

'I've had quite enough, thank you. I didn't come here on a social visit and I'm sure you didn't want me to go to the trouble of finding this place so you could play mother over the china.'

He smiled tightly. 'Of course not. I merely believe that business should always be conducted in the most civilised and courteous manner.'

He lifted the pot and poured a stream of thin gold tea into his cup.

'So this is business, then?' I looked around at the room. It was finely furnished. The panelled wooden walls glowed like new-minted chestnuts. Rows of bookshelves stretched between the windows, giving the place the air of a library. On the wall along from the door where I'd come in, there were several paintings of men, most of them in military rig. The braid on their shoulders and the gilt of their buttons caught the light from the fire. The rug underfoot was thick as a parson's lawn and the dark blue velvet curtains swagged around the windows pooled on the floor in a way that suggested whoever ordered them didn't have to worry much about cutting their cloth.

I sat forward.

'Whose business?'

I thought I might know the answer to that, but I wanted to hear it.

Vellum glanced at the fire where the papers had burned to a heap of glowing ash. He reached for a silver bowl on the tray and stirred a spoonful of sugar into his tea.

I plonked my own cup and saucer back on the table so hard the china rattled. 'Listen, I reckon I've taken a considerable risk coming to find you. The first time I saw you was at Great Bartholomew's that night when . . . when . . .'

When I murdered Peggy's Danny – good as, anyway.

That's what went through my head, only I couldn't say it.

'. . . when you were one of them, a Baron, I mean,' I carried on. 'But now, here you are tucked away Christ knows where, pouring tea like a bleedin' duchess, warming your feet at the fire and expecting us to have a cosy little chat like nothing's happened. For all I know, any minute now Lord Kite might walk through that door.'

Vellum took a sip of his tea. 'That would be most unlikely.'

'Why? Is it more unlikely than me being here?'

'You came here by choice and at my personal invitation.'

He regarded me with them clear grey eyes and I saw something dangerous there. I was minded of the old gent in the coach.

'When the time is right, Anthony Carstone will not be so fortunate.' He placed his cup and saucer back on the tray. The movement was careful, delicate even, as if to show me how it was done in polite circles. He looked up at the ceiling, his eyes roaming around like he was looking for something that had got lost up there. At last he fixed on a spot just above my head.

'As I told you that afternoon on the train, Miss Peck, and again today, I am not a Baron. I never was. My . . . connection was purely a professional matter.'

He rose and went to a bookshelf on the far side of the fireplace. I watched him scan the rows. As he reached to the shelves his frock coat fell away and I noted how spare he was, beneath all that gear.

Nothing a good meat pudding couldn't right. Nanny Peck's voice went off in my head. I was surprised; it had been a deal of time since I'd been reminded of one of the old girl's observations, but I was oddly grateful to hear her now.

Vellum selected two books, offered one to me and sat down again opposite to flick through some thin pages. I looked at the book in my hand, only to find it was more like a leather-covered brick, bound in cord and covered in scratches and symbols I couldn't begin to make sense of.

'What's this?'

'It is *The Art of War*, in the original.' He didn't look up. 'An ancient Chinese treatise on military strategy, but the principles are of universal application. I find it very useful. That copy is fragile and rather valuable. I rarely refer to it. This –' he raised the book in his hand – 'is a French transcription. One day, I intend to translate Sun Tzu into English, but for now, the Amiot will suffice. Ah, here. It is a little crude and loses some of the nuance, but . . .'

He began to read swiftly.

'"*It is said that if you know your enemies and know yourself, you will not be put at risk even in a hundred battles. If you only know yourself, but not your opponent, you may win or may lose. If you know neither yourself nor your enemy, you will always endanger yourself.*"'

He closed the book. 'What do you make of that?'

It was familiar. Hadn't Lucca said something very similar after we'd watched the Reverend at the Martingate Mission?

It is good to know your enemies.

I turned the peeling leather brick in my hands, recognising the marks and lines now as Chinese writing, much like one of Tan Seng's lists back at The Palace. I found myself thinking about the brothers. I wondered if they'd heard of *The Art of War*. Judging by the way they helped me to free Lucca and Sam on the boat, I reckoned they had. Or if they hadn't, they didn't need to. That little piece I'd just had read to me was all about the importance of knowing your enemies, but it was just as important to know your friends.

I thought about Danny's bloody broken fingers clutching the hem of my skirt. He'd begged me to save him that night at Great Bartholomew's, only I couldn't. Under the jacket I could feel the collar of my cotton blouse twitch in time to the blood pulsing in a vein in my neck. I tried to swallow it still.

'Well?' Vellum asked again.

I looked up. 'You . . . you were playing a part. You got yourself accepted into their number so you could find out about them.'

He nodded. 'Precisely.'

'In your *Art of War* it says that if you know your enemies you won't be put at risk.' I handed Vellum the old Chinese book. 'But there's no art to betraying your friends, and no risk neither. Not for you, leastways. You were there that night when they made me seal Danny Tewson into that pit and you did nothing.'

'There was nothing I could do.' Vellum looked away. 'I am sorry, but I could not allow myself to be discovered. It was a terrible thing they did to that man. And you must see it was *them,* not you, Miss Peck. Hold onto that, otherwise you will not be able to live with yourself.'

He stood and went back to the shelves with the books. Something came to me. I twisted in the chair.

'How did they test you? They always ask for a sacrifice to try your mettle. Danny was mine, what was yours?'

Vellum pushed the books back into place. He didn't look at me and he didn't answer, neither, but I knew from the way he kept his back to me and the way he moved, like one of Signor Marcelli's puppets, that he was fighting to master himself. When he finally turned, his face was taut and white as his cuffs.

'Your grandmother, Lady Ginger, was consumed by hatred for those men. I believe her cancer was a physical manifestation of that enmity. If you want to avenge Daniel Tewson, Miss Peck, and indeed all of them – the men, the women, the children – whose lives the Barons have tainted or destroyed, then I suggest it is anger you should feel, not guilt. You, of all people, have every reason to wish for revenge. Your friend Mr Fratelli? Your brother Joseph? Indeed, your whole family . . .' He paused. 'I understand that when your grandmother was . . . *tested*—'

'Not that!' I shouted aloud to stop him. I didn't want Vellum to finish that sentence, but it was too late. It all came squirming into my head – all the things I'd been trying so hard not to think about. That pain stabbed sharp and sudden over my left eye. It gouged and twisted deep. I scrabbled at my forehead, knocking the bonnet askew. The light seemed to drain from the room, leaching the colour and the shape of everything around me. I cupped my head in my hands and felt the bonnet tumble.

'Miss Peck . . . Kitty!' Vellum's voice came from far away.

I saw the Barons' faces as they gathered round my grandmother's tiny coffin. Lord Oak, Lord Mitre, Lord Silver, Lord Ferrous and the Lords Janus, joined at the hip and shuffling closer. I smelt the mountain of flesh that was Lord Fetch, even though he wasn't there, and I felt the spittle on my face from Kite's bloodless lips as he told me that any one of the men present could be my father.

*

'Miss Peck?' I was pulled upright. I felt a cool hand at the collar of my jacket. Someone loosened the buttons at my neck and pushed damp hair back from my forehead. The hand moved to my face, patting the skin of my cheeks. 'Can you hear me?'

For a moment, I wasn't sure where I was. Then I began to

cough as smoke filled my nose. Something was burning. There was a sour twang to the scent of it.

'Your hat!'

I was thrown back into the chair. The jolt brought me fully to my senses. I opened my eyes to see Vellum trying to extract my bonnet from the edge of the hearth with a poker. It had rolled too close to the edge and now the veil was alight. There was a spitting sound as the black straw caught, blazing with a bright and greenish flame. The bird sewn to the rim dipped lower and lower. Just before it flared into a spitting ball, I imagined I caught a look of regret in its beady black eyes. Now Vellum used the poker to push the ruined bonnet deeper into the hearth.

'That's two guineas gone up in smoke.' I sat up in the chair and watched the bonnet curl upon itself until it was a charred and twisted thing.

Vellum kneeled in front of me, taking my hands in his. 'You fainted.' He scanned my face. 'Are you recovered?'

I nodded. I wasn't entirely sure what had happened. 'Must have been the tea?' I tried a smile. My head felt as if it was stuffed with wool. Despite the heat of the fire, I shivered.

'I have something stronger. It might be wise.' He stood and went back to the desk. I heard a chink of glass and the sound of liquid being poured.

'Brandy.' He returned to the hearth and placed two full glasses on the tray between the tea cups. Sitting down again, he cleared his throat.

'I must apologise, Miss Peck. I spoke in haste and in anger. It was insensitive of me to mention your late grandmother in such a clumsy way. Forgive me, I did not realise that it would affect you so.'

I almost laughed in his face. He thought I was grieving for the old cow. That was rich.

He nodded at the brandy. 'Drink. It will revive you.'

I looked down into the dark liquid. I was minded of the ruby earrings that glinted in the hollows of my grandmother's stringy neck. I took up the glass and swallowed a mouthful, feeling the hot trail of it slip down my throat to my belly. It warmed me. I took another sip.

'You knew her well, then – my grandmother, I mean?'

Vellum flicked a speck lint from his sleeve. 'I cannot say I knew Lady Ginger well. I wonder if anyone could say that?' He stared at me over the rim of his glass; I knew he was calculating how much to tell me.

'We met once, privately, your grandmother and I. The meeting took place at her house in Sussex a week or so before she died. The Abbey is now yours, I believe?'

'I'm selling it. I don't need Fraines Abbey. As far as I'm concerned her money is tainted and I can find better things to do with it.' It was true enough. The Beetle was already drawing up plans. I didn't want my grandmother's fortune and I didn't want a hand in the pockets of the dirty trades that built it.

I sipped again at the brandy. 'So, you and her . . . you had a little chat then? That must have been a rare treat.'

Vellum turned his glass between long thin fingers. 'It was . . . enlightening. During that meeting it became very clear to me that we shared a common goal.'

'To bring the Barons down?'

He nodded slowly. 'She told me that you held the key.'

I stared at the wreckage of my bonnet in the hearth, a crumpled fist-sized lump atop a pile of ash. I bit my lip, wondering whether to try him on it. The brandy decided for me.

'I saw a name on one of them papers you was burning in the fire. It was a woman's name. A high name.' I cradled the glass in my hands; the liquor made me bolder. 'A royal name.'

Vellum's face, all angles and shadows, gave nothing away.

'You work for her, don't you? The Queen, I mean. When we met on the train you gave me the word of the Crown that the Beetle – Mr Telferman – wouldn't be harmed and just now the old gent who gave me a ride here in his carriage said the same. What is this place? And for that matter, if you're not a Baron – I think I almost believe you on that score now – what are you?'

'A shadow.'

'What's that supposed to mean?'

'It means precisely that, Miss Peck. I am a shadow, nothing more. I do not have a name or a title. In a hundred or perhaps two hundred years' time, when those with an appetite for such things examine documents and records to seek an understanding of our age, they will not find me and the others like me, nor will they find the man who brought you in his carriage to Little Sanctuary. They will not find a trace of the men you saw in the hall, or their many, many colleagues working in places you could not begin to imagine. But our shadows will fall across history. We make history.'

I frowned, trying to make sense of what he was telling me. 'You mean . . . *you* make the rules? You and all them others out there?' I waved my glass at the door. Brandy splashed over the crystal rim to spatter on the rug. Vellum looked down at the tiny dark stains, but he didn't give me an answer.

I tried again. 'What about the Queen, don't she have a say in all this?'

He blinked, but gave nothing more.

'Or Mr Gladstone? He's the bleedin' prime minister, after all.'

He swirled the brandy, the glow from the embers of the fire sparking the crystal. 'You work in the theatre, Miss Peck. I am confident that you are familiar with painted facades and actors playing a role.'

'You mean he's not real?'

Vellum laughed. For the first time he sounded genuinely amused. 'Oh, Mr Gladstone is very real, I can assure you of that. But the true business of government, the hard, brutal, bloody business of ruling an Empire that covers two thirds of the globe, is not in his hands, or for that matter in the hands of our queen. It would be an impossibility. She does not hold the reins.'

'And you do?'

He reached into a pocket, drew out a folded slip of paper and handed it to me.

'Read this, please.'

I opened it out. One word was written in small neat black capitals.

VINULUM

My heart skipped under the velvet. I glanced at Vellum, but he was staring into his glass. I screwed the paper to a little ball.

She told me that you held the key.

Of course! That's what he was sinuating earlier when he said he'd had an 'enlightening' conversation with Lady Ginger. Point of fact, I did hold the key. The code to open the Vinculum, the place where the Barons kept their greatest treasure, was scrawled between the printed lines on the tissue-thin pages of the Bible that my brother Joey had given me when I went to him at the Bethlem. There were only two people alive who knew that code. Joey had it locked in his head and I had it locked in a drawer at the bottom of my wardrobe wrapped in Nanny Peck's old plaid shawl.

Joey again! Even here I couldn't escape him, not entirely. My brother was the cause of so much trouble. I'd kept my side of the bargain and got him out of the Bethlem, but I didn't have the first idea of where he was now. I was content for matters to stay that way. It had taken me eighteen years to work him out, and at the end I found it wasn't worth the effort.

Tell truth, having the code wasn't worth much to me neither. I didn't know where, or even *what* exactly, the Vinculum was, so having the code to open it was about as useful as a farthing to a beggar. I knew one thing for a certainty, though: it was dangerous. People had died for that string of numbers, letters and symbols.

I tossed the ball of paper onto the smouldering hearth. Vellum watched it open out and blacken and then he took a swig of brandy.

'Did you recognise the word, Miss Peck?'

I decided the best course was ignorance when it came to anything connected to Joey Peck. There were already too many complications creeping out of the wainscots for my liking. I shrugged.

'Is it another made-up name like yours? Endymion, is it? That's what they called you at the door. Perhaps this Vinculum is someone else who works here? Either way, it means nothing to me.'

'Clearly.' He nodded and put his glass on the tray. 'The world beyond the Sanctuary is a perilous place, Miss Peck. The Barons, mostly, are the very least of my concerns.'

'You said, on the train, that they were . . .' I closed my eyes to get it exact. '. . . *as fleas on the back of a dog compared to what is coming.*'

'Good. You have an excellent memory. Your grandmother mentioned it to me, among other things. I can use that.'

I folded my arms. 'Don't I get a say in it?'

He took a flat silver case from his pocket, flicked it open and offered it to me. Inside, the case was gilded and full of long white smokes, the sort that Sam couldn't afford. I had a sudden rush of guilt. I realised I was almost enjoying sitting here in front of the fire. There was something about Vellum's manner of speaking and his company that . . .

I stopped that as quick as it had come. I took a smoke as much for something to do as for the taste.

'I had the feeling you were a modern.' He leaned across to light it for me and I smelt the richness of his cologne. He lit his own cigarette.

'Let me tell you a little of how I came to be among them, the Barons. Perhaps that will convince you.' He took a drag and sat forward, the cigarette dandling elegantly between his fingers.

'The association was not a long one, but it was, until the end, useful. As you know, Miss Peck, it is the habit of the Barons to favour their own. It took months of subterfuge and persuasion, not to mention forgery, to convince them that I was the natural heir of Sir Anthony Woolley, he being the previous Lord Vellum.'

'It's not your real name then?' I took down a lungful. I was right, it was a decent smoke.

'Of course it is not.' Vellum – or whoever he really was – looked pained, and disappointed in me, which cut. I knew full well it wasn't his name.

'I was just . . . just—'

'Interrupting.' He flicked his ash into the hearth and moved a silver dish close to my side of the table.

'We have known about the existence of the Barons for many years. My predecessors tolerated them as one might tolerate a dog of uncertain temperament.'

'Where I come from we wouldn't put up with a mutt like that.'

Vellum arched a brow. 'We are from quite different worlds, Miss Peck. There are bonds that go deep. The Barons are drawn from some of our oldest and most respectable families.'

'But they're a bunch of bleedin' criminals – the lot of them.'

He took up his brandy. 'An interesting word. Tell me, how do you imagine the greatest families in the land came by their wealth originally?'

Tell truth, I hadn't given the matter much thought, let alone imagination. But then I picked on something he'd said.

'The greatest families, you say? What about the brothers? The joined ones from the carnival folk? I can't *imagine* you carving a Sunday joint with them at your table.'

'The Lords Janus are regarded as kings within their . . . tribe.' Vellum's eyes strayed to the end of my smoke, which was threatening to fall on the rug. I tapped it over the tray.

'Go on then. If you put up with them for so long, what changed?'

'The times. Do you remember I told you on the train that the Barons are an anachronism?'

'A chronic what?'

I saw that sly grin again, but he masked it quick. 'They have no place in our modern world. The time has come to deal with them. They are an irritation, an impediment, a distraction . . .' He paused. 'And also a risk. I do not fear the Barons, Miss Peck, but I do fear that their existence may one day prove useful to others. It is those others I fear.'

He settled back with his smoke and his brandy. 'As you know, it is not an easy thing to become a Baron. We watched for our chance and it came in the form of Sir Anthony Woolley, who held a place at court. His official title was Master of the Queen's Velin—' He broke off and fixed his eyes on mine. 'Do you know what vellum is?'

I shook my head. 'I thought it might be another made-up word.'

'It is not. Vellum is a parchment, a sort of paper made from cured calfskin. It has remarkable longevity, which is why, for hundreds of years, the laws of this land have been recorded on it. The vellum rolls are stored in a variety of places. Many are stacked in the cellars beneath St Stephen's Hall at the Houses of Parliament. Master of the Queen's Velin – that, by the way, is the Old French for vellum – was something of an honorary title, but with it came certain grants of access to the original documents that enshrine government. In the right, or the *wrong* hands to be more specific, such information is extremely useful. This was most valuable to the Barons and to Kite – Carstone as we both know him – in particular. For a long time, Woolley was his great ally among that infernal pack.'

Vellum paused. 'But then, just eighteen months ago, Sir Anthony had a riding accident in Hyde Park. He fell from his horse in Rotten Row.'

I had a clarity. 'An accident? Or was it something else?'

He dashed away my question with a flick of the hand holding the cigarette. A plume of smoke wavered between us. 'The horse bolted. I daresay *something* must have given it a fright. Woolley was paralysed and bedridden. He lingered in that state for several months, but never recovered the ability to move or speak. That was when I made my move. I'd been waiting for an opportunity to infiltrate their number and Woolley's . . . misfortune was exactly what I needed. It was . . . lucky for me.'

He reached for his brandy and gulped down a mouthful. After a moment he continued.

'Woolley was childless. He had never married, but there were rumours about his dalliances with young, very young, women. He had a preference, it seems, for the younger daughters of minor titled families. It is a long and rather sordid story, but I managed to create some documents proving my connection to Woolley, and indeed the man's recognition of me as his natural son. With the help of some plausible character witnesses, and my own . . . associations with the machinery of government, I was able to convince the Barons that I was ideally placed to succeed my "father" and uniquely placed to do so. The advantage of living as a shadow means that you are able to slip easily into the darkest corners. I attended my first court three seasons before you also became one of them. And in that time I learned a great deal. Some of it surprised me, some of it was almost amusing – those pathetic ceremonies!' He laughed, a bitter short bark. 'But most of it disgusted me.'

We sat in silence. Vellum took a drag and blew a perfect ring of smoke. It lingered above his head like a halo on one of Lucca's painted saints. I watched it rise gently and spread out so thin it disappeared.

'I wondered about you, Miss Peck. I wondered what I would see when you came to give your first parable at the Barons' Vernal Court earlier this year.'

'And what did you see?' I gripped the stem of my glass.

'I saw someone who shared my disgust.'

He ground out his smoke in the silver tray between us, stood and went back to the desk. I heard a drawer open. 'There is something else I would like to show you.'

I had something for him too. I pulled my bag to my lap and delved inside for the page torn from *The London Pictorial*. I smoothed it flat on my knee. The man I'd been talking to for the last half hour was at the bottom right of the woodblock print, his smooth-shaven face notably fresh among so many old bristlers.

I read the text again, trying for the hundredth time to smoke out something useful there, and then I stared at General Denderholm. You could stuff a bolster with his whiskers. There was something about this news story, something important I already knew. I tried to catch it, but whatever it was slipped away. I heard footsteps behind me. 'Do you recall this? You ought to, it came from your own newspaper. Ah . . .'

Vellum was looking down at the creased scrap in my lap. Its twin was between his own fingers, although his version was smooth as a laundered bed sheet and neatly trimmed round the edges.

'I see that we share an interest in the General.'

I quizzed at him. 'It was *you* I wanted to know about.' I pointed him out on the paper, not that he needed reminding. 'When I saw the story, I recognised you straight off.'

'As did several others.' Vellum flicked his coat tails and took his seat opposite again. 'To my cost. Tell me how this came to be printed in *The London Pictorial News*.'

'First you tell me why you're there.' I jabbed at the picture.

'I should *not* have been there. That is at the heart of *everything*, Miss Peck.'

*

'You say it was a mistake?' He twisted the ring on his smallest finger.

I nodded. 'It came from a contact of Sam's – Sam Collins, that is. He's the editor, good as.' It felt odd talking about him, disloyal almost. 'There's something called the Bureau and when they're running short on proper news they buy in stories. Sam says as a rule it's dull as a curate's cassock, but it fills the space. This one –' I tapped the scrap on the table between us – 'was especially useful because it came with the block for the print. It filled an even bigger gap, see, just at a time when he needed it.'

Vellum's eyes wandered to a corner beyond the fireplace. He seemed to find something interesting there. 'And your friend's enquiries . . .?'

'They didn't come to much. His contact at the Bureau got into a deal of bother over it, scared he was. He told Sam it wasn't supposed to have been used so early. It had got into the wrong drawer or something of the sort. But that was the odd thing, because someone had gone to the bother of making a block print to go with it. And then . . .' I stared at the whiskered face in the centre of the picture. 'The man at the Bureau, the contact, went missing, just around the same time Sam started making his own enquiries about this man here . . .' I pointed at Denderholm and looked up. 'And about you.'

'And what did he find out?' Vellum was still staring at the corner. He put me in mind of a sighthound locked on a rabbit.

'Nothing about you, but it seems the General is recently back from India and the London Imperial Agency is something in the way of a job to keep him comfortable in his retirement. It was when Sam started sniffing around him that he got himself marked out by the Barons.'

Vellum's eyes narrowed. He seemed to find whatever it was he was searching for in the shadows. I leaned forward.

'What do you make of it then?'

He took up the paper and stared at Denderholm.

'Well?' I asked again.

'You have confirmed that the Sanctuary suffers from draughts, Miss Peck.' Vellum sat back. 'But that is, perhaps, to be expected. I will see that it is dealt with. More pertinently, I believe you have confirmed the existence of a connection between the Barons and this man. You say that it was when Mr Collins made enquiries about General Denderholm that his friend disappeared and he himself fell into danger?'

'It was more than that. The Barons took him prisoner. They were going to kill him. Lucca too. The pair of them nearly died because of me.'

'As I understand it, you saved them.'

'They wouldn't have been in danger in the first place if it hadn't been for me.'

I wondered where Sam was right now, what he was doing. He was still in danger out there somewhere while I was sitting here thinking . . .

That was it, wasn't it? What was I thinking? I didn't like to put a string of words to it, but a part of me was enjoying the present company, almost admiring it, you might say. I rolled that away and packed it tight in a place where I wouldn't easily come across it.

I shifted on the chair. 'Sam's sharp as a boning knife. As a matter of fact, he found something else out about this General Denderholm. It's another connection, or might be. When he came back from India, he moved into the Angevin Club in St James's and that's where—'

'Where Anthony Carstone resides when he is town,' Vellum finished for me.

'You knew?'

He nodded. 'Arthur George Denderholm is someone I have been interested in for some time. His appointment to the London Imperial Agency is not, as you suggest, a matter of convenience. He will wield considerable power and he will be privy to the deepest secrets of state. In time the Agency's work will have some bearing on my own affairs. These men –' he swept a hand across the paper – 'are indeed good men and I am to be their . . . conduit.'

I shook my head. 'You'll have to speak plainer. What's that?'

'Their connection.'

He didn't embroider that for me, but he went on. 'However, that connection should never have been made public. Someone added my face to that block print, and I will find them.'

There was something to his tone that almost made me feel sorry for whoever it was. I drained the last of the brandy from my glass.

'Why are you interested in the General?'

Vellum looked at me straight, his eyes calculating. If I was a sum, I obviously came out right.

'Because of this.' He drew a small grey card from his pocket. 'It was delivered by hand to the Sanctuary last week. I understand the postal service from India is affected by the monsoon season. This should have arrived three months ago.' He handed me the card. It was covered in tiny print and looping handwriting. I moved to catch the light from the gas lamp.

Certificate of Death
Issued by the Office of
the British East India Company, Madras

Surname: *Denderholm*
Forenames: *Arthur George*
Date of registration: *18th October 1817*
Date of birth: *23rd March 1813*
Cause: *Cholera*
Place of residence: /
Father: *Eustace Connelly Denderholm, Capt. (d)*
Mother: *Sarah Amelia Denderholm (d)*
District Registrar: *Sir William Vickery*
Burial: *St Mary, Fort St George*
Fee: *Alexander Richardson, Capt. 2/6*

'It can't be right.' I read it again to make sure. 'According to this, Arthur George Denderholm was dead before his fifth birthday. And he died in India nearly sixty-five years back.'

'That does, indeed, seem to be the case.' Vellum nodded. 'The document in your hand is a facsimile of the original, but I have no reason to doubt the information. Arthur George Denderholm died in October 1817 and his parents preceded him. You'll note the "d" after their names. It stands for deceased. My reading of the scant information in your hand suggests he had no other living relatives.'

I looked at the grey card again. 'How do you make that out?'

'The funeral of the child was paid for by another officer – a Captain Alexander Richardson. The fee was sufficient for a pauper's burial.'

'That's a sad thing for an orphaned child.' I shook my head. 'But what does it mean? Is it by coincidence they share a name?'

'What do you think, Miss Peck?' Vellum turned at the sound of a knock on the door. The Owl stepped into the room.

'It is time, sir. They are waiting. They have been waiting this last quarter.'

'Tell them I have been detained, offer my apologies. I will join them shortly.'

'Very good, sir.' The Owl blinked behind the panes of his specs. 'And the young . . . lady, sir?'

'She will require a carriage. If you would arrange that too, please.'

The Owl made a curt bow and went to the door.

'By the way . . .' Vellum called out and the Owl paused in the chink. 'You are quite right about those draughts in the

Sanctuary. Miss Peck here has confirmed them. We will need to take action.'

The Owl looked at me with something like respect. 'Very good, sir.'

Once he'd gone, Vellum rose and went to the shadows on the far side of the fireplace. He bent to retrieve a pile of papers bound with scarlet ribbons and threw them onto the hearth. In just a few moments, they caught from the smouldering ash. He leaned against the mantel, watching the papers burn, and then he turned to me.

'And the answer to my question about the orphaned child?'

I pushed a loose strand of hair from my eyes. 'It's no coincidence. Not all three names. Little Arthur can't be in two places at once. If he really has been lying in a pauper's grave in India for over sixty years then he can't be here in London, can he?'

Vellum shook his head. 'In which case we must ask ourselves who General Arthur George Denderholm really is. Furthermore, I think we would be wise to examine his relationship with the Barons, most specifically his connection with Anthony Carstone, Lord Kite.'

Something cold licked at my neck.

'*We?* What sort of "we" do you mean? Are you talking about the people here in the Sanctuary or . . .'

'I mean you, Miss Peck. On the train I asked if you would be willing to work with me. If you recall, I suggested that if your answer was yes, then you should seek me out. And here you are. If you want to bring the petty rule of the Barons to an end, this is your chance.'

His pale eyes caught the gold of the flames and for all his

smooth words and sleek gear I was again aware that there was a danger to him.

Of an instant, the sight of Signor Marcelli nailed to that chair, a pool of dark sticky blood spreading across the boards, came to mind. The stench came too, the metal of his blood and the foul sweetness of his mess. I didn't like to dwell on the way he'd suffered, but I knew he wouldn't be the last. Whatever Vellum was offering, it was better than nothing. And nothing was what I had.

He was right. It was a chance to make a stand, an opportunity to make sure no one near me suffered again. I thought about what Kite had told me about the day the Barons tested my grandmother. His milk-blind eyes shone like pearls as he told me how they all took turns to defile a drugged and senseless young woman while Lady Ginger was forced to watch.

I stood up, abrupt. The movement knocked my empty glass from the table. The crystal shattered into a thousand glittering fragments on the rug. There weren't enough tears in my head to wash away the thought of what they'd done to Elizabeth Redmayne, my mother.

I swallowed down a lump the size of a ball of butcher's lard.

'I'll help you bring them down, the whole stinking pack of them.'

Vellum didn't move from the mantel. After a moment, he spoke softly. 'Do you not see how necessary a world of pains and troubles is to school an intelligence and make it a soul?'

I didn't understand what he was driving at, but he carried on. 'You need not bother yourself with the pack, Miss Peck. The traps are already baited. I've no doubt you will read about it soon, perhaps in the pages of your very own newspaper.'

I took a step towards him. 'Then why am I here? What do you want from me?'

'Two things.' He pulled a red cord dangling by the marble hearth. 'The Barons are easy meat, all of them, except Kite . . . and one other.' Before he wiped it clear, I caught an odd expression on his face, something between anger and disgust.

'You will receive my instructions.'

'Instructions!' I couldn't help myself. 'I'm not your maid, Vellum, or whatever your real name is.'

He smiled thinly. 'Of course, you are not. But you are a person whose past activities could be held against you.'

I gripped the ivory handle of my bag. 'Is that blackmail?'

He shook his head.

'What is it then?'

'It is an . . . encouragement.'

'And what am I?'

He regarded me with those pale eyes. 'A shadow?'

The door opened behind me. I turned to see the Owl again. He cleared his throat. 'The carriage is ready, sir, for the young lady. With regards to your meeting, I must tell you they are most anxious.'

Vellum nodded. 'I am coming. Good day to you, Miss Peck. Please follow my colleague.' He gestured towards the door. 'You will be quite safe. I give you my word.'

I stood my ground. 'And whose word is that?'

'*My* word. I trust it has a value. Now, if you please . . .' He strode back to his desk without giving me another look. I was dismissed. He was right about the temperature here: just a few steps away from the hearth the room was cold. I shivered, turned back to the fire and took the scrap of print from

The London Pictorial from the table. I folded it straight across the middle of Denderholm's face and pushed it into my bag.

I glanced back to the desk. Vellum was busy gathering papers together. As far as he was concerned, I was gone. The Owl hovered as I reached up to tighten the pins holding my hair in place. Christ knows what I looked like without the bonnet. I'd certainly give the clerks in the hall something to rustle their papers over on my way out. I started for the door.

'Miss Peck.'

I turned at Vellum's call. He was staring direct at me, smiling.

'You made an error earlier. You will have to be more careful.'

I paused, uncertain. The Owl froze in the doorway and his eyes rolled towards the desk like a couple of marbles. Vellum laid down a sheaf of papers and stood up straight. His shadow flicked up the wall behind him.

'The word written on the paper you cast so casually into the fire was "Vinulum". You claimed not to recognise it and yet a moment later you said . . . let me get this quite right: "Perhaps this *Vinculum* is someone else who works here? Either way, it means nothing to me."'

I winced as he mimicked my voice. It sounded harsh and out of place, but what was worse was that, straight off, I knew he was right. Vellum was clever, I'll give him that. He'd waited until the last moment to reel me in. I searched for an answer.

'I . . . that is to say . . .'

He smiled. 'Come. There is little point in denying that you knew it, Miss Peck. It is not a common word, after all, and yet you pronounced it quite correctly, sounding the absent occlusive.'

'Elusive what?' I think I knew what he meant, but I was trying to think.

Vellum's smile widened. 'Oh bravo, Miss Peck. That is, in a way, quite correct, for I refer to the elusive C. You sounded that letter in the word "Vinculum" even though it was misspelt, quite deliberately, on the note I gave you. I must confess I am a little disappointed. That was too easy.' He planted his hands on the desk.

'The other thing I will require from you – when the time is right – is the key to the Vinculum.'

Chapter Ten

Vellum was good as his word. The carriage – a black anonymous hulk – was blocking the end of the passage leading to the peeling door of 33 Little Sanctuary. Once I was settled inside, I found that the heavy felt blinds were bolted to the woodwork so no one could see I was sitting there and, more particularly I supposed, I couldn't see where I was.

A candle lamp fixed to the wall above my head leaked a pool of light over the seat so at least it wasn't coffin-dark. As we clattered along, I cursed myself for making such a stupid mistake. Perhaps the brandy had gone to my head, or perhaps I'd allowed myself to feel a little too comfortable sitting in front of the fire? Either way, he'd got what he wanted. I'd given the game away myself, handed it to him on a silver platter. Sounding out a letter that wasn't there had been a fool's error. Now he knew that *I* knew about the Vinculum. The test was by way of a confirmation for *when the time is right*.

Whatever that meant.

And then there was the matter of the death certificate. One thing at least was clear, there was a deal more to the story that appeared in *The Pictorial* than Vellum was willing to tell me. I took the scrap of newsprint from my bag and flattened it out on my knee. If Arthur George Denderholm – the real one – was long dead and buried in a pauper's pit in India, then who was this staring up at me from the page on my lap?

I was missing something. I was sure of it. I had the feeling it was bleedin' obvious, but every time I tried to catch hold it slipped away. This picture of Denderholm and his wool-chopped worthies had something else to say to me.

A couple of years back I'd helped Lucca prepare some old painted flats in the workshops behind The Gaudy so they were ready for new scenery. It was a wonder to me then how a turps-soaked rag could wipe away a whole forest in less time than it took to fry a rasher of bacon. Only the faintest ghost of the original paintwork remained and that was a blurred and ugly shade of brown on account of the thinning and the mixing of the colours. Someone who'd seen the trees that used to be there on the panel might have a chance of making out the original design, but only if they knew how and where to look. That's how I felt now. I wasn't looking in the right way or in the right place.

*

The carriage rolled away into a rising fog. Hunched on the box, the coachman hadn't broken the vow of silence he'd clearly taken before he picked me up. The cobbles glistened in the light from the single lamp on the corner of Salmon Lane. The glass was clouded. A tangle of filthy spider webs spread beneath the cracked dome.

I pinched my collar against the damp and the chill and turned into the alley. The fog was thicker here, stirring itself about my skirts like a greasy cabbage stew. It even muffled the tap of my heels, not that it mattered. As usual, one of the double doors at The Palace swung open before I'd even put a foot on the steps. If there was such a thing as a sixth sense, Tan Seng had a seventh connected directly to that bleedin' door. I looked up. He was standing there now, just as I expected. Lucca was behind him.

'Fannella!' He flew down the steps into the fog and wrapped me in his arms.

'*Grazie a Dio!* What happened? Are you hurt? Where have you been all this time? We did not know what to do. We thought . . .' The questions stumbled to a halt in a series of half-formed fears. He hugged me so close I felt his heart thumping under his shirt. For the smallest moment I wished that heart to be working for someone else.

'*Grazie a Dio!*' he murmured again. 'We thought you were lost to us. That man in the carriage . . . was he a . . .?'

'No, Lucca, he wasn't a Baron. Quite the opposite in fact.' I glanced over his shoulder up at the doorway. Peggy and Lok were standing there now beside Tan Seng. None of them looked too clever. Peggy's face was white as a slice of boiled cod.

'Where've you been, Kit?' She shook her head. 'We've been in such a coil thinking about what might have happened to you.'

It came to me that given Lucca and Sam's experience with the Barons, the fact of me disappearing off a London street and into a great black carriage with a stranger was something more than surprising.

'Fannella?' Lucca was staring at me like I was a ghost back from the dead. He stepped back and gripped my shoulders. 'Why did you leave us like that? It was not wise.'

'I'm sorry.' I reached for his hand, squeezed tight and led him up the steps and into the hall. Tan Seng closed the doors behind us, his face rigid. He slipped silently to the stairs leading down to the basement without a word. After a moment, Lok followed him. As he passed me, he eyed my skirt and shook his head. His long grey plait, caught at the end with a thin black and red ribbon, flicked from side to side. A cat-tail of reproach.

'Well?' Peggy settled herself down on the stairs. 'Where've you been this time? We didn't know what to do. We just sat here, waiting and worrying. In the end, Tan Seng sent Hari off home. My nerves are like the notes of that old piano in the backyard at The Carnival. There's not one in the right place. I think we deserve an explanation.'

'*Sì.*' Lucca nodded. 'You must tell us where you went and what happened.' His eye lingered on my raggy hatless head. 'Did they hurt you?'

'No. And it wasn't a "they", it was a "him". I found him – Lord Vellum, I mean – or he found me, I'm not sure which way it goes. And I'm not sure what happens next.'

I loosened the buttons of my soiled jacket and kicked out the mud-caked hem of my skirt. Little shards of dried muck rattled across the black and white tiles of the hall. I must have looked a fright sitting there in front of Vellum's fire at the heart of Little Sanctuary.

'Listen, I'll tell you what happened, but first I need to get out of this gear and take a bath.' I glanced at the stairs leading down to the basement. 'Do you think the brothers will help with the water?'

Peggy sighed and stood up. 'I'll go and ask Lok for you, Kit.'

*

'So, it seems that Denderholm is perhaps not the person he claims to be, and Vellum is not a Baron?' Lucca frowned. He

133

turned as the tall parlour windows rattled in their frames. A wind had sprung up since I'd come back. The damp in the air had changed into rain again.

'Do you believe him?'

'Yes.' I nodded, trying to work out if that was entirely true. I didn't trust him, but that wasn't quite the same thing. Nothing he'd said had struck a flat key. I nodded again, more vigorous. 'I believe him on both counts. I'm back here, aren't I? I was safe all along.'

'But you did not know that. It was foolish to leave us.'

'It was all I had, *have*, Lucca. You saw what happened to S—' I broke off. *What happened to Signor Marcelli* was what I was going to say, but I didn't want Peggy to know about that. She latched onto something, though.

'Happened to who?' She winced and straightened beside me on the couch, her hands cupping her belly.

'You all right, Peg?' I watched her shift to a more comfortable position.

'He kicked, that's all.'

'It's a he, is it?'

She ran a hand over the mound in her yellow cotton dress.

'I reckon.' She looked down and smiled in a tight, private way. Just for a moment I felt like an intruder in my own parlour.

'Anyways, Dan wants a boy.' She twisted the circle of gold on the fourth finger of her left hand. She'd taken to wearing Dan's ring – the one she found buried in a pile of shit on her doorstep – like a wedding band.

She was still talking about him as if he were alive. I turned away from her and tucked my feet under the blue wrapper gown. The bath had cleared away the dirt of the streets, but not much else. I was juggling more questions in my head now than before I went to Little Sanctuary. I glanced at Lucca. There was a tic working in his jaw as he stared into the flickering hearth. They were still angry with me, all of them. The air in the room was thick with it. It was like I'd brought the fog back home with me.

When he'd helped with the hot water, Lok hadn't said a word, and even now, sitting either side of Jacobin's cage like a couple of bookends, the brothers were giving me the silence. I knew they'd been listening though; just occasionally I'd caught them exchanging meaningfuls.

What a picture we made, the five of us – six, if you include the parrot. I doubted there was another household like ours in London.

Peggy started up again. 'Go on then, you was saying – look what happened to *who*?'

'Sam and Lucca,' I covered. 'I can't let it go on. It's got to end. At that meeting on the train, Vellum made it clear that he hates the Barons as much as we do. And I didn't hear anything today to contradict that. Like I told you, he wants me to help him.'

'But you still do not know his real name? Or even where to find him again.' Lucca plucked at a thread in the arm of the chair. That was true enough. I heard a snort from Tan Seng. I sidled at him, but he was staring at his hands folded neat in the dark silk pleated on his lap.

Lucca stood and went to the fire. The parlour was cold, like Vellum's room at the Sanctuary. I thought again about the papers burning in that wide marble hearth.

'Do you trust him, Fannella?'

Lucca had gone straight to the question I'd been asking myself. I'd felt safe enough sitting there with him, but trust? That was a different matter. Vellum was clever and there was something else to him too, something dark held close just under the surface.

'Is he a looker?' Peggy shot me a question I chose to ignore.

'It is . . . *ingiusto.*' Lucca bent to shovel another heap of coal into the grate. 'This man, this Vellum . . .' He made the name sound like an insult. 'He knows so much about you, but we know nothing of him.' He took up an iron and herded the nuggets to a flame; the golden light shone up the good side of his face. I reached out to his shoulder.

'Thank you.' I wasn't talking about the fire.

Rain lashed hard against the window panes. The sound set Jacobin off. My grandmother's mangy grey parrot scuffled from his perch and latched his hooked beak and scaly claws round the brass bars of the cage. He fought with the metal, flapping his ragged wings and grunting like a docker. Lok stood and raised a hand to soothe him.

'Don't!' Peggy sprang from the couch. 'It'll take your finger off. Horrible, miserable thing.'

Lok made a cooing noise and Jacobin twisted his head to look at him. The bird's yellow-rimmed eye blinked twice. Lok pushed a finger through the bars and rubbed Jacobin's beak. I watched, amazed, as the parrot arched his neck to allow the small man to scratch the bald pink patches of flesh where feathers were missing.

Lok started to sing. He had a light, pleasant voice made sweeter by the accent he'd never lost. It was almost like listening to a child. The song, all about first love and second thoughts, sounded like something from years back, the sort that might have been sung in one of my grandmother's halls when she first took them on. Peggy sat down again and turned to look at me, her dark brows arched in surprise.

Jacobin was usually a ball of feathery fury, but now he swayed on his perch. After a minute, as Lok carried on singing, he closed his eyes and half tucked his head under a wing.

Lok finished the sentimental song and then reached down for the old broidered cloth that covered the cage at night. He pulled it gently over the bars and turned to me.

'He likes that. Long time. She sang to him.'

Of an instant, Tan Seng stood up and rattled out a string of Chinese to his brother.

'Lady.' He nodded at me and went quickly to the door, his grey tunic swishing out around him. He turned, billowing like a small storm cloud, and barked something at Lok, who was wringing his hands and staring at the rug. He bowed his head lower and went to join his brother at the door.

'Goodnight, Lady.' Lok didn't look up as they went out into the hall.

'What was that about?' Peggy quizzed at me. Jacobin was silent now beneath the faded scarlet cloth. I'd never seen him sweetened like that before. As a rule, that bird was a most obnoxious pet, but what could I do with him? He'd die in a day if I let him free. The Beetle once told me that Jacobin was at least sixty years old. Lady Ginger was fond of him, apparently. That didn't surprise me. Together, my grandmother and her bleedin' parrot made a nasty vicious pair.

In the flickering light cast by the fire, the shadow of Jacobin's cage massed and shivered in the corner. If I half closed my eyes it was like another person was in the room with us. I sat back on the couch. Jacobin was at least three times my age. I wondered about all the things he would have seen from his corner in Lady Ginger's parlour. I stared at the shadow. There was something more about that bird. Something else I knew about him along with his age. As I tried to track it down, Peggy patted my knee and stood up.

'I'm done in, Kit. You must be too.' She arched her back and the bulge of her belly strained against the primrose cotton.

'We're to our bed.' She smoothed the material over the lump. I noted the way she spoke of herself as a pair and felt a kick of guilt. It was because of me the child she carried would never see its father. She went to the crackled mirror over the hearth. For a moment I thought she was taking the pins from her hair, but then she turned and held out her hand. There was a green leather box, the size of a strike case, in her palm.

'I found it! I knew it was up here.' She smiled at me. 'Go on, Kit. I know I said it was a boy, but I'd like to know for sure. The old girl reckoned you had the knack, didn't she? Use the dice, let's see what they say. I'm writing to my cousin tomorrow – she had a boy too back in May. I could tell her what you think.'

I stared at Lady Ginger's dice box. I didn't want to touch it. It was true enough what Peggy said; there was a time at the start of this when I read my grandmother's dice in front of her and she'd said I had a rare gift.

She'd left them dice for me at The Palace on the day she moved out.

There were so many things she'd left me that turned out bad. I thought of the package of papers the Beetle had given me weeks back. They were my grandmother's, he said, but I hadn't wanted to open the parcel and look inside. Anything that came from her was tainted. I'd put them in the lowest drawer of the desk in my office, along with everything else that minded me of her. Every time I opened that drawer, which wasn't often, the smell of my grandmother's opium rose into the air like a genie from a flask.

I frowned. I thought the dice were there too.

Peggy took a step towards me, the little shagreen box in her hand gleaming in the firelight. 'I know I asked once before, but you never did it. Do it now, please. And perhaps . . . well, perhaps you could tell something about Dan? Where he is, I mean?'

Jesus! I didn't need the dice to put her straight there. I looked away from her eager face in case something showed in mine.

'Peg, I'm done in. Another time maybe, but not now.'

She carried on. 'One roll, just for the baby then. It'll give me something to dream about.'

'No!'

It was Lucca who answered her.

I turned, surprised at the force in his voice. He caught my eye and shook his head; it was a small, quick movement meant only for me. He cleared his throat. 'It is late, and we are all tired. This is not the time for games.'

'It wouldn't take a moment.' Peggy looked disappointed. Right on cue, as if in answer to Lucca's prompt, the dainty little clock on the hearth gathered itself to perform a delicate tinkling tune before starting to chime the hour.

He waited until the eleventh and final strike. 'You see? And you know it is always behind. It must be at least ten minutes

139

later. You must go to bed.' He smiled fondly at Peggy. 'Both of you.'

She grinned at that. 'Oh, all right. But I won't forget. You will read them for me, Kit, won't you?'

I shifted on the couch. Folded up beneath me, my leg had caught the cramp. I freed it from the folds of the wrapper and pointed my toes at the fire. 'Wouldn't you rather wait and be surprised?' I tried to sound like it didn't mean much to me either way, but that was a lie. I didn't want to see what the dice had to say about Peggy's unborn baby. If I was a superstitious type, I might have said it was like opening a door that ought to remain closed.

I wiggled my toes and watched her walk to the door. She caught the handle and turned.

'I don't like surprises, Kit. Never have. Surprises and secrets, when you think about it, they're much the same thing. It's always better to know.'

She closed the door behind her. I listened to her pad up the stairs to her room and thought how wrong she was.

'Fannella?' Lucca came to sit next to me. He took my face in his fingers and frowned. 'You are pale. I watched the colour drain from your face just now. *Come se avessi visto un fantasma?*' He shook his head, searching for the words. He clicked his fingers. 'A ghost. You have seen a ghost?'

I shook my head. 'It's late, like you say. It's been a long day.'

I looked away, sharp. Peggy had left the dice box on the low table beside the couch. I reached out to take it. If she couldn't see it or find it, perhaps she'd forget about it. I'd been grateful for Lucca's interruption earlier and now I could use it to turn the subject.

'Why didn't you want me to read the dice for Peg? You stepped in smart there.' I pushed the box into the pocket of my wrapper. The furrow between his brows deepened, pulling at the knot of skin that sealed his right eye.

'There are some things it is better not to know, Fannella.' Lucca glanced at the door to make sure we were alone, before facing me again. He spoke softly. 'Peggy does not look like a woman carrying a six-month child. She is too . . . *pesante*.'

I shook my head.

He mimed the bulge of her belly with his hand. 'Too heavy.'

'It's due around Christmas, that's what she reckons.'

Lucca chewed his lip. 'Impossible. She is nearly at her time, perhaps a little more than a month at most.'

I almost laughed. 'How do you know that? You're not a mid-wife in your spare hours, are you?'

'I have three older sisters. And my brothers have wives.'

'Well, it makes no odds.' My fingers strayed to the lump in the wrapper pocket where the little green case was lodged. I wondered how the box came to be there on the mantel. Of an instant, I had a clarity that Peggy must have put it there on purpose. I felt the chill on my neck and moved my hand.

'She must know her dates, Lucca. Peg can't be mistaken.'

He shook his head. 'Perhaps she wants to be mistaken? The father of her child—'

'Was Dan.' The name burned my tongue. '*Is* Dan, Danny,' I corrected myself.

'Is it?' Lucca stared at the fire. 'There could be another. When she was taken to the warehouse by that . . . *diavolo*.' He spat into the flames and shook his head. 'If I was carrying the child of a man who was capable of such things . . .'

141

It's always better to know.

Christ! If Lucca was right, no wonder Peggy wanted to see what the dice had to say about her baby. I often thought about the girls I saved from the warehouse back in February. Most of them, the ones that lived, were settled away from Limehouse and I'd made sure they was all comfortable. But Peggy now . . . she never told me what happened while she was chained in that cellar. Not all of it. And I never asked. But that didn't mean . . .

'It could still be his. Dan's, I mean.' I sounded more sure about that than I felt.

Lucca nodded. 'We must hope that is the case. But do not read the dice for her, Fannella, promise me.'

He was a good man to be wary of such a thing.

'I promise.'

I took his hand in mine, noting the stains across his knuckles and caught in the skin around his fingers.

'You've been painting again, Lucca?'

'*Sì*. It was the only way this afternoon . . . a distraction. We did not know if you were alive or . . .' His brown eye caught the light from the fire. 'You are telling the truth about what happened? You were not harmed?'

'I was well treated. Don't worry yourself on that score. He's a proper gentleman.'

'But there *is* something else, Fannella. I know you too well.' He stared at me, wary and expectant. And he was right. I hadn't told them about Vellum's parting shot – that little trap he set. Point of fact, I hadn't told anyone about the Vinculum. Was it better to keep it that way?

Lucca tilted his head. 'Well?'

I sighed and nodded. 'You're right. There was something

else.' I planted my bare feet on the rug and sat straight on the couch. 'Vellum wanted another secret . . . left to me by Joey.'

'Joey! *Ovviamente. Avrei dovuto saperlo!*' Lucca pulled away. 'Always Joey!'

'Well, you should know, he was your friend!'

'But he is a not a man to be trusted, Fannella. I thought you knew that now.'

We sat in silence for a long time. The only sound in the room was the spitting of the coals in the grate. The clock tinkled the quarter. Lucca waited until the pretty tune played itself out before he spoke.

'What is it then, this secret of Joey's?'

Chapter Eleven

Light was creeping through the shutters. I'd slept a little, but for the last hour I'd lain in bed chasing thoughts through a maze. The fact that Vellum knew about the Vinculum wasn't a mighty surprise. He'd been a Baron after all – and for a deal longer than I had. No, the thing I kept coming back to was the fact that he knew I had the key. As far as I could make out, the only person who could have told him was my grandmother, most likely when he'd made that trip to see her at Fraines Abbey.

That didn't help. It set off a dozen hares running in different directions. And, as Lucca said, once I'd laid it all out for him, there's no point in having the key to a door you can't find.

I rolled onto my side and looked at the wardrobe. An ugly great thing it was, the dark wood carved into Oriental curls and billows. Wide splayed feet gave the impression of a sly liveliness, suggesting it might cut a caper if your back was turned. The wardrobe was very much an object to my grandmother's taste. When I'd first taken this room as my own, we couldn't shift it.

The Bible Joey gave me that last time I saw him in the Bethlem was tucked away in the wardrobe's bottom drawer. The coded sequence to open the Vinculum was scribbled between the pages of the Book of Daniel. Which was appropriate, given the fact that my own grandmother had thrown me to the lions.

Learn it and then destroy it.

For a moment it was as if Joey was sitting on the end of the bed, whispering to me. I pulled up the blanket to ward off the morning chill. When I last saw my brother, the summer heat was so fierce it had sucked the air from his narrow cell, leaving behind the hum of sweat and piss and God knows what else. We'd sat close together on his bed at the Bethlem Hospital and my brother had told me a tale as ripe as the stink in his cell.

It all started a long time back, according to Joey, before either of us were born. Anthony Carstone had a fondness for our mother. He showered her with gifts and asked her to marry him. She wouldn't, and anyway she couldn't . . . on account of the fact that she was already married to another man. Kite's love had turned sour and his spite was bitter as spoiled vinegar.

That was bad enough, but what happened next made him vengeful.

Turns out there was once two Carstone brothers. Together they guarded the Vinculum, but it was Kite's brother Edmund, Lord Wren, who was the keeper of the key. They played it that way to make sure that the place where the Barons stored their treasure was secure.

Now, thanks to Joey, one of them was secure in a place there was no coming back from. See, when I saw my brother in the Bethlem, he also told me how he had killed Lord Wren and stolen the coded sequence to open the Vinculum.

That was the day I finally understood why the Barons wanted Joey so bad. Kite was the guardian of nothing if he couldn't open it. And beyond that, his own brother's blood was on Joey's hands. No wonder his hatred of my family was lodged so deep. It had become a part of him, festering like a sore that never heals.

I threw back the blankets and went to the wardrobe. The key to the bottom drawer was hidden up top behind a panel shaped like a wave cresting over the doors. I shifted a chair from the corner and balanced on the seat to reach behind the carving. As long as that code was written between the lines on those thin, transparent pages, Joey's Bethlem Bible was a dangerous thing. It was time I locked the code away in a place where no one could find it, except me.

The plaid bundle was hidden at the back of the drawer beneath a pile of folded blankets. I took it out and went to the window to open the shutters. The morning sky was a mottled grey, bruised with faded strips of purple, much like Nanny Peck's old shawl. The light was weak, but it was enough.

I sat cross-legged on the broidered bed coverlet. Taking the bundle onto my lap, I began to unwind the Bible from the folds of the shawl. There were stringy holes at the edges where moths had fed. Scraps of coarse wool turned to dust between my fingers as I pulled at the fabric. Nanny Peck's plaid was wearing away.

My eyes prickled. I was beginning to find it hard to bring the old girl's face to mind these days. Same was true of Ma. When I thought of the pair of them, it was like looking through a taproom window. There were people inside, but I couldn't make them out clear through the smoke and the smearing of the glass.

I wondered if there might come a time when I wouldn't catch their likeness at all. I swiped my cheek with the back of my hand, sat up straight and shook the Bible from the shawl onto the bed. It was a small, plain thing, printed cheap for the spiritual comfort of the Bethlem's lodgers. The black cover was creased and stained in the top left corner. It was all I had of my brother now.

I could see him clear enough. As far as I knew he was free from the Bethlem and far from London. I'd kept my promise. I ran the tip of a finger over the Bible's wrinkled cover. Wherever he was, I hoped he was safe, and I hoped he was settled, but somehow, knowing Joey, I didn't think he'd be either. Ramesh Das had sent word that the business of getting him free had been concluded and I hadn't asked for more.

My grandmother had relied on the Beetle, Mr Telferman, to run her books, and on Ramesh Das to keep her informed about the workings of Paradise.

'*I am your eyes, your ears and your tongue, Lady,*' he told me. '*My role is to ensure that nothing is lost, nothing mislaid, nothing misunderstood. I look into the hearts and minds of the far-born who carry out your bidding in the docks, on your ships and in your warehouses.*'

When I'd asked the dignified old man straight out if he was her spy, he'd called it a crudity, but all the same, when I needed something done about Joey, I knew where to turn.

And, of an instant, I knew where to turn right now. As I sat there on the bed, I finally caught hold of the thing in my head that kept dancing out of reach. Only it wasn't a thing, it was Ramesh Das.

The first time I'd visited him in his sweet-smelling rooms at Bell Wharf Stairs a scrap of print from *The London Pictorial* had been pinned to his desk. It was the same one I'd had in my bag when I went to find 33 Little Sanctuary – and the very same one that interested Vellum. I tried to remember what the old man had said about it. When I'd quizzed him, it was clear that it was General Denderholm who'd caught his eye. He'd tried to pass it off as nothing more than an old acquaintance.

'*One of the men is known to me. I had not seen him for many years. I was curious, that is all.*'

It was a lie. I smoked that straight off. Ramesh Das had stared at Denderholm's face on the paper in a way that could have scorched the General's whiskers to stubble. When I asked how he knew him, he wouldn't be drawn on the matter, but I had the most distinctive impression it was something that went way back.

'*You knew him in India?*'

The old man had brushed my question aside.

'*As I said – it was many years ago.*'

I leaned back against the brass rail of the bed. There were three of us interested in Denderholm. That added up to something more than coincidence. I glanced at the window. It was too early to pay a visit to Bell Wharf Stairs, but I needed to have a conversation about the past with Ramesh Das, whether he wanted it or not.

The morning purple had leached from the sky, leaving a sickly wash of greenish grey. Leaves caught up by the wind flattened themselves against the glass like little hands. The panes rattled and shuddered. A draught flipped open the frail cover of the Bible, startling the pages to a flutter. I was minded of what Vellum said about the Sanctuary. The draughts he was concerned about didn't come through gaps in the woodwork.

I took up Nanny Peck's fraying shawl and draped it around my shoulders, more for comfort than for warmth. Tucking a dandling plait behind my ear and out of the way, I pulled Joey's Bible towards me and turned to the Book of Daniel.

*

Blue-tinged flames licked at the edges of the pages, but the Bible was taking its time. I knelt and pushed the glowing mass deeper into the hearth with an iron and then I took up the fire shovel and added a scatter of coals. I wanted to make sure that it was nothing more than ash by the time the rest of them woke.

As I watched, it blazed up bright like a square of gold. Bleedin' thing was like them three prophets, untouched at the heart of the fiery furnace. There was an irony! For the last hour I'd been tracking Joey's cramped pencil marks – forty-five tiny letters and symbols – up the sides and across the bottom of the part of the Book of Daniel relating the story of Belshazzar's Feast. Old Shadrach, Meshach and Abednego were there too – a few pages earlier.

I had the complete sequence stored in my head now. It came easy enough. I only had to read it through twice with a purpose before I knew it. I'd tested myself a dozen times over on a sheet of paper before I went down to the parlour to light the fire.

I watched the charring Bible shift in the hearth and thought about the last time I saw Lady Ginger at Fraines Abbey. Even though she was so close to death she was practically shutting the door behind her, she was still playing me like a cat with an injured bird – more for the amusement of it than appetite. That's what I thought at the time, anyway.

Thing is, she was in earnest that day and never more so. My grandmother was testing me to see if I had the peculiar trick of memory that ran in the family. It was something Joey and I had in common, although, as it turned out, there wasn't much else these days to hold us close.

It came to me then that Lady Ginger must have summoned Vellum to Fraines Abbey at around the same time to tell him what she planned. She'd even told him about my gift for membrance, the gift she hoped I'd inherited.

Even though her mortal remains were rotting in the stone tomb she'd built for herself, my grandmother was still in the game and holding a close hand.

I poked the Bible again with the iron. It flared for a moment before finally collapsing into a little heap of gold-flecked cinders. The Word of the Lord put up a quite a fight before I was satisfied that no one would be able to read it again. I reached into the pocket of my wrapper and my fingers brushed against the rough shagreen of the dice case. I had half a mind to toss it into the hearth along with the Bible. I caught hold, but then I let go. The dice were uncanny. Maybe burning them would be unlucky. And didn't I already have a pile of misfortune on my plate?

Instead, I fished out the paper I'd used to test myself. As I screwed it to a ball, the edge nicked the side of my thumb. A smear of blood stained the crumpled sheet before I tossed it into the hearth, where it caught in an instant. The Word of the Barons was nothing. The paper was gone in less time than it took to say Vinculum, including the occlusive C. Whatever that was.

'Vinculum.'

I said it out loud, testing for meaning. Jacobin stirred in the corner. I heard the scrape of claws on metal and the flutter of wings. He squawked and started to call out the usual string of profanities. He carried on cussing and swearing under the broidered red cover, but then he started to talk in my grandmother's clipped little voice.

'*Deal with it. Deal with it. Deal with it.*'

I stood up abrupt and went out to the hall.

Lady Ginger had started this. If she'd still been alive, I could . . .

Could what, girl? Fact is, she never answered a question straight in her life. I paused at the foot of the stairs. Perhaps she *had* left me something I could use after all? I felt for the angular shape of the small green case through the cotton. If I rolled the dice just once and concentrated on the patterns that came, what would I see? What if I really did have the gift? Christ knows, there were a lot of questions I needed answers to – questions about the past, mainly. Questions about *my* past.

When it came to it, who was I, truly?

I snatched my hand away from the wrapper and studied the tiny bead of blood on my thumb. Whose blood was that?

It came again, that lick of cold on the back of my neck.

I pulled Nanny Peck's shawl around my shoulders. Her blood didn't run through me, but she was my grandmother all the same. Of an instant, I found I didn't want to know what the dice had to say on the matter. The truth was in my heart, not in my veins.

The Palace was silent as I crossed the hall and quietly opened the door to my office. It was so cold in there I could see my breath. Gripping the old shawl tight, I went to the desk and opened the lowest drawer. Immediately, the air filled with the sickly-sweet stench of the opium my grandmother favoured. Something moved behind me. From the corner of an eye, I saw the fine hairs come loose from my plait stir and rise on my shoulder. I whipped about smart, but there was just a wall at my back.

Draughts.

I bent to push the dice box to the back of the drawer. My fingers caught on string as I buried the little green case beneath a large rectangular parcel wrapped in brown paper. The package had been among papers the Beetle had given me after Lady Ginger died. The one I'd never opened. I hadn't touched it for fear of hearing her distinctive voice rising from the pages. And there was something else too. What if I heard myself there?

I tried to pull away but the smallest finger on my right hand had somehow got caught in the string. I wriggled it about, but on account of the angle I couldn't free myself. I reached into the drawer with my left hand and eased out the package. My finger came loose easy enough now.

I placed the parcel square on the leather worktop. The neat wrapping was the Beetle's work. The pang of guilt that jabbed whenever I thought of Marcus Telferman came again. I hadn't seen him since my grandmother's funeral. It was deliberate. I didn't want to be reminded of that day. Since then, we'd communicated about the winding up of Lady Ginger's interests (most of them) in a series of terse letters. I had every confidence he was parcelling up her estate in the same tidy, careful way he'd bound up the package sitting in front of me.

I sat down and studied it for a moment, and then I pulled at the strings and ripped at the paper.

There was another bundle inside. Something hard and square wrapped in dark red silk. The fabric was Oriental in design, shot with a pattern formed by swirls of golden thread. I tugged at the silk and it fell away from a book with a black cover.

I gathered the fabric into a ball. It was torn along the edge on one side and a jagged rip ran up through the middle, almost dividing it in two. Now I looked, the book was broken too. To be accurate, it was half a book. Beneath the cover, the pages hung loose from the binding threads as if someone had torn it apart.

I lay the book flat and lifted the cover, blocking my nose to the ghost of Lady Ginger rising from the papers.

Ten minutes later, when I couldn't stand it for a second more, I shut the thing up, wrapped it in the cloth and the paper again and stuffed it back into the drawer. I had enough of my grandmother's ledgers to tell me of all the dirty trades she'd run from The Palace. I didn't need another for proof on the matter.

I locked the drawer in case Peggy came prying and rested my head in my hands. My fingers stank of Lady Ginger's opium just from touching her bleedin' book and her Chinese silk.

Suddenly, hammering and calling came from below. Someone was beating on the door. The noise set off Jacobin again. I heard him cursing and raging in his cage. At the same moment, the clock on the mantel in the parlour jingled out the tune leading up to the hour. I sat there, trying to sort the commotion from the dainty music and Jacobin swearing in the dark. The clock finished up and poised itself to strike. It was seven o'clock.

153

Chapter Twelve

We stared at the body laid out on the desk. The head had been crushed to a pulp by something sharp and heavy, but to my mind, the worst of it was the big rusted nail driven through the back of the neck.

'Who could do such a terrible thing?'

Mr Chibbles gathered the matted bundle into his arms and rocked it to and fro. Tears the size of gooseberries rolled down his pitted pink cheeks. 'She was the best of them, my little Spark. Picked everything up straight off she did.'

He held the broken body close and buried his splayed nose into the bloodied fur. The muffled, reedy voice came again.

'None of the others will do the flaming hoop, not even for bacon rind.'

I glanced across the desk at Fitzy and Jesmond. The pair of them were standing. I'd taken the only chair. The distance between the men who managed my two remaining halls was as wide as my grandmother's wardrobe, but for once they weren't arguing.

As a rule, they didn't go near each other, but the death of what had once been Mr Chibbles' liveliest performing dog had made a sort of truce between them. We were in the sparse-furnished office at The Comet. The air was thick with the sharp, clean smell of fresh paint and new plaster. A neat pile of pots and rags was stacked in the corner.

On account of what had happened with poor Netta Swift, I still didn't trust Jesmond completely, but I couldn't deny he was doing a good job at The Comet. The best of the halls my grandmother had left me would be ready to open again in less than a month thanks to his management of the tradesmen putting it back together.

'Let me get this straight.' I planted my elbows on Jesmond's desk, careful to avoid the blood, and cradled my forehead in my hands. I concentrated on a little nick in the green leather worktop as I tried to figure out what he was telling me. 'I still can't see it. How did the dog—'

'Spark,' Chibbles interrupted. 'That was her name.'

I started again. 'How come Spark came to be here at The Comet at all? You were on at The Carnival last night.' I ran through the bill in my head. 'You went on after Dismal and before the Brothers?'

Chibbles choked out a great sob. 'That's right. But she wasn't at The Lamb afterwards. I didn't bring them, any of them, with me. I left them behind.'

It seemed like a long time since I'd been the girl who went to The Lamb with the others from the halls. It had been a usual way of rounding off the evening, especially at weekends. Nights at The Lamb had been filled with laughter and song and liquor. We all went – the acts, the girls from the chorus, the hands from the workshops, Peggy and Danny, even Lucca of occasion.

I looked across at Lucca now. He was leaning, arms folded, against the back wall by the newly painted door, staring at the limp little body in Mr Chibbles' arms. He shot me a look from under the brim of his hat and shook his head.

'What kind of person would do something like this?' Chibbles snorted and gulped down a mouthful of air as another sob wracked his small fat body. It was a fair question, although I reckoned I already knew the answer.

'Here, use this.' I took a square of cotton from my sleeve and handed it to him across the desk. 'You mean you went to The Lamb with the others after the last house and left the dogs behind at The Carnival?'

He snuffled. 'I've done it before. Just for a couple of hours. There's a space under the stairs out back. If you bolt the door and leave them with a bone or two or some butcher's scraps, they're happy as larks.'

'But you didn't go back for them last night? Is that it?'

Chibbles started to wail so loud, I reckoned the gilders putting the last touches to the plaster harps of the cherubs clambering up the sides of the stage outside would come running. They were good workers. A trio of Lambeth boys – brothers, Jesmond said. They didn't come cheap, but from what I'd seen I couldn't fault their work.

'No, I did go back, but . . .' He faltered and clutched the dog's body tight to his chest. Sticky dark blood was already smeared on his shirt. The violence of his grief made it worse.

'Thing is, I didn't count them. I can't lie, Miss, I'd had a few at The Lamb and when I went back to let them out, it was just a bit later than usual. When I opened up they all came tumbling out. Very eager to get going they was. What with one thing and another I didn't trouble to count. To be honest, I don't think I was capable of putting a number to them. To my eyes, on account of the gin, there could have been a dozen dogs running around the yard, yapping and wagging their tails. They followed me back to Rugg Street. It was only this morning when I woke that I found there were just five in the room. One

156

was missing. This one, Spark. Like I said, she was the best . . .'

His words were drowned by tears. He hugged that body so tight I thought it might burst. Lucca went to his side. He put a comforting hand on Mr Chibbles' heaving shoulder.

'And she was a fine, clever dog. Let me take Spark. I will clean her for you and then—'

'No! I'll do it. I want to . . . for her sake.' The little man continued to rock Spark's body like he was holding a baby. 'It's my fault.'

I turned to Jesmond. 'It was you who found her?'

'That I did, Ma'am.' His currant-black eyes sidled at Fitzy. He cleared his throat. 'As you know, Ma'am, after what happened with Ne—' He stopped himself and started again. 'That is to say, I make it my business to come every day before the workmen arrive. I don't take liquor, now – not ever – so I'm always early, always ready. Always keeping a close eye on things for you.'

He was nervous. I knew it from the way the sing-song Welsh in his voice came a note stronger than usual and the way he kept calling me 'Ma'am'. I caught the waft of his minted breath. Aubrey Jesmond was most particular about the way he presented himself, which was more than you could say for Fitzy.

'Go on, describe how you found her, Jessie.' Fitzy puffed out his cheeks. Faded ginger whiskers twitched beneath a nose that looked like a great strawberry smashed across his face. He nodded at me, in a most meaningful way.

'It wasn't a pretty sight, so it wasn't. From what Jessie said, it was . . . unnatural, Ma'am.'

He gave the word 'unnatural' a particular tone. I knew it was Signor Marcelli Fitzy was thinking of just then, not Mr Chibbles' dog.

Jesmond clasped the rim of his bowler, holding it in front of him like a small shield. I didn't much blame him for feeling uncomfortable, seeing as the last *unnatural* thing he'd found at The Comet was a filthy painting of me daubed twenty foot across the new plaster ceiling of the dome.

And that *had* been his fault, mainly.

He shuffled from foot to foot. 'She . . . the dog, Spark, was nailed to the back of the main entrance door, on the inside. See here . . .' Jesmond let go of his hat with one hand and pointed to the ugly nail puncturing the wiry brown scruff at her neck. 'I had to use the builders' pliers to get her off.'

'Bastard.' Chibbles stopped sobbing long enough to choke the word out.

'Like I said, unnatural.' Fitzy waggled his eyebrows at the dog and then at me with theatrical significance.

I folded my arms and sat back. 'She was a talent, Fitzpatrick, we all know that, but I don't reckon Spark got out a ladder, climbed up it and nailed herself to that door, do you? Of course it was bleedin' unnatural!'

The sobbing turned into a wail. I stared at the battered dog in Bertie Chibbles' arms and thought about Matthias Schalk and his hawk-headed cane. I pulled at the broidered collar of my blouse.

'Was there anything else, Jesmond? Was anything missing or moved, or left?'

'No, Ma'am.' Jesmond shook his head. 'It was just the dog. I recognised her at once as one of Bertie's.' He frowned. His tiny black eyes disappeared into pleats of skin. 'The door was locked when I came in first thing. Gave me a fright it did when I opened up, seeing all the blood on the tiles and the little bits of skull bo—'

I held up my hand. 'Thank you.'

I didn't want Bertie to hear too much detail. I didn't think it would be good for him.

'And after you found her, you went to Fitzpatrick?'

'Indeed I did, Ma'am. You've made it very clear to me that anything pertaining to the acts is his domain, so I took myself straight over to Paddy's . . . Mr Fitzpatrick's lodgings, and then I went to Rugg Street for poor Bertie here.' He nodded at Mr Chibbles. 'And Mr Fitzpatrick, now, he went direct to The Palace to fetch you.'

'And here we all are.'

'Indeed, Ma'am.'

I stared at the spots of blood on the desk's green leather. If I was to draw a line between them, they might shape something like a hawk's head. I looked up sharp.

'Tell me straight, Bertie.' I already knew the answer to my next questions, but I thought I ought to ask. 'Is there anyone who might have taken against you? Perhaps you've got a rival in the dog trade? Call it a professional jealousy. Or Spark, now, would there be someone who didn't like her for a particular reason? Was she a biter?'

He stared at me as if I'd hammered his dog onto the back of The Comet's front door with my own hands. I felt guilty for asking.

Chibbles opened his mouth and made a noise like a punctured squeezebox. He swallowed and tried again. 'I've never encroached myself on anyone's trade. And as for Spark, she was the very best of my girls. Everyone loves –' he gulped – '*loved* her, everyone, she . . .' The rest of his answer was muffled by another bout of sobbing. All I heard clear was 'sweetest of girls'.

Fitzy was staring at me. His bloodshot eyes bored into mine and his lips worked under the straggling tache at words he couldn't say in front of Bertie Chibbles and Aubrey Jesmond. Lucca patted the small man's shoulder again.

'I think you should take her home now, Bertie. Here, let me help.'

He turned and went to take up a square of painter's rag from the pile in the corner of the office.

'We can wrap her in this. You cannot carry her through the streets like that.'

I watched as Lucca tried to prise Spark gently from Mr Chibbles' arms. At first he resisted, but then he gave in and let Lucca take her. It was as if he'd finally recognised that his dog was gone. Lucca tucked the fabric carefully around the body and then, very respectfully, he handed the bundle back.

'Take her home and bury her. Do you have somewhere?'

Chibbles sniffed and nodded. 'There's a pear tree in the yard at Rugg Street. She liked to sit in the shade of it when we practised. I think I'll put her there, so she won't have gone far.' He shambled about and made for the door.

'Wait!' I stood up. 'Don't . . . Please don't tell anyone about Spark – what happened to her, I mean.'

Chibbles turned. 'Why ever not, Miss?'

'Because . . . because . . .' I slid a face at Lucca and then at Fitzy, who nodded.

I tried again. 'I'm very sorry for your loss, Bertie, truly. But I don't think it's the sort of thing we need getting about right now. Not when The Comet is about to open again. Isn't that right, Jesmond?'

'Quite right, Ma'am.' He nodded and fiddled with his

bowler. 'It wouldn't be good for business. And there's some who might see it as an omen. Not me, of course, I'm not superstitious myself – goes against the grain of my beliefs – but the others, see, especially the girls in the chorus, they might not take it too well.'

I nodded. 'They were fond of Spark. If they knew about this it would only upset them. You wouldn't want that, would you, Bertie?' I took a breath, uncomfortably aware that I was about to twist a man's grief to my own ends. I avoided Lucca's eye.

'You wouldn't want them thinking about Spark . . . *suffering* like that. It's not a way for them to remember her, is it? If anyone asks, I think it's best that you say she died natural in her sleep.'

Bertie shook his head slowly and his round blue eyes swam with fresh-squeezed tears. He looked down at the rag bundle in his arms and then at me.

'Why would anyone do such a thing? That's what I want to know.'

I couldn't answer him.

*

The door closed. We waited for a moment to make sure he was well on his way and then I turned to Jesmond.

'Does anyone else know about this?' I pointed at the door. 'What about the gilders out there?'

He shook his head. 'Before I went to see Paddy . . . Mr Fitzpatrick, I brought the dog in here and then I cleared away the mess in the hall. On my knees scrubbing I was. I didn't want anyone apart from me to see it. The workmen came in later. No one knows about it apart from the four of us here in the office and, of course, poor Bertie.'

'And the bastard who did it,' Fitzy added, unhelpfully.

'Well, that's the way it's going to stay.' I dabbed at the blood on the desk with the damp scrap of cotton I'd handed to Chibbles. It didn't do much good.

'Like I said to Bertie, I don't want this doing the rounds.'

I rubbed harder and the smear settled into the grain.

'Is that clear?' I looked direct at Jesmond because I was talking to him. As far as he was concerned the dog was the first dead thing to turn up in one of my halls this week, but Fitzy and Lucca knew different. Jesmond nodded, his little head bobbing like an apple in a bran tub. The light from the window shone up the bald pink dome of it and a greasy strand from the frill of dyed black hair slung low around his ears came loose. He patted it back into place. 'Indeed it is, Ma'am. It wouldn't be good for business as you said. I imagine it was in the way of a . . . a prank?' He grinned uneasily, showing off a set of small, unnaturally white teeth.

'Prank!' I sat down heavily. 'Christ, Jessie! If you think what happened to Bertie's dog was some sort of joke, it's a good thing I've Fitzpatrick here working on the acts. It was a threat – that's what it was, and I don't want word of it getting out. Go through it again, how you found her.'

'It's just as I said earlier, Ma'am.' Jesmond spun the bowler – I could see clammy dabs in the black felt of the rim as he twirled it between his fingers. 'I arrived early, unlocked the door and found her exactly as I said. To be frank with you, as soon as I opened up I knew there was something wrong from the smell – all that blood, see. And the buzzing of the flies.'

I was glad he hadn't mentioned that to Bertie Chibbles.

'The door was definitely locked?'

Jesmond patted his pocket. 'There's only the one set of keys and I have it at all times. After what happened before . . .' He tailed off. Fitzy looked at him and then he quizzed at me. If he was hoping for an explanation of 'what happened before', he was disappointed. That vivid, filthy picture of me, Joey and Lucca was still up there, hidden under layers of whitewash. And that was the way it was going to stay.

'No one else had access to the keys. I'd swear it on my old mother's grave, if that was a decent Christian thing to do.'

I drummed my fingers on the desk. 'You are telling me the truth this time, aren't you?'

He just nodded. For once his glibness disappeared. Oddly, it was the fact he didn't say anything that made me believe him.

'Thank you, Jesmond. And now, if you wouldn't mind leaving us for a moment. I have some matters to discuss with Mr Fitzpatrick.'

'But this is my office.' Jesmond flashed a look at Fitzy that suggested any truce between them was likely to be short-lived.

'I think you'll find it's mine, actually.' I pulled at the cuffs of my blouse and noticed a dark coin-sized stain on the pale blue cotton. Spark's blood was as thick and red as Signor Marcelli's. I pushed my hand into my lap under the desk.

'It won't take long and then you can have your chair back. It's just some business relating to the acts booked for The Comet when it opens. If this place is to be ready in three weeks' time like you promised me, Jessie, I reckon you'd be better off out there keeping an eye on the workmen than sitting in here on your ample arse watching paint dry.' I pointed at the door.

Jesmond's face flushed red as a robin's breast. For a moment he actually put me in mind of one of them furious little birds, always bobbing about and scrapping for a patch of nothing. He glared at Fitzy and then at me, but if there was anything he wanted to say – and I'm sure there was – he thought better of it. Instead he brushed the top of his bowler.

'I'll see how the gilders are getting on, Ma'am.'

He turned and went to the door, the back of his head stiff with dyed hair and spoiled dignity.

We waited in silence for a full minute, straining our ears to catch any sound that might suggest that Jessie was listening outside. When we were certain he wasn't I stood and went to the window.

'I think we need some fresh air in here.' I twisted the latch and pushed the window open to let out the smell of dead dog, blood and Fitzy's jacket.

I heard the rustle of the thicket in his nose as he drew breath to speak.

'Now, if I was a gambling man . . .'

'Which we know you are –' I turned from the window – 'so don't try to spread jam on a turd for my sake.' I didn't want him to think he was getting one over Jesmond when it came to favour.

Fitzy's tache rippled.

'What I mean to say, Ma'am, is that I'd be willing to lay a bet on the fact that whoever did that terrible thing to Marcelli saw to Bertie's dog as well.'

'Of course it was the same person, Fitzy. I would have thought that was clear as the nose on your face.' I sat at the desk again. 'You can't miss that either.'

I looked at Lucca. 'Spark won't be the last?'

164

He shook his head. 'I do not think so, Fannella, no.' He sighed. 'I am sorry for Bertie, but Spark was a dog. Tomorrow . . .' He let the thought of what might come next linger.

Fitzy came to stand closer to the desk. 'You know who's doing it.'

It wasn't a question. I drew a long breath. I didn't see the point of keeping secrets any more. I might as well tell it straight out for once.

'The Barons. Well, one of them in particular, but it might as well be all of them together for all it matters.'

Fitzy frowned. 'But you're one of them, so you are. You're a Baron just like she was before you – Lady Ginger, I mean.'

'I'm not. Not any more.' I shook my head. 'I never really was a Baron. I think that was the point when she left it all to me. She knew me better than I knew myself. You can ask Telferman if you like. I'm giving it all up – the dirty trades, the customs dodges, the opium dens by the river, the pleasure houses. He's working it out, going through the books and the ledgers. Once he's got it reckoned to the nearest farthing, I've told him to give it away, mostly.'

Fitzy's eyes bulged. 'What about us, what about Paradise?'

'Paradise will work well enough without a spider sitting at its heart, sucking the blood from every creature caught in the silk.'

'The Lady was our protection from the Barons.' Fitzy's big head swayed from side to side as he tried to digest it all. 'You can't just walk away. Now *you* are The Lady. She chose you.'

I shrugged. 'Well, I've unchosen myself. And don't worry about the Barons. I might not be one of them any more, but I've still got business to finish with them.'

I almost laughed at myself. They were fine words, girl, but what did they mean? I didn't have the first thought in my head as to how that business might be concluded.

'Jesus Christ!' Fitzy slumped against the desk, all the bluster and blarney leached from his body. 'That's if they don't finish us all first.'

I realised, with a jolt, he was scared too.

'It's just as your man Fratelli, here, says,' he went on. 'First Marcelli, then Bertie's dog. What comes next? Or who? I saw what happened both times. I don't mind telling you I haven't got the stomach for more. If you're not a Baron, what are you? You're no use to us lot, that's for sure. They talk about you, do you know that? The acts and the hands. You might have had their loyalty once, but you've worn it thin. You've patched it too many times to hold it together.'

I had a clarity then. I saw what Kite was at. He was trying to break the only thing my grandmother left to me that I cared about. He was trying to take the halls by seeding them with fear and doubt. It was a calculated act of vengeance. A spiteful boy ripping the wings off a fly before squashing it under a heel.

I swallowed hard. 'I'm your employer, Mr Fitzpatrick. And I need your help to make sure that the people in my halls are safe.'

'Safe!' He pounded the desk so hard it jumped. 'Like Spark? Like old Marcelli?' Fitzy's spittle pattered down on the leather.

'Fannella!' Lucca sprang forward, but I raised a hand to hold him off. Fitzy was old and baggy, but there was an ox beneath the fat. I stared at his big freckled fist on the desk. Years back he'd been a bare knuckler on the streets – one of the best, they said. It was where my grandmother had come across him, and then she found a use for him like she did with so many others.

I put my hand on his fist. 'What happened to the man you were, Fitzy? The man who used this and won again and again. As I hear it, there was a time when you were a champion. That's what I need now.'

Fitzy grunted and pulled away. He rolled his head on that big red neck, but I could tell I'd reached something deep inside. I carried on.

'You keep order in the halls better than anyone I've ever seen. Lady Ginger trusted you, and she trusted your fists as well. God knows, Fitzy, you've done some things in the past that give me a reason to hate you . . .' I looked up at his wrecked face and thought of the way he pawed at Peggy all those times, and other girls too.

But I needed him.

I glanced at Lucca. There were times when Fitzy had treated him with less respect than one of Chibbles' dogs. He was staring at the floor. He had his long coat huddled about him and he was plucking at the wool of his trailing scarf. Christ knows what he thought.

'Listen, Fitzy.' I folded my arms. 'We have to keep this quiet and I'm relying on you to make sure things are . . . secure. I want you to keep your eyes open at The Carnival. This isn't going to make you – or me, come to it – popular, but from now on there's going to be some order. I want everyone – the girls, the hands, the orchestra – to sign in and out every day and every evening, even when they come in to practise. I don't want Johnnies waiting out back – you're to clear them off. The girls are never to go off alone – anywhere or anytime – and no one is to go to The Lamb after last house.'

Fitzy laughed. 'And how am I supposed to make them agree to that? You know what they're like. It would be easier to bring Marcelli and Spark back from the dead.'

'I know.' I bit my lip and thought.

'I need you to put it about that it's just a temporary thing. Say I want to make sure that everyone is concentrating on their acts and their work, ready for the day The Comet opens again. Tell the girls I don't want a whiff of scandal to take the shine off the craft Jessie's gilders have put in. If it smooths the way for you, tell them there's an extra guinea a week for each and every one of them if they play me fair.'

Fitzy sniffed. 'They all like the feel of a coin in their pocket, so they do. If it's a temporary arrangement, they might be more amenable – at a price.'

'There's more for you too, if it works.'

I could see him considering my offer. He stared at the desk.

'This is likely to be a fine place when it opens again, so it is. Jessie now, he doesn't have the feel for it like I do. Wasted on him it is.'

I knew what he was sinuating straight off. He was punting for the chair at The Comet. Empty and boarded as it was, it was still a hundred times better than The Carnival. When it opened again it would be the finest of my halls. The pair I had left, anyway. I held out my hand.

'I think we have an accommodation, Mr Fitzpatrick.'

He gripped my fingers in his greasy paw. 'We do, for now.' His little watery eyes sharpened. 'So, after you've finished this business of yours with the Barons we can all sleep safe in our beds, is that it? One little girl against so many.'

A sudden draught of chill air made me shiver.

I stood up sharp, went to the window to close it, and turned back.

'I'm the *little girl* who went up in the cage night after night without a net to catch her. Don't you ever forget that, Fitzy, because I won't.'

He grinned; his chopped-liver lips squirmed beneath the tache. He opened his chequered jacket, letting the meaty heft of his body mingle with the scent of the paint and the plaster.

'And I almost forgot, Ma'am. I've a suggestion here for the opening night of The Comet – quite a draw, I reckon.'

He dug into a pocket and handed me a page from *The London Evening News*; I recognised the blue paper. Even Fitzy wasn't reading *The Pictorial* these days.

'At the bottom, marked out clear. You can't miss it. And there's something else. When I came here this morning, this was stuck to the door.' He delved into another pocket and produced a folded yellow sheet. He handed it to me and fumbled into the pocket again to bring out a raggy cigar and a dented brass strike case.

He nodded at the paper in my hand as he lit up. 'There was one pasted at The Carnival too, on the wall outside. And there are bound to be more. The ink's fresh. Call themselves the Children of Purity, so they do.'

Fitzy blew out a ring of rank smoke.

'I call them a fucking menace.'

Chapter Thirteen

The edges of the folded paper were torn where Fitzy had ripped it from The Comet's door. Thick white glue pasted on the back was still sticky in places. I prised it open, flapped it out and held the sheet at arm's length to give Lucca the benefit. The bottom of the paper curled in the muck on the floor of the hack.

BEHOLD THE WORDS OF THE LORD

For we will destroy this place, because the cry of them is waxen great before the face of the Lord; and the Lord hath sent us to destroy it. Genesis 19.

THE CHILDREN OF PURITY RISE.

We stared at the yellow bill poster. It was large – four foot high at least – and framed and lettered much like something Fitzy would have put together for The Carnival. The colour, that bilious yellow, was designed to catch the eye. If nothing else I could take a lesson from Auchlyne-Doune there. Fitzy was right about the ink. Not quite dry, the bold black letters on the paper had an oily shine to them. I wondered how many others like it were plastered on walls around Paradise.

I kicked the bottom of the bill away from my skirt. The glue made it stick to the moire, leaving little white streaks.

'What do you make of that?'

Lucca hitched back the blind on his side to let more light through the mud-spattered window. He wound down the glass a little to bring some air into the carriage. On account of the glue, the air in that rocking wooden box was noxious.

The skin around his eye crimped like the frill on a meat pie as he scanned the words.

'It is from the Bible.'

'I know that. It says so right there.' I flicked at the paper. 'Genesis 19.'

I was thrown back into the seat and Lucca reached for the strap as the hack took the corner from Margaret Street into the Commercial at a lick.

On the way back to Salmon Lane, I'd decided, on the spur, to go on to Bell Wharf Stairs. It was still an hour to noon. I had it in mind that a talk with Ramesh Das about old mutton head might salvage something from the day.

Still keeping hold of the leather, Lucca reached down to pinch the bottom corner of the bill in a way that suggested he didn't like to touch it. He pulled it towards him.

'It is the story of the cities punished for their wickedness. *Sodoma e Gomorra.* Two angels are sent with fire and . . .' He searched for the English, but gave up. '*Zolfo.*'

I recognised it exactly, now. Point of fact it was one of Nanny Peck's Sunday favourites. I heard her voice.

And that's why curiosity killed the cat, my girl. If she hadn't looked back, then she would have escaped with the rest of her family. And all things considered, now, wouldn't that have been a blessing for them all?

I didn't have an opinion on that. I'm not sure how the story ended because Nanny Peck always finished up with the pillar of salt and a little lecture on the perils of taking too close an interest in things. Looking back, I can see that, between them, she and Ma, Lady Ginger too, had a deal to hide, so it might well have been something more than a cautionary tale.

Lucca let the corner of the bill slip from his hand. He rubbed ink and glue between the ball of his thumb and the tips of his fingers. The white turned to grey. He frowned and wrinkled his nose.

'Do you know it, Fannella?'

I nodded. 'I do now, thanks to you. It's Lot and his wife. We'd call the cities Sodom and Gomorrah. They escaped – Lot, his wife and daughters – but then she looked back to see what was happening and got turned to salt. God destroys the wicked, that's the gist, isn't it? Come to that, he's not got much time for the curious neither. I always felt sorry for the wife.'

Lucca flicked a tiny pellet of blackened glue at the bill. It hit the paper with a hollow smack.

'There is no mercy. It is a story of anger and hate. The Old Testament is full of such tales.'

I tried to fold the bill to a more amenable size. The glue made it difficult. 'I thought you Romans went in for all this?'

'Those are not the words of my God.'

He turned away to look through the window. We were making our way west down the Commercial now. The hack was moving slowly in the press. Through the pane on my side I saw that we were behind a line of timber wagons making heavy weather under loads from the docks. A Baltic must have come in with the midnight tide on the river. The scent of cut wood lent a notable freshness to the frowse of dead horse.

The street was lively. People jostled for space on the narrow cobbled pavements. Before we left The Comet, I'd asked Fitzy to make sure every bleedin' yellow sheet pasted to a Limehouse wall was removed. But even so, since dipping their bread in dripping this morning, how many of them out there had seen one of the Reverend's bill posters?

It was the kind of day where colour was a luxury. The drabness of the clouds overhead seemed to seep into everything below. We passed a butcher's shop on the corner of York Street. Sides of pork caught by the trotters swayed from hooks beneath the striped awning. The meat was the colour of gruel and flecked with a glistening sheen that could almost be mistaken for sweat. There was something indecent about all that naked flesh and the delicate little feet dangling above the cobbles. Nanny Peck always held that no leg of mutton should be hung in a butcher's window without being properly dressed. Looking at the pork, I could see her point.

A gust of wind caught the brim of a man's tall hat. He tried to keep it in place, but he was too slow. In a moment it was flying down the street, tumbling and carting like it was grateful to be free from his greasy thatch. I watched it come to rest upright in the road in the path of one of the timber wagons. Before its owner was able to retrieve it, an iron-bound wheel as tall as a man crushed it to a cap.

I wiped my hand on the side of the hack. 'Christ! This stuff's persistent, Lucca. And the ink's just as bad.'

More glue stuck to my gloves as I struggled to fold the bill to a shape that would fit into my bag. 'He must have had the presses running in the early hours. That takes coin. And it doesn't take a parson to see what he's poking at. Even if you didn't know the Bible story, the message is clear enough. The halls are places of wickedness and vice, and the Lord's servant – that's how the Reverend presents himself – is coming for us with his heavenly army. The Children of Purity are the rabble he's gathering to his cause.'

The yellow paper tore. I swore under my breath. The soft grey leather of my gloves was streaked with glue and stained black from the ink.

'I don't need this. And I don't reckon I deserve it neither. If Auchlyne-Doune and his lily-faced daughter knew a quarter of what really went on in this city they'd have a genuine battle to fight. First Signor Marcelli, now Spark. I know she was just a dog, but Bertie loved her like a child. It's the beginning. There's enough trouble coming to the halls and everyone who works in them without this . . . this . . .'

I gave up trying to fold the sheet. Instead I screwed it into a messy ball and tossed it to the floor of the hack. I kicked it into the corner.

'This is just . . . a distraction. I haven't got time for it.'

I watched the paper unfurl again like a grimy yellow flower. I thumped the bench between us. 'Of course! That's it, Lucca.'

He turned from the window.

'It's a distraction. *He's* a distraction.'

I sat up straight.

'What if it's all connected? What if the Reverend is working for them? The Barons, I mean? If word gets out about Marcelli, Chibbles, and God knows who else if we don't take a care, then how do I keep them all on my side – the acts, the girls, the hands in the workshops, even Professor Ruben and the orchestra boys? No one within a hundred miles of London would want to be on the bill at The Carnival, or even at The Comet when it opens again. It would be like reading your own death warrant.'

Lucca quizzed at me. 'But I do not see how—'

'But I think I *can* see. It's not just the acts they're going for. For the past month Telferman's been parcelling off the trades so I don't have a financial interest in Paradise – not like Lady Ginger had – but I've kept hold of the halls. It's the one thing she left to me that doesn't feel dirty. It's the place I came from. The place I care about. The Barons know that. What if the Reverend isn't out for himself? What if Kite and the rest of them are using him to stir up the punters so I'm fighting a battle inside and out? They won't need to come for me – my own people will do the job for them.'

Of an instant, I was sitting in front of a fire with what looked like a leather-bound brick in my hand. I gripped Lucca's hand.

'When I went to find Vellum, he read me something from an old book. *The Art of War* he called it. Do you know it?'

Lucca shook his head. I wasn't surprised. He was a reader, don't get me wrong, and he had a pile of books in his room at The Palace, but they were mostly full of pictures and accounts of the lives of all them old-time painters. He was interested in art, but I don't think he had a taste for war.

'Even if you don't, you said something like it yourself. Listen to this.' I paused for a moment, marshalling the order in my head. Once I was sure I'd got it all correct I rattled it all off.

'"*It is said that if you know your enemies and know yourself, you will not be put at risk even in a hundred battles. If you only know yourself, but not your opponent, you may win or may lose. If you know neither yourself nor your enemy, you will always endanger yourself.*"

'Know your enemies. That's the key. The Reverend is an opponent all right, but if he's working for the Barons then at least I've got something on him.'

For the first time in a while I felt a flicker of hope. If I'd been a gambling type, it was like seeing a Jack in a fist of duds.

'If I'm right, then perhaps—'

I broke off as a cloud of thick black smoke filled the hack. Lucca pushed up the window, but it was too late. We spluttered and choked in the sudden darkness. The hack shuddered on its springs as a train crossed the Blackwall viaduct directly overhead. The bellow of the engine echoed off the bricks arching beside us.

The noise spooked the horse. It plunged forward into the bank of steam massing beneath the arch. I felt the driver pull hard on the reins as the hack bucked. I was jolted back and my head cracked on the wood. I heard the beads on my bonnet scrape on the panel.

In a moment, we were rolling along at a more sedate pace. The driver tapped the roof and pushed back the slat up top. Through the gap I saw him tug his cap by way of apology. 'Begging your pardon. Sampson's new at the game. I've only had him in the traces three weeks. He's not come across an engine before. Everything all right inside?'

He closed up sharp without waiting for an answer. I pulled my hat back into place. This one had a frill of black lace wafting at the brim. It couldn't make up its mind whether it wanted to cover my face for the mystery of it, or annoy me. I rolled the lace back and tucked it under the beaded ribbon at the crown to keep it busy.

I glanced through the window. We'd cleared the viaduct now and were down on Brook Street. Lucca wound down the glass again. The last of the smoke cleared, but it took a moment before we could talk free without packing our lungs with soot.

'Are you all right, Fannella? Your head?'

I nodded. 'It sounded worse than it felt.'

He took a 'kerchief from a pocket. 'May I?' He leaned over to wipe smuts from my face. The clean white cotton smelt of lemon cologne. Without thinking, I took it from his hand and repaid the compliment, suddenly feeling the roughness of his scars as I dabbed at his cheeks. I paused. I'd become so used to his face that it didn't look wrong to me. He stopped my hand and took the 'kerchief, silently returning it to his pocket. He cleared his throat.

'You were saying. *Perhaps* . . . what?'

I wondered whether to apologise for the dabbing. Deciding against it, I tried to answer his question. 'Perhaps I can use it. If the Reverend is working for the Barons, then I'm a step ahead. That's something, isn't it? There must be a way to turn that to an advantage.'

'But what if he is not?' Lucca rubbed his fingers over his cheek, then he pulled at his hat, lowering the brim to shade the scars. I'm not sure he even knew he was doing it, but it was a reminder that I'd taken a liberty. He turned to the window.

'When we went to the meeting at the mission, Fannella, I saw a man who seeks to control, not someone who can be controlled.'

'And I saw an actor who likes to hear the chink of brass in his pocket.'

He nodded. 'But that does not mean he is in the pay of the Barons. Auchlyne-Doune and his daughter seemed very able to take money from those who attended the meeting. It was professional, a business. It seemed practised.'

I picked at the glue on my gloves. They were ruined. I unbuttoned them at the wrists, peeled them from my fingers and threw them to the floor to join the crumpled yellow poster.

'Yes, practised, I'll give you that. But who brought them here and why now?'

Lucca shook his head. 'I believe they are the sort who travel from city to city, like actors.' He gestured at the street beyond the window. 'For so many, this is a hard place. It is easy to take despair and anger to make . . .' He shrugged. '*Non tutto è burro che viene dalla mucca.*'

I rolled my eyes. 'What's that supposed to mean, in London?'

'It is a saying from home. The cow does not only produce butter. The Reverend milks the people for their money, but there is also . . .'

'Shit?'

He winced, but I carried on. 'He's churning the shit. Is that it?'

Lucca nodded. 'In a way. That is how they work, people like the Reverend and his daughter. They create chaos and then they move on. It is a dirty trade.' He took my bare hand in his. 'You are right to be wary, Fannella. But I believe this is . . . *coincidenza.*'

I ran a finger over the dried paint on his knuckles. 'Well, coincidence or not, I've a mind to find out more about the Reverend. He didn't come from nowhere, did he? We need to sniff out every scrap of his past. I reckon he's left a stinking trail behind him.'

The hack juddered to a halt. The driver rapped on the roof and opened the slat up top again.

'Bell Wharf Stairs – near as. I can't go closer. That'll be two shillings.'

Chapter Fourteen

'I am glad to meet you properly at last, Mr Fratelli.' Ramesh Das sat back in the carved wooden chair. His dark, deep-set eyes scanned Lucca's face. 'The fever was severe when last we met. You are bound to be weakened.'

The voice was smooth and cultured. Ramesh Das spoke like a regular gent. And he carried himself like one too. He was tall and spare with a long mournful face. When he smiled, which didn't happen often, the years fell away and you could see, quite clear, the handsome young man who'd come to London more than fifty years back.

He swept a hand to his forehead. The broidered sleeve of his spotless linen gown fell away and I saw the scar coiled about his arm. I recalled it from the last time I'd sat here drinking chai, trying to pretend I wasn't surprised.

The snake – that was what the scar looked like – curled through the dark hairs on his arm, its flat head resting between the prominent bones of his wrist. It was likely a burn. The skin was puckered and healed, and a deal paler than the rest of him.

If Ramesh Das caught me staring again, he didn't let on. Instead he kept his eyes locked on Lucca's face.

'I fear it is here –' he circled a finger on his brow – 'that the frailty will persist.' He studied Lucca's face to a count of ten and then he reached to the brass-topped table set between us and lifted a jewel-coloured glass.

He was right about that. Lucca was getting stronger every day, and I was grateful to see it. The fact he was painting again was something too. But even so, since that time when the Barons had taken him (and Sam), it was like a little flame had been snuffed out somewhere deep inside.

Lucca didn't answer. He took up his own glass and swirled the sweetness around.

Ramesh Das caught my eye. I sidled at Lucca and nodded.

'I do not, for a moment, wish to cause offence, Mr Fratelli. But sometimes the mind takes longer than the body to recover from a great harm.' Ramesh blinked slowly and waved a hand at the glass on the table before me.

'The chai is to your taste, Lady?'

The red stone of the ring on his middle finger caught the light from the window over the river. The shutters were hooked back to let as much of the day into the room as possible.

The last time I came here I was blinded by the sun, but the world beyond the glass now was shrouded. It was impossible to make anything out clear. I remembered that Ramesh Das told me how the brilliance bouncing off the water reminded him of his childhood in India.

That was partly what I was here to ask him about. It was clear there was a score to settle between Ramesh Das and the man who called himself General Arthur George Denderholm.

He tapped the top of the copper pot on the table. 'I believe you tried this blend when you visited me with your friend, Mrs Tewson? Tell me, how is she – and the baby?'

'This is just as good as ever, thank you.' I raised a gilded green glass to my lips. 'And Peggy's doing well.' I thought about my grandmother's dice box and the conversation I'd had with Lucca about the possible father of that baby. I glanced at him, but he was busy acquainting himself with the contents of the room. I wasn't surprised it appealed to him.

The warren leading to Bell Wharf Stairs was a poor place, but this building overlooking the Thames had once been the home of someone who needed to keep an eye on his ships and the trades they carried home. The house had been carved into lodging spaces. Ramesh had a run of tall-ceilinged chambers on the top two floors.

The room where we sat together now was filled with wooden couches strewn with woven cushions. There was a particular aroma, not unpleasant, but not something I could put a name to. It minded me of the inside of old Pardieu's medicine bag. The floorboards were mostly hidden by a multitude of overlapping rugs, the different patterns contriving somehow to complement each other, rather than argue the toss. Book-lined shelves filled a whole wall, and everywhere you looked, all manner of ornaments – mostly of an Eastern variety – jostled for space.

Nanny Peck would have thrown up her hands in horror at all that dusting and clambering. Mind you, judging by the pristine state of the place, it was clear that someone here was a dab hand with a cloth. Probably Jani, I reckoned. The barefoot boy had brought in the chai five minutes after we'd arrived.

I sipped it now, feeling the sweetness and warmth slip to my belly.

Ramesh smiled. 'It has been some time, Lady. I am not so vain as to imagine you have come to see me today for the sake of my company or my conversation.'

I'd told him before that he didn't have to call me that – Lady, I mean – but like the brothers at The Palace he didn't seem able or willing to slip out of the habit. On both counts, I imagined it came out of a sense of loyalty to my grandmother, Lady Ginger. They'd called her that for years. Now I was in her place they didn't see a reason to use any other title.

It was still a wonder to me that someone like Ramesh Das was in my employ, in a manner of speaking. There was something about this gracious man that was at once a comfort and a puzzle. For a start, he had a way of looking at you that sinuated it wasn't so much your face he was interested in as your soul. I reckoned Lucca had just had the benefit of that.

And there was something else too, a danger. I was minded of Vellum at the Sanctuary. Something smouldered beneath the surface of his courtesy, something I wouldn't want to poke to a flame. I was grateful Ramesh Das was my friend.

I twisted the tea glass. The emerald facets threw back a dozen reflections of my face. The glass was a pretty thing, something chosen by a woman. Last time I came here with Peggy, Ramesh had told me about his wife, Siya. She'd died years back, but the way he talked about her suggested that he had hopes of seeing her again in this world. I tracked down the particular word he'd used. In my mind it was connected to flowers . . .

Reincarnation.

That was it.

I didn't pretend to understand what he'd meant when he told me that. It wasn't something they spread on a free bun at a Sunday Bible class, and that was as deep as I was prepared to consider the matter. But thinking about it now brought another question to mind. There was someone *I* didn't want to see again. Someone who'd only brought me trouble. The green-faced girls in the glass frowned.

'Well, Lady, you have a purpose?'

I looked up. Ramesh was staring at me expectant, watchful.

'Joey. I asked you to take care of him – get him free of the Bethlem.' I put my glass down on the table. 'Before we go any further I'd like your assurance that he's a long way from Paradise.'

'And you are wise to do so.' Ramesh nodded. 'Money – a great deal of it, I might add – proved persuasive. In the end it was an easy matter to buy a closed eye and a way out from that place. Joseph is indeed a long way from Paradise. The ship on which more of your money secured a passage was bound for Australia. I delivered him myself to a well-appointed cabin and watched the *Helena Mena* sail from London on the evening tide.'

I looked at Lucca. He was slowly twisting his chai glass on the brass table top. It caught the thin bar of light from the window, spilling a halo of blue on the metal. Despite their friendship, Lucca had tried to warn me about Joey so many times, but back then I wasn't in a place to hear what he was saying.

I felt a tightness in my throat. That bleedin' soot from the viaduct lodged everywhere.

'How did Joey take . . . I mean, was he . . . amenable?'

Ramesh shrugged. The nostrils at the end of his long nose flared. 'I do not believe that is a word that could ever be applied to Joseph . . . to your brother, Lady. But when I made his situation quite clear –' he held his hands open in front of him like Joey was slippering through them – 'he was forced to agree that this was an . . . *acceptable* solution. He would be a greater fool than I imagine him to be if he did not take this opportunity.'

I flicked a speck of lint from the moire. Part of me was glad, relieved to hear it. The more I'd learned about Joey, the more

I'd come to realise that the clever golden boy I'd worshipped in the days after Ma and Nanny Peck had left Paradise in London and moved on to the real thing had feet of mud. And that was putting it delicately.

But now I knew where he was bound, I felt an ache deep inside that would likely trouble me like a rotten tooth for the rest of my days. One of my eyes began to water on account of another speck of soot.

'So, he's gone then?' I swallowed the question.

'Yes, Lady. He is gone. And he will arrive in Australia as a new man, with a new name. It was arranged. The book of his past here is closed. There is no more to say of Joseph Peck.' Ramesh brought his hands together, in the way of a prayer, and sat back. 'What do you say, Mr Fratelli?'

Lucca looked up sharp like he'd been caught dreaming by a schoolmaster.

'Joseph will always be a . . .' He balanced his words on the scales. 'He will always be a troubled man, and I fear that a shadow will follow him wherever he goes. He did love you, Fannella. I know that, but . . . I agree that it is better this way. Mr Das –' he nodded at Ramesh – 'is right. There is no more to say.'

Lucca took my hand and squeezed tight. I felt a wetness slip down my cheek. I swiped it away. My brother wasn't worth tears, I knew that now. We sat in a silence that wasn't uncomfortable, but wasn't a consolation neither. After a moment Ramesh spoke.

'Joseph is not the reason you are here today.' It was a statement of fact, not a question. I reached for my glass and forced a mouthful of chai past the knot in my throat.

'You seek information about the Children of Purity, Lady.' Again, it wasn't a question. 'The Reverend Auchlyne-Doune is a . . . nuisance.'

'Nuisance!' I almost choked on the chai. 'I reckon he's a deal more than that. Menace is something more like it. I don't know what his game is exactly, but if he's a regular man of the cloth then I'm a bleedin' duchess. Just this morning someone left a bill plastered to the doors of The Comet. It was lines from the Bible finished off with something like a threat.'

Ramesh nodded. '"The Children of Purity rise."'

'You've seen it?' I quizzed at him.

'I am your eyes and ears, Lady. Even if you no longer wish to be closely involved in the affairs of Paradise, I still serve your interests and will continue to do so, as will my esteemed colleague Mr Telferman. You may rely on us, always, even if you avoid our company.'

He paused to let that sink in. I felt like a child reminded of its manners. Of course, Ramesh Das already knew about the Reverend and his dogs. It was his job. It was what I paid him for.

He sipped his chai. 'It is my understanding that these yellow notices, all of them, have already been removed.' He waved in the general direction of streets beyond the building.

'You . . . you've already dealt with it?'

He nodded. Once again, I had cause to be grateful, and surprised, that this elegant old gent was in my employ.

'Thank you, Mr Das.' I glanced at Lucca. 'I'd be obliged if you could let me know anything you find out about him, and his daughter too. Lucca thinks it's a coincidence that Auchlyne-Doune has washed up in Paradise just now, but I want to be sure it's . . . it's nothing more.'

'You speak of the Barons.' Ramesh blinked those heavy-lidded eyes. Again, it wasn't a question.

I swallowed. 'We both know they haven't finished with me. In fact, they're circling now.'

I told him about Signor Marcelli – how we'd found him and his puppets – and about Bertie Chibbles' dog.

'In both cases what happened had the bloody print of Kite's man, Matthias Schalk. I've seen his cruelty before.' I sidled at Lucca. 'I know the work of that cane of his when I see it. But what's to come next? Old Marcelli wasn't liked, and Spark . . . well, she was a bright little thing, but at the end of the day, she was a dog. What if . . . if . . .'

What if he came for one of the girls?

That was what went through my mind most distinctly, but I didn't want to put it into words, for fear of making it a truth. And if not one of the chorus girls, it could be another of the acts, or one of the hands in the workshops or, God forbid, one of the orchestra boys. For years after Ma and Nanny Peck had died, and before Joey had come back from the grave, the people in the halls were the closest I'd had to a family.

'I was aware of the death of the puppeteer, poor man –' Ramesh bowed his head in sorrow – 'but not of the dog.'

'It only happened this morning. Jessie – Mr Jesmond – found her when he came in. I've asked him to keep it to himself and I've taken steps to keep the others as safe as possible, under the circumstances. Fitzy's looking after that for me. It was him who found the bill stickers plastered over the doors of The Comet, and The Carnival too.'

'I will look into this also, on your behalf.' Ramesh appeared to consider the matter. His gaze roamed across my shoulder and came to rest somewhere behind my head. His eyes sharpened. I turned to see what he was looking at but there was nothing there except a table set against the wall, the surface cluttered with more of his ornaments – dancing figures, seated figures, riding figures, men with more heads and arms than was natural, a cow as big as a coal scuttle and a woman who – as far as I could tell – was mostly a snake.

'My sources may hear something of use, Lady.'

I turned back. 'I'm not sure I want anyone hearing anything. If word gets out, Auchlyne-Doune won't need his pious mob to close the halls because there won't be an act left in the Empire, let alone London, willing to work for me.'

Empire.

I'd reminded myself of the question I'd come here to ask. I put my chai glass down.

'Mr Das, when I came here with Peggy that time, you had a scrap of print pinned to your desk. I had its twin in my bag. Do you remember?'

Ramesh shifted back in his chair. His face was in shadow now and I thought it deliberate. I bent to my bag and retrieved the grimy cut of paper. It had been folded and poked at so many times it was almost coming apart along the creases.

'If you need a reminder, it was this.'

I opened it out carefully and laid it flat on the little table between us, so we could all see it clear.

'This man here.' I pointed at Denderholm's woolly face. 'You told me you knew him, from way back, before you ever came to London. I need to know more about him.'

Ramesh turned away. At first, I thought he wasn't going to answer. I watched as he reached to the row of open wooden compartments along the top of his desk. The papers lodging there like pigeons were neatly bound with ribbon. He idled a finger along the row and slipped out a familiar fold of print. He handed it to me, in silence. I flattened it out and laid it on the table next to mine, careful of the copper chai pot. It had a drip to its spout.

Three of us had saved that same story from *The London Pictorial*. I stared at the cuts laid side by side and tried, again, to make out what I was missing.

'I believe you also knew a man whose picture is there, Lady?' Ramesh twisted about to take something from the desk. I didn't see what it was, but I heard the jink of metal on metal as he closed his fingers to a fist to hold something tight. He settled back into the shadow, but that bar of watery light slanted across his lap, drawing the glow from the ruby in his ring.

'You said that you were familiar with the young man in the lower part of the engraving?'

'Him.' I pointed at Vellum, noting again the way he looked like a cherry floating in a bowl of eel jelly among the company on the page.

'I've had occasion to meet him now and he's not . . . well, he's not what I thought. He's not a friend, exactly, but I don't think he's an enemy neither. He works for the Crown. At least that's what he told me.' I paused. What did I really know about Vellum or who he worked for? I didn't even know his true name. I looked up and caught Ramesh Das staring at me. *Into* me is more like.

I drained the last of my chai.

'My . . . acquaintance here was interested in how his picture came to be in Sam's . . . *The London Pictorial*. We also had a chat about him . . .' I tapped a finger on Denderholm's face. 'And now I've got good reason to believe he isn't who he says he is. Last time I was here you told me that you knew him too. You recognised him and cut this scrap from the paper, same as I did. Why?'

He didn't answer.

I tried again. 'Where were you born, Ramesh? It wasn't here in London, was it?' I turned my own scrap of newsprint to face him. 'I need to know about this man. I think he's part of something that goes beyond the Barons, and – if I've understood it right – beyond anything my grandmother was ever caught up in. Who is he?'

There was a long silence, then: 'I knew him only as Denderholm.'

Ramesh opened his clenched fist and studied the contents of his palm. All the time he'd been holding a tiny metal figure, a dancing man with the head of an elephant.

'Do you remember this trinket, Lady?'

I nodded. 'You said it was . . .' I tracked the name. 'Ganesha . . . is that right?'

'Your memory is impressive, as Telferman always tells me. Take him.' Ramesh handed me the figure. 'What else do you recall of our conversation?'

I looked down at the little statue. The metal was heavier than you'd expect for something so slight. Balanced delicately on one leg, Ganesha peered up at me. There was amusement and a shrewdness in his expression, like he knew more than he was prepared to tell. The part of him that was a man was well fed, his ample corporation tumbled over a narrow belt. For all his grace, he had a heft.

I turned the figure between my fingers. 'You said he was lucky, for some, leastways. He removes things that get in the way of good fortune, but sometimes he blocks the way of those who don't deserve it.'

Ramesh nodded. 'Very good, Lady.'

He sat up straight in his carved black chair, arranged his hands in his lap and closed his eyes. After a minute or so, when he wasn't forthcoming, I quizzed at Lucca, wondering whether he might have nodded off. Lucca shook his head. A moment later, Ramesh opened his eyes. Flecks of amber glinted in the brown.

'I will tell you what I know of the man who calls himself Arthur George Denderholm. Then, perhaps, you will tell me what he deserves.'

Chapter Fifteen

'The ancient city where I was born has many names. The British called it Calicut and so did my father, who dealt in spice like his father and his grandfather before him. My father's family had come from the north originally, but we had always been merchants.'

Ramesh pointed at the little figure in my hand. 'It belonged to my great-grandfather. He said that a trader must be able to create opportunities and make obstacles appear in the path of his rivals.

'When I was born, the days of Calicut as a great port were coming to an end, but its position on the Malabar coast was valuable to our British rulers. My father spoke many languages. It was useful to be fluent in the tongues of the men with whom he dealt, and this talent was also a commodity. He assisted the British and, in return, their patronage brought us wealth and position. There was a time when we thought ourselves fortunate.

'We lived in a beautiful house overlooking the sea. We had servants, good food, fine clothes – everything we could desire. Peacocks walked in our courtyard and light reflected from the ocean shimmered on the walls and the ceilings. When I think of those days it is that light I remember most clearly, that and the sound of my sister Abha's laughter.'

Ramesh twisted the ruby ring.

'Our parents came late to parenthood. Abha and I were their only living children and they loved us fiercely. My sister was four years older than me. She was beautiful and she was clever. Our father made sure that we were educated together, which was unusual, but she had such a questing mind that, despite our mother's anxiety, he could not refuse her. I believe Abha was a better scholar than ever I was. By the time she was twelve she spoke many languages almost as fluently as my father himself. But that was a curse and not a blessing.'

He paused and ran a hand through his thick grey hair as if to smooth the thoughts tangling up beneath.

'When my father fell ill we prayed at the Tali Temple and gave offerings for his recovery, but it was his time. In less than two months he was a shadow. Our house had once been a busy, lively place, but now, in the days of his sickness, it fell strangely silent. Nobody called to pay their respects and I began to see that the servants looked away from me, unwilling to catch my eye.

'One evening, close to the end, my father called my sister to his room and asked to be left alone with her. The next morning no one could find her, but I knew where she was. There was a hidden place beyond our garden amid the rocks at the edge of the sea where we would sit and watch the coming and going of the ships and talk about all the places we would travel to one day.'

Ramesh fell silent and took up his chai. He stared at the glass in his hand. It was like he was seeing something in the dregs of the sweet liquid.

'I found Abha there weeping. Our life was built on nothing more than clouds, she told me. We had been blind to so much. Beyond the red-washed walls of our beautiful house and peaceful garden we had enemies – men who despised and envied our father, but worse, men who wished us harm because they saw him as a betrayer.

'Abha said that when our father died, as he surely would, he feared the British would not protect us from these men because we would no longer serve a purpose. That was why he had called her to his bedside.

'When he died, he said she was to go with me to the British at West Hill. We were to ask to see the district Collector and beg for help. Father told her that it was important to show the Collector how perfectly both she and I spoke in English. He said he wanted us to prove that we could be useful, just as he had been. He made Abha promise this and she agreed. But he was a dying man, sick in mind as well as body . . . his words were not wise.'

Ramesh swirled the glass and drank the last of the chai. He stared at the window. It was raining now. Thin trails of water streaked the panes.

'Calicut suffers greatly during the rains. The night my father died coincided with the first deluge of the season. We sat with my mother at his bedside until it was light, as was the custom, but when we left the room we found that my father had been right to fear. Every servant – except Ina, who was very old and who had been with my mother since she was a child – had gone. We were abandoned.

'Our mother was distraught. Nothing we said could persuade her to leave the room where my father's body grew cold. She knelt at his side and continued to speak to him as if he were alive. I remember standing at the door, listening to her whispering, but I could not hear what she said for the drumming of the rain on the stones of the courtyard.

'Eventually, Abha took my hand and led me away from that room to the gate. She had brought my cloak and my wooden street shoes, and I saw that she too was dressed for a journey. The rain was our friend that day, for the streets were deserted. The wind that always comes with the season tore the branches of the trees and snatched loose tiles from roofs. I was frightened. Protected by the high red walls of our home, I had never seen the city in such a rage, but Abha kept hold of my hand and told me that I must be brave . . .'

Ramesh broke off and reached for the copper pot. He refilled the glasses in turn and gestured at the table. 'Please.'

Lucca took his glass, but I sat still with my hands clasped in my lap, feeling the weight of the little metal figure in my palm. Ramesh raised his glass and the spicy scent of the fresh-poured chai filled the air.

'We walked through the old city, past the temple where we had prayed for our father's recovery and out through the western gate to the road. The residence of the Collector was not far, but the dust had already churned to a river of mud. We slipped and slid, and often we fell. Soon our sodden cloaks were heavy and soiled.

'Finally, when the rain came so hard that we could not go on, we sheltered beneath the arches of a roadside shrine carved from a single rock. It was an ancient place where travellers left offerings for safe journeys. I remember studying the figures and faded paintings of the gods on the stone roof above our heads. Flowers left against the pillars at the entrance were tossed aside by the wind and carried away on the torrent and I wondered if the gods would not be pleased.

'We could not go on. Neither could we go back. Soon, the

paved floor of the shrine began to flood. Dirty water swirled around our ankles. We climbed into a niche for offerings set high in the rock. It was deep and wide enough for us to lie side by side. Abha held me close and after a while I fell asleep.

'When I woke, she was standing below, talking in English to a tall man in a long travelling cloak. Beyond the entrance to the shrine I could see a horse stamping in the mud. I stayed hidden in the shadows, but Abha called to me and I crept forward. The man turned to look up at me and I saw scarlet beneath the folds of grey, and the glint of golden buttons.'

Ramesh set his glass down carefully on the table and took up the cutting from *The London Pictorial*. He moved it to catch the light from the window, holding it at a distance to see it clear.

A year or so back I'd visited the Zoological Gardens up west with Lucca when he had a fancy to draw the animals there. A solitary tiger had watched me from behind the bars of its circular cage. It had stretched out a lazy paw and yawned like it couldn't really be bothered, but its golden eyes gave the lie to that casual disregard. Experience had taught that tiger it couldn't reach me, but I was in no doubt that the thing it wanted to do most in all the world at that moment was to clamp its jaws around my neck. The fire in the eyes of Ramesh Das just now put me in mind of that tiger.

I looked down at my own creased bit of print. Until that moment I'd always seen something comical in the General's face with its luxuriance of whiskers. You could hardly see the man behind them, they bristled so thick. Now when I looked, there was nothing amusing there at all. Just a pair of hooded eyes staring up at me from the paper. I had a clarity as to where this story was leading. I waited, aware of a silence in the room that might burst your ears.

Ramesh folded the newspaper scrap many times over until it was a tiny square between his fingers. Tears doused the blaze in his eyes now. He drew a sharp breath. 'I was nine years old, and my sister was not yet fourteen. We were children.

'In the correct English my father had taught us, my sister introduced me to the officer and told me that when the rain allowed, he had offered to take her to the Collector's house. It was a lucky meeting, she said, for the captain was also on his way to West Hill, carrying a message from the Governor of Madras. Like us, he had been forced to take shelter from the rain.

'The captain smiled. He was a young man, not yet . . .' Ramesh ran a hand over his jaw. 'He had the palest skin I had ever seen and eyes that were such an odd light shade of blue that they seemed to be barely there at all. They minded me of the moonstones belonging to my mother that Ina called unlucky.

'He bowed his head to me, as if I were a man, and said he would happily take my sister to West Hill, as she requested, but that I should remain at the shrine because there was not room for us both to ride with him. He asked if I would mind being alone for a little while. I did not want to be shamed before my sister so I told him I would be happy to wait.

'I stayed in my niche and I listened to my clever sister chattering to the captain in his own tongue as easily and naturally as if he were a family friend. I was proud of her and I could see that the captain was impressed. At least, that was what I thought I saw.

'In a while the rain fell more gently. The captain said it was time for them to leave. He bowed to me again and took my sister by the hand. She waved up at me and told me – in our tongue – to wait in the shrine and that she would return for me soon. The captain led her out through the archway. I remember how little she looked beside him. He plucked her from the mud and swung her up high to the saddle of his horse. A moment later he seated himself behind her –' Ramesh looked to the window – '. . . and they rode away.'

The tears brimmed over and trickled down his face – streaks of silver on the dark skin. I glanced at Lucca who sat still as a marble figure. His eye was fixed on our host.

We waited, and we waited some more.

Ramesh rolled the square of paper between his long fingers. I noted how he squeezed it so tight that the skin around his nails went white. 'I stayed there in the shrine. Day became night. Abha did not return, but I was certain she would come. I sat there in the darkness, straining to hear the sound of a horse, or my sister calling my name above the wind and the rain. By daybreak I was hungry and so thirsty that I licked at the water that dripped from the carved figures, but I did what Abha had told me and I waited.

'Eventually, I wrapped myself in my cloak, rolled to the back of the niche and slept. I was woken by the sound of voices outside. English voices. I sat up, eager to see my sister again, but I heard a profanity and then muttered conversation. Something made me wary. If the men outside had been sent by Abha and the captain, why did they not call my name?

'I moved as quietly as I could to a place where I could see without being seen. Two British soldiers stood at the entrance to the shrine. I knew at once from their uniform that they were not of rank. One of them carried a knotted sack over his shoulder. He shrugged it free and it fell heavily to the mud. The other man stepped beneath the arch. I watched him push the bundle with his foot through the dirty pool until it rested in the furthest, darkest corner.

'I recall, most distinctly, what they said to each other that day. I will remember every word they uttered to the moment the very last breath leaves my body. The man who had entered the shrine called out to his companion: "Even if this isn't where he meant, I'm damned if I'm going to cart Denderholm's foul business a mile further. This isn't soldier's work and I want nothing more to do with it."

'I shrank into the niche as the other man ducked his head through the arch and stared around at the carvings and faded painted walls. He shook his head. "Not even a decent Christian burial, poor mite. Although, under the circumstances, I'm not sure that would have been right."

'The man standing below me replied, "There's nothing right about this. All I know for sure is that the young captain is a vicious devil. The sooner he's on his way back to Madras the better for all of us." I watched him remove his cap and bend to touch the bundle. It was a tender gesture. I heard him whisper something then he crossed himself –' Ramesh looked direct at Lucca – 'in the way, I think, of your faith.

'When I was quite certain they had gone, I climbed down to see what they had left. Stains darker than mud seeped through the sackcloth. My hands trembled as I loosened the cords at the neck. The first thing I saw was a mass of dark hair matted with blood. I pushed the hair aside and saw my sister's face.'

Ramesh swallowed. 'Abha was no longer beautiful.'

He struggled to master himself, then he spoke very slowly. 'The last time I saw my sister alive was when she left the road-side shrine in the storm with Captain Denderholm. I do not know exactly what he did to her. And that, perhaps, is a blessing.'

Chapter Sixteen

The sound of rain drumming on a window in Limehouse merged with the storm hammering on the stones of that road-side shrine outside Calicut. I couldn't breathe, and I couldn't speak. I was standing there in the gloom with a nine-year-old boy and the body of his sister. Lucca reached across to place his hand on Ramesh's arm.

'*Mi dispiace molto.*' He whispered the words again. I didn't need to pick out the meaning. I gripped the little metal figure of Ganesha so tight that I felt it digging into the flesh of my palm.

I will tell you what I know of the man who calls himself Arthur George Denderholm, and then perhaps you will tell me what he deserves.

For once I didn't have a ready answer. I stared at the news cutting – the ragged one from my bag – still sitting on the table, then I brought that tiny dancing god down so heavily on the image of the General's head that the brass rang aloud and the chai pot juddered.

Ramesh steadied the pot. He turned to the desk behind him and produced a pretty filigree strike box. He lit a Lucifer and held it to the edge of the tiny folded square of newsprint he'd been clutching while telling us his story.

In a moment it burned with a fierce golden flame, but Ramesh held it between his finger and thumb until it was a charred cinder. If it caused him pain he didn't seem to notice. Instead he stared at the tiny fire in his hand, the light of it flickering in his brown eyes until it died. He clicked his fingers and it was gone.

He took up the elephant-headed figure between his singed fingers and kissed it. I noticed tiny spots of red glistening on the metal. I looked down at my palm and saw blood where the metal had cut me. I felt the making of a pact between us. A dark one.

I shifted on the dainty chair. 'And now he's here in London. Denderholm, or whatever his true name is.'

Ramesh placed Ganesha very carefully and deliberately back on the General's face. 'So it would appear.'

I stared at the little elephant figure. 'I've seen a death certificate of a boy called Arthur George Denderholm who was buried in Madras more than sixty years back. It's not a common name.'

Ramesh nodded. 'It is a simple thing, for a man to buy himself a new name in a faraway place where the names of dead children are easy to come by.'

He scanned my face for a moment. 'Do you believe in fate, Lady?'

If you'd asked that question to the girl who cleared slops from the gallery at The Gaudy a year back, she'd have given a pert answer about having better things to think about than fortune telling, but she wasn't the same person sitting here now. I studied the complicated pattern in the rug beneath my chair. I couldn't see where it ended or where it began.

'I . . . I believe in justice, but that's not the same thing, is it?'

'Is it not? I think you are an instrument of justice. It seems we are bound by this man who calls himself Denderholm. And that is also our fate.'

On impulse, I reached out and caught Ramesh by the wrist.

'If you want to put an obstacle, a bleedin' big one, in his path, I'll help you. I give you my word on that.'

I felt the puckered skin of the snake-like scar beneath my fingers and quizzed at him. He furled back the sleeve of his tunic and held out his arm so Lucca and me could see the burn.

'Some scars heal more easily than others. What Denderholm did to my sister can never heal, here . . .' Ramesh brought a hand to his heart. 'What he did to me . . .' He shrugged and pulled down the sleeve.

'He did that to you?' For a moment, I was confused. 'When? After he took—' I stopped myself. 'I mean, did he come back to the shrine to . . . find you?'

Ramesh shook his head. 'No, but I will be brief, Lady. Abha's story is the one that cries for vengeance. I ran from the shrine and back to our house in the city. My father's enemies had been swift. The house had been looted and I found the bodies of my mother and Ina in the garden. The peacocks had been beheaded. Even the feathers from their tails had been stolen. There was nothing for me in Calicut. I gathered together what little I could find in the wreckage of our home –' he glanced at Ganesha whose expression now seemed to have more of sympathy than of slyness to the tilt of the eyes – 'and I made my way east to distant family in Madras.

'They took me in, but I was not favoured. I was another mouth to feed and I was unable to speak. From the day I ran from the shrine my tongue had become locked. My uncle – I called him that, although it was not really correct – sold cloth and I was set to work with him.'

Ramesh bent towards me. 'In truth, Lady, I went to Madras

for one reason only – to find Captain Denderholm. I remembered the words of the soldiers in the shrine and I knew I would recognise him. Each day I prayed to Ganesha that I might find the man who murdered my sister and, as you said, place . . . an obstacle in his path.'

'And did you?' I couldn't help myself from asking.

Ramesh nodded slowly. 'Yes, I found him, but it was not the proper time. I know now that the wheel turns slowly. One day, a fine young British officer with curling whiskers came to my uncle's shop with his fellows. I knew the captain immediately from those cold eyes. My hands trembled as I rolled bolts of cloth across the wooden floor. All the while I thought about my sister. And suddenly, my voice returned.

'I stood up straight and still in the middle of my uncle's shop and began to tell the British officers, in good English, a story about a boy and a girl who took shelter from the rain in a roadside shrine near Calicut. As I spoke, I took care to look into Denderholm's eyes so that he would know me. I had not gone very far in my tale before the blood drained from his face. He called me a dog and whipped me across the shoulders with his riding crop. Then he marched from the shop, ordering his comrades to follow.

'My uncle chased after them, begging them to return. He believed I had insulted the officers in some way and feared that he had lost trade through my insolence.

'When a party of British soldiers came later that day he was happy to let them take me. I was bound and silenced with a strip of rag and taken to a house in the poorest streets by the river. Denderholm was waiting for me there in the company of a huge man with a broken nose and the marks of disease upon his face. The soldiers swapped me for a bag of coins.

'Despite the heat, there was a brazier in the corner of that windowless room. The coals glowed red in the darkness. Denderholm was drunk, the air was thick with his whisky. His jacket hung from a hook on the wall, and his shirt was unbuttoned and loose. He reached into his collar, pulled a thick golden chain over his head and tossed it onto the coals. Then he nodded at the giant.

'The man with the pitted face kicked me so many times that the pain divided my soul from my body. I remember looking down at the room as if from a great height. I saw Denderholm smile as the giant's boot pounded my back, my stomach, my legs, over and over. Then he called out for the man to stop, but it was not over.'

Ramesh rubbed at the ashy, lumpen scar that emerged from the sleeve of his tunic and coiled to the back of his wrist.

'Denderholm went to the brazier. He removed the glowing golden chain with a pair of tongs. The giant hauled me to a stool and forced me to kneel. He cut the bonds from my arms, crushed my neck beneath his knee and held my arm ready for Denderholm's burning bracelet.'

'He branded you!' I brought my hand to my mouth.

Ramesh blinked slowly. 'I felt nothing, Lady. I had already retreated to a place where nothing could cause me more pain. Denderholm thought me to be dead. His giant took my body and left it where the stray dogs of the city could feed on my flesh.'

His dark eyes caught the light from the window. Something there put me in mind of Ganesha. It was the look of a man about to share a secret.

'The wheel has turned at last and debts long accrued will be paid. When Denderholm's man left me for dead fifty years ago on the banks of the River Adyar, it was not my time. I was alive when your grandmother's agent found me.'

He smiled. 'Now it is Denderholm's time. It is fate . . . and it is justice.'

Chapter Seventeen

I stared at the gin. Through the lace veil of my hat I could see a tiny black fly stuck to the rim of the glass, its wing twitching. Lucca turned from the bar to scan the crowd pressed around us. I knew it didn't appeal – and now I was standing here ankle-deep in sawdust and Christ knows what else, I couldn't blame him.

The Hope was a low sort of place, a dingy stand-up on the corner of Palmer's Rents and The Orchard. That last was a name to conjure with. There wasn't a living being who could recall when there'd last been a stump here, let alone an orchard. Five minutes at the bar of The Hope was about as much as a person could take without considering the irony of the name.

I thought about it now as I studied the fly.

We'd walked in silence as we made our way back through the narrow passages from Bell Wharf Stairs. Abha was lodged in our minds, her story playing out again and again like something you might see on a stage. Now I understood why Ramesh Das's eyes blazed like a glass furnace when he looked at that picture of the General. Five simple words rang in my head.

Abha was no longer beautiful.

A fire was burning inside me too. What sort of a man could do that to a child?

The Hope was the first building I saw when I led Lucca out of the warren and into Broad Street. The name was daubed in cracked red paint on the bricks over the door. I'd thought that the liquor might sharpen me up and cool me down, but the gin served over the counter here might just as well have been boiled from river mud.

The place was packed tight. The fug of cheap smokes – worse than the ones Sam favoured – clouded the air and made my eyes water. The man standing next to me at the bar reeked of sweat, but above that, an evil sweetness rising from his person told of his day in the horn sheds down Great Hermitage Street, where the bins and stacks of antlers, hides, ivory and whalebone filled the air and coated anything that came too close with the rich stench of death.

Joey had taken me there once. I can't have been much more than ten at the time. Looking back, it must have been when he was running an errand for Lady Ginger. We'd gone to a warehouse that took the Russian trade off the river and up Hermitage Stairs. Joey had left me in the stacks and gone off to find his mark. As I stood there among the bins and jagged piles, the smell of the place had clawed at the back of my throat, bringing tears to my eyes. I had to cover my nose and mouth against the burning. Above the sound of the warehouse men hauling and scraping, I could hear a buzzing. At first I'd taken it for the whir of machinery, but it had seemed to come from above. I'd looked up. There was a cloud of black smoke billowing beneath the rafters. It was a moment or so before I realised it was a swarm of flies attracted to the rotten flesh clinging to the bones and skins around me.

I flicked at the fly stuck to the rim of the rinser. The Hope wasn't the sort of establishment where you called for a cleaner glass. You couldn't even get a seat. The clients – men and women – weren't interested in their surroundings or even the quality of the goods. When they pushed a fiddler over the counter, it was escape they were buying.

I sidled at the man stinking next to me. He was about to empty his pot and was already signing the woman behind the bar for another. The skin of his lower arm was crossed with blue-grey lines that had once, most likely, been the name of a sweetheart, until he'd found himself another and had to remove the evidence. I turned my back on him, partly to ward off the smell, but also because the place was so full that standing sideways on was more comfortable. Now I found myself pressed up close against Lucca. The lemon of his cologne was a balm to the nose.

The fact of the matter was that I needed something strong to calm the fire in my head. There was a time, and not so long ago, when I'd happily lose myself for an hour to the company of one of my grandmother's black opium sticks. I might even have gone to Nanking Nancy's den, off Cock Hill, if it didn't hold such a bitter membrance of Joey, and the way the old girl had mistaken us for each other.

Anyway, I'd promised Lucca I'd never go back there. Now I raised my smeary glass to him. His own grubby cogue was still full to the brim on the counter.

'To hope.' I folded back the lace veil of my hat and tipped the gin down in one. Then I covered myself again. Lucca bumped close against me as a woman with a face like a donkey and a rump to match ploughed through the crowd.

'Jug of Tom.' She hoisted a brown pot to the counter and nodded at it, expectant. The tall, raw-boned woman behind the bar folded her arms.

'Not today, Cora, and not any day until I see bustle. The Hope ain't a charity.'

Cora tried again. Her rough voice was loud and carried. Punters turned to look.

'What about my Jim? He's come home dry as a camel. What am I to say to him?'

The tall woman shrugged. 'You owe a shiner. Until it's paid, that jug stays parched, just like your Jim.'

A man stationed a way up the counter called out, 'Jim Deeks won't take kind to his woman coming home empty-handed.'

'That right, is it?' The woman behind the bar jutted her flat-iron chin in his direction. 'Well, it's not my lookout. And I'd thank you to keep your opinions to yourself –' she smiled, thinly – 'unless you're offering to clear Jim's slate?'

There was a notable silence.

'No. I didn't think you was. You've got a big mouth on you. Pity you ain't got the pockets to match.'

The punters nearest the bar laughed. The hard-faced woman turned her attention back to Cora.

'Tell him to go whistle for his jug of Tom.'

Cora leaned across the counter to catch hold of her wrist. 'You know I can't do that.'

The woman swiped Cora's hand away, catching the jug as she did so. It skittered across the counter and toppled to the floor behind the bar. I heard the earthenware smash. Cora's eyes bulged. The bar woman bent to scoop up the fragments. She grinned and scattered them across the sticky board.

'There's your message, my love.' She flicked at the broken handle, which had sheared off in one curved piece. It spun about on the wood. 'You take that lot home and tell Jimmy Deeks that next time he wants his jug filled he should come himself, not send his bitch.'

'You cow!' Cora lunged forward and slapped the woman's face. The Hope fell silent. There was an edge to the silence, the sort that draws blood. The bar woman rubbed her jaw where the mark of Cora's hand glowed red. She opened her mouth, but nothing came out.

'That's the way to do it.'

The voice – a perfect imitation of Mr Punch – came from an alcove over to the left. A wooden panel set with an etched-glass window screened the man who'd called out. Shadows moved behind the pane. Through the smoke I saw a hand catch the side of the panel. Light from the candle lanterns gave the fingers a yellow tinge. The hand moved from the wood and fluttered mid-air for a moment like it was conducting an orchestra, then another voice came from behind the glass, a woman's this time.

'Yes, Cora, that's the way to do it.' Long delicate fingers waggled in the air. The woman's voice, firm and clear, came again. There was a ringing quality to it, something between a song and a sermon.

'If everyone here, with a slate to clear, was refused their beer, now wouldn't that be queer?'

There was a mutter of agreement from the punters. Punch took up the verse again.

'And poor Jim's jug, lying there all cracked. I reckon someone deserves to be whacked.'

The fluttering hand paused for a moment. I watched it count to a beat of four, then the woman spoke again very slowly, sounding every word like the chime of a bell.

'An eye for an eye. A tooth for a tooth . . .'

The word 'tooth' came out closer to 'tuth'. She repeated it again, and then again and again.

Slowly the muttering turned into a ragged echo. The punters

began to chant the Bible words under their breath. I peered through the smoke. There was something about that voice, something that plucked at a memory. There was something about that hand, too.

Mr Punch sang out again, his tinny voice shrill above the chanting. 'Cora, Cora, how we adore her. She's put up a fight, let's see her served right.'

Of an instant, Cora clenched up a fist and punched the bar woman's nose. I heard something crack.

'Fannella!' Lucca hissed urgently. 'We must go.'

He caught my hand and dragged me roughly through the crowd. As we neared the door the chanting built to something more substantial. I could feel excitement raw as the gin. The men and women around us were craning for a view and straining like dogs on a leash.

Just as Lucca pushed the door open, there was a crash from somewhere over to the left. I ducked as a tankard sailed over our heads and out into the street. The sound of splintering wood came above the sudden baying of the punters. Violence was free entertainment here. The rapture of it spread like a fever. I turned to look back. As the door swung to a close, the last thing I saw inside was a human knot of heaving backs, flailing legs and elbows working like pistons.

*

Lucca pulled his hat down low and twisted his scarf to sit higher on his shoulders.

'Do you have a wish for death, Fannella?' He tightened his grip on my arm as a man barrelled past, eager for a rumpus.

I could smell the sour sweat of his enthusiasm. The sound of the battle taking place in The Hope was attracting attention. You might think a person would shy away from trouble, but not here. People were poking their heads out of windows and doors to see what was what. And after an earful, a surprising number of them decided to trot down the street and join in.

'Why there?' Lucca herded me forward like I was a bleedin' lamb. If it hadn't been for the riot behind us, I might have had something sharp to say about that, but instead I answered his question as we clipped along.

'I needed something stronger than chai after that story. Anyway, no one was interested in us, if that's what you're worried about. My face was behind the lace most of the time we were in there, and you were hidden under the brim of that hat.'

The sound of breaking glass made both of us look back. The fight had spilled onto the street. We watched a ball of bodies burst through the door of The Hope. Even though we were fifty yards off we could hear the men grunting and roaring as they pummelled and rolled in the dirt.

Then an odd thing happened. Two people stepped out, a man and a woman. I couldn't see their faces clear as they were too far off, but their gear was good. He was wearing a long coat and a wide-brimmed hat and she was dressed in a dark cloak with the hood drawn up. They went a way along the street, paused to watch the brawl for a couple of seconds and then they linked arms and took off smart in the opposite direction. I frowned. They didn't look likely to be regulars. I thought about the couple hidden behind the screen.

And of an instant, I caught it, the thing about the woman beyond the glass that was familiar. When I'd watched that hand flutter at the edge of the panel, there'd been a black ribbon tied round the wrist.

An eye for an eye. A tuth for a tuth.

The voice had a Scottish lilt. I broke free from Lucca and tried to see where the couple had gone.

'This is madness.' Lucca grabbed my hand. We ducked as a brown glass bottle soared over our heads and smashed into a thousand pieces on the cobbles ahead. He stretched an arm around my back and propelled me forward, away from the fight. A couple of men jostled past us impatient to join in. One of them caught my shoulder and sent me toppling to the gutter. Lucca muttered under his breath as he helped me to my feet.

'Are you hurt?'

'No, I'm fine.'

He stared at me, angry and baffled.

'All right. It was a mistake.' I dabbed at the muck on my skirt. 'We probably shouldn't have gone there.' I bit my lip under the veil and twisted about to look back down the street. 'Did it remind you of anything?'

'Do you mean the story of Lot and his wife?' Lucca shook his head. 'Come, Fannella, please. This is not a time to be curious. If you must know, it reminded me that the world is brutal and ugly.'

'I wouldn't argue with you on it.' I straightened up. 'But the other thing it minded me of was the Reverend and the way he managed to . . . *infect* everyone at the Martingate Hall with his cant. It was like a spark leaping between them.'

'*Sì.*' Lucca nodded slowly. 'Like the people back there.' He glanced in the direction of The Hope. 'It made them feel . . . good?'

'More than that. I reckon it made them feel alive. The Hope was a tinder box waiting for a strike, just like the hall that night. And there's something else they have in common too . . .'

I was about to tell him about the woman with the mourning band when another bottle smashed on the stones a dozen paces behind us. I don't think it was meant for us; someone had hurled it up the street in hope of extending the entertainment. We started off again at a lick, Lucca shielding me with his back. We turned into a passage and when we'd gone a way, the bricks swallowed the sound of the fighting.

'*Bevono il vino della violenza.*'

'What was that?'

'It is from the Bible. I thought of it when you spoke of the Reverend – *and they drink the wine of violence.*'

'It was gin actually, and that was cut.' I caught myself making a note to mention it to the Beetle. Christ! The Hope wasn't my concern any more. Nor were *any* of the trades my grandmother had passed to me when she left me her interests in Paradise. Perhaps the Beetle had already passed it on?

It was late in the afternoon. The rain had stopped, but now a greenish mist was rising around our ankles. It crept up from the river, slicking the cobbles at our feet. Lucca tugged at my hand. 'We must find a cab, Fannella.'

I nodded. 'We need to go back up to the Commercial. This way's quickest.'

I gathered up my skirts to step over a puddle flecked with yellow foam. Looking down, I saw something blue blocking the grille that carried the water down to the drains and into the Thames. It was a newspaper. To be precise, it was *The London Evening News*, rival to Sam's *London Pictorial News*.

My *London Pictorial News*, to be even more precise. I still had Fitzy's crumpled page from it in my bag. For a moment I was happy to see the sodden blue paper down there in the drain amid the muck. Someone had thrown it away. A thought came, not a comfortable one. Seeing that paper minded me of something Sam had said before he went off.

Just make sure you buy every copy as long as it runs and keep a close eye on the announcements column at the back. My mother's maiden name was Simpson, Esther Simpson. Remember that.

Only I hadn't remembered. I'd been so caught up with events that I'd forgotten to read my own newspaper for the last two days.

*

The boy swiped the back of his hand under his nose and then he pointed at the newspaper I'd just bought. Both his hand and face were blotched with smudges of black ink.

'I don't sell so many of them these days. Everyone asks for *The Evening News*. I've got a couple left in the sack if you'd rather, Miss.' He looked hopefully at Lucca, who was watching the Commercial for a cab.

'You, sir?'

Lucca shook his head.

I fished in my bag for my purse. 'This is the one I want. I'm loyal to *The Pictorial*, even if no one else is.'

'Suit yourself.' The boy shrugged and sniffed. 'I'm just saying that *The News* is very popular.'

I was about to pay and walk away from his makeshift wooden stand on the corner of Caroline Street when a question occurred.

'And what do *you* think?'

'About what, Miss?'

'About the newspapers?'

He frowned. 'I don't think nothing, Miss. I can't read.' He grinned and cocked his head to one side. 'I like the pictures though, so does my brother Tom. He's still got one from that paper –' he nodded at *The Pictorial* in my hand – 'pinned to the wall next to his bunk. Some bird it was, not a garden one if you get me . . .' He winked at Lucca in a conspiratorial manner.

'The Limehouse Linnet, from the old Gaudy, that's who. Lovely!'

The boy gave a low whistle and curved his hands in the air in the rough simulation of a female form for Lucca's benefit, although he was missing his mark there.

'I wish I'd seen her in that cage. They say she was a wonder.'

I looked down, opened the purse and pushed a thruppenny bit into his hand, even though it was too much.

'You can keep the change.'

The boy stared at the coin and grinned. 'Tell you what, Miss. Seeing as it's late and you've been very generous, I'll throw in a *News* too.'

He handed me a roll of blue paper, licked his lips and winked again.

'I do like a pretty lady. I bet you're a proper stunner under all that lace.'

I turned away smart. My heels tapped out like a cobbler's hammer as I marched off. I heard Lucca snort behind me and whipped about.

'You can stop that.'

He smiled. 'But it was all true, Fannella. You were . . . *are* a wonder.'

I tucked the newspapers under my arm. 'I should have been keeping an eye on the announcement column of *The Pictorial* for a message from Sam. What if I've missed him?'

When we'd gone a little way along the Commercial, I halted. Keeping my arm clamped over *The Evening News* I shook *The Pictorial* out, flicked to the back pages and scanned the names in the announcements columns for *Simpson*.

First off, I was relieved to see nothing there, and then I was disappointed. Not a word from Sam then? I hoped Tan Seng had been keeping track of the paper like I'd asked. What if I'd missed a message?

I glanced up at Lucca and shook my head. He shrugged and turned from me to scan the street. There were plenty of cabs about at this time, but none were free. I rolled *The Pictorial* up again and tucked it beneath my arm with the other paper. I kept it because I had a curiosity to see what Sam was up against.

'We can walk, Lucca. It's not far.'

I felt a tap on my arm and turned, expecting the newspaper boy to be standing there with his tongue hanging out.

Matthias Schalk lifted his hat and tilted his head.

'Good evening to you, Lady Linnet.'

He looked at Lucca. Brilliant blue eyes disappeared above cheekbones that nearly cut through his pale skin as he forced a smile. 'And to you also, Mr Fratelli. How pleasant it is to see you again.' In his harsh, angular accent, the words sounded like rocks chipped from his throat. The street lamp behind him chose that moment to hiss into life. The globe filled with a sudden greenish glow that flickered in the gemstone eyes of the silver hawk head at the tip of Schalk's cane. The light caught on the sharpened point of the curved beak.

I felt Lucca tense. He – and Sam too – knew what that cane could do. I reached my hand out behind me and was grateful when Lucca took hold. I held him tight.

'What do you want, Schalk?'

A gust of wind snatched at his cloak, and it flew up around him, making his large frame seem even taller and broader. The light from the gas lamp turned his red-gold hair to brass. I was minded again of an angel, one that had fallen a very long way.

He turned and gestured at a large black carriage drawn up by the side of the road twenty yards distant. Two grey horses in the traces jinked about as a bus passed too close. Mist coiled around the bottom of the wheels. In an hour or so it promised to thicken itself into a right pea-souper.

'We were on our way to Salmon Lane, but fortunately I saw you in the street. My master would like you to join us.'

I frowned. 'You mean Kite's in there? In that carriage?'

Schalk nodded. 'He is waiting for you within.'

I almost laughed out loud at the absurd invitation. 'He's going to be waiting a bleedin' long time.' I felt Lucca's warning pull on my hand. I didn't care. We were standing in the middle of one of London's busiest streets in plain sight of a hundred people. Just to the right, not two yards off, a trader was pulling the dusty second-hand gear hanging off the front of his tatter shop with a hook on a pole. I smelt naphtha from the damp old cloth as it swayed on the hook above us and swooped down to the level of the street.

And I could smell something else too – the leather and spice of Schalk's cologne. Just for a moment, it brought back that night at Great Bartholomew's and what the man standing in front of me had done to Peggy's Dan. What he'd made *me* do to Dan, more like. I swallowed the membrance down hard. It burned like a coal in my belly, but it gave me fire.

I jerked my head at the carriage. 'Do you really think I'm going to climb in there, meek as a lap dog, and sit with him?'

'Lord Kite wishes to speak to you on a matter of importance.'

'Well, I've got nothing to say to him, now nor never. You can get back inside that carriage, lick his bony arse, or whatever it is you do for him, and tell him that.'

Schalk came towards me, but I stood my ground, all the while keeping a grip on Lucca's hand.

'Not a step closer.' As I raised my free hand to ward him off, the newspapers tucked under my arm fell to the ground. 'You must think me green as a cabbage if you reckon I'd trip along the street, climb up there and sit inside with you and your master. If he's really there.'

'I give you my word, Lady Linnet.' Schalk bowed again. 'And that of my master. You will not be harmed.'

'Your word!' I laughed. 'As far as I'm concerned, that's worth less than a rat's turd. As for your master . . .'

For once words failed me. If Kite really was inside that carriage, I had a fair idea of what he'd want to talk to me about. Only I wouldn't give him the pleasure. I could easily imagine the sheen in those stone-blind eyes of his as he smugly minded me of the extent of his reach into my concerns.

I balled my free hand to a fist. 'If Kite thinks he can get to me through my halls and the people in them, he's wrong. I know his game now and I'm ready. Point of fact we all are. Next time you come knocking at my door with that bleedin' fancy stick of yours we'll know where to shove it.'

Tell truth, I wasn't at all certain of that. Of an instant, the sight of Signor Marcelli strung up and mutilated like one of his puppets came to mind, and I thought of Bertie Chibbles' little Spark nailed to the door of The Comet.

I couldn't stop myself.

'What sort of a man would do the things you've done? A defenceless old man and a sweet-natured dog who'd lick your hand to the bone rather than bite it?'

Schalk frowned. I caught a look of confusion in his cold eyes. He opened his mouth as if to say something, but nothing came out. He glanced back at the carriage and then at me again. This clearly wasn't going the way he intended. It made me bolder.

'I'm not afraid of you, Matthias Schalk. As a matter of fact, I pity you. You must be lower than shit stuck to the sole of one of Kite's shoes to serve him like you do.'

That got through. I heard Lucca gasp as Schalk raised the cane, his gloved fingers smoothing the sharpened silver hawk head.

I shook my head. 'Not here you wouldn't. There are plenty of people on the Commercial with us this evening so we're quite safe. I don't, for a moment, think you or your master would be foolish enough to try something with so many witnesses. So, I think you'd better climb back into that carriage like a good dog and give him my message . . .' I paused for effect. 'Especially that bit about licking his arse.'

Schalk's angular face flushed with anger. It was the first time I'd ever seen a colour rise to his boiled cod skin. Despite

220

what I'd said, he took another step closer. Instead of raising the cane he bent down. For a moment I almost thought he was kneeling to me, but then I watched as he gathered the fallen newspapers together.

'I imagine that you are very happy, Lady Linnet?' His blue eyes burned like the depths of a fire as he straightened up.

'I'm happy to save you both the trouble of coming all the way to Salmon Lane only to have the door slammed in your faces.'

Schalk thrust the newspapers at me. It was such a sudden unexpected gesture. I dropped Lucca's hand to catch them.

'Enjoy your reading, Lady Linnet, but remember you cannot win.'

He turned abrupt and went back to the carriage. The door opened and after a short, muttered conversation he climbed inside. The greys jerked their heads at the crack of the driver's whip and the carriage started forward, drawing the mist in its wake. I heard a rattle as the window scrolled down. I tried to catch sight of Kite, but Schalk's dark bulk filled the entire frame.

He stared at me and turned his head slowly to keep me in view as the carriage rolled on past us.

'I will give you the gist of my master's message.' He leaned from the window, the lamplight lending a bilious tint to his hair and skin. 'This is not a victory, Lady Linnet. This is a beginning.'

Chapter Eighteen

I struck a Lucifer and put it to the curl of blue paper tucked between the coals. In a moment, a lacy green-tinged glow flickered along the edges. It was early in the year for a fire, but autumn had settled itself on Limehouse like the damp and frowsy skirts of a Billingsgate fishwife. I pulled Nanny Peck's threadbare plaid around my shoulders – more for the comfort than any warmth it offered – and blew to encourage the flames.

A beginning?

What did that mean? And why would Kite take a carriage ride to Limehouse to tell me that? I poked at the coals with an iron and watched the fire fight against the draughts in the room. I thought it might die to nothing, but once it got the hang of living I sat back on the rug, twisting the ends of that frayed old shawl between my fingers.

The encounter with Schalk had stirred up Lucca's memories. When we got back to The Palace he was pale and silent. He clearly wasn't in the frame of mind to go picking over the day and I didn't blame him when he said he needed to rest. Peggy, God love her, had fussed over him like he was her own child. I'd heard her talking to Lok about an infusion for sleep, and a little later, when she'd padded past the door on her way to Lucca's room above, she was humming a lullaby.

The house was quiet now. I was sitting cross-legged in front of the fire in my office. The panes of the window overlooking the yard rattled like marbles in a pouch as a raw east wind battered the back wall of The Palace. There was nothing grand about the house my grandmother had left me. It was falling apart . . . like everything else. The draught squeezing through the gaps of the splintered window frame lifted the corners of the creased cutting from *The London Pictorial* laid out in front of me. The paper was thin and the newsprint was smeary. The General's face was beginning to blur. No wonder people were turning away from *The Pictorial*. Even that clipped page Fitzy had given me with his thoughts about new acts for the opening of The Comet had come from a rival publication.

I glanced at the two newspapers Schalk had thrust into my hand when we were on the Commercial. They were rolled together and resting on top of the coal scuttle. If nothing else, they were useful when it came to feeding a fire. The blue front page of *The London Evening News* dandled over the edge of the scuttle, trembling in the draught. Despite the gloom, I could see the crisp bold quality of the print and the number of advertisements jostling for space in the columns.

Sam had his work cut out.

I wondered where he was and what he was doing right now. My head was so full of him tonight, there wasn't room for anything else. I badly wanted to tell him Ramesh's story to see what he made of it. Then there was that peculiar meeting on the Commercial. What was that all about? Sam Collins had an enquiring mind – surely he could pull some of the trailing strings to a knot?

That's what I told myself, anyway.

The truth of the matter, if I took it out and held it to the light, was that I badly wanted to see him. It was Sam Collins's arms I wanted to feel around my shoulders, not Nanny Peck's old shawl. I was angry too. If he really cared for me like he said, then why wasn't he here?

I won't deny I'd been disappointed not to see the name Simpson in the announcements column of today's *Pictorial*. Perhaps it was too soon? But then again, Sam could have left a message yesterday or the day before.

If Tan Seng had been buying copies for the last two days like I'd asked, they'd be down in the parlour. I made to stand, but a coal popped in the fire, sending a tiny glowing cinder from the grate to the crumpled square of print on the rag rug. It started to singe a hole in the paper next to Denderholm's head. I spat on it sharp, taking a pleasure in the fact that it was what the old bastard deserved.

I studied the General's fading face. If he wasn't Arthur Denderholm, who was he? The death certificate I'd seen at the Sanctuary suggested the boy who'd been given that name had been dead and buried for a considerable time before Ramesh Das and his sister had the misfortune of meeting the captain at that roadside shrine.

The hearth popped again. Now, when I looked into the flames, I saw the scarlet of Denderholm's uniform beneath the cloak and the glint of his golden buttons.

I shivered and held my hands to the coals. As far as I knew, Denderholm wasn't a common name like Smith or Brown – or even Simpson for that matter – and what was the likelihood that Arthur and George would end up tethered together with it? Just as Vellum had sinuated, it was more than coincidence. Someone somewhere knew who the General really was. I bit my lip and stared at the empty space above the mantel where a mirror used to hang. I could still make out the ghost of its outline on faded floral paper.

Everything left a trace. I looked down at the General's face again.

'Who are you?' Despite the fire, the air in the room was so cold I saw the question rise as frigid breath. There was a tap on the door. Tan Seng stood there, lit by the single candle on the tray in his hands. The flicker of the little flame made his oval face look like it was floating independent of a body.

'It is late, Lady.' He brandished the tray towards me. 'Cheese and bread.'

I wasn't in the mood for anything much, but it was a kindness. I heard my knees click as I stood and went to take it from him.

'Thank you.' I peered into the darkness beyond the door. 'Is everyone else abed?'

He nodded. 'Do you wish for anything more, Lady?'

'No, this is more than I need. And you should be turning in, not fussing about me. Here, you'd better take this to light your way.'

I handed him the candle and he bowed.

'Oh! There is one thing, Tan Seng.'

'Lady?'

'Do we have copies of Sam's . . . of *The London Pictorial*?'

He nodded. 'It is as you asked. A new copy for each day. It is arranged. They are in the parlour.'

As he stepped out into the hallway, Jacobin screeched from his cage in the room across the landing. After a moment I heard the rasp of his claws on the metal bars.

'Tan Seng!' I called out. 'Can you cover him for the night? None of us will get any rest if he keeps up that racket. And before you go down, would you bring me the copies of *The Pictorial*, please?'

'Lady.' He bowed again and folded his hands into the sleeves of his grey tunic. I watched him disappear in the darkness to the parlour opposite and then I closed the door to keep in the scanty heat. I took the tray to the fire and sat down. Examining the portion of cheese on the saucer I found that I might have an appetite after all. I broke off a corner and let the salty richness melt on my tongue.

Tan Seng wasn't one for conversation, but that tray was a sign of his concern. No, more than that, it was a token of his affection. It came to me that I had found something in The Palace – two things to be precise – to be grateful to my grandmother for. I still drew exception at her bleedin' parrot, mind.

Just then, I had a clarity about that bird. Or a membrance, more like.

Jacobin wasn't *her* parrot, was he?

I snatched up the lamp from the desk and ran to the parlour. Tan Seng was by the cage in the corner, crooning away in a soft low voice. I recognised the same lullaby sung by Lok. As he sang, he swayed to the old-time melody, moving the candle back and forth outside the bars.

The parrot's yellow-rimmed eyes were drooping to a close, but they snapped open when I tumbled into the room. Immediately he threw himself at the bars – a flurry of feathers and spite. The sound that came from him now wasn't so much a screech, as a string of profanities.

Tan Seng broke off, surprised. 'Lady?'

He had the old broidered cloth in his free hand. Behind him Jacobin rattled and swore. The shadow of his outstretched wings was huge on the wall beyond the cage. I came to stand level with Tan Seng and now the parrot shrank back from the light of the oil lamp.

'He was quiet, Lady, as you wished.' There was a note of reproach there. I held the lamp high to see the old man's face clear.

'Yesterday, when Lok was calming Jacobin down, he said it was a song he'd liked for a long time, a song *she* sang to him. I don't reckon she was ever much of a singer, my grandmother. So, my question is . . . who sang that song to him?'

Tan Seng's black eyes slipped to the floor. It was a confirmation. He bent to place his candle on the boards and then he wrestled with the cloth, twisting it between his fingers. I reached out to stop him, resting my hand gently on his.

'I know who it was, Tan Seng. It was my mother, wasn't it? Jacobin was given to her as a gift.'

The thing that had been pecking away at the back of my mind with regard to that parrot had come back as I'd sat there picking at the cheese on that saucer. I've often heard it said that cheese can give a person nightmares. Well, I didn't have an opinion about that, but what I did know was that my last conversation with Joey – in the Bethlem – had been the cause of every sleepless night I'd had since.

As we'd sat there in his dismal cell, he'd told me about Lord Kite's partiality for our mother.

. . . he followed her everywhere, he bombarded her with flowers and gifts. Mostly she returned them, but some she kept. Jacobin was one of his more imaginative offerings.

I held the lamp close to the cage to see this 'imaginative offering'. Jacobin blinked and opened his black beak as if to pass comment. He obviously changed his mind because he shuffled from foot to foot on the perch, and then he turned his back on me. There was a bald, raw patch visible on his rump through the mangy grey feathers.

If that parrot was supposed to represent love, it had gone the way of the man who'd offered it. Anything that milk-eyed monster had once felt for Ma had turned in on itself. It was a good wine that had become sour and noxious as cheap vinegar. And it stung like vinegar too. Kite's hatred of my family was like an open canker sore eating him to the bone.

Tan Seng backed away. He kept his eyes on the floor and didn't answer my question.

I tried again. 'Tan Seng, what really happened all that time ago?'

Long fingers pleated the broidered cloth. 'I promised that I would not tell.'

'You mean you promised my grandmother, Lady Ginger?'

He shook his head.

'You promised Ma?'

Again, he shook his head.

'Then who? Who did you promise, and why?'

'Forgive me, Lady. I must go.' His black eyes widened in alarm. 'Ah! Look there!' He pointed over my shoulder to the corner of the room. I spun about, but there was nothing behind me. And when I turned back there was nothing in front of me neither.

One second, Tan Seng had been there, the next he was gone. The old man and his candle had disappeared in the blink of an eye, leaving the cloth cover of Jacobin's cage in a little heap on the boards to mark the place where he'd been. The brothers had played my grandmother's halls. They knew how to pull off a vanishing act.

I stared at Jacobin's back. He didn't turn to look at me, and he didn't make a sound, which was a novelty.

'Nothing to say for yourself then?' I waited for a sour answer, but nothing came.

'That makes a nice change.'

I took up the cloth and threw it roughly over the cage. Then I fetched the newspapers from the side table next to the yellow couch. Taking the lamp, I went to the door.

There was a croak from the cage in the corner. I heard the rattle of a razor-sharp beak on the bars and the battering of wings. Then Jacobin started to speak. I say Jacobin, but it was my grandmother's voice that came from beneath that cloth. The parrot mimicked her odd fluting voice – a little girl speaking with a mouthful of nails.

'*Change. Change. Chains. House of Chains. House of Chains. House of Chains. House of . . .*'

I pulled the door shut behind me to block the sound.

*

I leaned on the door of my office. I could still hear Lady Ginger calling from the parlour, muffled now by distance and two layers of wood. I brought my hands to my ears and willed him to stop. When I listened again a minute later, he was silent. And so was she.

I pulled Nanny Peck's shawl close around my shoulders and crossed to the fire again. Kneeling on the rug, I spread a copy of *The Pictorial* out in front of me and leafed to the announcements at the back. I ran an ink-stained finger down the names. Sacher, Sanders, Sargeant, Scholes, Semper, Simes, Smith, Smith, Smith, Standish, Steddings, Tamblin, Tasker . . .

I pushed the newspaper aside and took up the next, but it

was the same story. Nothing from Sam and nothing from his mother neither. I wondered if the absence of a message meant that he was in trouble on my behalf, or whether he'd decided to cut his losses and run.

The air in front of my face misted up. It was bleedin' cold for the time of year. I reached across to the scuttle, intending to throw some more coals into the fire, and the copy of *The London Evening News* balanced on top slipped to the boards. It rolled slowly open, revealing a black-bordered page of close-packed copy topped and bottomed by two large woodblock prints.

The print at the top, wreathed in an abundance of wilting foliage, seemed to be very like the back of a penny, only Britannia had taken off her helmet, laid down her shield and spear and was weeping into cupped hands. The lion at her feet was staring up at her, its big watery eyes full of mournful concern.

But it wasn't Britannia that caught me so much as the headline beneath her, picked out on the blue paper in crisp black letters two inches high.

WILTON CRESCENT TRAGEDY: BRITAIN MOURNS PASSING OF THE BEST OF MEN

I pulled the newspaper towards me and began to read. When I finished, some ten minutes later, having read the article several times to be certain, and having checked and rechecked the printed faces of the six men gathered round the representation of the elegant five-storey townhouse that had unaccountably collapsed to a pile of rubble while they were dining together in Belgravia the night before last, I went direct to Lucca's room.

Chapter Nineteen

'Listen to this bit.'

I shifted to let the light from the candle on Lucca's bedside table fall across the paper. The blue made it difficult to read in the gloom. I thought I might mention that to Sam as a notable defect in a rival publication, when I saw him.

I leaned in close to the print.

It is too early to identify the cause of the tragedy; however, there is mounting speculation that remedial work below street level in an adjacent property may, in some way, have weakened the structure to the point that total collapse ensued.

Nevertheless, while the root of this most calamitous event remains shrouded in confusion, *The London Evening News* must report with dreadful certainty that it ended the lives of six fine men who had nobly devoted their lives to the service of Crown and State.

Be in no doubt, the reason these titans were gathered together to dine in Wilton Crescent would have touched upon the welfare of our nation. Never at rest, their entire thought and purpose was devoted at all times to the common weal.

Truly this was the night when the gayest and most brilliant flowers of Britannia's garden were crushed by the booted cruelty of Fate.

Now we must pray that they have found the repose they so richly deserve.

Requiescant in pace.

I stumbled over the last bit and looked up. 'What's that mean? It's from the Roman, I reckon?'

Lucca nodded. 'It is Latin, although not as I have heard it before. I believe it is "rest in peace".'

'"*Now we must pray that they have found the repose they so richly deserve.*"'

I read the line aloud again and smacked the page with the back of my hand.

'Well, it seems they got what they richly deserved all right, although not in the way the writer of this sanctimonial claptrap imagined. "*Truly this was the night when the gayest and most brilliant flowers of Britannia's garden were crushed by the booted cruelty of Fate.*" If only he knew.'

Lucca had been awake when I went up to his room, so I didn't feel bad about disturbing him. Anyway, I was bringing him the best news I'd had in an age. Sitting on his bed with the paper between us, I'd pointed out the faces of the men who'd secretly controlled every filthy trick and trade in the City of London, and far beyond. The six dead Barons looked like regular sober gents cut from quality cloth. From the arch of their brows to the curve of their nostrils at the ends of camel-humped noses, these were men whose families hadn't spent a night out of fine cotton sheets scented with lavender and roses since the days of Good Queen Bess. Maybe longer than that.

When I read Lucca the account of the 'Wilton Crescent Tragedy' for a second time, with pertinent comments of my own, I might add, he leaned back against the bed rail and stared up at the ceiling. The candlelight made the lashes of his left eye seem unnaturally long. They cast a shadow that curved along his cheekbone. He wasn't wearing a nightshirt, but he'd drawn the sheet up to cover the ridged marks of the burn that stretched down the side of his neck to his right shoulder. Over to the left his skin was golden. His bare shoulder was square and broader than I'd imagined under that scarf and droopy gear he hid himself away in.

I thought again, as I sat with him, that he was beautiful. It was an odd word to use for a man, but it was true. We made a fine pair, I reckoned, both of us waiting for someone to . . .

'But, what does it mean, Fannella?'

I was grateful when Lucca asked that. It meant I didn't have to follow that thought to its home and find myself disappointed when I got there.

'It means there's a dozen or so of them still alive. Shove over.' I scrambled into the bed next to him and pulled the cover over my knees.

'No wonder Kite wanted to see me.' I wriggled into a warmer patch under the blankets. 'Don't you see?'

Lucca nodded slowly. 'I think I am beginning to. "Enjoy your reading, Lady Linnet." I wondered what Sch . . . *he* meant by that.'

I noted the fact that he couldn't bring himself to name Kite's man.

'And do you remember what he said when he handed me the newspapers?'

'*Sì.*' Lucca frowned. 'I thought it was odd at the time. He remarked that you must think yourself very happy and then he said –' his eye fixed on a damp spot overhead – '"Enjoy your reading, Lady Linnet, but remember you cannot win."'

He brought his hand down on the blue printed page.

'*Oddio!* What if Lord Kite thinks that you are behind this, Fannella?'

I shook my head. 'I don't know if that's right. What Schalk actually said was "This is not a victory." He didn't say who for.'

The scars on Lucca's brow tightened. 'There was more – "This is a beginning."'

I took up the page and stared at the faces of the dead Barons. It was more in the way of an ending as far as they were concerned. As I regarded the whisker-clad chops of:

> six fine men who had nobly devoted their lives to the service of Crown and State

I had a clarity about what might have happened to the:

> . . . most brilliant flowers of Britannia's garden

To be more precise on the matter, I had a clarity on *who* might have been behind it. I sat back against the bed rail, twisting the ends of Nanny Peck's plaid.

'The beginning of what, Lucca? That's the question.'

*

'You mean the Barons are dead?' Peggy held the page out in front of her and stared at the men clustered beneath the weeping Britannia.

'Not all of them. But six is a good start.' I leaned across her lap and took in the printed faces again. There was a name wreathed in a looping black garland beneath each man. It was an odd thing to know who they really were when they were out and about in the world. I only ever knew them by the made-up names they gave themselves.

I jabbed at the page. 'That one, Sir Peter Whitlock, he's Lord Oak – something to do with the navy, he is. Or was, I should say. General Eustace Thurlwood, him just there –' I pointed at a man with a nose so bent you could hang a side of mutton from it – 'was known as Lord Iron. He was Oak's opposite number in the army. That fat one resembling a pig, bottom right – His Grace the Bishop of Roxton apparently – I knew as Lord Mitre. Above him, the weasel with the beady little eyes, Sir Nicholas Cantrip as it says there, goes by the name of Lord Silver – you can guess for yourself where his interests lie . . . *lay*.'

I corrected myself again. I was still finding it hard to take it all in.

'Money – coin?' Peggy held the paper further away, gripping the top two corners like she was hanging out washing. 'Old Nick certainly looks like a man who counted his brass by the light of a candle.'

I nodded. 'That's right. He was something to do with the Mint. See, it's easy once you get the way of it. And that one there –' I pointed out a grim-faced man bottom left – 'went by the name Lord Ferrous on account of his interests in mining.'

I stared at his face. Dark eyes set close beneath a prominent brow looked back at me. I chewed on my lip and examined another of them, the fat little bishop whose jowls hung like curtains beneath a jaw of uncertain projection. I didn't see a trace of myself in either of them. I forced myself to study them all, searching for a clue.

Most of the time I was careful not to give a thought to what Kite had told me on the day of my grandmother's funeral. I kept it locked away in a dark place where it couldn't thrive or breathe. But just now, looking at the six of them gathered together on the page, I heard Kite's voice again, taunting me with the possibility that any one of the men standing around Lady Ginger's tiny black coffin could be my father.

I tasted blood. I'd bitten down so hard that I'd broken the skin of my lower lip.

Peggy flapped the newspaper out in front of her. '"Flowers of Britannia's garden", are they? In that case she should have done some more weeding. It's not because I know different, Kit, but looking at this lot, there's not a man here I'd lend a shilling to in the hope of getting it back.' She narrowed her eyes. 'I wouldn't want to meet any of them on a dark night, no matter what they were calling themselves at the time. All them fancy made-up names. What was the point of that?'

I sat back on the yellow couch and picked at a straw poking through the padded seat. It turned out to be the end of a small grey feather. I pulled it free and twisted it between my thumb and forefinger.

'I think they hid themselves from what they were doing, *really* doing I mean, as Barons, by wrapping it all in ceremony. It made it feel . . .' I paused trying to find the right of it. 'I don't know exactly – it made it feel like a game, I suppose.'

No, that wasn't quite right. There was nothing playful about the Barons. Quite the opposite, in fact. There was a terrible earnestness to their ceremonies. I started again. 'The ritual of it all, the mysterious names, the rules and obligations. I think it made them feel part of something they could justify, something they actually felt *proud* of.'

I sat up straight as the truth came to me.

'Jesus, Peg! It made them feel clean – that's the joke of it.'

I brushed the little grey feather against my stinging lip. 'Clean! That's a word I'd never have thought to use about them, but I'm right. I know it.'

The Barons came from the highest circles in the land and yet what they did made them lower than toshers. As far as I could see, there was very little to choose between the poor sods who sifted for treasure in the sewers under the City and the men sitting in panelled rooms turning shit to gold. Perhaps the Barons caught a sense of that? All that cant and ritual was a way of shining their sins up so bright that they couldn't look at themselves direct.

'Bastards.' I stared at the dead men reverently arranged around the image of the elegant house that was now, according to the report, a pile of rubble.

'What about the others, Fannella?' Lucca was leaning against the mantel. Despite the early hour, a fire was already crackling in the hearth beneath. We were gathered in the parlour. No one had bothered to uncover Jacobin's cage this morning, and as far as I could tell from the silence in his corner, he was still asleep. Perhaps he'd exhausted himself, shrieking into the dark in my grandmother's tinny voice?

The only one of us missing was Tan Seng. I suspected he was downstairs in the basement rooms the brothers called home – avoiding me. Lok was sitting on a high-backed chair across the hearth from Lucca. He was studying the dusty toes of his pointed black slippers. He was so tiny his feet didn't touch the boards.

I considered Lucca's question. 'I imagine they're looking over their shoulders. If Lord Kite himself was setting out to see me at home, then they must be rattled.'

'He was coming here!' Peggy dropped the news page to the boards. Her hand flew to her belly.

I stared at Britannia, weeping near my foot. 'I think so. Lucca and me, we met him – well, it was his man Schalk – on the Commercial last evening. He wanted me to step into his master's coach for a little chat. Now I know why. Kite thinks I'm behind what happened in Wilton Crescent.'

'And are you?' Peggy's brown eyes sidled at me.

'Of course not!' It came out sharp.

She rubbed the mound through the sprigged cotton wrapper. 'I was asking a reasonable question. You've got so many secrets these days, Kit, I wouldn't have put it past you.'

'Well, you're wrong. It was nothing to do with me.'

The little porcelain clock on the mantel next to Lucca's elbow cleared its throat. There was a metallic click, a whirring sound and then it began to trip out the tune that came before it announced the hour. When the ninth chime faded, Lucca stepped across to take up the page Peggy had dropped.

I watched as he scanned the copy again. He looked up and the crease between his brows deepened, dragging at the scarred skin around his missing left eye. 'Perhaps it truly was an accident. It says the house next door was undergoing work? What if that caused the—'

'No,' I cut him off. 'It was no accident.'

I knew, without a shred of doubt, who was behind the execution, because that was what it was.

The traps are already baited. I've no doubt you will read about it soon, perhaps in the pages of your very own newspaper.

The man who told me that was mostly right there, except for the bit about reading it in the pages of my own newspaper. There was a soft tap on the door and Tan Seng padded into the room. He bowed and, as if he were obeying a theatrical cue, handed me a fresh copy of *The Pictorial*.

'As you wished, Lady.'

'Thank you.' I felt a stab of guilt as I took it from his hands. He wasn't hiding from me in the basement after all. He was out doing me a favour. I flicked to the announcements at the back and ran a finger down the names.

I caught my breath.

Simpson, Esther: 12 Lincoln's Inn Fields. Noon.

'Lucca!' I held the paper out to him. My heart pounded like a navvy's hammer under my nightshift. I could feel its rhythm fluttering in the lace at my neck as I watched him find and read Sam's scant message.

I stood up, catching my wrapper tight around me. 'He means noon today. We need to leave as soon as possible.'

There was a small cough and rustle.

'And there is this also.' Tan Seng reached into the baggy sleeve of his grey tunic and produced a small rectangular package wrapped in brown paper. 'I found it on the steps, Lady, when I returned with the newspaper.'

Before I could thank him again, he bowed, turned away sharp and went to the door. I caught a face pass between him and Lok as he slipped out into the hall. I couldn't make out whether that look was a warning or an agreement.

Confused, I turned the package in my hands. It was bound in thick red cord and addressed, sparsely, to me in an elegant looped hand.

For Miss Kitty Peck

'Aren't you going to open it?' Peggy craned from the couch, but Lucca raised a hand in warning.

'Be careful, Fannella. You do not know what it is or where it is from.'

Instantly, Peggy shrank back. 'He's right. What if it's poison, or a bomb?'

I weighed the package in my hands. Through the paper I felt the outline of a book with a hard cover. I turned it over and noticed a line of tiny writing – same hand – mostly hidden beneath the cord. I pushed it aside with my thumb.

Know your enemies

Was he an ally or an enemy? He needed me, he'd made that clear enough when I went to see him, but that didn't make him my friend. I considered the package, and then I pulled at the cord.

I heard Peggy gasp as I ripped the brown paper. A small brown book fell to the floor. The fine leather cover was tooled with scrolling flowers and leaves and, in the middle, set in a gold square over something that looked like a vase, there was a single name: Keats.

'It's safe, Peg. You can come out from behind that couch. I know who sent it. It's a message, of a sort – a confirmation.' I took up the book and caught the rich smell of new binding as I flicked through the pages.

Lucca quizzed at me. 'A book of poetry, Fannella?'

'Someone's sending you poems now?' Peggy's brown eyes sharpened.

Lucca bent to retrieve a white card that had fallen from inside the cover and handed it to me. I flipped it over to read Vellum's curt message.

It has begun.

Chapter Twenty

I dressed fast, but I took care with my gear, choosing something very fine but plain with it. As I stared at myself in the mirror in the hallway of The Palace, pinching my cheeks and tucking stray hairs beneath my best straw, I caught Lucca's reflection watching me.

I whipped round, stung by the accusation I thought I saw in his eye.

'Can you go down to the lane, please, and see about a cab?'

He nodded and wound his scarf twice over his shoulders. A handful of leaves scuttled across the marble tiles as he opened up and went out onto the steps. The wind snatched one of the doors from his hand and slammed it back hard against the wall.

The old double doors to The Palace were heavy things banded with iron on the inside – a protection, I guessed. The weight of one swinging back so sudden and vicious brought plaster from the wall. It pattered to the tiles.

At the same moment, the portrait of the young gent in blue I'd found in the attic rooms my grandmother had closed away slid down the wall and thudded onto the marble. The bottom of the old gilt frame crumbled into a hundred dusty pieces that skittered across the hallway like curls of charred bacon rind. Without a solid frame, the painting slipped to the side, so the gent seemed to be pointing at something on the floor rather than the house with white columns half hidden in the trees behind him.

Lok and Tan Seng came from below. I wouldn't say they were running, exactly, but the pair of them appeared within seconds of the racket. Tan Seng regarded the fallen painting and then said something to Lok in their own patter. Lok blinked and forced his hands into his sleeves. They stared at me expectant as cats when a pan of tripe is on the boil.

I stepped over the knubbles of plaster and joined Lucca in the doorway.

'It was the wind. It caught the door unexpected.' I pointed at the painting apologetically. 'I'd help clear it up, but we have to get going. It's no loss. I only put it there for the blue of his coat to brighten the place. It can go back upstairs where I found it.'

I glanced at the painting. The young gent was fair with a pointed chin and dark eyes. There was something of the dandy in the lace at his cuffs and the cut of his coat. More than once, Peggy had remarked on a family likeness. She reckoned the boy in the painting looked like me, but Lucca always said it put him in mind of Joey. And now here I was – clearing him away again. My brother was on the other side of the world and his double was going back to the attic.

'The Lady is leaving?' Tan Seng shook his head. 'It is not safe.'

'There's not much I can do about that – we have to be at Lincoln's Inn Fields by noon. The message in *The Pictorial* was clear.'

I didn't say it, but I reckoned there was a sort of safety in numbers – smaller numbers, that is. Lincoln's Inn Fields was a nest of legals. The last time I went there with Lok and Hari in tow, I'd swivelled more eyes than a French fan dancer.

Upstairs the painted clock in the parlour began to measure out a quarter.

'Come on, Lucca.' Without another word to the brothers, I spun about and took his hand. 'Let's hope there's a cab going our way.'

*

We stared up at the building. With its flat stone exterior dotted with statues and ornaments of a classical type, it wasn't quite like anything else in the row. Tall arched windows along from the door gave the impression it was amused to see us standing there. Or suspicious.

I smoothed down the skirt of my good visiting dress, wiping away the dust and Christ knows what else from the seat of the cab. Judging from the frowse in the box, the last passenger had been a dog, likely a dead one. I hoped that the bottle-green satin hadn't taken up the stink.

Lincoln's Inn Fields was a spit from Sam's office, so it wasn't surprising he'd called a meeting here. Now we were standing outside number 12, I was reconsidering the matter.

It wasn't a legal's office, as far as I could make out, but it didn't look like a regular residence neither. Of all things, it most put me in mind of a stage set Lucca had painted a couple of years back for a solo engaged on the fly by Fitzy. The old chaunter always had a weakness for flesh shows.

Madame Regina was, apparently, famous for her tasteful classical attitudes with musical accompaniment. Famous fifty years back, that is. By the time she arrived at The Gaudy, all decked out with ribbons and painted like a carnival ride, Regina was the size of the bull rather than Europa. The punters took one look and showed her what attitude really meant in Limehouse.

It was a shame, really. Lucca had painted up a lovely set of flats for her performance – a wooded landscape full of statues and broken columns much like the ones ranged about the house in front of us now.

Although it was the height of the day it was gloomy. Clouds the colour of old men's socks balled overhead and the wind shook the trees of the square battering showers of leaves to the grass and pavement.

Someone was at home at number 12. Glass lamps glowed in the lower windows, their reddish light leached onto the pale stone sills, turning them pink.

A single bell began to chime. Half the notes were tossed away on the wind, but I didn't need to count. It was noon and Sam was waiting inside. I breathed deep and my corset clamped tight. It felt as if my heart might burst in its whalebone cage. Them haughty windows raised their brows.

Lucca clamped his hat to his head and stepped back onto the cobbled road to take a better view. He nodded to himself.

'I have always wanted to visit this place.'

'You know it?' I was surprised.

'*Sì.*'

'What is it, then? It don't look like the rest of the houses on the square.'

'It is the home of a famous collector, Fannella, and full of wonders.'

A gust of wind lifted the skirt of my dress. The dark satin rustled and billowed out around me. I stared up at the studded door at the top of a short flight of steps. Was Sam really here? Was that likely?'

My heart seemed to have climbed to my throat. I swallowed

hard, but it wouldn't go back down to its rightful place. One of the ribbons from my bonnet slapped across my cheek. It stung like a whip. I flattened a hand on the crown to keep it in place and turned to Lucca. 'I don't understand. If it's someone's house, what are we supposed to do? Go up there, knock, say hello and just walk in?'

Lucca nodded. 'That is exactly what we shall do.'

Before I could give an opinion on the matter, he strode up to the door, his long coat flapping in the wind. He took hold of a large metal ring and knocked. Even from the foot of the steps I heard it echo beyond the door.

I went up to join him. When no one answered he tried again. After a moment or two we heard footsteps and bolts being drawn. Someone coughed and the door opened a little. A man peered at us through the crack. He had a neat moustache and wore a small fabric hat broidered with flowers. Dark eyes danced behind round gold-framed specs.

'The house of Sir John Soane is not admitting today.' He coughed again, delicately. 'Visiting hours are displayed on the board attached to the rail below. I am sorry if this is an inconvenience, but I cannot make exceptions.'

He started to close the door, but I placed my gloved hand on his arm.

'Wait, please. We haven't come to see Mr Soane.'

The man studied the affrontery of my hand and cleared his throat. He brought a 'kerchief to his lips and coughed again, quietly.

'No one has visited Sir John for forty-four years. He died in 1837.'

I thought the 'kerchief masked a smirk and tightened my

grip. 'It's not him we're here for. I'm looking for Mr Collins, Sam Collins of *The London Pictorial News*. I had a message to meet him here at noon.'

'Ah.' Gently, but firmly, the man removed my offending hand. 'Then perhaps you should have said that, Miss Peck. It would have saved us both an embarrassment. Do come in.'

The door opened wide and the scent of beeswax polish, lilies and dust came rushing at me. I could see the man in the broidered hat clear now. He was small, thin and difficult to put an age to. He had the lined, leathery skin of a traveller, but behind the glasses, his eyes were large, lively and amused, giving the impression of someone much younger.

He smiled and offered Lucca his hand.

'Signor Fratelli, I have heard a great deal about you. Good afternoon.' He bowed and turned to me, absently patting my outstretched hand.

'And Miss Peck, good afternoon to you also.' He took a step back and studied me through the lenses of his small gold specs. I had the distinctive impression he was sizing me up.

He nodded. 'Good, very good. Mr Collins is waiting for you in the crypt.'

*

We followed the man through a wooden cubby just inside the door into a stone-flagged hallway. On the side was a vast arrangement of lilies a day past their best. The floor beneath was powdered with streaks of yellow pollen. Dark-painted walls were cluttered with paintings and all manner of Oriental decoration. It struck me that my grandmother might have felt herself at home here. Lucca removed his hat and turned about slowly, taking everything in. It was like he'd entered a church.

Through an open door to the right I could see a fire crackling in a hearth set between two leather chairs. The dancing flames sparked up the mirrors and crystal set around the room and glowed in the glass doors of rows of cabinets stuffed with books. Marble classical statues, dozens of them, gleamed like pearls. Although the room was painted the deepest red, light seemed to bounce from the walls and the objects.

The man wiped a finger along the pollen-dusted shelf and tutted.

'This way, please.' He beckoned us to follow him. On the left a grand staircase twisted upward, but he led us through a curtained arch to the end of the passage where another set of stairs curled down into gloom. He paused at the top and adjusted a lamp, moving the glass to allow more light to fall onto the steps.

'Candles are romantic, but what the place needs, in my opinion, is more daylight.' He tutted again. 'Soane was a genius, of course, but it can be exceedingly dim here at times, especially in the winter months. Still, my reordering will rectify the problem.' He pushed his glasses to the end of his nose and examined the hallway. 'Yes! Yes, it most definitely will.'

He nodded in agreement with himself, and motioned briskly towards another arched passage in the shadows behind him.

'This is the parting of the ways. I go down here and you go that way –' another flap of the hand – 'along to the end of the corridor, turn right, follow the colonnade round and down the stairs to the crypt. Try to avoid the buckets . . . There's another leak from the dome. If you encounter a small, heavy-set person muttering obscenities, don't be alarmed. It *won't* be a ghost. It *will* be Mrs Scovell, the weekly char.'

He started off down the stairs. I wondered if this was a trick. Perhaps we'd walked into a trap. I leaned over the rail.

'Wait, please.'

'You have a question, Miss Peck?' The man paused. As he looked back up at us, the light from the candle lamp turned his glasses to shining pennies. First off, I was minded of Lord Kite's blindness, but then another membrance came. I'm not sure which was worse. They were bleak days when Joey and me had laid out Ma and Nanny Peck. People say that the placing of coins on a corpse's eyes is done to pay the ferryman, but I know from experience it's done to stop those dead eyes opening again and staying that way.

I gripped the rail.

'I just want to . . . to make sure he . . . that he . . .' I tried again. 'How do I know that Sam, Mr Collins, is really here?'

The man smiled.

'You're quite safe, I assure you. However, if you were to ask such a question, I was to give you this exact reply – "Peters makes terrible tea."'

Under the bottle-green satin, my heart leapt like a salmon. I knew it was from Sam. His elderly assistant at *The Pictorial* had the habit of making tea that tasted like Billingsgate slop water. Peters was a good man, but his tea was diabolical. The very first time I met Sam he'd warned me against it.

I nodded. 'That sounds about right. Thank you.'

The man gave a small bow. 'You'll find young Samuel by the sarcophagus of King Seti, the first of that name. Dreadful thing – and very difficult to clean. Scovell can't even reach the bottom. It's certainly not the finest example of New Kingdom Nineteenth Dynasty funerary work. It should have stayed in Egypt. And the price! Soane was robbed, if you ask me. But no one ever does, even though I spent six years there.' He coughed again. The white 'kerchief fluttered like a dove in the gloom. 'At the foot of the stairs, follow the passage round to the right into the crypt. You'll see when you get there – I lit the way for him earlier. Good day to you both.'

He turned and after a moment more he disappeared into the darkness at the bottom of the stairs. We heard the echo of footsteps on a stone floor below and then the sound of a door closing.

Samuel? I didn't understand much of what I'd just heard, but I liked the way the man called him that. I took a deep breath to fill myself with something more than the thumping of my heart.

'That way?' Lucca pointed at a curtain-swagged arch at the end of the passage.

I nodded. 'That's what he said. Then around to the right and down the stairs to the crypt. That's a place where they bury the dead, isn't it? I don't understand. Why would a house on Lincoln's Inn Fields have a bleedin' crypt?'

'It is more than a house, Fannella. This place is extraordinary. It is . . . *un colpo del teatro.'*

Lucca stared wistfully over my shoulder at the door to the glowing red room with the books, the statues and the inviting fire.

'*Questa casa è una meraviglia.'*

I didn't need a translator to know he was hankering after a tour. 'Come on.' I took his hand. 'We need to find *young Samuel* next to the sarcophagus, whatever that is.'

*

I didn't envy Mrs Scovell. There were *things* everywhere – busts, vases, statues. You couldn't see clear to the wall for dust collectors. A hundred pairs of stony eyes watched as I picked my way around the balustrade, with Lucca following just behind.

An array of ancient stoneware was balanced along the edge. I had to mind the size of my hat and hold my skirt close for fear of dislodging something. I peered over into the depths below, where a flickering glow suggested the presence of candles. It was like being in the gallery at the old Gaudy and looking down over the rail to the pit. I could make out shapes down there, but not much else.

There was something, though. A faint smack of cheap tobacco laced the air. Now I looked, I could see thin wisps of smoke rising from below. I knew just one person who favoured that brand. I drew it down into my own lungs and thought about calling Sam's name, but somehow it didn't seem right. Anything above a reverent whisper seemed wrong here.

I plucked at Lucca's sleeve to get his attention. His eye was on a stalk.

'Is this place a sort of museum then?'

'*Sì.*' He nodded. 'But it was also a home. Among many other things, Sir John was a great collector. When he died he made provision for his house to be preserved exactly as it was and opened to the public.'

He paused in front of a life-sized statue of a man not quite wearing a cloak. It was another one of the classical types he liked. I studied the carefully placed cabbage leaf just above Lucca's head.

'It doesn't leave much to the imagination, does it?'

He shot me a pained look. 'It is the Apollo Belvedere, Fannella. A copy of one of the greatest sculptures of ancient Greece – *è magnifico.*'

I noted that he was whispering too. There was no need for candles in this part of the house (if you could call it that), but it wasn't what you'd call bright neither. Bilious light, filtered by the glass dome overhead, gave the impression we were moving underwater. At the end of the balustrade, we had to step round a bucket, just as the man in the broidered hat had warned. There was a tapping sound from above. I looked up and a splash of water caught the end of my nose. He was right about the leak too.

Beyond the dome, the shadows deepened. After rounding another set of life-sized statues I was grateful to find a second candle lantern marking the top of the stairs, but when I turned to point out the way, Lucca wasn't there.

'Where are you?' I whispered as loud as I dared. A moment later he stepped into the circle of light, twisting his hat.

'I . . . I found the picture room, Fannella.' He glanced back over his shoulder. 'The Canalettos, the Hogarths . . .'

'Christ!' I planted my hands on my hips and forgot to whisper. 'Tell you what, why don't you just stay up here and have a nose around on your own, Lucca Fratelli. Don't mind about me.'

The echo of my voice rang out around us.

Don't mind about me. Don't mind about me. Don't mind about me.

Someone somewhere on the floor below started to laugh.

Chapter Twenty-one

Just as the man who let us in had said, the crypt was lit with a score of candle lanterns; the flames danced like fireflies trapped in the little metal cans. Sam's top half was mostly hidden in shadow on account of the placing of the lanterns on the floor around him.

For a moment I could hardly breathe. I wanted to reach out and touch his face, mainly for assurance that he was actually there, but something about the way he leaned back on the edge of that big stone bath with his arms crossed about him and a smoke dandling between his fingers made me hold myself in. Lucca put his hand on my shoulder and I was grateful to feel the pressure of it.

'Good, you're on time.' Sam nodded at us in turn, took a drag and straightened up. The light from a single candle lantern flickering in a niche on the wall fell across his features. The shadow cut a firmness to his jaw that sent a sudden rush of heat from the base of my spine to the top of my head. My hair prickled under the bonnet as I stared at him. The beard had gone, but something had come back.

I couldn't stop myself. 'Your eye! How? I mean, how come there are—'

'Two of them?' Sam grinned. 'It's glass. Rather a good match, I think? I've a friend who is training to be a surgeon at Moorfields. He found me a replacement. It's damned uncomfortable after a while, but useful. An eye patch is quite distinctive and where we're going I don't want to take any more risks than absolutely necessary. I certainly can't afford to be recognised, and neither can you. We don't have long, Kitty.' He crushed out the glowing stub of his smoke on the edge of the bath. 'You'll need to change down here.'

He reached down into the bath and his voice echoed from the stone.

'I've borrowed these things from Wild. He goes to a lot of formal dinners. The pair of you are about the same height.'

This wasn't the meeting I was expecting. I don't know what I actually *was* expecting, but it definitely wasn't this. Lucca squeezed my shoulder. I reckoned he was as confused as I was.

'Here.' Sam thrust a bundle at me. Something glinted in his hand, but he shifted position to hide whatever it was behind him and leaned back against the bath again. I heard the chink of metal on stone as he dropped it down inside.

'You can change in the Monk's Parlour just down there.' He pointed at an arched passage behind me. 'Wild has lit some candles for you.'

I studied the pile of clothing in my hands. A pair of dark breeches was folded neatly on the top. There was a starched white shirt beneath them.

'This is men's gear.'

'Nothing gets past you, Kitty.' Sam reached into a top pocket for his smoke case. It came to me then that the smokes were likely a nervous thing. Sam Collins was such a coil of thoughts and deeds he needed something to keep his hands busy. When he wasn't waving a roll-up about, he was forever fiddling with his bleedin' fringe and leaving ink on his face.

There wasn't a smudge on him today. The Sam in front of me now was crisp as a new-cut lettuce. His hair was clipped neat and he was dressed a deal smarter than the last time we met. Quite the toff he looked in his sleek black tails.

He flicked open the case. 'As I explained, they belong to Wild. Put them on, please. We don't have much time. We have to be there at two-thirty prompt.' He offered the contents of the case to Lucca. 'While we wait?'

'No, you wait!' Furious – about a lot of things – I flung the clothes to the floor. 'I came here expecting . . .' I paused, unable to finish that off with a certainty. I swallowed and started again. 'Before anything else, I reckon I deserve an explanation. For a start, who's this Wild you keep dropping? I don't know him from Adam, and now I'm supposed to wear his bleedin' breeches. It seems to be taking a liberty – with the both of us!'

Sam cupped his fingers and lit a new smoke. He blew a ghostly ring that floated upward to the statue-lined balcony overhead.

'Actually, you do know him, Kitty. He let you in just now. James Wild is the curator of this remarkable place. We met in Lincoln's Inn Fields in the same week I started out at *The Pictorial*. It was summer and we had both taken our lunch outside. We shared a bench and began to talk. At first, I admit, I saw him as a useful contact. He is very well connected, after all. But I soon realised I was wrong – not about his connections, of course – but about him. Wild is eccentric, I grant you, but he is also one of the most intelligent, well-travelled and interesting people I have ever met, and I am proud to call him my friend. He helped me to arrange this meeting and –' Sam pointed his smoke at the heap of clothing at my feet – 'offered the disguise you have treated so casually.'

He balanced his smoke on the edge of the bath and knelt to gather the clothing together. 'Now, take these and change into them. Lucca and I will wait here by old Seti's sarcophagus. We can help with the collar and the studs if you need assistance.'

'And then what?' I took the breeches and the shirt from him. As my hand brushed against his, I felt a tiny jolt, almost a spark, jump between us. I looked up to see if he'd caught it too, but he turned away sharp and leaned into the bath.

'Then I will have to cut your hair.' He held up a pair of silver scissors. 'With your permission, naturally.' I saw a challenge in his expression. I didn't answer, but as I stared direct into his brown eyes, both of them, a fire started to burn in my belly. I won't lie, the feeling wasn't unwelcome.

Lucca stepped between us. 'This is going too far.'

Keeping my eyes locked on Sam's, I draped the gear over one arm.

'I went out with you dressed as a man once, Lucca. Remember?'

'But your hair!' He spun round. 'I did not ask you to do that. *Che follia!*' He swung back to face Sam. 'Where are we going?'

'Ah, that's another thing.' Sam picked up his smoke again and took a drag. 'I'm afraid you'll have to wait for us here. Kitty will need to change back into her clothes later and then I must ask you to accompany her safely back to The Palace.'

'*Cristo questo è ridicolo!*' Lucca wrung the brim of his hat like a flannel. I could see he was building to argue the toss on the matter, but Sam rested a hand on his arm.

'I'm sorry but you really can't come with us. You'd be too notable and that would be dangerous . . . for Kitty. I've asked Wild to give you a private tour and there are some sketches and prints that might interest you.'

'Fannella?' Lucca turned to me in appeal.

I brushed a smear of plaster dust from the pile of clothes in my hands. It was quality gear all of it, a gentleman's rig. I had a clarity.

'I know where we're going, Sam.'

'Do you?' He stared at me expectant. He grinned wide, his lean, handsome face shaping itself into a pleasing collection of angles and shadows. His eyes really were a good match. The only thing that gave it away was a certain stillness to the glass one, that and a lack of lively enquiry. Again, I fought the urge to reach out and touch him. Instead, I hugged the bundle of clothes close, spun about the stones and headed towards the passage.

Sam called out. 'You didn't answer me, Kitty.'

'It's bleedin' obvious, isn't it?' I didn't turn around. 'We're going to the Angevin Club in St James's.'

Chapter Twenty-two

'He sent you poetry?'

Sam rested the notebook on his knee and sucked the end of his pencil. The page in front of him was covered in his short-hand scrawl. In the afternoon traffic, the Angevin Club was a half-hour ride from the museum but given my unfamiliar rig we'd decided that taking a cab was safer than walking. Besides, the journey gave Sam a chance to quiz me and write it all down. It seemed easier to talk about what had happened with Vellum, Ramesh Das and little Spark than anything else. I finished up with an account of the 'Wilton Crescent Tragedy', pointing out Vellum's involvement and the proof he'd sent.

'And he really calls himself Endymion?' I heard him snort.

I turned to him sharp. 'That's what other people call him.'

'Do you trust him, Kitty?'

I noted that Sam asked the very same question about Vellum as Lucca.

I nodded. 'He's been as good as his word.'

The movement of the cab made Wild's black hat tip forward on my head. It was a little too large for me, but Lucca had stuffed a strip of 'kerchief into the band to make it true. Sam had hacked out a sort of fringe to 'give my face some cover', but at the back I could feel the unfamiliar press of the rim through the stubble of newly shorn hair. Sam was a dab hand with the scissors. After five minutes I was standing in the crypt surrounded by a pile of ringlets that shone like golden rope in the candlelight.

It was an odd thing, but I didn't regret it for a moment. My head seemed to feel lighter and lighter as he went to work. Tell truth, there was a pleasure in the brush of his hands on my neck as he angled the scissors and snipped at the curls. His fingers smelt of soap and smoke.

And I thought there was a tremble as he smoothed the strands aside.

On the way out of the museum I caught sight of myself in one of the mirrors in the hallway. I looked a regular masher. Mr Wild himself adjusted the stiff white collar and pushed a golden pin into my tie. He arranged the hat on my head, tilting it a little to the side, and smiled at me in the mirror.

'There are new gloves in the inside pocket. This will be quite a performance. I suspect you'll do very well, Miss Peck.' He flicked a speck of lint from my shoulder, stepped back and turned to Lucca who had come to see us off. He had a face on him that told a story.

Wild pushed his spectacles to the bottom of his nose and regarded Lucca with a certain sympathy. 'I understand from my friend Samuel that you have an interest in art and that you are a gifted painter?'

Lucca shrugged. He shot me a look from under his thick black mop. His hair was longer than mine now. I knew he didn't approve of our visit to the club, but he didn't have much say in the matter.

'Come with me, Signor Fratelli.' Wild patted his shoulder and walked back along the curtain-swagged corridor. 'We can begin in the picture room and there are some sketches I'd like you to see too. I'd value your thoughts on the Piranesi drawings.'

'Fannella?' It was a last appeal.

I shook my head. 'Sam's right. You're a notable person. It's going to be hard enough getting *me* through the doors of the Angevin Club, let alone—' I broke off, for fear of hurting him. 'Go with Mr Wild, Lucca. We'll be back before you know it.'

I turned away from the look in his eye and studied myself again in the mirror. If you didn't peer too close there was a fine young man standing there. I pushed aside the blunt-cut hair poking out from under the brim of the tall hat and nodded at Sam.

'Let's go then.'

I held onto the brim of that hat now as the wheels of the cab rumbled over a series of ruts. Once we were rolling along smooth again, I let go and pondered Sam's question about trust.

'Six of the Barons are dead and Vellum was behind it. That book of poems was his proof to me.'

'And what's he like, this Vellum?' It came out casual, but I thought I caught an edge to it. I sidled at Sam, but he had turned away from me to look out through the window.

I considered the man I'd met in the draughty rooms at the Sanctuary.

'He's with us and against them. I'm sure of that.'

Was I?

A couple of years back Fitzy had booked a novelty act for The Gaudy. Direct from the halls in Brussels and Paris, where he'd created quite a sensation, Herr Gebhardt took to the stage with Russig, a black panther the size of a bleedin' donkey. During the act, he let that creature nuzzle his boots, lick his hands and rest its dinner-plate paws on his shoulders. At one point, to the delight of the audience, Russig allowed himself to be dressed as a baby and tucked up in a bed complete with pillows and blankets. His great yellow eyes burned from under the lacy frills of the bonnet and sometimes the tip of his tail poked out from the sheets and twitched in a lively manner. The climax of the act was a toothache routine, when the panther opened his jaws wide enough to allow Gebhardt to poke his head inside.

According to his master, *süsse* Russig was mild as a kitten. But I don't think the stroller who lost four of his fingers backstage on what turned out to be the last night of Herr Gebhardt's engagement would agree.

I held tight to the brim of the hat as the cab juddered over another rut. 'I wouldn't turn my back on him, if that's what you're getting at.'

It came to me then that there was something else about Russig that minded me of Vellum. Under that flimsy bonnet, the panther's eyes were angry and sad.

We turned a corner and the cab lurched to the left. For a moment I was thrown up close to Sam. I caught his soap, his smokes, his warmth and just the faintest dash of his sweat. I breathed him in and straightened up smart on the padded leather. I clutched the strap by the door for fear of catching hold of him and never letting go. A silence followed, until I broke it.

'Anyway, I've told you everything – not that it's much. Now it's your turn. Where've you been, Sam?'

He pulled the pencil from his lips and scratched out some more notes in the book on his knee. He snapped it shut and looked at me direct. His good eye roamed across my face, from the tip of my chin to the brim of the hat. It was all I could do to stop myself from moving close to run a finger down the side of his clean-shaven jaw. Instead, I held onto that strap so tight my nails dug crescents into my palms.

He grinned and my heart fluttered like a moth under Wild's fine linen.

'It suits you, Kitty. I daresay you could work it into an act. Male impersonators are the rage – look at Vesta Tilley. You'll need something sensational for The Comet when it opens again. Why shouldn't it be you?'

Part of me was flattered, I'll admit it, but another part was frustrated that all Sam could think about at that moment was business. I pulled at the waist of the breeches and shifted on the seat. 'I haven't got the time or the inclination to work this rig up into an act. Anyway, Fitzy says he's got something in mind for The Comet.'

I turned away to look out of the window. The cab was at the bottom of The Strand and turning into Trafalgar Square. A sheet of blue newsprint flattened itself against the glass. It rustled there for a moment, before the wind snatched it away again.

As I watched the thin paper buck and flutter towards the square like one of Swami Jonah's dusted pigeons, I remembered that I still hadn't looked at Fitzy's suggestion. The bit of blue print he'd torn from *The Evening News* for my consideration was crumpled at the bottom of my bag back at the museum.

'It's not far now.' I let go of the strap. 'You haven't answered me. Where've you been?'

'Here and there.' Sam tapped the book on his knee. 'I've made some interesting discoveries about our friend who calls himself the Reverend, for example. I have to say, it was you who put me on the right track there.'

'Calls himself? You mean he's not—'

'Not what he seems, Kitty. After the meeting at the mission hall, you said he had them blowing hot and cold. It was "practised" – that was your exact word. You said that Auchlyne-Doune reminded you of an act?'

I nodded.

'Well, that rang true. Taking your observation as my cue, I made some general enquiries about the good Reverend's past. It's impossible to arrive in London without leaving a trace. If you know where to look and who to ask, it's generally quite simple to smoke an odd fish, especially one that stinks. One of my . . . acquaintances suggested that the Reverend's trail led directly to Glasgow, to the Bridewell Prison in Duke Street to be precise. If I'm right, then Auchlyne-Doune's real name is Billy Downie. Apparently, that was quite a name in the Scottish halls a decade back.'

He paused and quizzed at me.

I shook my head. 'It's not one I'm familiar with. Are you saying he was an act?'

He nodded. 'Downie was – and perhaps still is – a mesmerist. A draw, by all accounts, and particularly popular with women. That was his undoing. There were complaints of impropriety both from the women in the halls where he worked and from certain society ladies of Glasgow and Edinburgh for whom he performed what I suppose could be termed *private* engagements. It seems that plain Mr Downie didn't just take advantage of their persons while they were under the influence, he also stole from them. He either believed that his powers of mental persuasion would be so strong that the society women wouldn't accuse him, or he was confident that they would be too embarrassed to reveal their folly.'

The cab clipped the side of a kerb and I steadied the hat again. 'How did he end up in the block then, if he was so sure no one would tell?'

'Given the delicacy of the matter, it fell to the women in the halls to make the accusations. From what I've learned, I infer that those women, who did not have reputations to lose in quite the same way as their society sisters, were paid very well to bring him to justice. And for a change, they were listened to. I understand that the sister of a prominent judge was one of the women Downie used so shamefully.'

I pulled the hat from my head and thumped it down on the padded leather seat between us. A cloud of dust rose into the air. 'Isn't that always the way of it? It doesn't matter how many poor girls he pawed and swindled, after all, they don't matter. It's only when a toff's sister gets the treatment that anyone bothers.'

Sam frowned. 'You're right, of course, but look at it this way – at least Downie went down for his crimes.'

I traced a pattern on the silky crown of the hat. 'But not for long it seems. Now he's out and he's down here. What's his game?'

'That's a good question, and I'm afraid it's one I have no answer to, yet.'

I drummed my fingers on the top of the hat. The hollow sound echoed in the box of the cab.

'If it's true, then we have a weapon, Sam. If the Reverend was revealed as the lying bastard he really is, his claque might not be inclined to lap up his every word like it was milk and honey. In fact, I'd say they might turn on him. Having seen them up close, that wouldn't be pretty.'

Sam nodded. 'The Children of Purity would make cat's meat of him. As you say, the truth would finish him. But before we can take it any further, I still need to find a way to confirm that the Reverend William Auchlyne-Doune and Billy Downie truly are one and the same man.'

I looked up. 'What is it that makes you so certain they are?'

'Ah, well, first there's the name – Doune and Downie have a similar stamp to them, don't you think?' Sam stared direct at me. He was pleased with himself. I recognised the fox in his lean features. 'But mostly,' he went on, 'it was a report I found in the archives of *The Edinburgh Evening Courant.*'

'Edinburgh. You mean you've been up in Scotland?'

No wonder I hadn't heard from him.

'Only for a day. I slept on the train there and back.' He opened the notebook, flicked through the pages until he came to the place he was looking for and began to read his shorthand.

'"*On hearing the sentence passed by Sheriff Lord Whitesayle, Downie's wife – present in the gallery – was heard to cry out: 'What will become of the three of us now, Billy?' The woman was advised to be silent, but her dreadful protests continued to the consternation of all present. Indeed, Mrs Downie's incontinent display led to her ejection from the court. She was accompanied by her daughter, whose most apparent meekness and shame on hearing the catalogue of sins committed by her sire had won her no little sympathy during the trial from those present. This remorse was revealed at the last to be as feigned as the innocence so loudly proclaimed by the prisoner in the dock. In an act of reckless defiance, the young woman paused at the gallery door, removed her veil, uttered a word that cannot be repeated in the pages of the*

Courant *and spat in the direction of the bench. She then ran from the scene of her outrage.*"'

Sam looked up and grinned. 'Well, what do you make of that?'

I thought about the milk-faced girl minding the door at the Martingate Mission Hall. She'd had a black ribbon of membrance tied round her wrist, just like the woman behind the screen at The Hope; the woman who'd taken a delight in fanning the embers of an argument to a raging fire. Billy Downie's daughter was learning her father's trade. Likely it was the pair of them I'd seen stepping out onto the street.

'The daughter in court – it's the pious mouse in mourning who took the money that night at the mission. Downie and his girl are still working together.'

He nodded. 'That's exactly what I thought. But there's a difference between thinking something and knowing it to be true. I need absolute proof.'

Of an instant, I thought of someone who might just be able to give me that proof.

'Dismal!'

Sam chewed the end of his pencil. 'I admit it won't be easy, but I won't give up.'

'No.' I twisted on the seat to face him. 'I mean Dismal Jimmy, he's a patter man – one of my acts. You said this Billy Downie worked the Scottish halls?'

Sam nodded.

'So did Dismal, a long time back.' Originally, Jimmy had learned his trade in Glasgow – a scar over one eye was a reminder of the dangers of playing Trongate. Limehouse punters liked his lazy convoluted delivery and they respected the salt he showered on those unwise enough to heckle. For myself, I respected the amount of whisky he was able to put away, before, during and after a show. That and the fact that he turned up regular as a bedbug, no matter how much alcohol was swilling around in his belly.

'He might know something, Sam. It's worth a try?'

The carriage jerked to a halt and the driver rapped on the roof.

'The Angevin Club, sirs. That'll be a shilling apiece.'

Sam slipped the notebook into the inside pocket of his tail coat and reached for the handle on his side. He motioned for me to open my door and waited. It was a moment before I cottoned on. I was a man now – no one was going to do it for me. I took up the hat, slid across the seat and stepped down to the street. Sam came round the cab to stand next to me.

We looked up at the grand, soot-crusted building looming over us. The Angevin Club was four storeys high and took up a whole block between two streets. It looked very sure of itself. There was no sign or name attached to the rails or the wall to give it away to anyone who didn't have a right to be there.

Wide stone steps led up to a canopied entrance. Even though it was mid-afternoon, the doorway was burnished by flaming torches held in the claws of two creatures positioned at either side at the top of the steps. I couldn't rightly make out what they were supposed to be. From where I stood, they seemed to have the top half of a bird and the back end of a lion. One thing was clear, though: they didn't look pleased to see me. I felt myself scrutinised and found wanting. The torches guttered in the wind and the effect brought a ripple to the muscles of the creatures' flanks. I swept Wild's hat onto my head, pushing at the fringe so it was tucked under the brim, and turned back to Sam who was paying the jarvey. A moment later the hack rolled away.

Sam studied me. 'It's always gloomy in these clubs. That will help. Act as if you own the place. Stand tall, take up space, don't speak. Leave that to me. Gloves.'

I reached into a pocket in Wild's tail coat and retrieved a pair of lavender-scented, grey kid gloves. As I eased then onto my fingers, Sam continued. 'The other thing I've been doing since we last met, Kitty, is calling in favours from some old friends. As a matter of fact, you're about to meet one of them.'

I stretched the new leather at the tip of a finger and sidled warily at the doorway. 'As I recall it, Sam, you said you had a connection here. Your friend gave you the list of members.'

He nodded. 'And now he's going to let us in.'

Chapter Twenty-three

We didn't even knock. The shiny black door swung open of its own accord as we reached the top step. A bald man with a drooping tache and the poker-backed bearing of a former militarian bowed low.

'Good afternoon . . . Mr Simpson.' There was the slightest hesitation in the greeting that told me that this was Sam's 'old friend'.

'Atkins! Just the fellow. A very good afternoon to you too.' Sam stepped boldly into the hallway like it was his second home. He cast a meaningful look in my direction. 'And this is the guest I mentioned, Mr Thomas Lassiter.'

'Sir.' Atkins stared at me and tilted his head. If he caught anything amiss, his face didn't show it. Then again, on account of the general blandness of his expression, I got the impression he was careful as a widow with a sizable fortune when it came to giving anything away. I imagined that came with the territory.

The Angevin Club smelt of polish and old men. The pillared hallway was panelled with dark wood. Portraits in ugly gilt frames leaned out from the walls, giving the impression that the subjects – all of them men and most of them wearing wigs down to their elbows – were straining to hear the business going on below.

A listless fire smoked in a wide tile-clad hearth beyond a long table with swollen legs. At the centre of the table a silver bowl was surrounded by tall black hats, all of them identical to the one on my head. A stag's head mounted high on the wall above the hearth kept watch over the hats. I noted a dusty cobweb strung between its antlers. The strands swayed a little in the draught from the open door. Scores of lit candles were set about the walls in moulded brackets, but they didn't make much of a dent on the dim.

A broad staircase rose on the left from the mottled stones of the hall. The stairs followed the line of the wall, turning about on themselves again and again, forming a series of square galleries on the floors above until they disappeared into darkness.

Atkins moved around me to catch the door. There was a sad sigh and a soft thud as he closed it. I had the feeling of being sealed in. The back of my neck prickled as the thought of Danny rotting in the pit at Great Bartholomew's came rushing at me. The stones of the floor seemed to shift and rearrange themselves as I tried to push the memory of that night back into its box and lock it down tight. The prickle beneath my starched white collar turned to something more like the pinch of cold fingers. I fumbled at the gold pin and reached out to a pillar to steady myself. Sam turned about sharp.

'Ki—' He stopped, aware that a stooped elderly man with a head like a tortoise poking from its shell had entered the hallway from a door beside the hearth and was creeping to the stairs.

He began again, his voice a loud, braying imitation of the toffs who usually frequented places like the Angevin Club.

'Careful, Tommy. That champagne we had at luncheon has a powerful kick.' He stared at me. 'Are you all right there?'

I nodded, although I wasn't right. I thought this might be easy. Back at the museum I even imagined it might be exciting to be out and about with Sam alone. But now I was standing here in the club, the look of it, and most especially the smell of it, minded me of them. It brought back most forceful what they were and what they'd done. This was the Barons' territory, even if half of them were dead. I felt like a cod gasping for breath on a marble slab.

Atkins regarded me with his watery blue eyes. He sucked on the ends of his tache for a moment and sidled at Sam. We waited in silence until the tortoise had climbed to the first landing. It took him a full three minutes.

'Your hats, sirs?' Atkins held out his hand.

I glanced at Sam, who nodded. He took off his hat and passed it to Atkins. I did the same, pushing the newly cut fringe across my forehead to give my face some cover. Atkins's tache rippled as he stared at me. I thought he was about to say something but instead he balanced our hats on the crook of his raised arm in a professional manner and produced two red tickets from his pocket. Keeping his arm raised and his back straight as a plank, he went to the table, placed the tickets on the wooden surface near the bowl and then, with a great show of reverence, he positioned our hats over them.

'The numbers are twelve and sixteen. Now if you would sign the day book, sirs.' He indicated a ledger lying on a clerk's desk behind his post at the door. The ledger was closed, but I supposed a blue satin ribbon poking out from the pages marked the place where he meant us to write our names.

'Perhaps, Mr Simpson first.' Atkins ushered Sam towards the ledger. He patted the leather cover and cleared his throat.

'The Angevin is very quiet today, sir.'

'Is it?' Sam opened the ledger at the ribbon and ran a

271

finger down the rows of signatures. He turned to me, his good eye bright with intent. 'This is most unfortunate, Tommy. We appear to have missed our friends.'

He motioned for me to look at the page.

'See here, and here also.' He tapped lightly on two signatures. I bent to read them, tracing a gloved fingertip across the lines. Two names leapt out at me. '*Carstone*' had left the club at ten o'clock that morning and Denderholm had followed him an hour later.

Atkins cleared his throat again.

'Perhaps the gentlemen would care to wait in the library?'

'That is an excellent idea.' Sam grinned. 'Do you suppose we'll have long to wait?'

'Oh, I rather think so, sir.' Atkins sounded gloomy. 'There was talk of an evening engagement.'

Sam winked at me. 'Can't be helped, I suppose. The library it is then.'

Atkins stepped closer to Sam and murmured so quietly I only just caught the words. 'First floor, fourth door on the left. The rooms are on the third. The rest is up to you.'

'Splendid.' Sam spoke up loud and bright. 'And would you arrange for two brandies to be sent to the library?' He handed the man a small brown envelope. In return Atkins pressed something into the palm of his hand. Sam pushed whatever it was into the pocket of his breeches and spun about towards the stairs. He moved so fast his coat flapped and divided behind him like the tail of a swift.

'Come on then, Tommy. Let me introduce you to the delights of the Angevin Club.'

*

The library, first floor, fourth door on the left of the gallery over the hall, was almost deserted. There's a saying of a place being quiet as the grave. The room we found ourselves in now was pretty much the last stop on the way to that great silence, apart from the snoring.

Three old men, who looked likely to have been members since the club first opened its doors, appeared to be soundly asleep in vast leather chairs set about as far apart from each other as it was possible to be without sitting out on the landing. A ripe chorus of grunts, snuffles, whistles and peculiarly moist popping sounds was the only thing that told you they were still with us.

If I was to describe the place with one word, it would be 'brown'. I was expecting to see rows of books, but instead the panelled walls were sparse, except for a couple more of them leaning portraits set either side of the hearth – this time a small solemn-faced man perched on a mad-eyed horse with an arse the size of a barge end, and a lily-faced, long-nosed fellow whose stockinged legs emerged from puffed breeches that finished an unfeasible distance from his knees. He minded me of a principal boy from a pantomime, only with a beard.

Considering that this was supposed to be a library, there didn't seem to be much in the way of reading matter, other than a rack of carefully ironed newspapers standing near the door.

Like the hall below, this was a gloomy room, lit only by the glow of the fire (there was a more enthusiastic blaze up here) and candles mounted in two large chandeliers dandling from plaster roundels at either end of the ceiling. Gaslight hadn't been introduced to the Angevin Club. It was clear that time stopped at the door, which was probably what the snoring gents were banking on.

I'll say one thing for the library, it was warm. The heat from the fire was trapped in the room by heavy velvet curtains at the windows along one wall. They were all drawn close against the afternoon light.

Sam selected a newspaper from the rack and motioned for me to do likewise. We went to an arrangement of high-backed chairs gathered around a stool in the only corner of the library without a slumbering occupant. He flipped his tails aside and the old leather creaked as he sank into the seat. I took the chair opposite.

I leaned forward and whispered, 'What now?'

He rustled the newspaper and opened it to form a sort of shield between us and the rest of the room. 'We're going to take advantage of the absence of Carstone and Denderholm and search their rooms for anything that might prove useful.'

He spoke very quietly and angled the newspaper towards me, pointing at a paragraph that appeared to have captured his interest. He bent his head low and continued, 'We have plenty of time. Atkins says they won't be back until evening and fortunately the club is quiet today.'

I nodded as if to agree to whatever it was he was showing me. 'But, how do we know where their rooms are?'

'Atkins told us downstairs when he took the hats. Their rooms are on the third floor, numbers twelve and sixteen.'

'That's all very well, but . . .' My head shot up as one of the old men let out a snort that could have stood in for the last trump. Although it might have woken the dead, it didn't do anything to rouse the sleepers in the library. I watched them close for a moment, but when none of them even twitched, I felt a little bolder.

'But what, Tommy?' Sam grinned at me over the top of the newspaper. I could feel a loose board joggle beneath my boots (well, Wild's boots stuffed with paper, to be accurate) as Sam's foot tapped out a rhythm known only to him. He was in his element, I could tell. He was on the scent of a tale and revelling in the success of his scheme. His hair was springing back to its usual untidy state, quivering brown strands jumping free from the oil he'd used to keep it neat.

I resisted the urge to reach out and smooth them back into place. Instead, I spread my own paper wide and shook it out to look natural. I answered from behind the page. 'But how do we get in? It's all very well knowing their room numbers. I can't believe they're not locked, even in a place as fine as the Angevin Club.'

'I have the master key. Atkins passed it to me downstairs.'

I remembered that the doorman had pressed something into Sam's hand.

I quizzed at him around the paper. 'Why would Atkins have a master?'

'They need it when members die in the rooms. Happens quite often apparently.' Sam folded his paper to a square and checked on our sleeping companions. 'The question is, how can they tell?'

I almost laughed out loud, but buttoned it tight. Sam shifted forward and his chair wheezed like a pair of ruptured bellows.

'In a moment, I fully expect that Atkins will send us two

brandies. If he does, it's a sign that the third floor is clear and that we can go up there without fear of being noticed.'

'And what if he doesn't?'

'Then we wait. As I said, there's plenty of time. If the worst comes to the worst, all we have to do is go back down the stairs, collect our hats and allow Atkins to usher us out onto the street. No one will be any the wiser.'

'What exactly are we looking for, S— *Mr Simpson*?'

He studied me, his eye suddenly quite sharp. 'I rather think that's up to you, Tommy. I'm sure you have some ideas – after all, you know these men better than I do.'

I shook my head. 'Only Kite. He's the one I've had . . . dealings with. All I know about Denderholm is what Ramesh Das told me, and that's not much.'

Sam stared at me. 'It was enough for someone. You will recall that it was when I made enquiries about the General and this London Imperial Agency that . . .' His fingers strayed to his jutting cheekbone just below the brown glass eye. 'You've been holding all the cards very close . . . including the King of Diamonds.'

I looked away, confused. I knew he was talking about the night when he and Lucca had been forced to make a terrible choice on the turn of a card. When Lucca had drawn the King of Diamonds, the only one-eyed king, Sam had swapped places with him to save his sight. It was a brave thing he did. But was he mentioning it now to tell me I held him in my hands, in a romantic way, or was it a reminder I owed him dear?

I heard the creaking of the leather as he moved nearer. 'After what happened on that boat, Kitty, I needed to find out more about that card. It haunted me. I needed to put it to rest or use it.'

'And?' I could hardly bear to look at him.

'It seems that despite his loss, the King of Diamonds is the most powerful card in the pack. In some traditions, he is Caesar and in others he is Odin, the king of the Norse gods who bartered an eye for knowledge of all things.'

The warmth of his breath on my cheek made me flush. I wondered if he could see me shining like a beacon in the gloom.

'Was it . . .' I swallowed and tried again. 'Was it a good bargain?'

Sam settled back in the chair. 'That depends. I rather think it—'

Whatever it was he thought, I wasn't to know. At that moment the door opened and a man carrying a silver tray entered the library. He paused and scanned the room, head bobbing over his collar like a bird feeding a nest of chicks. He dialled us in the corner and picked his way between the herd of brown chairs. I pretended to be interested in the newspaper.

'I believe you ordered two brandies, sirs.' He placed the tray on the footstool between us and lingered. He turned away to survey the room, coughed and traced a pattern in the Turkey rug with the toe of his shoe. Sam produced a coin and dropped it into the cupped hand that waggled like a fish behind the man's back. Neither of them said a word, but the deal was done. The hand was whipped away. Grateful that Sam knew what to do, I watched the man head to the door and out to the galleried landing. He didn't look back.

Sam took up his glass and rolled the brandy around. It glowed deep amber in the candlelight and a little rainbow danced in the crystal. He raised it to me.

'To the third floor.'

Chapter Twenty-four

The corridor was deserted. We waited and listened for a moment to make sure we were alone and then Sam fitted Atkins's master key to the lock on the door of number 12. He turned it to the right and there was a loud click as the teeth bit true.

He stood aside to let me go first. Inside it was as dark as the rest of the club, but faint pale lines on the wall opposite the door suggested a row of windows. I went across and pulled a heavy curtain aside, allowing brackish light to seep into the room. Sam did the same to the next window along, tucking the trailing ends into a braided loop hanging from the wall to keep it in place.

Number 12 overlooked a square courtyard at the back of the Angevin Club. I peered through the glass. There was a well at the centre of the yard and beyond it an archway leading out to the street.

Sam caught my sleeve. 'Careful, Kitty. We can't be seen in here.'

He didn't whisper, but he kept it low. I twitched the curtain over a little more to shield us and turned to the room. It was larger than I'd expected. An ugly bed with a half canopy stood along from the door and next to it there was a washstand with a china jug and bowl. An old-fashioned, dark wood wardrobe with a full-length mirror between two doors took up most of one wall and a heavy desk with clawed feet stood guard between the windows. There was a hearth set ready with coals and tapers. Two leather chairs drawn up beside the hearth completed the furniture arrangement. In the corner beyond the windows was another door, leading, I imagined, to a closet.

The surprising thing about the room was the wallpaper. The sprigged rosy pattern clambering up the walls was the last thing I'd expected to see. Where the rest of the club was brown, this room was pink and blousy as a bangtail's boudoir. It smelt of carbolic and cologne laced with embrocation.

'Which of them lodges here?' Sam came to stand next to me.

I shook my head. I couldn't imagine Kite in this room, but then again, it was difficult to imagine the monster described to me by Ramesh Das bedding down amid the roses.

I went to the desk. It was neat and clear with three rows of drawers stacked behind a fine silver pen stand. The inkpot at the centre of the pen stand was shaped like a man holding an umbrella riding an elephant. The umbrella was hinged so it could be tipped back for the dipping of a pen.

'Sam!' I whipped round. He'd opened the wardrobe so quietly I hadn't heard a thing and now he was on his knees peering into the compartment on the right. Dandling white shirt sleeves flapped over his head as he delved inside. I heard a bump as he dislodged something at the back. He rocked back on his heels and stood up, a small brown box in his hands.

'I know whose room this is, Kitty.'

'So do I.' I pointed at the inkstand. 'Isn't that just the sort of memento a man might bring home from India?'

'Perhaps in a case like this?' He walked softly to the desk and held the box to the light so I could see the faded gold letters embossed on the leather: A.G.D.

'Arthur George Denderholm.' I found myself whispering the name in case it conjured him into the room.

Sam nodded. 'There's a pile of monogrammed boxes and cases just like it stacked at the bottom of the wardrobe.' He flipped up the umbrella cover of the inkstand and dropped it back into place. Then he did it a couple of times more. 'And you're right about this too. Anything else here?'

'Let's see.'

I tried to open one of the drawers at the back of the desk, but it wouldn't budge. In fact, I couldn't open any of them. I thought the single lock at the top of the middle row might do for them all, but there wasn't a key.

'Let me try.' Sam took the pin from his tie and bent forward. He pushed it into the lock and wiggled it around. After a deal of jiggling and poking there was another click.

'Got it!' He sidled at me. His hair had given up the ghost on the oil now. It was flapping over his forehead like a mop. He was closer to his natural state and I liked him all the better for it.

'Where d'you learn to do that?'

'A journalist has to be a master of many talents, Kitty. Tricks of the trade and all that.'

'Some might call it a liberty, Sam Collins. That's a trick that could get you into trouble.'

'I'll let you be the judge of my talent, then.' He pulled the top drawer open. A sheaf of folded papers tied with crimson ribbons bristled to attention. I pulled off my gloves, pushed them into a pocket and carefully lifted the bundle of papers from the drawer. I laid them down on the desk and took up the one on the top of the pile. The paper was fine stuff, thick and very white. I pushed at my fringe, surprised by the unfamiliar bluntness of it.

'Whatever we do, Sam, we have to make sure that we leave

this room exactly as we found it. This lot have to go back in the same order they came out.'

I slipped off the satin ribbon. As I opened the paper, I felt something raised beneath the tips of my fingers. I held it to the light and saw a pattern pressed into the top of the sheet. I frowned and scanned the elegant writing. Straight off, one word set my heart pounding like a steam hammer.

Sir John Rathmole
Vinculum juris

For as much as I, the undersigned, have sworn allegiance to Her Majesty to accept this honour and undertake this great service, I hereby offer my word and bond to uphold the interests of the London Imperial Agency and its instruments in all matters and degrees necessary.
    Signed:
    This day:
    Witness:

Vinculum?

I read it again to be sure I hadn't missed anything but that was all there was. One sentence and a mention of the Vinculum. I took up another paper from the pile and slipped off the ribbon. It was exactly the same, this time for the attention of Sir George Massingham, Bt. I handed them both to Sam and reached for a third. Same again, this time for Major General Sir Magnus Cowper; the next was for Admiral Nathaniel Staggers, Lord Staggers of Lympstock; and the fifth was for the Right Honourable Julius Gussing.

In all there were twelve unsigned documents, each one intended for a titled person or a notable.

I coiled a length of ribbon round my finger.

'What do you make of them?'

Sam glanced at me. His eye shone bright as a new-minted penny. I could see he was wound up tight like one of them puppets on a spring that leap from a painted box, but he was trying to keep a lid on it.

He began casual. 'I recognise most of the names. Some are very rich and some are very well placed. Most of them have long-standing trading interests overseas. This one –' he held out the paper intended for the Right Honourable Julius Gussing – 'owns diamond mines in Africa and is said to be the wealthiest man in Yorkshire. Black gold.'

I quizzed at him.

'Coal. In the last two centuries, his family has made a fortune from mines. Now their interests are further afield. And this one . . .' He shuffled the papers until he reached the one he wanted. 'Massingham. He has recently been made a privy councillor.'

'That don't sound like a plum job to me.'

Sam snorted. 'It means adviser, Kitty. Adviser to the Queen. Although in the most literal sense you're probably right. Creeping around the Widow of Windsor is not a job for the faint-hearted.'

He flicked the edges of the papers with a thumbnail and then he looked direct at me.

'Most pertinently, I believe that these are the men whose faces were printed in *The Pictorial* by mistake alongside Denderholm a couple of months back. Do you remember I told you there'd been a mix-up with the print blocks?'

I nodded. 'The story came from the . . . Bureau? You said it was dull stuff as a generality, but you use it when you need to fill space. The story about the London Imperial Agency and Lord Denderholm appeared too early, or perhaps should never have appeared at all? Your friend got into trouble when you asked about it.'

'More than that, Kitty. He disappeared.' Sam stared at the monogrammed case near his foot. I thought he might kick it.

'Has he turned up?' I reckoned I knew the answer to that, but I asked all the same.

Sam shook his head. 'You asked me about that story because of your friend, Vellum. The one who sends you poems. He was one of the men whose face appeared with Denderholm and you wanted to know who he was. Perhaps one of these letters is intended for him?'

I sat back on the edge of the desk. 'He's not my friend. I thought he was a Baron, that's why I wanted to find out about him and why I asked you about that story. As I recall, it was you who took it on yourself to ask questions about General Denderholm and the Agency. You thought it might be a story for *The Pictorial*. What do you think now?'

'I think . . .' Sam looked at the papers in his hand. 'I think we've strayed into enemy territory without the benefit of a map.'

The hollow sound of a carriage clattering through the arch and into the courtyard below made us both go to the window. We stood behind the curtain and watched the long backs of the horses and the square black top of the box curve around the well, but we were badly placed to catch sight of its purpose.

The carriage drew up under a stone canopy two storeys below and then, a minute or so later, it rolled off again. We listened, but we couldn't hear voices. It was impossible to tell whether it had picked someone up or delivered them to the back door. A bell marked the hour. I listened to four solemn notes and then another bell joined in, followed by a third and a fourth. The churches round here ran time ragged.

'It's getting late. We've still got another room to try, Sam.' I went to the desk and sorted the papers back into the proper order, taking care to memorise all the names and the titles. Before I tied the ribbon around the paper intended for Sir John Rathmole, I read it again to make sure I hadn't missed a trick. It occurred to me that I hadn't told Sam about the Vinculum.

'Sam?'

He was putting the leather box back into the wardrobe, pushing it to the back as far as it could go.

'Do you know what this "Vinculum juris" means? It's written at the top of every one of these papers.'

He straightened up and ran a hand through his fringe. There were stains on his fingers from fiddling with the lid of the inkwell.

'I assume it's Latin. There's something familiar about it, but I didn't pay much attention in class. The Latin master stank like a ferret, a dead one. Now, this is interesting. I've just found—'

The door opened wide and Atkins tumbled into the room. His face was as pink as the roses on the wallpaper.

'Back! They're back.' He could hardly get the words out for panting. His eyes swept the scene for evidence of our presence.

'They're on the way up. Both of them.'

In confirmation, I heard Kite's stringy voice echo along the gallery. He was calling for fresh water and a cloth.

Every nerve in my body pulled tight as a bow string. I pointed at the closet, but Sam shook his head.

Another deeper voice came from outside. Christ! Denderholm was almost at the door. I scanned the room, searching for a place to hide. Meanwhile, Atkins lunged for the curtains, pulling them close. Everything went dark.

I heard Atkins fling himself across the room. A light flared just for a moment. I saw him kneeling in front of the hearth, a strike case in his hands. The light died and there was a clattering sound. I reckoned his hands were shaking so much he'd dropped the case on the tiles.

'Blast and damnation!'

There was more fumbling and scratching, then Atkins appeared again outlined against the mouth of the fireplace as a flame caught a taper end. He lit another taper poking from the coals, the thin yellow light shining up the dome of his bald head.

'Bed.' He circled a hand wildly behind him and blew on the trembling flames. 'Under the bed!'

Chapter Twenty-five

Sam's head cracked against mine as we dived under the bed from opposite sides. I muffled a yelp and rolled onto my back. As we lay there rigid in the darkness, I felt Sam's hand brush against mine. I tried to master my breathing, certain that Denderholm could hear me. My heart was lodged in my throat, fluttering like a bird trapped in a chimney. I closed my eyes and gulped down a mouthful of air that tasted of dust, old wood and naphtha.

Of an instant I was minded of the Beetle. The thought had a comfort to it.

A board creaked close to the bed. I opened my eyes. Someone crossed the room to the window. There was a rustle. A frill of cold light spread around the fringed edge of the bedcover. I shifted my head to the side. In the two inches visible, a pair of shining black shoes swivelled on the rug.

'What the devil are you doing there?' Denderholm's deep, rasping voice was throttled by years of smoke and good living. Sam clutched my hand.

'Good afternoon, sir.' From the sudden scrambling sound, I pictured Atkins springing to attention. I breathed out silently. He cleared his throat and corrected himself.

'Good afternoon, *sirs.*'

So, they were both in the room with us, Denderholm and Kite?

Atkins answered the General's question. 'I am lighting fires in all the occupied rooms. The Angevin Club is renowned for the attention it pays to the comfort of its guests.'

'Tell that to the cook.' Denderholm grunted. 'Yesterday's mutton wasn't fit to saddle a mule. Off with you then.'

'Sirs.' I watched Atkins's feet move quickly to the door.

'Wait.' The voice belonged to Kite. Atkins's feet turned. They shifted uncertainly from side to side as if they were considering making a run for it.

Kite spoke again, his voice a thin drawl. 'How did you enter this room? The General has the key.'

The feet shuffled. 'There is a master key suitable for all the rooms, sir. Only the most trusted servants of the Club are allowed access to it.'

'And why would such a thing exist, Atkins?' Kite's voice was sharp as a gimlet. I pictured him in court, swathed in judicial red, blind white eyes gleaming like twin moons under a grey curled wig.

'It is sometimes necessary in cases of . . . need.' Atkins coughed. 'The master key allows us to gain access to a room where one of our more senior members has, er, has most unfortunately . . .' he faltered.

'Died? Is that what you're trying to say?' Denderholm snarled. 'For Christ's sake, stop primping the word like a trollop's abbess. Every man dies in the end, even members of the Angevin Club.'

'Indeed, sir. Died – that is correct.'

'Then why didn't you say so? That will be all. Send up a bottle of the claret.'

'Very good, sir.'

Atkins's feet disappeared speedily from view. A moment later I heard the door close. The bed springs rasped and bulged above my head as someone sat down. I watched a pair of large freckled hands work at the laces of enormous shoes less than half a yard from my face. Sam's grip on my hand tightened.

'Strange. In all the years I have lodged here, I have never come across one of the servants in my own room.' Kite's voice came from over near the hearth. I heard the scrape of a chair on the boards. I shifted myself soundlessly to a place under the bed where I could get a clearer view. Beyond Denderholm's feet I could see Kite seated now in one of the chairs beside the fire. The light flickered on the line of his profile, making his long, narrow nose seem sharper than ever. As he pushed back a wing of white hair, the rubies in that silver bird-head ring of his sparked red.

The bed springs complained again as Denderholm stood and went to the hearth.

'Judging from what the man just told us, I'd be grateful for that, brother.'

Brother?

That was impossible. According to Joey, Kite's brother was dead. My own brother was in a place to know. After all, he was the one who'd killed him, cracking his head open with a fire iron. It was the same night that Joey had stolen the code to open the Vinculum.

I peered through the fringe of the bedcover.

Denderholm removed his coat and flung it to the bed. The tails draped over the edge but didn't block the view. He took the seat opposite Kite. I couldn't see his face clear on account of the winged sides of the chair, but I could see the top of his head, notably thatched it was, and the curved ends of his whiskers bristling out at the side.

He unclipped the cuffs of his shirt and tossed them into the fire. The stiff white circles caught light instantly, curling in on themselves. Bright flames tinged with purple leapt into the throat of the chimney.

Denderholm stretched out his hands. I glimpsed the breadth of his back and the roll of his shoulder. He was a man who took up a lot of space in a room. As I watched him warm himself, holding palms the size of paddles to the flames, I thought of Ramesh and most especially of his sister, Abha.

I remembered what those hands had done and felt rage boil inside me. Where was justice in the fact that a man like him could ease himself into the highest levels of society? Wasn't the Queen herself supposed to be partial to his service, setting him up on a comfortable perch in gratitude for his years of service in India?

He sat back and belched loudly. 'You might have the guts of a lizard, Anthony, but I'm grateful for the fire. This country is cold as a nun's quim, but not as dry.'

Kite flicked at his hair as if he was batting at a fly. He was, I thought, irritated by the crudeness of his companion. I wasn't wrong about that.

'India not only made you coarse, it made you soft.' Kite sniffed. 'You were away too long, brother.'

There it was again – *brother*. I frowned, catching at a likelihood. Perhaps it was a manner of speech? In their ridiculous ceremonies, the Barons always referred to each other as 'brother'. What if Kite was setting Denderholm a place at the table? After what happened at Wilton Crescent, there were plenty of spaces free now. Perhaps that was what the London Imperial Agency had been about all along? Kite was shuffling the pack and placing a new Baron in the spread.

There was a rap on the door. A reedy voice piped up.

'Your claret, sirs.'

'Bring it here.' Denderholm watched the servant, a thin young man with arms too long for his coat, settle a tray before the hearth. Two glasses and a silver-topped crystal jug glinted in the firelight. The young man lingered meaningfully for a beat longer than was comfortable and then he gave up and made for the door.

'Here, boy!' Denderholm tossed something at him. The silver coin bounced on the edge of the rug and then it rolled under the bed, bumping to a rest against my chin. The man hovered, uncertain what to do. He stared at the bed and then at the men by the fire.

Denderholm laughed.

'Fetch!'

Grateful for the dim light, I pushed the coin, a mere tanner it was, out beyond the fringed edge of the bedcover, careful not to make a sound. After a moment more, the young man swallowed his pride. He came to the bed, bent down and ran his fingers back and forth over the wooden boards. He was so close I could see the hairs on his wrist and the stains on his cuffs. I willed him to find that coin. I thought he might start scraping under the bed, but at last he came to it, straightened up and left the room.

Denderholm filled two glasses, handing one to Kite. 'They keep a good cellar here, I'll say that for the place. My return has its compensations. This turns to vinegar in the heat. I missed it.' He raised his glass 'To absent friends.'

Kite lifted his own glass, took a sip and leaned forward in

the chair. The firelight brought an eerie glow to the whiteness of his skin and hair against the crow-black of his gear.

'And to new friends.' He raised a second toast. 'In good time it seems. You have the documents ready?'

Denderholm nodded, not that Kite would have noticed. 'The wording is just as you specified. Although I can't see the point—'

'*I* can see the point,' Kite interrupted him, 'and that is all you need concern yourself with. Men are easily flattered. If they believe themselves to have been chosen, to have been personally singled out from the many by the highest personage, there is nothing I cannot . . . *we* cannot . . . persuade them to do in her name. The signing in the presence is theatre, the last flourish. If there is one thing I have learned, it is the power of ceremony.'

'Is that why you've set up this bloody pantomime next Thursday?' Denderholm scratched his foot. 'Seems like a waste of time to me.'

'On the contrary.' Kite rolled the wine in his glass. 'It is not often that we are able to gain access without drawing attention to our interest. We will have an opportunity to examine the problem at close range. The ceremony is not a pantomime – you are quite wrong about that. It will bind them and blind them, while giving us time to proceed in plain sight. And how appropriate it is that the moment of creation should take place there. My only regret is that we have been forced to move earlier than intended.' He ran a finger along the arm of the chair. I heard the leather squeak. 'When news of the London Imperial Agency appeared in that rag, brother, I admit I was unprepared and surprised. But now I see how useful it was.'

Denderholm grunted. 'Useful! I call it damned lucky. The

sketch man from the Bureau was skulking in the hallway at Windsor Castle when we were waiting to go up to the presence chamber. Even you couldn't miss him, Anthony. He stank like a wet dog. He'd walked from the station in the rain. When you consider that forty men were present, it was an extraordinary stroke of fortune that he caught Vellum. To be frank, if it wasn't for the image in that damned rag, I don't even think I would have remembered Vellum being there at all. Do you still think it was just a mistake?'

Kite sipped his wine. 'As a matter of fact, I do, now. The man questioned by Matthias was a fool, but he had nothing to hide other than his poverty . . . and a second family in Clapham. It was a tale of need. He stole the story and the blocks from the Bureau but couldn't find a buyer for such apparently dry fare. In the end he sold low. It was how you ended up in the pages of *The London Pictorial*. And how the thief ended up beneath the Euston dust heap.'

Sam nudged me as Kite continued.

'I do not think that particular newspaper will trouble us much longer. An ecclesiastical writ will be served within the month.' He turned his face to the fire. 'It seems that *The London Pictorial* did us a great favour.'

Denderholm thumped the arm of his chair. 'You mean you flushed him out, like a rat from a drain.'

Kite nodded slowly. 'A rat? In a way that is quite true. I had suspected for a while that he was not what he seemed, but that image proved it. My friend at the Sanctuary recognised his superior and immediately brought the matter to my attention. Matthias confirmed that the man on the page was the man known to me as Lord Vellum.'

Kite had someone at the Sanctuary, did he? I bumped Sam's elbow. When we got out of here, I'd have currency for Vellum.

The windows along the wall opposite the bed rattled violently. Fed by the sudden gust, the fire in the hearth rippled and flared, sending huge shadows of the chairs to the edge of the bed.

Kite took a prissy sip of wine. 'In the end, Vellum's subterfuge was futile. If only he knew how he has worked against himself. I would take pleasure in that. I do not often regret the loss of my sight, but I would enjoy his expression.' The rubies in his ring caught the firelight as he turned the crystal around and around again. 'The days of the Barons were limping to an end, but it would have been difficult to persuade them to . . . retire. Inadvertently, our enemy has done us a great favour. He has helped to clear away the dead wood and prepare new ground. We live in an age of opportunity with vast horizons before us. Modern times call for modern solutions. I will not mourn the passing of the brotherhood. Instead, I will celebrate a new beginning.'

He raised his glass and Denderholm echoed the toast.

A new beginning?

That was close to what Matthias Schalk had said in the street a day back. My head was a tangle of loose ends now. Denderholm took a mouthful of wine and grunted. 'Dead wood, you say? We're not out of the trees yet. Are they warned, the ones left?'

'I cannot be linked to any of them.' Kite sniffed. 'They are aware that our . . . circle has been broken and that their lives are in danger. Wilton Crescent proved that. By now most of them will have left the country. I understand the Brothers Janus have taken their carnival to Spain, indefinitely.' He took a mouthful of claret. 'It is, after all, a land with a taste for the . . . unusual.'

I thought of the men joined at the shoulder and hip, two arms, three legs between them. They were Barons, but cast in a different mould from the rest. The Lords Janus came from the travelling folk. I remembered the sharpness of their minds and the gold on their ears and fingers.

And I remembered again Kite's sinuation at my grandmother's funeral that one of them – any one of the Barons, he meant – might be my father. I harried the thought from my mind. If I allowed it to fester it would spread like mould through a wheel of cheese. I took a silent breath full of dust and clenched up my free hand so tight the nails dug into my palm.

Keep yourself sharp, girl.

Kite's drawl continued. 'Of course, in his condition, Fetch cannot move, or be moved. I hear he is near to death. Perhaps that will be for the best. He was useful once, but now he has served his purpose along with the others. If he lingers beyond his time, he could become a problem. I might be forced to send Matthias to him. A final mercy.'

Mercy! I fought against the memory of that stinking mound of flesh. Lord Fetch was so vast he couldn't fit his body into normal gear. Instead he wore a dark gown that billowed over his bloated form. I'd seen him only once, that night at Great Bartholomew's, and that was enough. I still wasn't sure of his trade but of all the Barons he was a mystery I didn't want to solve. He came to me in nightmares. Rolls of fat smothering me, fetid skin stopping my breath until . . .

I forced myself to concentrate on what Kite was saying.

'The events at Wilton Crescent were—'

'A bloody shambles,' Denderholm interrupted. 'What were they doing there? Did you know they were meeting?'

'Of course I did not.' Kite's reply snapped the air like a whip. 'They *thought* they were meeting me. It was Vellum's trap. I received the information via the usual source yesterday. My contact at the Sanctuary has also indicated that the Peck girl had nothing to do with it.'

Sam's grip tightened again.

Denderholm belched louder than before. He reached for the jug and poured a stream of claret into his glass. 'I could have told you that. I don't know why you bothered to seek her out. What's the Limehouse place called again? The Palace, is it?'

Kite nodded slowly. 'She is a . . . resourceful young woman. There was a possibility that she might have had a hand in what happened in Wilton Crescent. She has reason to stand against us. I had to be sure.'

'And now?'

Kite was silent for a moment. 'After the meeting next week, no one will be able to stand against us again. I have selected our new . . . *friends* with care. There is not one among them without a secret to be exploited. Once they commit, I will bind them tight and bury them so deep in the labyrinth of the law that they will never find their way back. They believe themselves to be serving the Crown, but they will be mine –' he corrected himself and raised the glass – '*our*s. Lady Ginger's songbird is an irritation. My contact tells me that she has made a visit to the Sanctuary. I wonder . . .' He cupped the wine glass in both hands and seemed to stare into the flames.

The wind shook the window panes again and I was minded of what Vellum had said about the Sanctuary being full of draughts. At the time it was clear that he and his owl-faced friend were worried about housekeeping, and with good reason. I had a ripe tale for them both now.

'She might live in a palace, but she's no queen.' Denderholm took a swig of wine. 'She's nothing, Anthony, a drab from the gutters like her mother. I can't understand your obsession with that miserable chit from the halls or her family. They are nothing to us now.'

There was a sharp crack as the bowl of Kite's glass snapped from its stem and smashed to a hundred jagged pieces on the hearth. Glinting shards of crystal scattered across the tiles and tumbled across the boards between the chairs. Spilled claret bled into the edge of the rug.

'You cannot begin to understand.' Kite's voice was coiled like a serpent about to strike. 'You were on the other side of the world. Our brother Edmund—'

'Lost us the key.' Denderholm wiped the back of a hand over his mouth. 'And now you can't forgive him.' He snorted. 'If we still had the damned code half of this charade next week wouldn't be necessary. Even then we're likely to be disappointed. Admit it, you don't have a clue how to open it, or even what's inside it when . . . *if* we do.'

Kite rose. 'On the contrary. I know exactly what it contains and the value of that holding. It is our insurance of success. Without Edmund it has been difficult to gain access, but if nothing else, we can assure ourselves of its integrity. There might be a way—'

'And there might be a mountain of gold locked inside.' The whiskers on Denderholm's face twitched. 'But it's worth nothing if we can't get to it.' He loosened the collar of his shirt and scratched at his neck. I was minded of a bear. 'Still, now the others are out of the way, if we ever get the blasted thing open again, all the more for us, brother. Just the two of us now. I stand by what I said. Edmund was a careless fool.'

It was the Vinculum he meant, I was certain. I flattened my cheek against the boards to see them as clear as possible through the fringe of the bedcover. Even though he was blind, Kite seemed to stare at Denderholm. The firelight made his white hair glow like a halo.

'How little you know, Rufus.'

Fat fingers rasped through bristle. 'I know enough to understand that Edmund was a sodomite. That's what killed him.'

'He was murdered by Joseph Peck.' The way Kite said Joey's name shrivelled my stomach. From beneath the bed, I watched him ball his free hand into a fist. He released it, stretched his fingers wide and clenched it again, repeating the movement like he was squeezing the life from a mouse. All the while the ruby eyes of the bird-head ring glowed in the firelight.

Denderholm stared at the spilt wine. 'That's a waste of a good vintage. I'll have more sent up, and another glass for you, brother.'

'That will not be necessary.' Kite's voice cut like the shards of glass on the hearth. 'I will dine at the inn this evening. The meat here is not to my taste.'

'You were always too delicate, Anthony, even as a child.' Denderholm splashed the last of the claret into his glass and slumped back in the chair. 'Do you need a man to guide you down?'

I caught an insolence in the question.

Kite stiffened. 'I have lived at the Angevin for a decade. Do you imagine I do not know the way?'

He turned, his shoes crunching on the broken glass, and went direct to the door. If you didn't know he was blind you'd never have suspected he walked in darkness. Kite reached for the handle and paused to stare with sightless eyes at the man I now knew, for a certainty, to be his brother.

'I will leave you to consider all I have done for you, Rufus. And consider this also: there was another reason I intended to visit the girl at the house in Salmon Lane. Jacobin lives.'

'Good God!' Denderholm spluttered his wine. 'The bird must be fifty years old. I gave it to Edmund when I . . . left. He always admired it.'

'But he could not keep it. After several weeks he found he could not breathe if it was near him. I found another home for it.'

Denderholm sneered. 'Poor Anthony. Gave it to your little lady love, did you?'

His question was answered by the slamming of the door.

Chapter Twenty-six

The man who called himself Arthur George Denderholm sat in front of the fire for a long time. He didn't call for more wine; instead he stared into the flames, one hand still dandling an empty glass over the edge of the chair. He twisted it by the stem and a rainbow of sparks played over the hearth and the wall as the crystal cast off the light from the flames.

Afternoon edged into evening and the corners of the room were lost in shadow.

I thought he might fall asleep, but at the sound of bells chiming a new hour from all round St James's, he roused himself, and went to fetch two candles from a bracket near the door. Sweeping the glass aside with the edge of the tray, he knelt in front of the fire, his bulk blocking the light from the flames. He was a brute of a man, broad and tall, the very opposite of his reed-like brother.

I didn't know which of them to fear most.

There was a click of bone on gristle as Denderholm rose with lighted candles in each hand. He pushed one back into the bracket by the bed and took the other towards the desk. I couldn't see him now. The bed groaned and sagged low over my feet. Denderholm had parked himself on the end. He belched again and the springs rasped and bounced. A moment later a pair of breeches and a shirt flew across to the floor, landing in a heap just beyond the fringe of the bedcover on my side.

The bed rocked. I heard footsteps and the squeak of a hinge as a wardrobe door opened. Sam squeezed my hand and shifted himself silently over to his side of the bed. He had the view of what was happening now.

I listened. There was a deal of banging and scraping followed by a *thwump* as something of a material nature was thrown over the cover above us. A moment later water was poured into a china bowl. I heard the slap of Denderholm's hands on his whiskered cheeks. Carbolic came on strong, then the waft of his musky cologne.

He started to hum, and then he came close to Sam's side of the bed. From the rustling, I reckoned he was dressing again for the evening. Denderholm grunted like a sow in labour as he worked at his fresh rig. His heavy tread went back over to the mirror, where I imagined he admired himself, and then he came back to the bed on my side. The humming started up again. Just occasionally he rode the tune.

I froze as a hand brushed aside the fringe not six inches from my face. Denderholm retrieved a black shoe and tried further down for its mate. His hand found something, but not the other shoe, which I could see lying on its side on the rug. The hand was whipped away. Denderholm straightened up.

'What the devil is this doing there?' He muttered the question to himself. On account of the discarded clothes tangled in a pile beyond the bed, I couldn't quite make out what he was at, but I heard him go to the hearth and poke an iron at the coals. The boards groaned as he stepped back.

'Ah!' He found the other shoe and, judging by the creak of the leather, sat down in one of the wing-back chairs to deal with the laces. Less than a minute later he rose and went to the door, now whistling that same song.

*

The key turned in the lock. Neither of us moved.

'Give it fifty,' Sam whispered. 'We need to be sure.'

I counted under my breath, straining to hear a voice or the squeak of the boards in the gallery outside. When we were certain he wasn't coming back, we rolled out from under the bed.

'Jesus! I thought he'd never leave, Sam.' I arched my back and stretched my arms above my head. I had a crick in my shoulder where I'd lain at an angle.

'More to the point, I thought *we'd* never leave.' He rounded the bed and paused, wrinkling his nose. 'What's that?'

He was right, there was an odd smell in the room now. Not just Denderholm's carbolic and cologne, but something sour with a smoky tang of the farmyard to it.

'It's from the fire.' I went to the hearth. A glove shrivelled at the heart of the coals. I put a hand into my pocket and found just one of the pair Wild had given me. Now I knew what Denderholm – it was hard to think of him as anyone else – had found when he poked around under the bed for his shoe. The glove must have fallen out when I dived for cover.

'Is it yours?' Sam stared at the blackened leather. The fingers had curled to a tiny fist.

'Not exactly. It's Mr Wild's. We're lucky the General isn't the curious type.'

'We'll be luckier to get out of here.' Sam went to the door and listened.

'It's quiet. Are you ready?'

I shook my head. 'Neither are you. Look at us. That jacket was black when you came in. Now it's grey and covered in hair

301

and God knows what else. Mine's no better. The Angevin Club might be the grandest, oldest establishment in London, but a century goes by before anyone pokes a duster under the beds. We can't go back out there like this.'

Atkins watched us as we came down the stairs. I wasn't entirely confident our gear was free of dust, but I'd done my best, patting Sam's tail coat until it seemed black again in the candlelight. He'd done the same for me. Atkins was back at his post by the door. I reckoned he was waiting there just to be certain we left.

The club was busier now. Clusters of men in evening dress stood talking in the hall; their voices came so loud I wondered if they might be deaf. When they laughed they put me in mind of a herd of goats.

'Bold steps, Tommy, remember.' Sam nudged my arm. 'Walk tall.'

He went to the table and I followed. The stag with the cobweb between its antlers watched us. There were more black hats jostling for space around the bowl now. No wonder you needed a ticket to find your own.

'Is everything in order, sir?' Atkins was suddenly at Sam's shoulder. His large blue eyes sidled between us while his brows worked at the real question.

'Excellent, thank you.' Sam scooped his hat from the table and swept it to his head. He patted Atkins's arm and moved his hand deftly to the man's upturned palm. I knew he was returning the key.

'The Angevin Club never disappoints.' He turned sharp and headed direct to the door. I pulled my hat onto my head and went after him, taking care to walk big. Wild's breeches were pulling now in places where fabric didn't ought to be. I'd be happy to see my own gear again.

We were five foot off the entrance when a hand clamped down on my shoulder.

'I know you, don't I?' I swallowed and turned. A young man peered at me through a monocle. If it hadn't been for the glass he would have looked very like a rabbit, a stringy one. He stared at my face and frowned.

'Yes, I do believe I know you, sir. You are very familiar.'

It wasn't a question exactly, but he waited for an answer, furling his damp top lip over teeth like ivory gambling sticks.

'Yes!' He nodded with an enthusiasm I couldn't match and the glass fell from his eye. It dandled on a thin gold chain down the front of his frock coat.

'It's coming back to me. I believe we met in Limehouse of all places. One of the halls there. A low sort of place, but plenty of tail?'

Sam stepped between us, raising a hand to the brim of his hat. 'I'm sorry. My cousin is newly arrived in London and speaks little English, Mr . . .?'

'*Viscount*. Viscount Ouselby.' The Rabbit collected the monocle and screwed it back into place. The lip went higher. 'And you are . . .'

'In a great hurry, I'm afraid.' Sam took my shoulder, propelled me to the door and out onto the torchlit steps of the Angevin Club. The stone creatures either side of the entrance looked ready to swoop down and tear out my lights.

*

In a hack on the way back to the museum we went over it all, trying to match up parts of the conversation we'd heard to what we already knew. Sam took out his notebook and wrote it all down, cursing the state of the streets when his pencil jumped.

I repeated the exact words on the ribbon-bound documents we'd found in Denderholm's desk and I listed the names and titles of all the men the papers were intended for. If Sam was impressed he didn't show it, but just kept scribbling away.

'And you're sure they're brothers?' He tucked the pencil behind an ear and reached up to adjust the candle lantern set between us on the back wall of the box. It was around seven and darker than the hour gave credit for. Rain drummed like impatient fingers on the roof overhead.

'I wasn't at first, but I am now. When Kite called him *Rufus*, I knew it for a certainty. Last time I saw Joey he told me that Kite had two brothers. He thought the oldest, Rufus, had died in India years back. But now we know he didn't. He's here in London wearing a dead child's name. When I went to the Sanctuary, Vellum showed me an old death certificate. He'd had it sent over from India. The dead boy – a pauper and orphan – was called Arthur George Denderholm, and he'd been buried in Madras sixty years back. Vellum sinuated that the General had stolen the name.'

Sam rubbed the skin beneath the glass eye. 'Just before Atkins came to warn us, I found a box at the back of the wardrobe. Do you remember I told you I'd found something interesting?'

I nodded. 'But you didn't have a chance to say what.'

He took the pencil from its lodging. 'It was a collar box, an old one, pushed to the back of the wardrobe. The leather was battered and cracked, but it was clearly marked with the letters R.J.C. At the time I thought it odd, but now I see they must have stood for—'

'Rufus Carstone!' I watched Sam scrawl another line and wondered what the 'J' stood for. Judas came to mind.

'And did you recognise the rest of what he said, Kitty?' He didn't look up from the notebook. 'About your brother, I mean . . .'

The cab jerked. I caught the brim of Wild's hat to stop it slipping from the seat. There was a lot of muck on the floor below. I took a deep breath. 'Joey murdered Edmund Carstone – he was known as Lord Wren, another of the Barons. The night it happened my brother stole something from him.'

I studied the spirals of black satin on the crown of the hat, wondering how much more to say.

'It's a long story, Sam.'

'We have time.' His voice was casual. 'The rain has made the roads busy. In this traffic it will be a while yet before we come to the Fields.'

*

Once I got going it was hard to stop. Sam took it all down as I rattled on. The squeak of his pencil skating across the paper set my teeth on edge. He flipped to a new page in his notebook as I finished up with an account of how the key to the Vinculum – whatever and wherever it was – came to be lodged in my head.

'You sent your brother to Australia?'

'Not personally, but yes, that's where Joey's headed.'

'And now you're the only other person who knows the code to open the . . .' He studied his shorthand.

'Vinculum,' I finished. 'It was why I asked you about the words we saw on the papers, "Vinculum juris". It's more than a coincidence, I reckon. I know the code to open the Vinculum, but only Kite knows exactly where it is. That was the way of it.'

Sam frowned. 'Does Kite know that Joey gave you the key?'

'No. I'm quite certain of that because he would have been after me by now. The way they spoke about this meeting they're holding, it seems to me that it must be connected to the Vinculum. Denderholm said something that struck me – something about the "charade" next week and how it wouldn't be necessary if they had the code.'

Sam nodded. 'From what I heard it certainly seemed as if they needed an opportunity to examine something. If it's where the Barons have hidden their assets, no wonder Kite is anxious to keep an eye on it. *Vinculum . . .*' He chewed the end of the pencil. 'There's something about that word, but . . .' He shrugged. 'If it's a Latin term we can find out what it means easily enough.'

He stared at me, his face hollowed out by the thin light of the candle lantern. 'That's quite a tale, Kitty. If I wasn't in . . .' He paused. 'If I wasn't involved I could make my name and a considerable fortune with it.'

I shifted on the bench. Of an instant, I wasn't entirely com-fortable with the way he looked at me. 'What will you do?'

'Help you, of course.' He tapped the notebook with the pen-cil end. 'It's all here. Now it's just a matter of fitting the pieces together.' His eye locked on a tear in the leather on the seat opposite. We'd taken a growler. It was the first cab to come along King Street after we'd tumbled down the steps of the Angevin Club and run like a tiger was on our tails.

'Two things strike me.' From the jogging of his foot on the boards I could tell Sam was wound like a clock ready to strike. 'Firstly, Kite didn't mention the halls at all, or more specifically, he didn't mention your puppet man . . . Marconi, was it?'

'Marcelli. Signor Marcelli. And there was the dog, Spark. What happened to both of them had Schalk's marks all over it. I'd know his work anywhere.'

Sam nodded. 'As would I, Kitty.' We sat in silence for a moment. I picked at a wrinkle in the fabric of my breeches.

'But think about this,' Sam started again. 'If Kite or his man was involved, wouldn't he have crowed about it? He talked about you, after all. He knew you'd gone to the Sanctuary, for example.'

He had a point there. It minded me of something important. 'He's clearly got a fly on the wall at the Sanctuary. Did you notice how he mentioned a "source", and later on he talked about his "contact".'

'Indeed.' Sam frowned as he concentrated on the tear in the leather. 'Secondly, did it strike you that Kite didn't seem terribly concerned about the fate of the Barons?'

I nodded. 'It was like they were the past as far as he was concerned. In fact, he was pleased that Vellum has done his dirty work for him.'

Vellum?

It came to me that something Kite had said was very similar to a comment made by Vellum when he spoke of the Barons. *They have no place in our modern world.* I rifled for Kite's version. *Modern times call for modern solutions. I will not mourn the passing of the brotherhood.*

307

I had a clarity. 'He's already setting up a new business! The letters, the names . . .?'

'All highly placed, respectable, wealthy, powerful men. I agree.' Sam studied the tear like he could see something through it. 'The Barons are dead. Long live the Barons. Or in this case, perhaps I should say—'

'Long live the London Imperial Agency!' I thumped the top of Wild's hat so hard I left a dent in the crown.

*

I stepped through the archway and back into the crypt. Sam, Lucca and Wild were waiting for me. Wild was perched on the edge of the bath, a smoke between his fingers. He was still wearing the broidered hat and now he'd added a pair of slippers to match. The air was pungent with spice and something like the stuff they used in one of Lucca's churches. I took it to be the Eastern blend of Wild's tobacco.

Candles still burned in pierced cans on the floor and in niches set into the walls. The place seemed a deal more welcoming than the Angevin Club. I went over to Wild and laid his folded gear over the side of the bath.

'Thank you for the use of these. I'm sorry if there's any dust, and I'm sorry about the hat too,' I added. 'I reckon you can fix the crown. I'll pay for another if you can't.'

He smiled and took a pull on his smoke. 'My pleasure, Miss Peck. I hear you've had quite an adventure this afternoon.'

I looked at Sam, who was flicking through his notebook. He also had a smoke clamped between his fingers.

Wild smiled. 'Finest Egyptian, unlike this monstrosity.' He

patted the side of the stone bath. 'And unlike the usual abominable stuff favoured by our friend.' Digging into a pocket he produced a golden smoke case. He flipped it open and offered it to me. 'Care to try one?'

I shook my head. 'Thanks, but we should go. Lucca?' I quizzed him and was gratified to see a smile.

'I don't know what Peggy'll say to this.' I ran a hand through my shorn hair. I quite liked the feel of it. I hadn't realised how much natural weight I carried around on the top of my head.

Sam looked up. I noted the return of the eye patch and remembered what he said about the glass being uncomfortable. He grinned. 'Perhaps you'll set a fashion, Kitty. Or buy a wig?'

Lucca handed me my bonnet. 'Sam tells us that your journey wasn't wasted.'

'You might well say that. And what about you? Have you forgiven me for leaving you here?'

He glanced at Wild. 'Now you have returned, Fannella, yes. This place is wonderful.'

Wild pushed his glasses to the end of his nose and regarded Lucca with interest. 'And you have been a very perceptive guest, Mr Fratelli. I hope you will come again.'

Lucca returned the compliment with a small formal bow. 'It was a privilege, sir.'

Glass splintered somewhere above. Someone let out a great wail that echoed from the walls.

'Scovell! She is in the breakfast room. Excuse me.' Wild started for the stairs.

A thought occurred. 'Mr Wild, sir?'

He turned, wincing as another ominous thud echoed from the gallery overhead.

'You're a scholar, that's what Sam says. Do you know Latin?'

He peered at me. 'I am proficient in Greek, Hebrew and Aramaic. I can read Egyptian hieroglyphs spanning eleven dynasties and I have a working knowledge of Demotic script. Of course I know Latin.'

His answer was a mite sharper than I expected. Sam took a drag on his smoke and gave me a sly smile of encouragement.

'*Vinculum.*' I said the word clear. 'That's Latin, isn't it?'

Wild nodded.

'What's it mean?'

He tilted his head. 'I believe there are several definitions. The term can be understood as a mathematical instruction linking two parts of an equation. It can also be interpreted in a legal sense as a bond between two or more parties. In the purest translation of the Latin, "vinculum" should be read as that which imprisons or binds – a fetter or chain.'

'*Sì!* Now I know this word.' Lucca turned to Wild. 'It is like *vincoli*? *San Pietro in Vincoli?*'

Wild nodded. 'Good, yes, Mr Fratelli, go on. Explain to your friends.'

'At home many churches are named for this. It is from the Bible, the New Testament. When St Peter was held in chains by King Herod an angel set him free. The word for "chains" is *vincoli.*'

Wild was clearly impressed. 'You didn't need me at all, Miss Peck. Mr Fratelli is quite right. Many churches are named after this picturesque episode. I came across several in Egypt – Coptic naturally. Indeed, there's one within two miles of here. At the Tower of London, the chapel is dedicated to St Peter ad Vincula. Now, if you'll excuse me I really should find out what Scovell has broken. You know the way out, Samuel. Good evening to you all.'

We listened to his footsteps on the stairs and then the sounds of a heated discussion from above punctuated by more wailing from Mrs Scovell. Poor woman. If she was the only cleaner here she had a battle on her hands.

I plonked the bonnet on my head, surprised by the fact that now I didn't have a yard of hair wound up on top it was several sizes too large. I pushed it back to get a clear view and turned to Sam.

'You'd better let us out then.'

At the door, just as we were going down to the street, Sam caught my hand tight. I spun round to look at him. The patch gave him a rakish air. He bent his head close to mine and my heart swooped like a swallow in spring.

'Keep buying *The Pictorial*, Kitty. And keep an eye out for Mother.'

Chapter Twenty-seven

Tan Seng shut the door behind us. He had to put his back to it on account of the wind. In the lamplight of the hall I saw Lok halfway up the stairs with a tray in his hands. I caught the particular smoke-laced scent of the tea the brothers favoured. It was an acquired taste – one I'd acquired but Peggy hadn't.

Tan Seng bowed. 'There are visitors, Lady. They wait in the parlour with Mrs Tewson.'

'At this hour?' I untied the ribbons of the bonnet and pulled it free. 'Who are they?'

Tan Seng handed me a small square white card. His eyes strayed to my hair and lingered. Credit where it's due, he didn't say anything. From the look on his face he didn't have to.

I flipped the card over and read the single name printed in neat black letters across the middle. I glanced warily at the stairs, imagining him and whoever he'd come with sitting up there with Peggy and the parrot.

The question was why? I showed the card to Lucca, who was removing his street coat. He pointed at the white gloves and tall black hat sitting on the hall table. A silver-topped cane rested against the wall.

'And there is this, Lady.' Tan Seng reached into the loose grey sleeve of his tunic and produced a letter. 'The boy said it was urgent. There is no need to reply.'

It wasn't sealed so I imagined Tan Seng had had a look. I opened it up to see Fitzy's ugly scrawl covering half the sheet.

Seeing as I have not heard from you, Marm, I have taken it upon myself to arraynge a try-out for the act I brought to your attenshun. I have arsked her to come to The Comet tonite and she is willing, coming on direct from The Golden Ball at closing. I told her to be set for 11. We don't need word to get round so I thought The Comet would be the best and most private place. She could be a draw for the opening. Jessie says works near compleet so this is also by way of a chance for you to see what you payd for and for me to see how it plays.

    F

I handed the paper to Lucca. He scanned the lines quickly.

'What will you do, Fannella? It is late. Today has already been . . .' He shook his head and looked at the hat and gloves on the hall table. 'And you have a visitor.'

*

Endymion set down his china cup and rose from the couch as we entered the room. He was in evening dress. Over by the window a man in a long grey coat watched the lane. He glanced at me over his shoulder, dipped his head and then turned back to his post.

'Good evening, Miss Peck.' Vellum bowed. If he dialled my hair, he didn't seem affected by it. Cool grey eyes held mine for a moment more than was comfortable. It was an odd thing, but in the lamplight he seemed at once younger and older than I'd thought him to be at the Sanctuary. He stood straight and his movements were elegant and assured. If you didn't know more or look too deep, you'd take him to be a regular masher out on the town. On the surface he was cut from the same pattern as the buck-toothed viscount at the club, but the fine strands of silver in Vellum's black hair and a tightness to the skin around his eyes told a different story.

'I must apologise, both for this unexpected visit and for the lateness of the hour.' He turned to Lucca.

'Mr Fratelli, is it?'

Lucca nodded. For the flick of a cat's eyelid, Vellum took him in and then gave a shallow bow.

'Delighted to make your acquaintance, sir.' He gestured at Peggy, who was perched on the edge of the chair by the fire. 'In your absence, Mrs Tewson has been a most attentive hostess. We have been having a very pleasant conversation, have we not?'

Peggy smoothed the skirt of her dress. It was a new one. I'd bought it for her to accommodate the baby. The dark red fabric whispered as she ran her hands across her lap.

She nodded and stared at me, her dark eyes round as saucers.

'Your hair! What happened to it?'

'Later.' I flicked a look at Vellum. 'You've been entertaining, I see?'

'Mr Endymion has been here for the last half hour.' She sidled at him in a meaningful way, her brows arching themselves into the question that was eating her up.

'Lok just brought up tea. Mr Endymion –' I could tell she enjoyed wrapping her lips around that name – 'tells me he prefers the Eastern blends, just like you, Kit . . . Kitty.' She sat there expectant, her eyes bouncing between us.

'Did he now?' I went to the tray and poured myself a cup

of Lok's tea. I took a sip and rolled it around my mouth, wondering what to say next. What was he doing here? Over in the corner, Jacobin was curiously still in his cage. I could see the glint of his black eyes as he watched us through the bars.

The mantel clock whirred, paused and tumbled out the tune marking the half. I thought about Fitzy's message.

Seeing as I have not heard from you, Mam.

That was an accusation. Despite the hour and despite the events of the day, I had to show willing. I'd been neglecting the halls.

Vellum sat again and I took the seat by the fire opposite Peggy. Lucca stood behind me, his hand resting on my shoulder. I could tell he was taking the measure of the man on the yellow couch, returning the compliment you might say.

I set the tea cup down. 'I reckon Limehouse is a way off your usual patch. What brings you here?'

'The pleasure of your company.' Vellum smiled and sipped. Peggy's eyes widened. I could see what she was thinking easy enough. First poems, then a personal visitation.

He sat forward. 'As you are aware, I am in the process of concluding some complicated business matters, Miss Peck. My friend and I –' he indicated the man at the window – 'thought that a visit to the delights of the eastern fringes might provide some respite from our labours. Naturally, I thought of you. No one is better placed to offer a personal recommendation, although the delightful Mrs Tewson has been most informative.' He acknowledged Peggy with a tilt of the head. She fluffed herself up like a bantam hen.

He set the cup down on the tray. 'I also wonder if we might speak in private for a moment. I have some delicate details of the recent negotiations that can only be divulged to an associate of the company.'

I felt Lucca's fingers tighten on my shoulder. I rested my hand lightly on his to reassure him and stood up.

'We can go through to my office. As a matter of fact, there are some things I'd like to go through with you. This way.'

I went to the door and felt Peggy's eyes burn twin holes in my back.

*

'Brothers?'

Vellum stared at the faded patch over the hearth where the mirror used to be.

I nodded. 'I thought at first it was just show – part of the ceremony the Barons favour, brother this, brother that. You of all people know how it goes. As they talked it became clear. His real name is Rufus Carstone, but he is—'

'Dead?' Vellum twisted the ring on his smallest finger.

'Yes! I mean, no! Rufus Carstone has been in India all this time and now he's back with a new name. You were right about that death certificate and that poor child. And I know all about him in India. I have a . . . friend, a Mr Das. He dealt with my grandmother's business and now he deals with mine – not that I'll be carrying it on much longer, you understand. Anyway, the point is that this Rufus – Denderholm . . . whatever he calls himself – did a terrible wrong to my friend. He murdered his sister. We weren't the only ones interested in that news story when it came out, by accident. Ramesh Das recognised him too from the picture.'

'His sister . . .' Vellum frowned. 'Was she young?'

'Abha, that was her name, was just thirteen. Denderholm took her away and he . . .' I couldn't finish that. The thought of Ramesh peeling back the sodden sacking in that flooded roadside temple came to me.

Abha was no longer beautiful.

There was a world of pain and meaning in his words. Vellum drummed his fingers on the desk. 'Thank you, Miss Peck. You have confirmed something I should have seen. Idiot!'

He must have caught the look on my face.

'I am sorry, I am referring to myself, not the child. I should have seen the pattern, the connections. I should have known my enemies, even the dead ones.'

I quizzed at him.

He sat back. 'I have made a study of the Carstone family, but I should have looked closer.

'Forty years ago, Rufus Carstone, the oldest of the three and not yet twenty-five, was connected to a series of violent assaults: women, all of them very young. Some of them were actresses from the halls. Rufus was an enthusiastic habitué of the lower forms of theatre.' He paused. 'I am sure you know how difficult it was for a girl from such a background to make a case against a man such as him.'

I nodded, thinking of the women who'd testified against Billy Downie. The only reason they were listened to was because they were really speaking for others with reputations to lose.

'Things haven't changed much in forty years. You said "some of them". Who else?'

'He also abused servants in houses known to his family. For a long time, the Carstones were able to hide the evidence of his crimes, or bribe people to ignore them. They were successful until his depravity went too far and they could not shield him. There was a particularly violent and gruesome death, this time the teenage daughter of a coachman. I won't go into detail other than to say that at first it was thought that she had been savaged by a wild animal. The child was a favourite of the household, not just the servants. It could not go on. An investigation was ordered. Rufus Carstone disappeared. His body was discovered several months later in a lodging house. The corpse was in such an advanced state of decomposition that identification was only possible through personal items found with it.'

'But that body wasn't his.' I scratched the back of my head where the short hair prickled on my neck.

Vellum nodded. 'The Carstone family were able to buy silence and even a respectable burial. But it is very clear that the man they buried was *not* Rufus Carstone. By the time the body was found, the real Rufus Carstone had escaped his crimes and was travelling to a new life and a new name.'

It came to me also that if we were talking about the past, there was another Carstone brother in this story. The one Joey murdered with a fire iron when he stole the key to the Vinculum. If Vellum had made a study of the family, like he said, what did he know about that? I considered what to say, and what not to say, wondering where the wrong question might lead.

I decided on something simple.

'There were three brothers, you said?'

Vellum reached into a pocket and pulled out his smoke box. He offered it to me.

'We need not concern ourselves with Edmund Carstone, Miss Peck. He is dead and buried with the full honour and ceremony accorded to a member of the royal household. He was, I understand, very close to the Queen.'

I took one of the smokes and glanced at Vellum's face. He was watching me close.

'He was also the Baron known as Lord Wren, as I am sure you already know. Your own brother, Joseph Peck, killed him.'

I sat poker-straight ready for more but Vellum shook his head. 'That, for the time being, is all I have to say on the matter of Edmund Carstone.'

He leaned in to light the end of my smoke and I caught the lavender of his cologne. My eyes strayed to his, but he looked away.

'You have been most helpful, Miss Peck. You and your friend Mr Collins from that troublesome newspaper.'

I took a pull on my smoke to get it going. 'That picture of Denderholm and all those men in *The Pictorial* . . .' His eyes flicked back to me, sharp. 'It got printed by accident. That's what I heard them say. You were there by accident too. That day at Windsor when the first meeting of the London Imperial Agency took place, there was a press man doing quick sketches, wasn't there?'

Vellum pushed a lock of hair back from his high forehead; a lit cigarette dandled between his fingers now. He nodded. 'I remember a small man with a patchy beard and a distinctive odour. He was lurking in the hallway, downstairs, not in the presence chamber. I did not think he had noted me. I was careful to be discreet.'

I shrugged. 'Well, whatever that means, you weren't doing it carefully enough. He was there for the Bureau and at some point he took your likeness. That's how your face got into *The*

Pictorial along with the others. It really was a mistake.'

Vellum closed his eyes. He moved the cigarette to his lips and considered the matter.

'I see.'

I thought he was about to say something more, but he blew a smoke ring and settled back to watch it rise between us. 'The documents you found in the desk, Kitty, were they signed?' He was off on another tack now.

I took a drag. 'No – but there was space for a signature at the bottom of each one and a place marked for a witness to sign too.'

I rattled the names off for him. I had them locked in my head. There were a dozen in total. I gave him the men's titles too. Vellum sat very still as I counted them off. When I got to the last one, I tapped a curl of ash from the end of the smoke into the brass tray between us on my desk. 'The way they talked it was as if they were building up to something. Denderholm – I still can't think of him as Rufus – said something about it being a waste of time.'

I frowned and tried to get the words just right, sorting through the order as my lungs filled with the richness of Vellum's tobacco. His smokes were a deal better than Sam's. There was a particular word that struck me as odd.

'What he actually said was that he couldn't see why Kite had set up a "bloody pantomime next Thursday".'

Vellum sat up straight, his clear grey eyes sharp as a new shaved pencil.

'That would be the twenty-seventh?'

I nodded. 'That's right, next week. Five days before we open *The Comet*.'

I wondered what time it was now. In all likelihood, Fitzy was waiting at The Comet with this act of his. I made up my mind and stubbed out the smoke on the tray.

Vellum was in no rush, even if I was. He took a lazy drag and studied me close. 'This has been most useful. I am glad we have had this conversation, Miss Peck. Your information about Kite's connection to the Sanctuary is not a surprise. However, it adds to the evidence already collected against the suspect.'

'Not the Owl?'

Vellum stared at me, a smile pulling at the edge of his lips.

'I mean the man with the round specs, only he seemed very—'

'Loyal,' Vellum finished for me and smiled properly. 'No, it was not the Owl. You need not concern yourself with the identity of—'

There was a crumbling, pattering sound. We both stared at the hearth, where a sudden gust down the chimney fanned the coals to a blaze. Something tumbled out from the chimney onto the fire. I stood and went to prod at the coals with a poker. The remains of a nest hissed and crackled there now, along with a tiny ball of bones and feathers that might once have been a sparrow.

I pushed at it with the poker until it was buried beneath the coals. 'What's his real name, then?' I turned to face Vellum. 'The Owl, I mean. What do you call him?'

Vellum tapped ash from the end of his smoke onto the tray. 'As I told you before, we do not have names in the Sanctuary. Owl will do. It is rather appropriate. Now, I have a . . . request.'

I reckoned I knew what he wanted. He'd caught me out on it when we met at the Sanctuary. I needed time to think about the Vinculum and what I was going to tell him.

I wiped my hands. Soot from the poker had blackened my fingers. 'Well, unless you're willing to come to The Comet with me right now, you'll be waiting a long time for an answer.' I could see he was about to refuse, but I shook my head. 'Oh no, that's not how it goes. You can't just come here and tell me what to do. I have obligations too. I've got an appointment this evening. If you want something from me, you'll have to wait here or come out with me. It won't take long.' I folded my arms. 'You might as well. A night at the halls might do you good.'

Chapter Twenty-eight

The double doors to The Comet were closed, but gaslights flickered beyond the new glass panels. I rapped twice and waited. Behind me I heard Vellum's grey man muttering to the coachman. I turned to see what he was at. Two bay horses fretted in the traces, rain pattering softly on their backs. The man nodded up at Vellum and came to the foot of the steps. A second later, the carriage, a bleedin' great black thing, rumbled forward on the cobbles and disappeared round the corner.

One of the doors opened. Fitzy studied us all for a moment, clearly confused. We made a curious party. Me, Vellum and his man, Lucca, Peggy and Lok too had all crammed ourselves inside Vellum's carriage. All the while we'd been at The Palace the coachman had been idling up on Salmon Lane. When I'd made it clear that I was going to The Comet, Vellum had offered to take me – and everyone else. Tell truth, I didn't give him an option on it.

I'd done my best to put Peggy off, but she wouldn't take no for an answer. I reckon her curiosity about me and Vellum would have taken her to the rim of a volcano if she thought she could get a better view. Besides, she already knew the contents of Fitzy's message – Lok must have told her – and saw it as her duty to sit beside me to pass judgement on a new act.

'It's late, so it is.' Fitzy opened the new painted door wider. His eyes strayed to the man in the long grey coat. He could sniff out the law dripping on his doorstep like a dog could sniff out cooked bacon.

'She was on the verge of leaving, but I got her to wait for ten minutes more.' He stood aside to let us in.

We filed into The Comet's freshly decorated hall. Plaster cherubs winked at us from the arched ceiling, their plump little hands clutching tiny golden harps to their chests. Gas lamps housed in etched glass cups threw off a soft yellow glow.

Vellum's man didn't follow us inside. Instead, he took up a new position at the top of the steps beyond the doors. I could see his back through the frosted panes.

Fitzy held aside a heavy blue velvet curtain and pushed at one of the gilded double doors leading into the hall. He sniffed. 'Jessie's done a good job. I can't deny it. See for yourself.'

The smell of sawdust and paint was the first thing that struck me. The second was the light. The old Comet was always the grandest of Lady Ginger's halls, but, on account of all the plaster mouldings painted gold and coated in years of dust and smoke, I'd always had the feeling that the place was pressing down, squeezing the air from my lungs. Now it seemed open, like someone had taken the lid off a box.

The gilding had been held to a minimum – a harp here, a crown there, a garland or two – and the walls were stripped back to the plaster. The old wallpaper – brown it was, either from design or years of punters' tar – had been replaced by blue fabric panels.

I took off my bonnet and turned about slowly. Along the back, one whole wall, including the doors in the middle where we'd just come in, was now a mirror. I was surprised for a moment by the sight of my hair. Burnished to an unlikely shade of gold by the lighted gas jets hissing in the brackets along the bow of the first balcony above, it glowed like a helmet.

Beside me, Lucca's reflection stared up at the topmost gallery. I knew what he was thinking.

I spun about and went through the rows of tables and chairs until I was standing right under the dome. I took a deep breath and looked up. It was when I'd taken a tumble from a cage hung seventy foot above the heads of the punters here, dragging half the ceiling with me, that The Comet was closed. But it wasn't so much that memory that came back to me now. No, I thought of the night when me and Jesmond had gone through a dozen pots of whitewash to cover up the filthy picture that had covered the ceiling up there. A picture that Lucca had been forced to paint.

I went back through the rows, took his hand and led him towards the stage.

'What do you think?'

'I do not recognise it, Fannella.' He removed his hat and turned to take in the room.

'Molto elegante.'

Of the three halls in my possession, The Comet was never my favourite. That would always be The Gaudy, even though it was now just a hole in the ground four streets away. So many bad things had happened here that I couldn't quite forgive it. I had to admit, mind, as I stood there with Lucca taking in the new decoration, the polished wood, the shining mirrors and the scrubbed furniture, that Fitzy was right. Aubrey Jesmond had done a fine job.

Right on cue, Jessie came out from the side door leading to the office. He dabbed his bald head with a 'kerchief and scuttled towards me.

'What do you think then, Ma'am?' He stared at my hair,

blinked and waved a hand to take in the hall.

'It's good, Jesmond. You've done well. Is it ready?'

'Indeed it is, Ma'am. The gilders finished last week and the carpenters say there's barely a day of work left – loose boards in the lower balcony. Apart from restocking the cellar we're quite ready to open. All it needs now is –' he glanced nervously at Fitzy – 'is something to bring them in. A draw, as it were.'

Fitzy grunted, pulled out a chair and sat down at one of the tables strung along the apron, right in front of the stage.

'Our draw has been waiting for the last half hour in the office with you. Bring her out, Jessie.'

Jesmond looked at his feet. 'There's something not quite . . . I don't feel it's right to . . .' He swallowed and started again. 'As the Bible tells us—'

'I don't care what the fucking Bible tells us, Jessie. All I'm interested in is what the takings tell us. As I hear it, tonight Madame took a month's worth at The Golden Ball.'

Fitzy swung round and grinned at me. If he'd noticed the change to my hair, it didn't bother him. 'Did you read the cutting? She'll bring 'em flocking.' He tapped his pitted nose. 'It's the coming thing, so it is.'

I nodded, even though it was a lie. I sat at the next table along and motioned for the others to follow. Peggy and Lok took the table on the left. Vellum and Lucca sat with me.

Peggy clapped her hands. 'Well, this is quite like old times, Kit. Or maybe I should say it isn't quite like old times, the place being so fine now. I know it's late, but can we go out back afterwards to the workshop? When Dan sees The Comet now he won't believe it.'

I couldn't look at her. I rested my hands in my lap and

rubbed at the smuts of soot that hadn't wiped away. My fingers were black and that seemed about right. Beside me, Vellum opened his smoke case again and offered it to me. The silver gilt interior caught the light from the jets, sending a shiver of light up the blue velvet curtain drawn across the stage.

I shook my head, but Lucca took one. The only other person present who knew the truth about Peggy's man was sitting next to me. I sidled at him. Vellum was studying the dial of a pocket watch.

'How long will this take, Miss Peck?'

'I thought you said you were looking for entertainment? You're in luck.'

I looked over at Fitzy and nodded. 'We're ready.'

He grinned and delved into his lairy jacket for a cigar. He twisted off the end, lit up and turned to Jesmond. 'Tell you what, Jessie, as we've taken such a trouble, why not try the works this evening?' He rolled his big head at the stage. 'Curtains, limelights, everything. I'd like to get a feel for the place. And we need to make our new friend feel at home. We wouldn't want her to go running off to New York, so we wouldn't.'

Jesmond's little black eyes flicked to the door at the side of the stage. He dabbed at his head again. Tiny beads of sweat glinted in the gaslight.

'She said . . . she told me some . . .' Jesmond shuffled from foot to foot. 'It will take some time to set it all up. Five minutes at least. And there's only me here.'

'She's waited this long. What do you say, Ma'am? You're the boss.' Fitzy coated the last with an insolence I chose to ignore. It occurred to me that I could retrieve that cutting from the bottom of my bag and read it. At least I'd know what I was letting myself in for. Judging by Jesmond's reaction, it was probably a flesh act of some sort. That would be Fitzy's natural choice, but it wouldn't be Jessie's. Despite years in the halls, he hadn't quite thrown off his chapel upbringing. Although, of occasion, alcohol eased his conscience when it came to a well-turned ankle. Poor Netta Swift had proved that.

I pulled my bag onto my lap. 'We might as well do what Fitzpatrick suggests. It would be good to see how it comes together after all your work.'

I scratched around and pulled out a folded square of blue newsprint, the one Fitzy had torn from *The Evening News*. I flattened it out on the table.

I scanned the grimy paper.

POISONOUS BEAUTY

Raised in the Orient and schooled in the mystic traditions of her fakiri forefathers, The John of Jerusalem proudly presents Madame Salima Zosta, handmaid to the Snake God. As a child initiate to an ancient and sacred order, Madame Zosta offered, most willingly and most trustingly, the tender flesh of her infant wrist to the caress of the Cobra, rendering herself immune to the venomous attack of the serpent species. See the fearless Madame Zosta clothe herself in the living, writhing skins of her fifty deadly specimens, each chosen for the fatal power of its kiss and the strength of its scaly embrace . . .

It went on for several lines more in the same vein. I could see why that would appeal to Fitzy. It was a flesh act involving a pretty girl wearing little more than God gave her and a box of fangless snakes – most likely smoked or drugged to keep them docile. And I thought he wanted to try something new?

I looked up. Jesmond hovered near the side door still dabbing away with that 'kerchief. His currant eyes seemed to be searching the room for a means of escape. It came to me that he was frightened, not nervous.

'Off you go then, Jessie.' Fitzy waved his stinking, flaking cigar like a conductor's baton. 'Remember, we're expecting the works.'

*

The gas jets died to a whisper. We sat in the comfortable gloom, staring up at the new blue curtains. The soft light brought out the sheen of the velvet. I wondered how much they cost. And then I wondered about Madame Zosta and her snakes. It was very quiet up there. I hadn't heard a sound from behind the drapes. Did she have them in a box? If she did, I hoped it was secure. The last thing we wanted before The Comet opened again was a bleedin' python on the loose.

A familiar hiss from the cups along the apron told me that Jessie had turned the taps for the limes. A moment later the cones sputtered and burned into life, sending a wall of brilliant white light up the curtain. It was so bright and so sudden we sat back, shading our eyes, but once the flow came more regular the flares died back.

Just along from me, Peggy settled in her chair. I could see

the glowing red mound of her belly. Lok leaned forward. He planted his elbows on the table and cupped his small lined face between his hands. Vellum pulled the newsprint towards him and held it to the limes to see it clear. He took a pull on his smoke and then he blew a ring that rose above the tables and floated up towards the dome, widening until it was stretched out so thin it vanished.

'I assume this is the act we are about to see?'

I nodded. 'It reads like the sort of thing favoured by my manager Fitzy.' I nodded along the row. 'Don't get your hopes up. I haven't.'

Vellum laid the scrap back on the table. It rested on the edge for a second before slipping to the boards. I didn't bother to retrieve it and neither did he. A violin started up behind the curtains, a right dirge it was, the bow coaxing only the lowest, most mournful notes from the strings.

As I sat there, I began to feel the music. Professor Ruben, who led the orchestra boys at The Carnival, wept when he played or heard certain tunes, but that was an emotional thing. This was quite different. I glanced at Lucca. He was staring up at the curtain. Of an instant, he winced and brought a hand to his ear as if to stop the noise.

I turned to Peggy. Her black hair had fallen forward to cover her face as she bent her head. I watched as she ran a hand over the bump of russet satin as if to protect her unborn child from the sound. It wasn't because the playing was bad, the notes were true enough after all. No, when I say I could *feel* the music coming from behind the velvet, I mean just that. It was like the bow was sawing across every nerve. It was as if we were the instrument. Every one of us was being played.

It didn't mention music in the scrap Fitzy had cut out for me. I shifted to get a look at him. He was sucking on that cigar and staring at the stage, but he didn't seem worried. I reached down for the fallen paper. My fingers scrabbled across the boards under the table. The violin stopped just at the moment I found it.

The limes flared brighter than ever and the curtains parted.

On account of the sudden light I shielded my eyes. There was someone standing dead centre, but I couldn't see them clear. The limes spat and fizzled down until they pooled a dim greenish crescent at the front of the stage. I heard footsteps and a woman holding a violin at her side stepped into the light.

Madame Salima Zosta wasn't what I was expecting. For a start she was buttoned up to her neck in black crêpe. Jet beads glittered in the folds of her narrow-cut skirt, at her cuffs and in a curling pattern that spilled over her shoulders. She was tall, around six foot I reckoned, and the black hair coiled and pinned on top of her head gave her several inches more.

You wouldn't call her young neither. White powder made her face seem to float above the beaded collar of her dress. The powder had settled into grooves around her mouth and nose. It brought an eerie, pearly glow to her hawkish features and made her long black eyes, the lids painted beetle-wing green, seem at once too large for her face and set too deep in her head. Her shadow flicked up the brick wall at the back of the stage, straight and narrow as a blade.

She took another step forward and dipped into an angular curtsey, holding the violin and the bow out stiffly to the sides. Her arms were almost as thin as the bow.

'Greetings.' She rolled the 'r' over her front teeth and

straightened up. I was wrong about her height. She was taller than six foot. In fact, she was taller than any woman I'd seen.

Madame Zosta looked at us all, her eyes moving slowly down the line. She turned away to place the violin and bow on a small black table set to the side of the stage. When she came back to stand at the centre again, the lights made the beads on her dress shimmer like scales.

I wondered where the snakes were. The woman was so thin she couldn't have hidden them up a sleeve and there didn't seem to be much room under her skirt neither. Then again, perhaps Jessie was keeping hold of them somewhere out to the sides? That would account for his nerves. I sidled at Fitzy. If he was expecting a fresh young piece flaunting flesh along with the fangs, he was bound to be disappointed.

'My music calms them.'

I turned back sharp. Madame Zosta had crossed her arms over her breast. Her eyes were closed. The green lids fluttered and I could see the rise and fall of her breathing from the winking of the beads on her chest. She began to speak quietly, but we were all close enough to hear what she said. It was clear from her accent that she came from somewhere a long way from London.

'Come. Come, my dear friends. You have heard my call. Now you will obey my summons.'

I folded my arms. I knew what came next. I'd once seen an old fakir at The Gaudy who played this trick or something near it. The Great Narnuk came from Bolton and he used music to make his cobra rise from a basket to perform a winding dance. That was just the one snake, mind. Didn't the newspaper piece mention more? There was definitely something about seeing the fearless Madame Zosta clothe herself in the living, writhing skins of her fifty deadly specimens, wasn't there?

I put the scrap of newsprint onto the table top to check.

'Answer my call. The journey is not far. The threshold may be dark, but the light will guide you. Come, friends, come.'

Madame Zosta was chanting now, her voice growing louder and sharper as she repeated the summons. Streaks of sweat left glittering snail trails in the white powder on her forehead and down her cheeks. She was quite a spectacle, all things considered. If I were a snake, it was Madame Zosta I'd be frightened of, not the other way round. Credit where it's due, this was something fresh. In a way.

I angled the scrap of newsprint to the limelight to read it again.

DEATH IS NOT THE END

Direct from Austria, where her extraordinary abilities have been scrutinised and not found wanting by students of both Medicine and Philosophy at The University of Vienna, Madame Liljana Toth-Varda brings her remarkable discoveries to London. Death is not the end. Madame Toth-Varda has devised and patented a scientific method to facilitate communication with those who have passed beyond the veil. Tomorrow she brings her message of hope to the grief-stricken of London for one engagement only before travelling onward to New York. Seek and ye shall find. Believe and ye shall be rewarded. The Golden Ball, Farringdon. Doors at seven o'clock sharp.

I flicked the paper over. Madame Zosta and her bleedin' snakes were on the other side, but now I looked properly I could see Fitzy's 'X' next to the words 'Death Is Not the End'. This was the act he was talking about all along; it wasn't a flesh act he was interested in, it was Madame Toth-Varda.

She carried on chanting as I scanned the page again.

'*Passed beyond the veil.*' Something cool brushed the back of my neck as my eye went to that line.

Madame Toth-Varda gasped. It sounded like she was hawking up something lodged in her throat. I looked up from the print to see her body stiffen. Slowly, graceful as a ballerina, she unfolded her arms from her breast and stretched them out to the sides. She took a great shuddering gulp of air and her painted eyelids snapped open.

'And now we go to work.'

Chapter Twenty-nine

Last night she came to me, my dead love came in
So softly she came that her feet made no din
As she laid her hand on me and this she did say:
'It will not be long, love, 'til our wedding day.'

When the singing stopped, Fitzy was sobbing. It was uncomfortable to hear it and to see his wide shoulders working themselves up and down like a laundry press, but not as uncomfortable as listening to the sweet, girlish Irish voice that came tripping again from Madame Toth-Varda's lips.

'I waited, Paddy. I waited a long time, but you never came.'

Fitzy wiped a cuff across his streaming nose. 'I tried, Nora. I tried my best, so I did.'

Madame Toth-Varda shook her head. The beads at her neck rustled. 'You were a fine man once. *Slán.*'

'Wait! Don't go.' Fitzy stood and stretched out a hand like he was trying to catch hold of something. It was clearly too late. Madame closed her eyes again. Her still silence was almost as unnerving as what we'd just seen.

Fitzy sank back onto his seat. He swiped at his damp cheeks, took a deep breath and swivelled his glassy little eyes warily to the rest of us to see what we were thinking. I noted that on account of his dignity we were all careful to keep staring direct at Madame on the stage.

Vellum moved close to whisper in my ear. 'A parlour trick, Miss Peck. Anyone who knows your manager – Fitzpatrick, is

335

it?' I nodded. 'Well, anyone who knows him could have passed on the details of his long-lost love. These people are clever. They research their subjects very thoroughly. I trust that it was your manager who made the arrangements for this evening?'

I nodded again. 'There you have it.' Vellum sat back, satisfied with his assessment.

I shifted on the chair. Vellum was right, of course. Fitzy wasn't one to keep a secret. I'd never heard him mention this Nora, but he could have burbled out that sentimental story when he was in his cups to anyone drunk enough to listen.

Madame Toth-Varda was good, though, a gifted actress if not in the flush. The girl's voice had been clear and very different to her own. And Fitzy seemed to recognise it straight off. When he'd heard his name called out in that soft lilting accent, he'd stopped chewing on that cigar and sat there still as a rat when a cat's on the prowl. I watched his jaw sag to his collar as 'Nora' talked of her father's farm, of the beach where she and – a much younger – Fitzy had met in secret and of his promise of marriage.

I pulled the neck of my coat close and turned up the collar. It was bleedin' cold in the hall. We sat in a silence that seemed to last a very long time. The only sound was the rattling of the limelight cones along the front of the stage. At the next table Peggy waved to catch my attention. I shifted over to listen, but Madame started up again.

I say Madame, but now she sounded like a young man. The voice was low and musical, and it wasn't speaking English.

'*Oddio.*' Lucca jumped up so abrupt his chair clattered to the boards. He crossed himself, gripped the brim of his hat and stared wildly at the door. Madame Toth-Varda paused and stared at him. Her dark eyes sparked like jewels. She spoke again, in the new voice, the words tumbling from her lips. All the while Lucca seemed torn between standing his place and making a run for it. The hat went round and round in his fingers. When she stopped, he nodded, his long black curls falling forward to cover his face.

'*Sì.*' He whispered the word.

The voice came again. Lucca looked up and smiled. In the limelight I could see tears rolling down one side of his face.

'*Ti penso spesso, Giacomo.*'

Madame raised a hand. It was either a blessing or a farewell. The voice of the young man came once more. Lucca took a step forward.

'*Grazie.*'

Madame closed her eyes. The jet beads rustled as she brought her hand back to her side. There was a ring with a tawny stone the size of a thrush egg on her middle finger. I tried to catch Lucca's eye, but he sat down again – a little apart from the rest of us now – and rested his forehead in his hands. I got the impression that he wanted to be separate.

Vellum opened his smoke case. This time I took one when he offered.

'What did you make of that?' I whispered as I leaned in for him to light it. He shook his head.

'She is very practised. But it seemed cruel.'

I took a drag and quizzed at him. 'You mean you understood what she said?'

He nodded. 'Most of it. I speak several languages.'

'Why cruel?'

'Because she played on your friend's . . . vulnerability. She spoke

337

of private matters.' His fine-cut nostrils flared with distaste as he stared at the still figure on the stage. 'Her informants are clearly very thorough.'

'Are you there?' Madame Toth-Varda started up again. Her green-lidded eyes opened. The new voice, a man's, came again.

'Jonathan?'

From the corner of my eye I saw the smoke in Vellum's fingers tremble. He was leaning back in the chair, one arm draped casual over the back.

Madame spoke again. 'Why did you do it?'

She waited for an answer that didn't come.

'You betrayed me, Jonathan. You threw me to the wolves. Why?'

The smoke between Vellum's fingers quivered again, ash falling to the table. He raked the other hand through his hair.

'This is becoming tedious, Miss Peck. How much more time are you prepared to waste on a charlatan?' He didn't bother to keep his voice low.

'Is that what she is?' I studied his profile. A tiny vein pulsed in his temple. A long time ago Joey had taught me to read a gambler's face. I was reading one now. I took a pull on my smoke and turned my attention back to the stage.

The hall was so cold I could see Madame Toth-Varda's breath. She took a single step forward and studied us all, her eyes flicking along the line. When she came to Vellum she stopped, her gaze unblinking. He just sat there, cool as a penny lick.

Madame closed her eyes and the man's voice came again, as if from somewhere far away. I wasn't sure how she managed it.

I had a dove and the sweet dove died;
And I have thought it died of grieving:
O, what could it grieve for? Its feet were tied,
With a silken thread of my own hand's weaving . . .

The last line echoed in the hall. Vellum didn't move. The smoke between his fingers burned near to the knuckle before the ash dropped to the table. I knew for a certainty he recognised that voice – and so did Madame Toth-Varda.

If she was a charlatan, like he said, she was the best I'd ever seen. If she wasn't—

'Tell them, Kit. You'll make it right, won't you?'

I sat up straight. Madame Toth-Varda stared direct at me. Dan's cracked and broken voice came again.

'You've come for me, haven't you?'

Jesus Christ, no! Not that.

I stood up. 'Jesmond, bring up the lights. I've seen all I need.'

Madame reached out a bony hand. Dark flecks deep in the amber stone of her ring seemed to weave and twist about.

'It's dark, Kit. So dark.'

'Jesmond! The lights!' I bawled the order and backed away from the stage. 'Now!' I called again. There was a hissing noise. The painted cups around the balcony jinked in their new brass fittings as the gas came through. Seconds later they began to glow. Light spread through the hall like a ribbon unfurled.

Madame studied me from the stage, but at least she was silent now.

Peggy turned on her chair. 'Why did you stop her? Someone had a message for you. Who was it?'

My heart leapt with relief. Peg hadn't recognised Dan's

339

ragged, desperate voice. He hadn't been speaking from beyond the grave so much as in it. I had to stop it. I had to stop him.

I shook my head. 'No one. No one I recognise, Peg . . . Besides it's just a trick, all of it. It's late. I've seen and heard enough. We all have.' I caught Vellum's eye. He struck a Lucifer along the side of his gold case and lit a new smoke. He knew who it was, all right. He was there at Great Bartholomew's that night.

I swallowed, aware that every eye in the room was on me. Lucca frowned.

'Fannella?'

Fitzy gestured at the stage. He'd recovered his dignity and was doing his sums. 'A bloody marvel, so she is.' He bobbed his head. 'Pardon my manners, so *you* are, Madame. Once word of this gets out, we'll have them queuing round the block three times a night.'

I went closer to the apron. Madame Toth-Varda didn't move a muscle or make a sound. Her black eyes held mine.

I put a hand to my collar. 'I'm sorry.' Chill breath rose into the air as I spoke. 'I'm sorry, Madame, but I won't be offering you an engagement.'

Fitzy grunted and spun round, his little eyes lost beneath the thicket of tangled brows.

'You are very . . . talented, I'm sure, but I don't think . . .' I gathered my thoughts. She was a bleedin' marvel just as Fitzy said, but not one I wanted within a thousand miles of me.

I started again, aware of Lok and Peggy, heads close, muttering to each other. 'The point is this, I don't think you're right for The Comet. This place is too big for your act. You need somewhere much smaller, much more confined . . .'

Somewhere much further away.

Madame still didn't move or speak.

'As I understand it, you're headed to New York?' It was a question, but she didn't answer. 'Well, I reckon you'll do well there, better than here anyway. The Limehouse punters like a bit more . . . show.'

Christ! I'd never seen a show like it.

The door at the side of the stage opened and Jesmond came out into the hall. He cast a nervous look up at Madame and hurried towards me.

'Well, what did you think, Ma'am?' His icy breath rose like Vellum's smoke rings.

I knew what he meant, but I didn't answer him straight. 'That curtain must have cost a packet, but The Comet looks good. I think we're ready.'

He looked at Fitzy and then at the woman looming above us. 'And, this evening?'

I shook my head. 'Madame's not right for us.' I turned to the stage. 'Thank you for coming tonight and at such a late hour. I'll see that you're paid for your time and for your trouble.'

Still she didn't move. Her eyes were closed now; the green paint on the lids looked cracked and smudged in the softer, more natural light of the gas jets.

'Shift yourselves.' I motioned for the others to get going. 'I'll leave you to lock up, Jesmond, and to arrange transport for Madame Toth-Varda. Fitzy, you can deal with the money. I don't want her out of pocket.'

I just want her out of my hall.

Without looking back, I took up my bag and bonnet and started to make my way through the chairs and tables to the door. In the mirror I saw the others rise from their seats to follow. I noted the confusion on Lucca's face. Peggy and Lok moved together, heads bent close. Vellum lifted the smoke to his lips and took up his hat.

Behind them, the woman on stage raised an arm.

'Katharine.'

Madame Toth-Varda's reflection stretched out the hand with the ring to point direct at me.

'Katharine.' Lady Ginger's strange, sing-song, girlish voice cut the air like a diamond on glass.

'He is your brother. At the end remember that.'

Chapter Thirty

Peggy arched her back and shifted on the couch. She pursed her lips and picked at the end of a feather poking from one of the bolsters. Lok swirled the small china bowl in his hands and took a gulp of tea. The brothers never took alcohol.

'Spit it out, Peg. I know you've got something to say.' I lifted my glass of brandy and waited.

The journey back to The Palace in Vellum's carriage had been a silent one. As I stared out of the window the sound of my grandmother's voice ran through my head again and again like a tune lost in an ear. She was talking about Joey. That was rich; there was nothing new there. Even though she was on the other side – and he was on the other side of the world – he was still in her thoughts. And now he was in mine again. What did she mean?

I glanced at Vellum, his face in shadow. Of all the people at The Comet tonight, I reckon it was me and him who'd been rattled most by Madame's performance. He'd called her a charlatan, but we both knew that wasn't true.

When the carriage halted on Salmon Lane I invited him, and his man, back to The Palace. He didn't refuse. And he didn't refuse my offer of brandy neither. Tan Seng brought a tray set with a bottle and five glasses up to the parlour a little while after we returned. I sent a glass out to the grey man, who insisted on standing watch on the steps.

And now here we were, sitting together in the empty hours, all of us sifting through the questions in our heads. Peggy plucked the feather free and twisted it between her thumb and forefinger. Eventually she threw a black look at me.

'I can't forgive you, Kit.'

The brandy lodged in my throat. Peggy went on, 'It wasn't fair, stopping her when you did. Anyone could see she was working along the row.' She turned to Lucca. 'You got a message, didn't you?'

'*Sì.*' He took up his brandy glass. He didn't add anything more, but that was enough for Peggy, who wasn't inclined to look for anything deeper than agreement.

'And there was Fitzy and his Nora.' She counted on her fingers. 'Then there was that other one, asking for Jonathan . . .'

Vellum's face gave nothing away.

'He didn't seem right, I grant you. And neither did the one with the hoarse voice who called you by name, Kit.' She shrugged. 'But that last one, the one that came out as we were leaving, I knew her straight off. Lady Ginger, it was, to the life. Your own grandmother, Kit! I wonder you didn't stay to hear what she had to say.'

Tan Seng stared at me. Then, for confirmation, he looked at Lok, who was examining the contents of his tea bowl. Lok must have felt his brother's question. He nodded without raising his eyes from the china.

'It was an act, Peggy. I didn't want to waste any more time.' I took another sip of brandy, grateful for the warmth of it slipping to my belly. I seemed to have brought the chill of the hall back with me. 'It was late and it was cold in there.'

'It was selfish.' Peggy pulled another feather from the bolster. A black one. 'You might not have wanted to hear from anyone, but I did. What if my mother had come over, or *my*

344

grandmother? That would have been a comfort.' She pulled the feather apart. 'And I could have asked them about Dan. Where he is, I mean.'

Peggy was set on the fact that Dan was alive and simply hiding himself from a bad debt. She couldn't allow herself to think anything else. I slid a look at Vellum, who set down his glass.

'It was indeed a fascinating performance, but I must agree with Miss Peck. It was nothing more than an act. You are a perceptive and intelligent young woman, Mrs Tewson. You will, of course, have noticed that some of Madame Toth-Varda's . . . communications fell on stony ground?'

Peggy frowned. I could see she was caught between enjoying Vellum's attention and her resentment.

'I understand that this is generally the way these performers work,' Vellum continued, his voice smooth as silk. 'They gain accurate information about at least one of the people expected to be present in their audience and use that material to their advantage. The rest is padding. It is a remarkable feat of memory and research, nothing more.'

Lucca sat forward. He pushed a hand through his hair and was clearly about to say something. A sharp look from Vellum stopped him.

'Madame Toth-Varda is an accomplished artiste.' Vellum smiled at Peggy. 'But she is not a vessel through which the dead speak. As a rational and modern young woman, you must surely agree with me?'

Peggy took a dainty sip of brandy. I could tell she was flattered. And I could see that Vellum's little speech had gone a way towards persuading her.

She sighed. 'Well, I know you're both right. It's just that it would have been . . .' She winced and put a hand to her side. 'He kicked.' She smiled at the bump in her dress and rubbed it gently. 'I think he's telling me it's a long way past his bedtime. And mine.'

*

'She was real, wasn't she?'

My question was meant for them both.

'She was remarkable, Fannella.' Lucca held his hands to the fire. The good side of his face shone like bronze. '*Terrificante e meravigliosa.* I never thought to hear his voice again.'

'It was Giacomo?' I asked lightly. Lucca's past, and most likely his future, turned on that name. He nodded, keeping his face to the hearth.

'And you?' I turned to Vellum.

He glanced at Lucca. 'I found the woman . . . convincing. There is nothing more I wish to add.'

The door opened. Tan Seng came back into the parlour with a bucket of coals. Despite the brandy, we were still so cold that we needed the warmth of the fire. He scattered another shovel-load onto the hearth and sat down opposite me, his hands tucked into the grey sleeves of his tunic. Lok had gone to make Peggy the special herbal concoction she took every night for the sake of the baby. I'd asked him to come back to us as soon as he was done.

The clock on the mantel whirred and jingled its tune, then it chimed twice. I poured myself another brandy and offered the bottle to Vellum.

'Before we went to The Comet tonight, you said you had

something else you wanted to talk to me about. It's late, but I don't imagine any of us are in the mood for sleep. You might as well go ahead now.'

Vellum shifted on the couch. 'The matter is private.'

'There's no one in this room I haven't trusted with my life. You're free to speak in front of my friends.'

At that moment, as if I'd summoned him, Lok came back. He went to a lacquer stool against the wall near Jacobin's cage and sat down.

'Very well.' Vellum took the bottle from me and poured himself a brandy. 'I have a request.'

Here it comes, I thought. *He's back on the track of the Vinculum.* I waited to see how he'd frame it. I still hadn't made up my mind on the matter. It seemed to me it was the only card I held.

He swirled the brandy around.

'You will carry a message for me to the Baron who calls himself Lord Fetch.'

I fought to still the glass in my hand as I thought of that rancid heap of flesh. Vellum's request wasn't what I'd expected.

'He's still alive then?' The question came out thin and high. I cleared my throat. 'Only, at the club I heard Kite say he was near to death. He reckoned it was a mercy.'

Vellum took a gulp of brandy. Fiery stuff, it was. It must have burned a track down his gullet and into his belly. He wiped the back of his hand across his lips. Just for a moment all his sleekness and control had vanished.

'There is no mercy for that man. There is, however, a compromise. I want the book of names. You will tell him that if he gives me this, I will . . . *allow* him to die in his bed. If he does not, I will drag his living carcass through the streets of London to Newgate Prison in an open cart.'

I put down my glass. The thought of being near that man, the reek of his body filling my nose, made my stomach clench tight as an oyster. Vellum stared at me, firelight dancing in his grey eyes.

'I can't.'

'Why not?'

I looked away. 'There . . . there was something Kite told me at my grandmother's funeral. It's haunted me since. To be exact, *he*, Lord Fetch, has haunted me since. Of all of them, he's the one I think about. I don't want to look at him again, in case I see something that . . . that—' I broke off.

'What did Kite tell you, Kitty?'

I noted he used my name. I couldn't read the look on his face as he studied me from the other end of the couch.

He asked again. 'What?'

'He said . . .' I took a mouthful of brandy and let it scorch my tongue. I stared at the rug, following the pattern with my eyes. There were so many trails knotting themselves around and around again.

I swallowed. 'He said that any of them – any of the Barons, I mean – could be my father.'

The room was completely silent. I looked up. Tan Seng and Lok were signing furiously at each other. When I caught them, they froze, casting their eyes downward. Lok seemed to shrink to half his normal size. It was as if he was trying to make himself invisible.

'And do you believe that?' Vellum spoke softly.

I shook my head. 'No. I mean, I don't think so. I can't let

348

myself dwell on it. But I know this: if I looked into Fetch's eyes and saw something, *someone* I recognised . . .'

'I understand.' Vellum sat back. 'Kite is a liar, Kitty. He twists the truth in his professional capacity both as a judge and as a man. He is blind, but his compensatory gift is the capacity to see the weak spot in others and use it.'

'Then it's not true?'

He didn't answer. Instead, he took out his smoke case, offering it first to Lucca and then to me. I took one and went to the fire to light it for myself. As I stared into the flames, I considered what Vellum had said. And what he hadn't said. I straightened up to face him.

'Why can't you go to Fetch yourself?'

He struck a Lucifer along the side of the case. 'Because I could not trust myself.'

He didn't offer anything more. I waited, but it was clear the question was a dead end.

'Well, what's this book you want? At least tell me that.'

Vellum pulled on a new smoke. 'It is a list of the . . . recreational procurements Fetch has made for many of the most prominent members of society. It lists the names of those capable of gross depravity and their *particular* interests. Men, women, children, the deformed, the deranged, the deluded, the desperate. Fetch believes it to be a secret thing, known only to him. In the wrong hands it could do great damage. In the right hands it is a priceless tool.'

'You mean you're going to blackmail them?'

'That is an ugly word. I prefer *encourage*.'

Wasn't that the very word he'd used when I went to the Sanctuary? I still wasn't sure whether the man in my parlour

349

was a friend or something else.

'If it's a great secret, how do you know about it?'

He dandled his smoke between his fingers and considered the question. His eyes strayed from Lucca to the brothers in turn, then he looked into the fire.

'I made a grave error when I sent a . . . colleague to investigate Fetch's circle. He found out about the book and communicated its existence to me before, before . . .' He took a drag on the smoke. '*Auribus teneo lupum.*'

It was clear he didn't intend that for anyone other than himself.

'I don't understand.' I sat down again. 'You've got all the men at the Sanctuary. Why can't one of them go for you?'

'Because in addition to the book, I also want the answer to a simple question. In the wrong hands that information could be . . . compromising.'

'You mean it could be dangerous for you?'

He pushed at his black hair. The gold ring on his smallest finger glinted in the firelight. 'It could, perhaps, undermine me.'

Of an instant I had a clarity about what it might be. I glanced at Lucca. He was studying Vellum with something between sympathy and surprise.

'It's something personal you don't want getting out. Is that it . . . *Jonathan*?'

Vellum didn't react. The mantel clock sounded the half. He cast the end of his smoke into the fire and stood up. He looked at his reflection in the mirror and straightened the pin at his neck.

'It is late and I must go. Will you do this?'

I folded my arms. 'It's not a request, is it?'

He stared at me in the glass. 'I asked you to work with me, Miss Peck.' I noted we were formal again now. 'It is a business transaction. I will send you my instructions. When you collect what I need, I will give you something in return. Something of value to you and those close to you. Something you *need*.'

I snorted. 'First you use blackmail and then you try to land me like a fish. What exactly are you offering?'

He turned to face me. 'Information. The question is what are *you* offering? That interests me. You have already proved to be an excellent . . . associate, you and your partner Mr Collins. The conversation you overheard between the Carstone brothers. You mentioned a "pantomime"?'

I nodded. 'On Thursday next week, the 27th, that's what Denderholm said.' It came back to me that when we'd talked in the office earlier, Vellum had recognised that date.

'What's it to you?'

He took up the smoke case from the arm of the yellow couch and pushed it into an inner pocket of his fine tail coat. 'The nature of my work allows me access to certain diaries, Miss Peck. Next week, on the 27th, an extraordinary meeting will be held at a Royal Peculiar.'

'A peculiar what?'

He smiled. Bleedin' superior again, he was now.

'It is a term applied to a church or chapel that lies within the direct jurisdiction of the monarch rather than a bishop or diocese. It is an ancient term, but these anomalies persist. On Thursday next I am aware that the Queen will attend a private function at one of the Royal Peculiars within the city. The purpose of that meeting was not stated in any papers I have seen. I will need to make further enquiries. It is most odd.'

Of an instant, there was a rustle from the corner.

'*Odd, odd, odd. Sweeney Todd. Sod.*'

Jacobin let off a stream of ripe obscenities and then he began to sing in a man's rough voice. It was another old song from the halls. As I recall, it had a crude chorus. I flicked a look at Vellum, who was staring at Jacobin. It was plain he didn't like what he saw, and I don't imagine he thought too highly of what he was hearing neither.

Sweeney Todd was a thieving sod, but his pies were good and hot.
His meat was lean and the trade was keen – each day he sold the lot.
Then one night a maid took fright, when she bit down on her pie,
For looking out, right beneath her snout was half a bloody eye.

Jacobin stopped and studied us for a moment, before launching into the chorus.

> *It could have been worse, it could have been worse,*
> > *good people don't you mock.*
> *Imagine the fright of the maid that night if she'd taken*
> > *a mouthful of c—*

'Enough!' I stood up abrupt and clapped my hands three times. Jacobin stopped singing, which was something. If I remembered the rest of the song rightly, it didn't get any daintier. The parrot stared at me, black eyes defiant and spiteful. Then he leapt to the bars. The cage rocked on its stand as he attacked the metal with his claws and beak. Lok sprang from the stool and tried to calm him. Humming that gentle old melody I'd heard before, he stretched out a tiny hand to strum along the bars. He yelped and pulled back, a dark smear of blood on his fingers.

Satisfied to be the centre of attention, Jacobin stretched out his wings, held his head to the side and watched us all through one yellow-rimmed eye. He arched his scruffy neck, opened his black beak and swore again. Lok showed his hand to his brother and then he spat on the wound and rubbed at the torn flesh.

Vellum brushed his sleeve as if something noxious had attached itself to the fabric. He looked at Jacobin and then at me. 'This evening has confirmed that I do not have a taste for the entertainments offered by the halls. You will await my message, Miss Peck.'

'Sounds like I don't have a choice, do I?'

'We all have choices. It is important to make the right one.' Vellum took a last look at his pale, narrow face in the mirror. 'As I said, I will summon you. Be ready.' He turned to the door but now Lucca blocked the way to the hall.

'I will go with her.' He turned to appeal to me. 'You do not know this man, Fannella. Wherever he sends you, you cannot go alone.'

'Loyalty is a great virtue.' Vellum smiled thinly. 'She will be safe, Mr Fratelli, I give you my word on that. But when I send for your linnet, she must travel alone. Now, you will stand aside.'

Lucca didn't budge. Vellum went slowly towards him. When he stopped, the space between their faces was uncomfortably close. They minded me of a pair of cats marking their territory.

Lucca flinched as Vellum took in his scars in a leisurely way.

'It has been a long and tiring evening, Mr Fratelli. My man will be chilled to the core. I could call him up and offer him the opportunity to . . . warm himself at the fire, but I imagine that for him, like me, the pleasures of Limehouse have become stale. He too is loyal. If I call, he *will* come.'

After a long silence Lucca stepped aside.

Chapter Thirty-one

Grey light seeped into the parlour. If I'd slept at all, I didn't notice. I'd tossed and turned in my bed, thoughts slipping through my head like eels in a barrel, until dawn showed through the gap in the shutters. I padded softly over the boards and stood in front of Jacobin's cage.

After Vellum left, we'd sat for a while watching the fire burn low. None of us had anything to say. Lok kept rubbing and spitting on the wounds on his fingers. Occasionally he darted a look at Jacobin's cage, the expression on his face lodged somewhere between hurt and disbelief. I don't reckon that bird had ever caught him before.

In the end, Tan Seng threw the broidered cloth over the cage. He muttered something to his brother and the pair of them nodded to me before slipping down to the basement. Lucca went a little while after. I caught his sleeve, thinking to thank him for making a stand, but I couldn't find the right words. I let go and he didn't look back as he left the room. I went to my own bed a little while after.

The parlour was silent and shadowed in the early light. If Jacobin knew I was standing there, he didn't let on. I reached up to drag the cover from the cage. The parrot kept his scraggy grey back to me. I might have thought him to be asleep if it wasn't for the way his claws tightened on the wooden bar of the dandling swing. A cuttlebone savaged by his beak lay beneath him. I covered my nose at the stink of bird shit and rotten fish and carefully turned the cage about, so he was facing me.

Black eyes locked on mine.

Jacobin lives.

That's what Kite had said to his brother. Why would he be concerned with the life of a mangy old parrot?

The crude song Jacobin had rattled out last evening was an old one. The story of Sweeney Todd and his pies filled with human flesh was popular in the halls years back. It must have been packed away in the bird's little grey head going on forty years. I wondered who he'd heard it from. It wasn't Lady Ginger this time. The voice had belonged to a man, and if I knew anything about that bleedin' parrot, I reckoned it was a fair impression of the singer.

Joey said Jacobin was Kite's gift to Ma and, from under that bed at the Angevin club, I'd heard Denderholm say much the same. But it wasn't Kite's voice I'd heard.

I thought I might try something to jog his memory.

'Eliza.' I whispered Ma's name through the bars. Jacobin's head jerked up. He turned to fix me with a single eye, rolled his head and opened his beak. A small grey tongue wriggled like a worm.

'Pretty girl. Pretty girl.'

The truce didn't last long. In less than a blink he flung himself at the bars, claws and beak straining for my face. I was too quick for him, stepping back before he could catch me. The parrot's fury was like a caged thundercloud. He squawked and scrabbled at the metal, all the while beating his raggy wings against the confines of the space. Peggy was right. It was a horrible thing to see. Even Jacobin, vicious as he was, didn't deserve to suffer like that.

I remembered the song that Lok and Tan Seng used to calm

him and started to hum. As I reached the chorus, Jacobin dropped to the floor of the cage next to the cuttlebone and arranged himself back into the shape of a bird. At the same moment, something fluttered in my mind. There was something about this tune I was missing.

I carried on humming and after a moment or two, eyes closed now, he began to sway in time. He started to sing along – it was a man's voice again – but the words didn't belong to the tune. Jacobin wasn't crooning about first love or second thoughts. I couldn't make head nor tail of it. The words fitted the melody perfectly, but they were meaningless.

Lucius Magg, clocksmith, appointed to serve the Crown.
True to the last as brother and master he rests in great renown.
A pious life, a grieving wife, these he has left on earth.
Beneath this stone, along with bone, is the total of his worth.
A rose, a lion, a crown, a star, compass his remains.
For Lucius Magg is free at last from the mortal house of chains.

I kept on humming and Jacobin sang the nonsense verse through three times before hopping up to his perch and turning his back on me. I stared at the raw, bald patch in his feathers.

House of chains . . . He'd said that before, hadn't he?

I closed my eyes and chased the parrot's words through the maze in my head.

House of chains. Chains . . . chains?

I opened my eyes as I finally caught up with it.

Not that it did much good. On account of the sudden knocking and thumping from downstairs, I didn't have a chance to turn it about to face me.

'If Fitzy's sent you to change my mind about Madame Toth-Varda, you've had a wasted journey.'

'It's not that, Ma'am. Indeed, it is not.' Aubrey Jesmond caught one of the double doors leading into the hallway and grappled with it. A gust snatched the rim of his bowler and sent it tumbling across the tiles. I went to fetch it.

'As a matter of fact, I very much agreed with you last night. There was something . . . *nasty* about that woman. I was in the office with her for near an hour before you came. Most of the time she didn't say a word, she just sat there with her eyes closed. I thought she was asleep, but . . .'

He swallowed and fluttered a small fat-fingered hand to his forehead to hook back a strand of oily hair come loose. I helped him to close the door. Dirt and leaves were scuffling in from the lane. I handed the bowler back to him.

'Did she . . . speak to you too?'

Jesmond nodded. 'Well, not her, exactly. It was my grandfather's voice I heard, see. Now, he was a violent man both in his words and in his deeds. And last night he . . . he wasn't peaceful. If I didn't know better, I'd say what she did wasn't an act at all. But in that case . . .'

He stared at his shiny black shoes and shook his head as if to clear out the alarming possibility that Madame Toth-Varda had brought his raging grandfather back from the dead.

'I don't know how she did it, Ma'am. But if you want the truth, I'd rather she didn't do it again. No matter what Fitzy says on the matter.' He looked up. 'He's not happy you sent her away. After he packed her off in a cab last night, he was quite . . . put out. You ought to know that he said some things about you that don't bear repetition.'

I pulled my wrapper close. Jessie had come early to The Palace to spread tittle-tattle, and I wasn't even dressed. The place was unusually quiet this morning. I was surprised that Tan Seng hadn't opened the door when Jesmond knocked.

I scratched the back of my neck where the short hair bristled at the skin.

Jesmond cleared his throat. 'All I'll say on the matter is that Fitzy is not a gentleman.'

I almost laughed out loud. 'I don't need the services of Madame Toth-Varda to know that, Jesmond. And don't worry – I heard his thoughts on the matter clear enough when I left The Comet last night. Is that it then? Is that why you came this morning?'

He shook his head. My neck prickled again. Without hair to cover my shoulders, I felt the chill in the air. I pulled the cords of the wrapper tight. It came to me that there might have been another cruelty connected with the halls.

'What is it now, Jessie?'

He stashed his bowler under an arm and delved into a pocket. 'I came about this, Ma'am. I found it in the early hours when I got back from The Comet. Every house on Spread Eagle Street had one. If they couldn't get it through the door, they'd left it on the steps under a stone or poked it through a crack in the brickwork. It was the same for all the streets nearby and probably further. I cleared as many as I could, but there must be hundreds of them all over Limehouse. Take a look.'

He handed me a folded yellow sheet.

A CALL to the CHILDREN OF PURITY

**Will YOU stand at the side of the
Reverend WILLIAM AUCHLYNE-DOUNE in the CRUSADE
against the MENACE OF THE MUSIC HALLS?
BROTHERS and SISTERS, take up your ARMS and JOIN
the BATTLE against all that is CORRUPT and FOUL.
The HOUR IS NIGH. Even now, the FORCES of the JUST and
the RIGHTEOUS gather to do HIS WILL.
TONIGHT let us LIGHT A LAMP in LIMEHOUSE that will
never be extinguished.
Cotton Street Seamen's Rest, six o'clock.
Refreshments will be supplied.**

I heard the Reverend's voice rise from the paper.

HIS WILL ? I reckoned he wasn't referring to God there.

Jesmond sucked at his borrowed teeth. There was a wet sound as they shifted on his gums. 'I thought I should bring it to your attention. I know there's been other meetings and such like, but this one seems quite specific. It sounds . . .' He blinked.

It sounds like trouble, I thought. As if I didn't have enough of that on my plate.

He pattered on. 'It sounds like something you ought to be aware of, Ma'am. Some of the words there are fighting talk. It can't be good for us, not with The Comet about to open and all.'

I couldn't argue with him on that. I scanned the paper again and frowned.

'I thought the mission on Cotton Street closed two years back?'

Jesmond nodded. 'It's been shut and boarded ever since. But it's no distance from The Comet and that's what worries me.'

He was right about that too.

'I'll keep this.' I stuffed the paper into the pocket of my wrapper. 'Thank you for bringing it to me.'

Jesmond shrugged. 'I thought you should know, Ma'am. Now, I'd best be off. The carpenters are coming in to finish the work in the lower balcony. They like to start early.'

He put his bowler back on and turned to the door. As he opened up, a rare shaft of sunlight streaked across the chequered tiles.

'Jesmond,' I called as he stepped out. He waited, one hand tugging at the ring of the knocker to keep the door steady in the wind.

'Your way takes you past Dismal's lodgings?'

He nodded.

'Tell him there's a sovereign from me if he doesn't touch a drop today. And tell him if he wants to collect it, he can meet me this evening at The Saracen on the corner of Arthur Street at quarter to six sharp.'

*

I sat on the stairs to read the paper again. The Reverend's liberal use of the capital letter was a war cry. The thought of standing there in the Seamen's Rest while he whipped the rabble to a pitch where he could set them off to do Christ knows what in HIS name made my belly shrivel. But I had to go, and if Sam was right about Auchlyne-Doune and Billy Downie from the Glasgow halls, I had to take Dismal Jimmy along with me.

I wished I could get a message to Sam too. Wherever he was.

The sunlight from the fan over the door slanted to the foot of the stairs. Just next to the post, one of the narrow ribbons Lok used to tie the end of his plait curled on a square of black marble. I wouldn't have noticed it if it hadn't been for the red.

I picked it up and rolled it between my fingers. It was clear that Tan Seng and Lok knew a lot more about the past than they'd ever said. Every time I tried to ask them about it, they avoided the question or simply ran away. Ran away from me, to be more exact. Last night when we'd sat in the parlour with Vellum, I'd caught the pair of them throwing faces at each other when they didn't think I was looking.

I twisted the ribbon until it was coiled into a tiny ball and stood up. A conversation about the past with Tan Seng and Lok was long overdue . . . whether they wanted it or not.

The door to the rooms in the basement that the brothers had made their own was shut. The smell of smoke, spices, clean laundry and coal filled the little square space at the bottom of the steps. I wondered whether to knock or just walk in.

The matter was decided for me.

'Lady?' Tan Seng opened the door to a crack and peered at me. It was uncanny the way he always knew where I was. I didn't know what to say. This was their domain. I was an intruder down here. I held out my hand, the ribbon in my palm.

'I found this. It's Lok's.'

Tan Seng opened the door a little wider, took it from me and bowed.

'He went early to the market, Lady. I will give it to him when he returns.'

Before he could shut the door again, which I could see he was itching to do, I put my hand to the lintel. If he closed it now he'd crush my fingers. His eyes slid to my hand and then to my face.

'Lady?'

I took a deep breath. 'I want to talk to you, Tan Seng – about the past.'

It was as if I'd thrown a pot of scalding fat into his face. He shut his eyes and screwed his features tight against me. If he stood there long enough like that, I imagine he thought I'd disappear. I moved my hand to his arm.

'Please.'

He thought to take advantage of the movement and tried to slam the door, but I'd been too quick for him. My leg was wedged in the gap now.

'I'm not going until we talk.' I pushed at the door, but he fought back. It was the first time either of the brothers had refused me. We tussled in the small lobby at the foot of the stairs, each trying to gain the upper hand. Tan Seng was old but I knew he had the strength of ten men half his age. It was hopeless. I stood back and the door slammed shut. I stared at the blind knots in the wood.

'Why won't you talk to me, Tan Seng?' I thumped on the door and called out. 'Don't you think I have a right? I just want to know about my mother . . . and my father.'

I didn't know that was what I wanted until I spoke that last word aloud. I could hardly get it out. It lodged tight in my throat, choking me. I stood for a moment more, staring at the door and then I crumpled to a heap against the wall at the foot of the stairs. Tears that I'd fought so hard to keep back rolled down my cheeks. I hid my face in my hands and tried to muffle the sound of my sobbing.

I heard a click.

'Lady.'

I swiped at my eyes and looked up. Tan Seng bowed and gestured towards the wide-open door behind him.

'I will make tea.'

*

I rarely came down to the basement. It was the brothers' home and I respected that. I sat at the long deal table watched by half a dozen versions of myself reflected in the copper pots and pans hung along the wall. Pressed white sheets were draped on a rail suspended from the ceiling, the corners folded to perfect squares. A bowl of vegetables stood next to the stone basin under the window. Tan Seng had clearly been peeling and chopping when I stood outside in the lobby. Half a potato sat on a board by the bowl. The knife had been placed carefully next to it. Both the blade and the pale slices of potato gleamed in the light streaming through clean glass panes.

The stones beneath my bare feet were cold. I hooked my toes over the bottom rung of the chair and watched Tan Seng work at the range. His movements were precise, elegant you might say, as he went about making the tea. The grey silk tunic that reached to his knees was crisp and the loose black breeches that folded over his leather slippers were unmarked by dust or grease. Everything was neat and clean. Everything had a place. Everything down here was exactly as it should be.

He turned from the range and brought a steaming pot to the

scrubbed table. Then he went to the dresser against the back wall and studied the china ranged along the shelves. He took his time, but at last he picked out two small blue and white bowls and set them between us. We sat in silence, waiting for the leaves in the pot to stew. Tan Seng twisted the bowl in front of him, examining the pattern on the china.

He looked up. As a rule, it was difficult to read his round face. It wasn't lined like Lok's, but even though his skin was smooth, it had the look of something softened by years of use. Today I saw sadness in eyes as black as the tea he poured into my bowl.

He lifted his own bowl and held it to the light from the window. 'This pattern tells an old story, Lady.'

I waited, cupping my hands around the steaming bowl in front of me.

Tan Seng cleared his throat. 'Many years ago, a woman gave birth to a daughter. As was the custom of the time, the daughter was sent away to be raised by a servant in a distant village, but when she came of age she was brought to the city to live with her mother. By this time, the mother had become very rich. She was proud, powerful and feared by many, but she found that she loved this child, more than she thought possible, and could deny her nothing. The girl was her only weakness.'

He paused, placed the bowl on the table and poured tea into it. I didn't make a sound. I didn't even breathe for fear of stopping him.

'The city was very different to the country. The girl soon had many suitors, but she was young and she was foolish, not used to such attention. She did not yet know that promises, even the most binding and serious ones, are made to be broken.' He tapped a long nail on the table top. 'There came a time when the rich woman was tricked by a . . . young magician who envied her power and wealth. She found that she owed a great deal of money to this man and to his brothers. The magician had admired the woman's daughter for a long time. He had spoken of love and given her many gifts. He told the woman that if she allowed him to marry her daughter, he would make her debts vanish.'

I thought I might know this tale. It wasn't a pattern on a bowl. I'd heard something very like it from Joey when I went to the Bethlem. I sat completely still as Tan Seng stared into his tea. Truly, it was the most I'd ever heard him say in perfect London English in one go.

He turned the bowl between long narrow fingers. 'The woman accepted the magician's offer, but when she told her daughter that she was to be married, the girl said it was impossible. She was already married, and she was with child.'

Tan Seng glanced up. His eyes met mine before he returned his gaze to the bowl.

'The magician was furious; he swore vengeance on the woman and her child. To protect her, the woman sent her daughter to the country again with her old serving woman, and the child was born in safety. The only other person who knew the secret of their hiding place was the girl's husband. When he could, he visited his wife and, in time, his son. For a while they were happy.'

He fell silent. I waited for him to finish, but he didn't make a sound. I sat there willing him to carry on, but he didn't even look up from the bowl.

'Then what?' I couldn't help myself. 'They were happy, you said, but what happened next?'

He shook his head; a small, quick movement.

'You can't stop there. What about the girl's husband? What happened to him?'

Tan Seng raised his eyes from the bowl. Along with the sadness, I caught something else there – fear. He looked away sharp. I put my hand on his.

'Finish the story, please.' He didn't move. We sat still and quiet for a long time, but eventually he nodded to himself as if he'd made up his mind about something. When he started the story again, it came as a whisper.

'The girl found that she was to have a second child. When she told her husband, he left the secret place and never returned. He had grown tired of the country, of his young wife and of his infant son. He was too young, he said. He was not ready to be a man of responsibility. He had made a mistake.'

Tan Seng's eyes flicked warily from the door to the window. He was speaking so softly now, I had to lean across the table to hear him.

'But it was too late. The marriage had taken place in the proper way and there were witnesses. The girl's mother reminded him of his duty, but he ignored her. A few weeks later the jealous magician discovered where the girl was hiding. He sent men to take her from her place of safety and he . . . punished her. The rich woman always believed that her faithless son-in-law had betrayed her daughter, his own wife, as a warning.'

He took up his bowl and drained the contents in four large gulps.

367

'As a warning against what?' I shifted on the chair.

'As a warning never to speak of the marriage.' Tan Seng turned the side of his bowl to face me. A painted hare leapt over something that resembled a small house with a gnarled tree growing at one side. A pair of dark butterflies fluttered overhead and a small winged insect rolled a tiny blue ball away from the scene around to the other side of the bowl. Above it all a crescent moon sailed on a coiling wisp of cloud. Next to it there was a star.

'Anyone who knew of the marriage was turned into a night creature, to remind them of the darkness of the grave.'

Tan Seng stood and bowed. 'That is the story painted on the bowl, Lady.'

He went back to the vegetables on the side. I heard the sound of the knife slice through the potato.

'Is that it?' I stared at his grey back outlined against the stark light of the window. He reached for another potato. The chopping sound came again.

'The tale you just told me. It was my mother, wasn't it? And Lady Ginger too, and Lord Kite and . . .' I tried to sort it together. 'Who was she married to, Tan Seng? My mother, I mean?'

He carried on chopping. Light glanced off the blade and shimmered on the wall as he worked.

'What about the night animals, what do they have to do with it?'

He turned. I couldn't see his face for the brilliance streaming through the panes behind him.

'It is an old legend from the land of my childhood, Lady, nothing more.'

He went back to the potatoes, pausing only at the thump of the door as Lok came in through the back entrance from the yard. He froze when he saw me at the table. At the sound of the knife he swivelled about on the stones to stare at his brother's back. He clipped out something sharp and fast.

Tan Seng paused for a moment. 'The Lady wanted tea, and now she goes.'

Chapter Thirty-two

Dismal Jimmy – James McKinnon to give him the dignity of his real name, which no one ever did – was waiting for us outside The Saracen. The promise of early sun had faded to something closer to the threat of rain and there was a bite to the air. I was glad to see him muffled against the chill. His long coat, woollen cap and scarf went some way to disguise his more notable features. Dismal had hair as red as a cardinal's cape and a prominent nose to match.

I'd pulled the veil of my hat to cover my face again and my drab street coat, much like a thousand others worn by London women, was buttoned high at the neck. Lucca's broad-brimmed hat and the scarf wound several times over his shoulders covered most of his face as usual. We couldn't be recognised.

I waved at Dismal and crossed the road to join him.

'Ma'am.' He tugged at his cap. There was a time when he would have called me Kit, but I was 'Ma'am' to them all now. My grandmother had seen to that. He glanced hopefully at the smoked glass door to The Saracen.

'I haven't taken a dram, just as you asked.' His Glasgow growl was cracked by years of whisky, smoke and bawling out to the hall.

'Good.' I patted my bag. 'I know it must have cost you, Dismal, and I'm grateful. Like I said, there's a sovereign in it.'

He scraped at the side of his face. His ruddy skin was pitted and freckled, but underneath it all you could just make out the handsome lad he must have been once. Dismal was a tall, big-boned, broad-shouldered man and the coat covered the low-slung paunch that had grown with his appetite for liquor. His bulk was an asset on nights when sailors put into the halls with stale time on their hands and fresh coin in their pockets.

He shuffled aside as the door behind him swung open. The fug of the tavern roiled into the street. 'I know what this is about, Ma'am.'

I nodded. No doubt Jesmond had told him about the meeting at the Seamen's Rest four streets down.

He scratched again. 'She's gone off before, but only for a night.'

I quizzed at him through the net.

'It's nearly three days now. Bella reckons she'll come back when she's ready. Thing is, Ma'am, I don't know why she'd go. We haven't rowed in weeks.'

I looked at Lucca, but it was plain he didn't have an idea what Dismal was talking about.

'I don't want you to think badly of me, Ma'am. I've never laid a hand on Marnie, not even when I've been . . .' He jerked his head at the door to The Saracen.

Marnie?

I knew the pair of them was a couple. Marnie Trinder was a bit older than most of the girls working at The Carnival, but she was a looker in her way, and sensible too. We all knew she kept Dismal on a long leash. They didn't live together as such, but their lodgings were two doors apart on Emmett Street, near West India Docks. Marnie shared a landing with big Bella Cundle, whose prime talents could poke your eyes out.

I patted his arm. 'You need to start at the beginning. What's happened to Marnie?'

'Well, that's the question, isn't it? She's gone, but she hasn't taken anything with her. I went to her room this morning with Bella – she's got a spare key. Everything was in its place as usual – Marnie likes to keep things tidy – but . . .' Dismal shook his head. 'Bella hasn't been there for a couple of nights. She's got a new man – a baker over in Poplar – so she hasn't seen Marnie coming and going. She reckons it's nothing, but I'm grateful you've taken an interest, Ma'am.'

He was wrong about that. Marnie Trinder wasn't the reason I was here. All the same, I could see he was worried. I knew she had a mother and grandmother still living; perhaps one of them had been took ill? I stepped into the gutter to let a man enter The Saracen. As the door opened another blast of smoke and liquor made Dismal's nose twitch. He turned to stare longingly into the pub.

I pulled at his sleeve. 'Marnie's got family in Barnet, hasn't she? Perhaps she got called away? It's only been a couple of days, and like you say, she's been gone before. Why are you worried about her?'

'Because of the blood.'

My spine prickled as Dismal went on. 'There was a handprint on the wall just by the door. The light's not good there, but I swear it was blood.'

I felt Lucca's hand on my shoulder. 'Fannella?'

I heard what happened to old Marcelli and Chibbles' dog Spark in his question.

The gaslight over the entrance to The Saracen fizzled into life. The flame bobbed and flickered behind the smeary glass panes, casting a pool of piss-coloured light down the soot-crusted bricks and into the gutter where we stood. It was almost six.

I looked away from Dismal's worried watery green eyes. I opened my bag, took out my purse and pressed the sovereign into his hand.

'I'm sure Marnie's fine.'

I wasn't, but there wasn't time just now to go haring off to Emmett Street. I felt guilty about that coin. It came to me that if something had happened to Marnie Trinder, there weren't enough sovereigns in the world to pay her man for his time tonight.

The wind gathered a handful of dust from the gutter and hurled it at my coat. 'If she's not back tomorrow, we'll have a think about what to do. Thing is, Dismal, I didn't come here about Marnie, I came about this. I want you to come to the Seamen's Rest with me and Lucca.'

I took the sheet Jesmond had found from my bag and handed it to him. He frowned as he read it to the end.

'Why?' He looked up.

'Because I think there might be someone there you'll recognise.'

*

The Cotton Street Seamen's Rest reeked of damp and dead mouse. There was a faint suggestion of old cabbage in the air too, a remnant from the days when bowls of stewed charity were ladled out for the destitute. Poor sods. You'd have to be desperate to get that down.

Most of the windows high along the wall were still boarded over. The ones that weren't were clouded with dirt and shrouded in cobwebs. Just below the arched ceiling, a gallery ran around three of the walls. The rail was broken in places and even from the door you could see where the boards were missing.

A dozen oil lamps flickered along the walls on each side. More lanterns burned along the front of a platform at the far end. The light quivered on the folds of a brown, moth-eaten curtain suspended from the gallery.

Despite the threadbare surroundings, the Reverend's call had attracted another sizeable audience. If anything, there were more people here tonight than at the Martingate Mission. The rows of seats near the platform were already full. Rather than sitting further back, some people were standing at the sides near the front to get a clear view.

The air was thick with old soup and expectation.

The three of us queued at the back of the hall, waiting to sign the ledger guarded by the Reverend's daughter. As we shuffled forward I studied her through the gaps between people's backs.

Just as last time she was dressed in grey and black. Her plain blouse was buttoned high at the neck and her thin, dun-coloured hair was plaited and wound into a knot. The 'voluntary' donation box was larger now and set more prominent on the desk beside her. I watched her blue eyes flick to it occasionally, calculating the value of the coins the punters posted through the slot. As she turned to a new page in the ledger, I caught a glimpse of that mourning ribbon tied around her wrist.

Miss Auchlyne-Doune had been at The Hope that evening. I was certain of it. Even though I hadn't seen her face, I'd dialled the ribbon and heard that voice . . .

A tuth for a tuth.

It seemed odd that such a soft-spoken woman should revel in violence. I watched her sitting there, prim-faced, straight-backed, all meekness and piety as she sheared her father's flock. I remembered the account of the trial Sam had found in *The Edinburgh Evening Courant*. Billy Downie's daughter had acted modest in court – people had admired her for it – but she spat like a hellcat when her father went down.

We got to the desk and Dismal signed first, bending low to scratch a name in the ledger. The girl patted the donation box. 'We do not ask for money, but the work of the Lord is costly. You will find refreshments at the table on the left.' She pointed to a trestle set along the wall. The Lord had been busy buttering bread.

Dismal glanced at me, wondering whether to dig for a penny. I shook my head. I didn't see why he should pay. The girl saw his question and turned her attention to me and then to Lucca. Her pale eyes sharpened. I saw her hand resting on the ledger tighten to a bony fist.

'We've met before, I think? When my father preached in Whitechapel?'

She smiled, but it didn't come natural. It was like she was trying it out for size.

'In Raven Street.' I nodded. 'We were . . . impressed.' I indicated Lucca. 'My brother thought we should come again and we brought a friend.' I pointed at Dismal, who was over at the trestle filling his pockets. Marnie's disappearance hadn't gone to his stomach then.

'You've moved east.' I looked up at the boarded windows. 'This place is . . . much plainer than the mission.'

The girl stared at us both. 'The word of God does not need a fine setting. The word is more precious than gold and shines in the darkness. My father answers the call of the Lord. He has summoned him to this place of need and in good time. Do you not see . . .?' She gestured at the people filling the hall. 'The Children of Purity rise. Your names, please.' She pushed the ledger across the desk and we bent to sign ourselves as 'Smith'.

As we walked to take seats near the back of the hall, I felt her eyes on me.

Dismal leaned across Lucca, who sat between us. 'It's the Reverend you're interested in, am I right?'

I hadn't told him about Billy Downie. I thought it best to let him make up his own mind. I sat back as a woman with a chin like a mason's mallet squeezed along the row to one of the last remaining seats. Once she settled herself I bent forward again to answer him.

'That's right. We're here to see the Reverend Auchlyne-Doune. If you recognise him, let me know. Do this as a sign.' I clasped my hands together and rested them on my knees. 'Make sure you stretch out so I can see.'

Dismal nodded. He reached into a pocket for a slice of bread, sat back and stared at the stage, his big jaw working at the Lord's generosity.

We sat there for a few minutes more before the organ started. It was so soft at first that it went unnoticed under the hubbub. As it gained in force and dignity the talking gradually stopped. By the time it was thumping out an anthem that could rip the ears from your head, I felt someone swish past me.

I turned to watch the girl snuff out the oil lamps along the side, one by one. She kept the cash box clamped under an arm as she went from bracket to bracket.

The last of the lamps along the wall hissed and died. The only light now came from the candle lanterns along the edge of the platform. The girl's shadow passed in front of the curtain. A moment later that bleedin' organ racket stopped.

The hall was completely silent. If you could bottle anticipation and sell it by the ounce, this was the place to trap it.

The ragged curtain trembled and then it parted in a series of jerks.

Auchlyne-Doune stood at the back of the platform. He was turned away from the punters, shaggy grey hair falling to his shoulders. He rolled his head from side to side and a great ripple went across his broad back. I was minded of a knuckler preparing for the ring.

He stretched his arms out to his sides and his huge crucified shadow filled the brick wall. A murmur rippled through the hall. Keeping his arms out straight, he turned and advanced slowly to the lights. His eyes shone and his teeth gleamed through the bristling bush of his beard. He brought his arms together like he was gathering us all to his heart.

'Brothers and sisters, I bid you welcome. Welcome, Children of Purity.'

Dismal leaned forward in his seat, hands clasped firmly on his knees.

*

'. . . And the breath of Satan himself will pour forth onto your streets. It will caress your soft and innocent flesh. It will fill your mind with thoughts of carnal pleasure. It will intoxicate you, feeding the flames of unspoken desires until you are powerless to resist in mind and body.'

He gave that last word, especially the 'O', a quivering relish.

377

From the corner of my eye I saw the woman with the chin sit forward and fan herself. Billy Downie's performance was going down like a roast beef dinner in a workhouse. By listing the vices available in the halls, he was allowing the punters to dwell on them in some detail and perhaps think about having a go.

He'd been at it for at least twenty minutes now. One woman had fainted. She'd been carried out on her chair. Billy's voice had a rare quality, I'll give him that. One moment you could almost feel it somewhere deep inside your head, planting ideas and opening windows to glimpses of things you wouldn't mind taking a closer look at. Next, it felt like it was dragging you out of your seat, pulling you towards him like a fish on a line. Of occasion I had to fight against the influence.

I looked direct at the stage again. Billy was holding his big hands together in prayer.

'The Devil will tempt you with earthly delight to lead you to Hell. You will taste the fruit of temptation and feel the rapture of his embrace. Do not be deceived. When the jaws open they will devour all that is righteous and spew forth a stream of iniquity and corruption.'

He paused, allowing the candlelight to strike sparks in his eyes.

'Will you be ready?' He whispered and took one step forward. 'I ask again, will you be ready when Satan's maw opens?' It was still a whisper, but delivered with such a practised skill that everyone in the hall heard it.

A man two rows ahead stood up. 'I'm ready now.' He turned to the punters, eyes alight with piety and zeal. 'We all know where the good Reverend means, don't we? I don't want that filth on my doorstep. Burn it, that's what I say. Burn The Comet to the ground before it opens again.'

All around me, people leapt to their feet. At first their howls and yells were a formless thunder of anger, but gradually the sound gathered a rhythm and a focus.

'Burn it! Burn it! Burn it!'

Lucca gripped my hand. Dismal pulled his cap down low and shot a look at me. He rolled his eyes to the door.

'Burn it!'

They were stamping in time with the words now. I looked to the platform. Billy was over to one side, talking to someone hidden behind the curtain. He snatched a look at the hall, turned back and shook his head. I caught a glimpse of a stringy hand jabbing at him from the other side of the moth-eaten fabric.

He came to the centre of the stage again, holding his broad palms out flat as if to push back the noise.

'Children,' he called above the chanting. 'Children, hear me.'

The punters came to a ragged halt. They shuffled on the boards, hungry for a sign.

Billy shook out his mane, produced a 'kerchief the size of a flag and dabbed at his eyes. He was turning on the taps again. Smiling, he allowed his glassy eyes to sweep the rows. He took his time about it. I swear every person there felt the individual force of his gaze.

At last he gave a great sigh.

'I am humbled. Humbled by your love for the Lord who guides us in all things. But tonight He has spoken to me and I must ask you to listen . . .'

As it turned out, the Lord reckoned he wasn't quite ready for the Children of Purity to burn down The Comet, although it was clearly on his list of things to get round to.

Billy was wily. He calmed them down and smoothed the angles off their passion, mindful, I reckoned, that the last thing he needed was to be responsible for loosing a mob on the streets of Limehouse.

He gave a long speech about the natural abundance of God's good fruit in the Garden of Eden, before Adam and Eve – especially Eve – gave in to temptation. Everything in the garden was just as it should be before she persuaded him to eat that apple.

In Billy's account, which included a lot about the pair of them frolicking through fields clothed in nothing more than innocence, Eve came over as quite the villain of the piece. She was an actress, masking her true sinful nature in a way calculated to lead poor Adam astray. I got the impression that it wasn't Eve he was talking about.

Billy ended up with a homily on harvest and the importance of picking your time with care. Ripeness was all, was the gist of it. Without actually saying as much, he sinuated that the best way to damage The Comet was to wait until it was on the point of actually opening its doors again.

At the end, the punters were docile as lambs. Something in his voice had soothed them, replacing their anger with drowsy satisfaction.

*

We stood at the back of the queue for the door, watching them file out to the street. Some yawned and rubbed at their eyes. Not a quarter of an hour earlier they'd been an army bent on destruction; now they were ready for their beds. The only light came from a single oil lamp on the table by the door. Billy's daughter stood behind the table, smiling and nodding occasionally if a punter passed a comment on the evening.

As we shuffled forward, I nudged Dismal's arm and spoke low. 'You knew him then?'

'Straight off, Ma'am.' He snorted. 'But he wasn't a man of the cloth back then. He was a devil for money and skirt. The last I heard of Billy Downie was that he was in the Bridewell. And that was no great surprise.'

I was glad to hear Dismal give the Reverend his real name without me putting it in his head.

'You're sure that was him?' I glanced at Lucca, but he'd turned to look back. He was interested in something up on the platform.

Dismal nodded. 'I'd know him anywhere. The act's the same. He's serving the same dish with a different spice. He was a clever one, that Billy. He could make the punters do exactly what he wanted. That was his undoing, in the end.' He frowned and shook his head. 'So, he's taken against the halls then? That's not good, Ma'am.' He cleared his throat. 'I reckon I need a dram, after that.'

There was a great thump from behind the brown curtain. The sound was followed by a yell. Immediately Billy's daughter abandoned her place at the door and rushed to the platform. She climbed up the rotten steps at the side and disappeared behind the dingy material. I could see a thin line of light beneath the ragged edge.

'Fannella?' Lucca pointed to the platform. 'It is as before?'

Apart from a man leaning on a stick and a couple of old women shuffling along arm in arm, we were the last punters in the hall. No one would notice if we stayed a little longer.

I nodded, turned and made my way quietly to the platform. Lucca and Dismal followed.

Someone was singing up there. It was a sweet, simple tune in a language I didn't understand. The girl – it must have been her – had a fine voice. Boards creaked in time to the song as if she was dancing or swaying. There was another sound too, a gulping snuffling broken occasionally by a yelp or muffled howl.

The girl broke off her song. 'Hush now, Donal. There's nothing to hurt you.' She started to sing again and the other noises faded. I quizzed at Lucca. He shrugged. Dismal fished in his pocket for another slice of bread.

Heavy footsteps sounded behind the curtain. The boards rumbled and the howling came again.

'You coddle him.' It was Billy who spoke now. I concentrated on his voice, trying to work out what was going on. Dismal paused, slice in hand, to listen.

'He's frightened. You didn't help this evening with your talk of hellfire and damnation.' The girl's accent came on strong when she was angry. 'He was at the side all the time. There was nowhere else for him to go because of the rain. He couldn't sit in the yard tonight. He heard it all. Hush now . . .' She tried once more to calm – Donal, was it? – who'd started to whimper again.

The sound didn't seem to bother Billy.

'It loosened their pockets. How much did we take?'

'Enough. But you went too far. We can get another night, maybe two, out of this lot before we move on. You nearly ruined it. We could have had the law breathing down our necks. You should take more care, Father.'

'Are you saying you could do better, Ishbel?' There was a dangerous tone to Billy's question as he continued. 'It seems to me that there's only one reason you're so keen to stick around here and it's hidden under your skirt, not in the cash box.' A sudden silence behind the curtain was broken by a sharp slap.

Billy growled. 'Don't you ever raise your hand to me, girl.'

The boards groaned and the curtain trembled. There was a series of tumbling thumps. Somewhere behind the moth-eaten fabric Ishbel gasped.

'You're not fit to wipe his shoes.'

'Is that a fact?' Billy's voice was coarse now; the silky tones he'd used for the punters was sandpapered down to Glasgow grit. 'Thing is, Ishbel, I reckon you'd need every trick I've taught you to get a man into your bed. You're not a woman, you're a broom handle.'

Donal started to howl like a chained dog.

'See what you've done now.' Heels tapped across the boards. 'Donny . . . listen to me, listen . . .'

Lucca grabbed my arm and hissed, 'I do not think it is safe.'

Dismal pushed the half-eaten slice of bread into his pocket. 'Lucca's right. Billy always had a violent streak.'

As if to confirm that, there was a roar and the sound of wood splitting. Someone up there had either trodden through a rotten board or ripped one up. The thought of Billy tearing back the curtain and finding us standing there wasn't appealing. I pointed back at the door where we'd come in.

We darted back through the rows of chairs. Rain slanting through the half-open door was beginning to form a dark puddle on the worm-eaten boards just inside the entrance to the Seamen's Rest. The water glinted in the light from the oil lamp. We filed outside, bending our heads into the wind. At the foot of the steps, under a painted sign that was hanging askew over the door, we paused as a howl of terror or pain, or perhaps both, came from the hall.

Now someone inside was running towards us. Their tread was heavy and uneven. A huge shape filled the doorway, but whoever it was slipped in the puddle and crumpled to their knees. I caught sight of a chalk-white face half-hidden by a hank of thick black hair. Despite the bulk, it was a boy, eyes wild with terror. He tried to scramble to his feet, but his hands flailed at his sides like he was trying to catch air. His lips twisted to the right and opened, but the only sound that came was a high-pitched keening.

'Donny!' More footsteps from the hall.

I put my finger to my lips and motioned for us to huddle in the deep shadows beyond the steps. We watched as Ishbel Downie gathered the giant boy to her breast and rocked him to and fro. After a moment she started to hum. The two of them sat there, locked together, as the rain streaked down their faces and soaked their clothes to their skin.

Chapter Thirty-three

Buckets had been set out around The Carnival to catch water dripping through holes in the roof. Rain had fallen all night. It was still hammering overhead now. I stepped over a puddle on the stage. If I were a punter, this was the last place I'd spend my shillings. Once The Comet was turning a profit I'd have to do something about the state of things here.

If I ever got the chance.

The Carnival, The Comet and the wreck of The Gaudy were the only things my grandmother had passed down to me that I cared about. Look what I'd done to them. No wonder Fitzy was boiling himself to a stew about the opening. It was all we had left to bank on.

And now I wasn't sure about that.

Neglect.

That was the word that came to mind as I looked at the shambles. The cold grey light from a fan-shaped window set high in the bricks at the back of the stage showed everything clear. Paint peeled from the walls. Damp bloomed in the corners and under the boards. The joints of the sticky tables and spindly chairs were held together with hope.

Fitzy came out of his office. He closed the door, folded his arms and waited. His pockmarked face was a study in surly exasperation. Jesmond stood two yards distant from him, examining the crown of his bowler. Everyone was here now.

The last time I'd stood on this stage and talked to them all, a giant painting of me – leering, naked and pissing a stream of golden coins – had hung at my back. It was a sight I'd never forget, and I doubt there was one of them in front of me now who wasn't thinking of it. Fitzy had burned the thing. It was the first and the last time he'd shown any feelings for me.

I sidled at Lucca, who had more reason than most to remember it. He was staring at his hands clasped tight in front of him.

I pushed the thought of that crude painting away and took a breath.

'Thank you all for coming this morning. I'm grateful.'

None of them looked at me direct. They leaned against the scuffed brown walls or slumped at the tables, careful not to dignify me with their consideration. If they were curious as to why I'd asked them in, they took care not to show it. Only Lucca, Dismal, Fitzy and Jesmond knew why I'd called a gathering.

I glanced over at Professor Ruben and the orchestra boys. It cut me to see the way they studied the puddles at their feet. The girls from the chorus whispered together. A quivering knot of feathers and frills, they switched between pouting at the hands from the workshop and darting eyes sharp as broken glass in my direction.

Mr Chibbles' dogs, just the five of them now, lay at his feet. Occasionally Bertie fished into a pocket and offered them titbits of rind to keep them quiet. Barney Knuckles yawned and studied the pages of the *Sporting Life*. He was a fiend for the horses. The Brothers Cherubimo sat at a table near the stage, flicking broads at each other. This morning their muscular acrobat bodies were hidden beneath identical coats that made them seem lumpy and old.

There was a stale frowse in the hall, which wasn't entirely

due to the damp, the smoke and the alcohol. It was just as Fitzy said. They'd had enough of me.

I started again. 'First off, I owe you all. Without you . . .' Drops of water pattered on my bonnet from one of the holes in the roof. I looked up. The rain came through a square of grey-green sky high above me. The roll of canvas that had been tacked across to keep it watertight had come loose. Grey fabric swayed between the wooden rafters. Water spattered on my face.

I swiped it away and carried on. 'Without you, this place would be nothing.'

A man's voice came from the back of the hall. 'That'd be a step up then?'

People laughed.

'Listen.' I shouted to make myself heard. 'Mr Jesmond's done a fine job. The Comet is a hundred times better than it ever was. When we open and the money comes rolling in, I'll use the profit to make The Carnival somewhere you'll be proud to work in too. And in time, I'll do the same for The Gaudy. It'll be like the old days – you'll have three halls to fill. You'll always have work here in Limehouse, I promise you.'

'Fine words, Kit, but we've heard it from you before.' One of the hands dropped a smoke to the boards and ground it under his boot. The atmosphere was hard as flint and ready to spark. I was glad that Tan Seng had insisted that Hari should come with us. He was outside, guarding the entrance, but the thought of him being there was a comfort. I never thought I'd feel threatened by my own.

I glanced at Professor Ruben. He shook his head slowly, but at least he held my gaze. His sad eyes were full of doubt.

I swallowed. 'I've called you all here this morning because I need your help.'

'Think yourself the queen of it all, don't you?' The new voice belonged to Effie Wragg, who was somewhere between a slop girl and an extra for the chorus. She was young, dark and pretty in the way of a big-eyed cow, but her soft looks belied a sharp tongue and a fondness for rough liquor and men to match.

'This time last year you was mopping out the gallery and now you're the one giving the orders. That don't sit right with a lot of us.' She stepped out from the cluster of women and planted her hands on her rounded hips.

'We all know you've called us here to lecture us about keeping regular hours. Fitzy's made it plain that you want us to keep ourselves straight. But you can't tell us how to live our lives. You don't own us. If I want to go to The Lamb of an evening I will. I've had enough of you giving it out. I reckon we all have.' She turned to take in her audience. There was a low rumble of agreement. 'Tell you what, *Kit* . . .' She looked at me again and raised a hand. 'You can take this and shove it.'

A penny bounced onto the stage. It rolled along a board and came to a rest, Britannia side up, against the toe of my boot. There were dark spots on the wood around the hem of my skirt where the rain had fallen. Another coin landed behind me, this one thrown with more force. It was followed by another and then another. One vicious shot caught the side of my face. I clapped my hand to my cheek against the sting of it. When I looked there was blood on my fingers.

I bent my head against the sudden shower of pennies that pelted the stage from all sides. The volley came so hard it knocked my bonnet askew. Of an instant, I was aware of

388

Lucca at my side. Shielding me from the hail of tiny missiles, he turned on them all.

'*Smettete subito!* Stop! Stop this now.' He pushed me behind him and I saw pennies bounce from his shoulders to the stage. 'This is madness. There is something you should know. Something important.' He raised his hands partly to ward off the coins and partly to quiet them. 'If you think you have something to complain of now, you know nothing. Listen, please, and then make up your minds.'

The pennies stopped coming and the hall fell silent.

'You make a fine pair, Lucca Fratelli. You and Kit.' Effie came closer to the stage and stared up at my shorn hair uncovered by the slip of the bonnet. 'Christ! Look at her now.'

Her lip curled. 'Tom!' She spat the insult, turned away, swaying her hips for the benefit of the hands, and jerked her head back at me. The gesture wasn't lost on the chorus, who clucked and fretted like hens.

I ripped off my bonnet and threw it down. 'Take a good look. What of it? It's no business of yours. My hair will grow again, but I tell you this, if you don't listen to me now you won't have a decent place to work in, and I very much doubt I'll be able to bring it back.'

I gripped Lucca's hand and squeezed tight, then I released him and went to the edge. They were all looking at me now.

I ran a hand through the ragged fringe Sam had left me. 'If The Comet burns to the ground before we open again, it won't grow back on the same spot, unlike my hair. Dismal . . .' I beckoned him. 'Come up here, stand by me and tell them what we saw on Cotton Street last night.'

Dismal was one of their own. They listened, quiet as mice in the skirting, as he described the meeting in the Seamen's Rest in his rusted voice. He didn't make a show of it and he didn't make them laugh. I was grateful for the power of his words and his person.

It turned out he wasn't the only one who could've recognised Billy Downie. The Brothers Cherubimo had shared lodgings with him and his family during a season in Paisley a dozen years back. Apart from a grudging admiration for his mesmerical act, they didn't have a good word to say about him. According to them, Billy was a loud, rough-natured brute who used his wife like a boxer's bag. He didn't treat his children – a girl and a younger boy – any better. As they described him in their flat Birmingham tones (it was a good thing the admiring women in the audience never heard them speak), I thought about Ishbel and the big lad I'd seen her comfort on the steps of the Seamen's Rest.

The pair of them were likely brother and sister. It would account for her particular and unexpected softness when it came to his care. The mourning band she wore must have been in membrance for their mother. I didn't want to interrupt the brothers' reminiscence, but as I stood by listening, something Sam had said about Billy's trial came back:

. . . *Downie's wife was heard to cry out: 'What will become of the three of us now, Billy?'*

I'd taken her to mean herself and her daughter along with her husband, but it must have been poor damaged Donal she meant. I wondered how he came to be such a shambling wreck. When I thought of Billy's great hands with knuckles like pebbles, it didn't take long for me to reach a conclusion on that.

Fired by Dismal's account of the Cotton Street meeting and by the brothers' assessment of Billy's character, the mood in the hall changed. Everyone present was prepared to do their bit to protect The Comet in case Billy's torch mob came calling. I didn't flatter myself that it was me they was thinking about; it was themselves. And I didn't blame them.

Jesmond and Fitzy took the names of the willing and promised to send round a watch list by the end of the afternoon. As I looked at them all filing through the doors at the back and out onto the streets, I was almost grateful to think they'd found a new enemy.

Dismal was one of the last to leave. I'd seen him talking to a couple of the older girls who were close to Marnie. I went over and patted his arm.

'Thank you. You spoke well.' I looked over to the stage where Lucca was talking to Professor Ruben. 'If it hadn't been for the pair of you, I don't think they would have listened.'

Dismal lifted his cap to his head and screwed it down tight on his red wire hair. 'He has to be stopped, Ma'am. There was always something dangerous about him, even if things were going his way. If you ask me, Billy's taken against the halls.'

I frowned. Something rang true there. 'You mean it's a punishment for what happened?'

He nodded. 'Aye. Revenge maybe. It's something like that, I reckon – and so do the brothers. They know him for what he is. There's a madness to him. He's . . . uncanny. It's part of his power.'

'Here.' I pressed a guinea into Dismal's hand, knowing it wouldn't be long before he turned lucre into liquor. 'Any news of Marnie?'

He shook his head and turned the guinea between his fingers. 'No one's heard from her.'

'Give it another day. It must be a family matter that's called her away.' I wished I was as certain of that as I sounded.

'I hope you're right, Ma'am.' He lifted a finger to his cap and turned to the door. I watched him add his name to Jesmond's list. Fitzy clapped a hand on his back.

I went over to Lucca and the Professor.

'That was brave.' I pulled at Lucca's sleeve. 'I didn't know what to do when they started to throw them bleedin' coins at me.'

'They needed to hear you, Fannella. They still do not know the full—' He stopped himself and flicked a look at the Professor. 'We have been talking about the meetings. I told the Professor about the first evening at the Martingate Mission.'

Professor Ruben nodded. 'I had heard of this *Reverend* and his Children of Purity.' He shrugged. 'London is full of fanatics – why would one more trouble us? But Lucca described his power over the crowd and now I understand that there is truly something to fear. And the threat is so close.'

He scanned the shabby hall and clearly found it wanting. 'Tommy's lungs are weak. The smoke is bad enough, but the damp in here . . .' He thumped a hand on his chest to demonstrate. 'I'm sorry, Ma'am, but if we lose The Comet, the boys and I will have to move on.'

I nodded. 'You and everyone else.'

Professor Ruben didn't disagree. He smiled in that melancholy way of his, collected his coat from the back of a chair, and went to sign his name on Jesmond's list.

There were just the four of us in the hall now – me, Lucca, Jesmond and Fitzy.

Jesmond piped up. 'That went very well, Ma'am, indeed it did.'

'Do you think so?' I glared at him. The cut on my cheek still smarted. 'If that was going well, I wouldn't want to be here when things were going badly.'

He stroked the felt of his bowler. 'I've taken plenty of names, Ma'am. Enough to stand guard round the clock until we open.'

Fitzy snorted. 'Even then we're not out of the woods. Thanks to you, we don't have a draw, Ma'am. Madame Toth-Varda was perfect, but you sent her packing. Even if you've changed your mind, it's too late. That ship sailed from Southampton this morning. She's not coming back, so she's not.'

Jesmond's little eyes caught mine. He cleared his throat. 'I don't think she's much of a loss. I'm happy to say I didn't take to her.'

'I don't care whether you took to her or not!' Fitzy brought a fist down on the top of the chair next to him. The bar splintered in two. 'The fact is,' he continued without apparently noticing the damage, 'she was fresh. Word would've spread. With her topping the bill we could've packed the place out for weeks.'

I could see what Fitzy meant. Madame was a draw, right enough, but she was bleedin' deadly too. I wouldn't want to be stuck on a ship with her. Of all of us gathered at The Comet, two nights back, Fitzy and Lucca were the only ones who'd received messages that brought a sort of comfort. As for the rest, I still couldn't rid myself of Lady Ginger's voice and I didn't think Vellum had heard words of consolation neither.

I shook my head. 'I've made up my mind. On this occasion, I agree with Jesmond. What that woman did was a clever trick, nothing more.'

Fitzy swore. 'We'll need more than a clever trick to fill The Comet on the opening night – if we get that far. We'll need a fucking miracle. We can't just send out the same old acts. Knackered as pit ponies, they are. We need a draw. What do you say, Jessie?' For once he appealed to his rival.

'Well, I do think . . . That is to say, I believe that Fitzy, Mr Fitzpatrick, here might be quite correct on some details. It's a fine hall now. We need something lively to bring them in.'

I turned to the stage. I didn't have the time or the inclination to listen to the pair of them squabble.

'I'm sure the two of you can deal with it. It's what I pay you for.'

I went to the steps and reached for my bonnet. The straw was soaked through. There was a peculiar slimy thickness to the wetness.

I looked down. My fingers were smeared with red.

'Jesus!' I threw the bonnet down. It skittered across the boards of the stage, the dark green ribbons trailing behind it.

'Fannella?' Lucca came up behind me. I turned and opened my hands to him.

'*Madre di Dio.*' He took a step back, and then a step forward, grabbing my wrists. 'What have you done? Are you hurt?'

Fighting the urge to wipe the blood on my skirt, I pulled myself free from his grip and climbed the steps, careful to hold my hands away from me. There were dark spots on the boards of the stage. Earlier I'd thought it was rain, but now I saw the truth.

I looked up and saw another truth. The swaying grey fabric I'd taken to be canvas come loose from the hole in the roof was a woman hanging from a rafter.

Chapter Thirty-four

'Poor Marnie.' Tears brimmed in Peggy's eyes. 'She was always kind to us, Kit, back when we . . .' She swallowed the rest of what she had to say about 'back when' with a sob.

I pulled the wrapper tight. The first thing I'd done when I got back to The Palace was to ask Lok to bring a bowl of hot water to my room. I'd scrubbed my hands and then my whole body until the skin was raw, but I could still feel the blood on my fingers – and worse, I could smell it.

'She was a good woman. One of the best of that lot. Last time I saw her she said she was knitting me a blanket.' Peggy gulped and dashed the tears from her cheeks, but they kept coming. 'Does he know yet?'

I shook my head. All things considered, I reckoned it might be a kindness for Dismal not to know what had happened to Marnie and – God forgive me – it might also be best that way for The Comet.

I plucked at the sprigged blue cotton of the wrapper, careful to avoid her eyes. 'The only people who know are Fitzy, Jessie, Lucca, Hari, me and now you. They're not going to spread it about and I don't want you to say a word, Peg. Please.'

'But surely you have to—'

I rattled on sharp. 'Hari helped bring her down. He was the only one who could reach out that far from the gallery to pull her in.'

Peggy dabbed at another trail of tears. 'You don't think it might have been . . . that she . . .' She rested a hand on the swell of her belly and took a breath. 'Did she do it herself?'

The question caught me. To be fair to Peggy, it wasn't unusual for a girl brought low to take matters into her own hands. Plenty in the halls took that route out, but not Marnie.

'No. I'm quite sure of that.' It came out more forceful than I intended. 'Why would she? Anyway, she was strung up below the roof right over the middle of the stage. It would have been impossible.'

Impossible. What I didn't tell Peggy was that the body Hari brought down from the rafters looked like it had been savaged by an animal.

We rolled Marnie in a strip of canvas from the side of the stage and then we followed Hari as he carried her to the workshops out back. Fitzy said it was the best place to hide her away until he could deal with her. I didn't look too far into that. If it came to it and people started asking questions, we could always say she'd gone north. Taken a job in Leeds like Signor Marcelli.

As we crossed the yard, drops of rain scattered like diamonds from the long black bundle in Hari's arms. We made a poor funeral procession, the five of us. Out of respect Jesmond kept hold of his hat. Thin trails of the dye he used on his hair trickled to his collar, staining the white with a tidemark of grey.

We went to the far end of the workshop and stepped through to the storeroom beyond. It was cluttered with broken furniture and bits of peeling decorative business never likely to see the limelight again. Just as Fitzy said, the place was deserted. The hands had nothing new to keep them busy until The Comet opened its doors.

'Behind there. That would be best.' He pointed to the far end where a row of painted flats – the last remnants of Mrs Conway's days as a virgin shepherdess – divided the space in two. Hari picked his way through the debris, moving with surprising grace for a man of his size.

Finding Marnie like that had affected him as much as the rest of us. I was glad to see the solemn, respectful way he carried her like a precious thing. We went behind the screen and watched in silence as he laid her down gently on a pile of moth-eaten red velvet that had once been a curtain. Even Fitzy took his hat off now.

The only light came from a narrow window set high in the brick wall at the back. The air was full of sawdust, which caught in my throat. I glanced at Lucca and saw that he was silently mouthing a prayer.

Behind him, backed into a corner and lying at an angle, was the brassy skeleton of the cage where I'd performed night after night as The Limehouse Linnet. On one side it was bent a little out of shape. In the thin light I could see the glass-beaded ribbons that threaded through the bars on the night it fell, with me perched inside, from the ceiling of The Comet. Now the ribbons hung limp and dull, a tawdry reminder of how I came to be standing here.

How we all came to be here.

Marnie deserved more than this. She should have been laid to rest with flowers and surrounded by loved ones, not hidden in a corner of a dusty workshop crowded with tat and circled by a knot of acquaintances too scared to tell the truth.

'If it wasn't . . . *suicide* –' Peggy whispered the word like it was a profanity – 'who do you think did it, Kit?'

The question had been clanging in my head like the cracked bell at St Anne's all the way back to The Palace. From what

I'd seen when Hari brought Marnie down to the stage, it was Schalk's handiwork. Kite's man took a rare pleasure in inflicting pain.

I'd always remember what Lucca told me about Old Peter's mutilated body when the orchestra boys, Tommy and Isaac, found him at Pearman's Yard. He said the gentle cornet player's innards had been *draped around the room like a bloody Christmas garland.* The description had lodged itself in my mind and would likely never leave it.

Then there was Big Red, the girl from the Bethlem, who'd carried a message from my brother to Telferman. The Beetle had told me what they found when she was fished from the river: *The woman's tongue had been cut from her mouth and forced into a part of her body.*

There was a cruelty inside Matthias Schalk that served Kite well. What had happened to Marcelli, Spark and now Marnie was stamped with his hallmark. But if it was his work, if he'd been set loose on me and mine, it was odd that Kite hadn't mentioned it in all his talk with his brother. In fact, Sam was right, he'd hardly touched on me or the halls at all during that meeting. Looking back on their conversation at the Angevin Club, it was as if Kite had his sights set on something bigger. And there was also that meeting on the Commercial when Schalk had tried to persuade me to climb into his master's carriage. I'd thrown a clear accusation of what he'd done to an old man and a sweet-natured dog into his face and he'd looked . . .

I brought the moment to mind again and studied Schalk's cold eyes. *Confusion* – that was what I'd seen there. It struck me as odd at the time, but I hadn't had a chance to dwell on it. Matthias Schalk took a perverse pride in his work. I'd offered him a chance to crow and yet he hadn't risen to it. Why?

The china clock on the mantel jingled out the tune for the half. The tinkling notes were a poor accompaniment to the thoughts jostling for space in my head. The sound set off Jacobin, who attacked the bars of his cage, plucking at them like the strings of an iron harp. Closing his black claws around the lowest bars, he rattled, swore and battered his ragged grey wings against confinement.

'He'll do himself a mischief if he carries on like that.' Peggy rose from the couch and went over to the cage. 'I don't like him, but I hate to see him like this.' Standing well back, she began to hum. After a moment, Jacobin quietened. Still gripping the bars, he turned his head to one side and watched Peggy with a single furious bead-black eye.

Peggy stroked her belly as she hummed. Silhouetted against the window I could see her clear. Judging by size, the baby's time was surely near no matter what she said about Christmas.

She broke off. 'See, he's calmer now, Kit, he likes this. It always works. Lok taught it me.'

Taking up the tune again, she swayed from foot to foot, careful to keep a safe distance from that nutcracker beak. I listened. It *was* an old song from the halls, but it was something more too. I concentrated, following the swoop and fall of the chorus, which was something like a carol.

And now I recognised it! The tune Lok had taught Peggy was exactly the same as the one Denderholm had attempted at the Angevin Club. It was the one he'd hummed and whistled as he readied himself for the evening. It hadn't come to me earlier on account of the fact that he couldn't place one right note in a dozen.

400

The parlour door opened. I looked away from Peggy, expecting to see Lucca, who'd gone to his room after we returned to The Palace. Instead, Vellum's grey-coated man came into the room, followed by Lucca, who was wiping paint from his fingers with a rag. Tan Seng brought up the rear. For once I could read his expression clear as a soap wrapper. He was angry.

'I was coming down to the parlour.' Lucca flicked a questioning look at Vellum's man. 'I heard the knock and went to the door at the same time as Tan Seng. Your . . . visitor was very . . . determined.'

The man nodded at me. His face was blank as a Billingsgate slab, but I felt naked under his scrutiny. I huddled the sprigged cotton close, pulling it tight at the neck.

'Lady. There is this.' Tan Seng bowed and produced from his sleeve a fold of white paper sealed with a circle of red wax. He handed it to me in silence.

I looked at the grey man. 'I assume this is from . . . your employer?'

He nodded, but didn't offer anything more.

'Will you need an answer?'

He shook his head and pointed at the message. I turned the paper in my hands, knowing and dreading what I'd see inside. I ran a fingertip over the wax seal.

'Kit!' I looked up. Peggy was craning out of the window. 'There's a carriage at the end of the lane and two men are standing with it.'

Chapter Thirty-five

Heavy black blinds obscured the view from the windows of Vellum's carriage. I couldn't see out and, more to the point I supposed, no one could see in. Two brass candle lanterns, one mounted on the wall above my seat and the other directly opposite, lit the rocking box.

At first, I got a sense of where we were on account of the noise from the streets and the smell. The Commercial always had a notable flavour. After that, I thought we were still going west, but that was all I could make out. Gradually the street sounds faded until all I could hear was the rumble of the wheels and the occasional whip crack and whinny from the horses.

Vellum's men, one next to me and two opposite, sat in silence, studying gloved hands folded in their laps. They all looked alike in a bland sort of way. Brown hair, muddy eyes, faces with no irregular angles or prominent features. A particular smell rose from the identical damp grey coats that reached to their ankles. It wasn't unpleasant, but after a while it filled the space with a musty sweetness that made me want to open the window and gulp fresh air.

I opened my bag and took out the message. I read Vellum's tight, sloping hand again. The writing was very small. It was difficult to read without holding it close, and even then it was hard on the eye. I knew why. There was something private tucked away here he didn't want people to know about.

Miss Peck,

This communication is for your attention only. When we last met, I demanded a great favour of you. The time has come. I must ask you to accompany these men. You will be safe. I give you my assurance on this, and the assurance of the Highest Authority. You will give him my message regarding the item in his possession and bring the item to me.

In addition, you will ask him what happened to AF. That, apart from your discretion, is all I require.

E

Also, at the end tell him this: Cotidie damnatur qui semper timet

All I require! It was bleedin' easy for him to write that.

The man he was sending me to see haunted my dreams. The thought of him and Ma, even though she was too drugged to know what was happening, was something I tried to lock away. But it still came to me in nightmares. There were times when I woke unable to move, fighting for breath, smothered by flesh that pressed me to the sheets, the stench of sweat and unwashed body stopping my nose.

Bile rose into my mouth.

I crushed the paper into a ball, but then I smoothed it out again over the dark grey satin of my skirt, folded it neat and pushed it back into my bag. I caught the eye of one of the grey coats. He looked away sharpish. I didn't bother to make conversation with them. They'd made it quite clear as soon as I took my seat in the carriage that small talk, or any kind of chat come to that, was a thing to be avoided.

I'd dressed myself as a lady. The black velvet jacket, beaded with jet at the collar and along the sleeve, was stiff like armour and the cloudy satin skirt of my dress stood out a yard. I chose it deliberate to keep him distant. I'd taken a new hat, never worn, from the tissue of its box at the bottom of the wardrobe. It was veiled and crowned with grey and black ostrich feathers that curled down over the veil and over my face. The hat was a fine thing and the tissue it had rested in for months had been scented with jasmine and lavender. I reckoned I'd need that under my nose.

There was a rap on the top of the carriage. Vellum's man, the one who'd come to collect me, looked up from his gloves.

'We are almost at our destination, Miss Peck. I have been asked to assure you that you will be safe.' His voice was as bland as his face. He wasn't a toff like Vellum, but he didn't speak London like I did. Everything about him was so very ordinary that he stuck out like a gouty toe.

He smoothed a strand of mouse-brown hair over his forehead. 'I have orders to accompany you to the chamber, but I cannot enter with you. I understand that you have been fully informed.'

I nodded. The black feather bobbed in front of my eyes. 'I know what's expected, if that's what you're asking. He wants the book of names?' *And he wants something else too*, I thought, *only he doesn't trust anyone else to ask for it.*

Vellum's man didn't answer. The carriage jolted right and the blind shifted. Through the crack I caught sight of the moon, almost full and new-risen in a darkening sky. It sailed above a shadowy line of trees. The wheels turned on gravel now. We sat in silence for a short while and then the carriage came to a halt.

The house in front of me was old. The layers of beams and bricks looked as if they had been thrown together in a random pattern without a thought for neatness or symmetry. The central doorway set beneath a large window with a hundred tiny panes skewed to the side as if pushed by a giant hand. Blousy summer roses still bloomed in the dark leaves that clambered around the door and up the wall. The rich, sweet scent of them filled the air.

It wasn't what you'd call a grand house, but it wasn't small neither. I don't know what I was expecting, but it wasn't this comfortable country residence with golden lights flickering at some of the windows and a garden filled with flowers.

From somewhere behind I heard a pattering sound. I turned. Vellum's men were standing on the gravel beside the carriage. Just beyond it a fountain sent jets of water into a stone-circled pool. The water spurted from the mouth of a man with the tail of a fish and tumbled over the lip of the vast shell in his arms. The statue and the water in the basin gleamed like milk in the moonlight. Apart from the burble and patter of the water it was silent here, peaceful almost.

I couldn't imagine that reeking pile of flesh at home in a place like this. Of an instant, the fetid, meaty stench came strong. Just thinking about him conjured it up. I took a deep breath, trying to fill my lungs with jasmine, lavender and roses.

'Miss Peck?' Vellum's man stepped forward and gestured at the house.

I tightened my grip on the ivory handle of my bag and went towards the door. Above me scores of tiny moons glinted in the panes of the window. I stood by as Vellum's man took hold of an iron ring and knocked twice.

Footsteps sounded beyond the door. I heard the grate of a bolt being drawn back and then the click of a key in a lock. The wooden panels swung inward.

A boy dressed in a loose scarlet robe stood just inside the door. Light from a candle-chandelier hanging in the hall behind him burnished the golden paint on his face and naked torso. It caught the silver powder glittering in his curled blond hair.

Dark eyes, almost hidden beneath heavily lamped lids, slid lazily from Vellum's man and then to me. He smiled, revealing a full set of beautiful, even white teeth, but his eyes – which suddenly struck me as very old in such a young face – gave the lie to the welcome.

'The house is closed to visitors. I am sorry you have had a wasted journey.' His voice was light, musical almost, with a definite trace of the north to it. It was a surprise given his exotic appearance. Just for a moment I was minded of the broad scouse Swami Jonah slipped into at the end of a night in The Lamb. Poor sod – he'd liked to pass himself off as something more than he was too.

The golden youth made to close the door, but I clapped a hand to the wood. I felt Vellum's man move in behind me.

'We've come to see . . .' I paused. The youth arched a brow. I saw now that he was a deal older than I'd thought, but skilfully painted and rouged to resemble a boy.

'I am here to see . . .' I wondered what name to use. The Barons gave each other titles. It was part of their ritual. I didn't know who he really was.

406

'I am here to see your . . . employer.'

'He is not receiving.' The man pushed at his silver-gilt hair and turned to look back into the hallway behind him. Three more young men, half dressed in a similar fashion, and a plump girl with red hair down to her ankles and not much else to cover her modesty stood in the shadows beyond the pool of light cast from the candles mounted on the chandelier. The man hissed. Instantly they melted back into the darkness.

I recognised the scent of opium rolling out from the house and into the night air. Christ! If ever there was a time when I might fall into the habit once more, this was it. My tongue stuck to the roof of my mouth as I spoke again.

'I know he's ill. Near to death as I hear it, but I need to see him. Tell him . . .' I stared into the young man's black eyes. The rest of him glowed and shimmered, but those eyes were flat and dead. I didn't see what you might call a soul looking back at me.

A shudder rippled from the top of my head to the base of my spine. I wondered what he'd done, or been forced to do, to lose so precious a thing.

'Tell him what?' The youth ran the tip of a finger down his golden chest, careful to let the scarlet fabric part to show his frame to the best advantage. 'You're right that he is . . . indisposed. Perhaps *I* can help you?' He licked his rouged lips and pouted at Vellum's man.

I pushed past him into the hallway. The youth tutted. He stared at my hat and then his eyes travelled down my body, calculating the worth of the rest of my rig.

'Or you, Miss.' He gave that hiss to the last. 'Do you have any particular requests for the Manor?'

407

I shuddered again.

'Not if it was the last place on earth. Tell Lord Fetch that Lady Linnet is here.'

*

We waited in the hallway for a time, the pair of us standing in silence and a fug of opium. All the while I was aware of being watched. I didn't see anyone, but somewhere deep in the Manor music was being played. Occasionally I heard laughter and the sounds of footsteps overhead. The old beams creaked as someone moved above us.

Whatever Golden Boy said to Fetch it did the trick. He shimmered back to us, candle in hand, and motioned for us to follow. We went to the end of the hallway and turned to the left, where a broad oak staircase rose into darkness. The painted man led the way, pausing at the broad first landing to make sure we were still behind him. The little flame licked at varnished paintings lining the walls. There seemed to be a lot of pale flesh on display. I stared up at them, trying to work out what was going on in them, and then, when I caught on, I wished I hadn't.

I badly wanted to feel Nanny Peck's old plaid draped around my shoulders instead of the rows and whorls of glittering jet. There was something good and simple and pure about that old, handmade piece. This place was corrupted and foul.

I glanced through the net of my veil at Vellum's man. His eyes bored into the back of the man with the candle. I got the distinct impression that an order from above to remove vermin from the Manor would've been welcomed.

We followed Golden Boy along a moonlit passage and stopped outside a doorway topped by an elaborate wooden carving. I didn't look too close at the workmanship this time.

'You can go in. He is expecting you.' The man leaned against the wall and stared at us both. He allowed his scarlet robe to fall open and I saw that he was completely naked beneath it, apart from the paint.

'Old friends, are you?' The way he asked the question made it obvious he didn't believe that for a moment. 'It's good that someone has bothered to visit the old bugger. He doesn't have long. To be frank with you, we're moving on, all of us. We've been packing for days. You were lucky to find someone to let you in.'

He set the candle on the floor. 'I'll leave this. I know my way around here blindfolded. I've done it often enough. Oh, the games we used to play.' He smiled, straightened up and reached out to run a red-nailed finger down the cheek of Vellum's man. I saw the twitch of the man's Adam's apple above the collar of his long grey coat and knew what he wanted to do.

'You'll let yourselves out then, unless there's anything else you want, that is. If you can pay, we can provide. The Manor is a house of requirement – right up to the end.'

He swayed off down the passage, the robe swirling around him. We watched him go in silence. When he had disappeared into the darkness I turned to Vellum's man.

'You're to wait here for me?'

He nodded and reached into his coat. 'There's this, Ma'am. For your safety. You are to leave it with him . . . at the end.'

He produced a small parcel of green cloth and handed it to me. I knew what it was as soon as I took it. I could feel the shape and weight of a little pistol through the silk. I quizzed at the man, but he looked down at his boots, where the reflection of the candle flame danced in the polished leather at the toes.

I put the parcel into my bag, snapped it shut and stretched a hand to the door.

Chapter Thirty-six

A wide window stretched from floor to ceiling directly opposite the door. Some of the leaded panels had been opened out to the night. The panes of glass caught the moonlight, casting a pool of silver across the boards. I reckoned someone had intended to freshen the place, only it hadn't worked. The air was thick with the stench of a body. Sweat, piss, shit and the rancid sweetness of disease came strong, but cutting through it there was something else too.

Once, I'd carried a note for Joey to a catgut maker in White Horse Alley, up Clerkenwell. The old man had a side job as a tally boy. A debt needed paying and Joey reckoned that if he sent his little sister he might gain a few days' grace. The lanes around Turnmill were a rookery and no place for a child. I didn't question it at the time. It was back when I'd do anything for my brother.

I made the mistake of cutting through Smithfield Market that day and I was unlucky. The Welsh drovers had brought cattle to London. They usually went to Copenhagen Fields in Islington, but on this occasion, on account of the numbers, they'd had to take a hundred animals to the city's old slaughter ground.

The Smithfield boys were brisk and jolly. Their broad backs were soaked with sweat and their leather aprons were red with blood as they went to work. It took less than a count of ten for a hobbled beast to sink to its knees once its throat was slit. The live ones knew what was coming, I swear it. They rolled their eyes, cried out loud and tried to break free but they were tied and held so close they could hardly move.

I'll always remember the smell of them – fear and shit, rising above the metallic stew of steaming organs the butchers drew from the carcasses. It was the fear that stayed with me. I never knew it left a trace, but it did. Sour like turned milk, fear was sharp as a knife, cold as a blade, and it stabbed you in the belly.

Fetch's chamber was rank as Smithfield Market, and above everything else I smelt fear.

Cold light from the window showed the place clear. Apart from a huge wooden chest to the right of the door where I'd come in, the room was bare. It was silent too. I wondered if Golden Boy had played us for fools, but then I noticed another door at the other end of the room. Perhaps that was where he was?

'Hello?' My voice echoed in the emptiness. There was a fluttering sound from outside the window, most likely a bird in the greenery disturbed by the sudden sound. I called again. When no answer came, I clamped a hand to the veil to cover my nose and went to the window, thinking to open another of the panels. The stench in there clawed at the back of my throat.

Something rustled. It wasn't no bird this time.

Someone spoke . . . or tried to. I gripped my bag tight and turned about slow, expecting to see a low bed or at least a couch backed to the wall behind me, but the chamber was empty except for the chest and a mound of pale rags piled against it.

Moonlight slicked the rags. There was a sort of pattern to the material, dark patches spread across it like flowers in bloom. The way it glistened put me in mind of the silver threads me and Peggy used to sew into the skirts of the chorus at the halls.

The shine caught the lights and drew the punters' eyes to a well-turned ankle.

The voice gurgled again and my belly squirmed. This wasn't something to draw the eye. The sound came from the midst of the naked sweating pile that was Lord Fetch. Disease had eaten him alive from the inside and now he was a puddle of flesh. The skin that once covered his immense body hung loose, rolling itself into mottled folds and creases that slumped across the boards. Punctured and collapsed, Fetch was hobbled by the vastness of his empty hide.

Wedged between the chest and the panelled wall, he shifted, struggling to raise his head from pleats that had once been a neck. The sound came again, a burble rising from his throat. I caught what he was saying now.

'Water.'

Something in the mound moved. A bony hand with bracelets of skin gestured weakly to a pottery jug and a small tin mug stationed against the wall several yards away. I reckoned it was deliberate. The water was out of his reach but close enough to taunt him. I wondered what to do, but then I decided it would be best to show willing.

The jug was full of water. As I poured it into the mug, Fetch started to moan. I turned. He was staring at me direct, black eyes burning like Lucifers in a shrunken face. The tip of his tongue crept out from cracked lips. I thought he was after the water, but there was something obscene about the way he moved it back and forth.

'Lady Linnet.' He sucked at my name. 'I'd know you anywhere.'

Christ! He was repulsive. I thought of Ma. Surely this heap

413

of slackened skin wouldn't have . . . couldn't have been capable of . . .?

My hand trembled and water spattered to the boards. I tore my eyes from his, afraid he might see my weakness, even through the veil. I hooked the bag over my arm and straightened up, clutching the tin mug tight.

Fetch's eyes went to the mug. The tongue appeared again. There was a sticky clicking sound as he ran it over crusted lips. Vellum was right – Kite too – Fetch was near the end, but it was difficult to tell when that would come. A light in his eyes suggested the life in him would burn down to a stub the size of a sixpence before it went out. He could linger like this for a long time, days even, if I gave him the water.

It came to me that the mug was a better weapon than a pistol wrapped in silk. I breathed deep, trying to hold jasmine and lavender in my nose. The stench of fear in the room was sharp. Fetch had been abandoned and he knew it.

Get it over with and then get yourself out, girl. That's what I told myself as I knelt and offered the water to him.

'You want this bad, don't you?'

He muttered and tried to take the mug from me. I snatched it away. 'I'll give it to you, but I want something in return. Two things, in fact. First, I want the book of names.'

The muttering stopped. Hooded eyes slid from the mug to my face. I saw a flicker of surprise there that told the truth.

'That is not what I thought . . .' He swallowed and tried again. I had to lean in close to make out what he was saying, even though the stench rolling off him almost felled me.

'Who sent you, Lady Linnet?'

I swirled the water. The slopping sound, hollow in the tin,

414

made Fetch open and shut his sticky mouth like a stranded fish. I brushed aside a feather bobbing from my hat to see him clear. His eyes were locked on the mug.

'This isn't a social call. I want the book of names.'

He tried to sit straighter. It was almost pitiful watching him haul himself together, but I couldn't waste feeling on him.

'I do not know what you mean.'

Liar! Now I was used to it, I could catch what he was saying more freely. He jerked his head like he was gulping something back.

'Was it that whoreson, Kite?' He took a throttled breath. 'Did he send you?'

The way he spat out the name told me there was no fellowship left there. I remembered the way Kite had dismissed Fetch, left him for cat's meat you might say, in that chat with his brother at the Angevin Club. He'd even threatened to send Schalk to put him out of his misery.

A thought occurred to me.

'I don't think Kite knows about your book, does he?'

Fetch's eyes glinted. 'What book, Lady Linnet?'

He started to laugh, a horrible sound somewhere between a choke and a wheeze.

Anger rose in me. How dare this . . . this *thing* find anything to amuse him. I remembered what Vellum had told me about the book of names:

It is a list of the recreational procurements Fetch has made for many of the most prominent members of society. It lists the names of those capable of gross depravity and their particular interests. Men, women, children, the deformed, the deranged, the deluded, the desperate . . .

415

It hardened me. I poured a little of the water from the mug to the boards, letting it trickle slowly and deliberately right in front of him.

'That was careless of me. And there's not much left where it came from. Now, back to this book you don't know about. If you want to play it that way, I can always tell Kite about it and see what he thinks. Would you like me to do that? I'm sure he'll be pleased to send his man Matthias to you.'

The laughter stopped.

'No.' Fetch stared at me. 'Please.'

I got the distinct impression that wasn't a word that came natural. I studied his face. Yellow skin stretched tight over jutting bones. Even without the blanket of flesh, he would have been a heavy-set, big-boned man. I stared direct into his eyes. There was nothing of me there. Nothing at all. I remembered what Vellum had told me about Kite's lies and at last I believed him. A knot loosened in my heart; a heaviness that had lodged there for weeks fell away. Fetch was no kin of mine.

Maybe none of them were.

I spilled more of the water and he let out a thin, high wail. His blackened fingers scrabbled towards the little puddle.

'The painted man who let us in downstairs said he was clearing out. They all are. They've been packing for days he told us, but I don't think they're planning to take you with them. When they've all gone you'll die in this room parched and alone. This –' I raised the mug and threatened to spill more – 'might ease you. But it's all you've got left. Give me the book and I'll let you drink.'

'Who is it? Who knew?' Fetch couldn't take his eyes from the mug.

I considered my answer. I could tell him about Vellum, or I could take another route. Which was best? I settled on the last.

'A . . . higher authority told me to give you a message. I have it exact here.' I tapped the brim of the hat. '"I want the book of names. You will tell him that if he gives me this, I will *allow* him to die in his bed. If he does not, I will drag his living carcass through the streets of London to Newgate Prison in an open cart."'

I sat back on my heels and placed the mug on the boards behind me out of his sight. 'You might not be in your bed just now, but . . .' A shiver went through me. I didn't know much about Vellum, but I knew, of a certainty, he'd meant every word of that.

I carried on. 'There's a carriage outside and three armed men with it. I don't think anyone here's going to lift a hand to stop us if we cart you away. It seems to me you have a choice – not the best, I grant you – but a choice it is. Give me the book and I'll give you water to ease you. I promise that. Otherwise . . .'

I thought I'd let him work it out for himself. Vellum's message was clear and vivid enough to help him decide. I stood, went to the jug and refilled the mug, careful to let Fetch hear the spatter of water on tin. From the clicking, rasping sounds behind me I knew he was desperate. When I turned back, the way he stared at the mug in my hand could have boiled the water inside it. I rattled the tin and it did the trick.

'There . . . there is a loose board.' He glanced to the far end of the chamber. 'Against the panelling near the door. Marked with a rose.'

I went to the furthest wall. The silvery light from the window showed everything plain enough. I saw where he meant

417

immediately. In the corner along from the door, one of the wooden floor planks was uneven and raised. You wouldn't pay attention to the irregularity if you hadn't been told to. I knelt and brushed away the dust. There was a pattern on the board – a rose, just as he said. Fragrance to mark filth. I set the mug down and caught the edge. It came up easy, revealing a small dark space beneath. I reached inside and the tips of my fingers brushed across something hard and square. I pulled out a package wrapped in dark cloth.

'Water.'

I ignored Fetch's bleat and went to the window, grateful to take in clean air.

'You must think me green as a country pasture. I need to take a look at this first.'

I unwrapped a book with a dark leather cover from the cloth. The spine was old and broken and the thing fell open in my hands. I held it to the moonlight. Tissue-thin pages had been split into four columns crammed with tiny close-packed script. On the left of each page there was a list of names. In the next column against each name, a brief description of a particular interest. Next came dates and in the final column, figures.

I ran a finger along the first row.

Sir William Corton. Boys (unbroken, not above 10 years).
10 July 1869 / 13 February 1870 / 20 September 1870 /
5 January 1873 / 17 March 1874 . . .

I swallowed. The dates continued for another two lines. Corton had paid Fetch over three thousand guineas in the last decade. It was just as Vellum had said, and, now I saw it written down in a clerk's tight hand, worse than I'd imagined. I went to the next line.

Augustus Thoyle (Reverend). Females (pliant, insensible, deranged – prefers old). 3 August 1864 / 6 December 1864 / 16 January 1865 / 11 March 1865 . . .

And the next:

Lucian McKew, Surgeon. Twins (male or female). Orphans. Fair (blue-eyed). Young . . .

And the next:

Venetia, Countess of Savernake, Art Collector. Tattooed males. To be delivered alive . . .

I didn't need to see more. I clapped the book shut and wrapped it tight again. Vellum might have the stomach to look through the book of names, but I felt soiled just from touching it. God knows, my own ledgers for the general business of Paradise were nothing to take a pride in, but they were a hymn book compared with what I'd seen on the page that had fallen open. And there were two hundred more.

I pushed the book deep into the bag still hooked over my arm and walked slowly back to Fetch. I'd left the mug over in the corner near the rose-marked board. When he saw I didn't have it, he started to shuffle and whine. The thought of giving him relief went against the grain of me now, but there was something else I wanted. I went to retrieve it.

'Don't worry, you'll have your water.' I raised the mug in a mockery of a toast. 'There's another thing I need first. What happened to A. F.?'

Understanding glimmered in Fetch's coal-chip eyes.

'Ah!' He took a rasping breath. 'So, that's how you know. The *spy* found out about the book, did he?'

I didn't have an answer to that. Fetch shifted in his puddle of flesh and wheezed on.

'An army man, was he? I think he was. Alexander Felstead was foolish. He had not seen much of the world before he came sniffing to the House of Requirement. Such an appetite he had, that handsome young officer.'

Fetch's voice came stronger now. After days of silence, he was wearing it in again. As he spoke it seemed to me that he took an odd pleasure, what you might call a professional pride, in telling the story. He grinned, the toad mouth splitting his face in two.

'Everyone has a secret and a weakness.' He sucked at his lip. 'I know who sent you now. It was me who brought Alexander Felstead to the Barons the night we tested Lord Vellum's loyalty . . .' Black eyes locked on mine. 'Just as we tested yours, Lady Linnet.'

The floor lurched beneath me. I heard Danny Tewson's voice and saw his fingers catching the hem of my skirt. I was back in that musty old church, watching the Barons seal Peggy's man alive beneath a flagstone. It was another of their rituals, designed to bind. There was no going back once you'd betrayed a friend, a lover . . . or a daughter. The night they tested my grandmother, Lady Ginger, they'd used Ma. My stomach clenched tight. I fought against the images that crowded my mind.

Fetch spoke again. 'Tell your friend that his spy paid the price in full.'

I snatched at his words, grateful to think of something, *someone*, else.

'That's where he is then, this Alexander, under that stone at Great Bartholomew's?'

Fetch shook his head. He blinked and gulped. 'Water.'

When he didn't offer anything more, I swiped up the jug along with the mug and went to the window. I flung the contents of the mug into the night.

'There's a drop more here.' I waved the jug at him. 'But it's going the same way unless you tell me what I need. If Alexander's not at Great Bartholomew's, where is he?'

Fetch grinned. 'I brought Felstead, drugged and insensible, back here that night, after Vellum's trial. You could ask him what we did to his friend. I am certain he remembers it well.' He grunted and scratched at the slack rolls of flesh that had once been his belly. 'My only regret is that I didn't mark the *professional* connection between Vellum and that pretty young man until it was too late. It would have served me better to offer Kite the truth, rather than an . . . entertainment.'

'What do you mean, "the truth"?' I stood my ground with the jug.

'If you are in league with Vellum then you already know it, Lady Linnet.' Those black eyes sharpened. 'Vellum hid his purpose from us quite successfully – at first, but he could not hide his true nature. He was indiscreet and I was watching. I always watch, Lady Linnet. I took advantage of his weakness. I thought it was an amusing coincidence that one of my customers should have an affectionate . . . *connection* with our newest

Baron. It was I who decided it would be the perfect test of loyalty if we were to present the new Lord Vellum with a trial that demonstrated the extent of our reach into the lives of the brethren. To his credit, he didn't bat an eye that evening.'

Fetch licked his lips with a tongue pale as a worm. 'I have given you enough. I need water.'

'Not until I have an answer.' I held the jug to the window. 'Where is he now? Alexander, I mean.'

'I do not know.' He gasped, wracked by a pain somewhere deep in the crumpled mound of his body. He began to choke. 'Water. I must have . . .'

'Not until you give me what I need. I mean it. I'll count to five and then this goes out of the window. One, two . . .'

An arm flailed; it was a sign of defeat.

'One hundred and twenty-seven . . . Lady Sarah Carew. There is never a body.'

I set down the jug and delved into the bag for the book. I took it to the window again and flicked through the pages. I saw now that they were numbered. When I reached page 127, I scanned the names. She was there, halfway down.

Lady Sarah Carew, hunts with hounds. Men (muscular).
Not above 25. Must have stamina.

Christ! I ran my finger to the end of the line. She'd been doing it for years. The last times Fetch had provided her with quarry were:

23 January 1877 / 12 November 1878 / 12 February
1879 / 14 December 1880

Alexander must have been the last of them, poor sod. I forced the book back into my bag. Part of me wanted to throw the rest of the water into Fetch's face, but that would have made me as low as him. I felt a need to prove myself better. Without a word, I filled the mug, took it to him and set it down where he could take it if he had the strength. I put the jug close by too.

As I straightened up, I remembered the green silk parcel in my bag. I wondered if Vellum would have offered such a mercy if he knew what had happened to his friend. I watched as Fetch hooked the edge of the mug with a finger and dragged it closer. The tin scraped on the boards. I'd kept my side of the bargain, but I wouldn't help him drink.

At last he had the mug in his grasp. His hand shook as he lifted it awkwardly to his lips and tipped it back. I waited until the greedy slurping stopped.

'More.' He stared into the empty mug and then up at me. I pushed the jug nearer to him with my foot.

'You can serve yourself. Before I go I have a last message. I was told to tell you this – *Cotidie damnatur qui semper timet,* whatever that means.

Fetch began to choke, but then I realised he was laughing again.

'Such a scholar, isn't he, your fine friend?' Those little dark eyes sparked with malice. 'You mangled the Latin.'

I held my bag close. The corners of the book jabbed through the fabric into my belly. I took out the green silk parcel for fear of setting the pistol off by accident.

'That don't make no odds to me. I've done what I promised. There's this too – he asked me to give it to you when I left. It's up to you what you make of it.' I put the parcel along from the jug, careful to leave it a fair distance from him. 'I'll add this . . . as a mercy. You'll be alone when I've gone. Once you've finished what's left in the jug, that's it. Just you, the pain and a thirst like sawdust in your throat. It might take a long while. I'll let you consider that.'

He looked at the parcel and then at me.

'"He who is constantly in fear of death is every day condemned." That is Vellum's final message. A parting gift, you might say.'

I turned on my heels and started for the door. There was nothing more I wanted from him.

He called out. 'I have one last request for you, Lady Linnet. Before you go would you open the window a little wider? Please.'

I thought about refusing, but it was such a small thing. I crossed to the window and reached up to unhitch a latch on one of the higher casements. It was stiff with rust and I had to push hard. That bleedin' feather came dandling down in front of my eyes as I tried to free it. I batted the feather away and rattled the panes. Below I saw the carriage on the gravel drive. Two of Vellum's men were leaning against the sides. The end of their smokes glowed red.

A shuffle and a clank of tin told me Fetch was trying for the water. He spoke again, his voice quite clear now. 'When you arrived, I thought you had come with a question of your own. I foolishly imagined you might be here to ask about your father.'

My hand froze on the latch. A drumbeat started under my jacket. The jet beads shifted on the velvet in time with my heart. I didn't turn. I couldn't look at him.

'Who . . . who is he?'

That throttled laugh came from behind.

'A customer.'

I heard a click. A crack of gunshot tore the air and a sudden brilliant light blazed in the tiny glass panes of the window. I spun about. The pistol was still in Fetch's hand and the contents of his head were spattered up the panelled wall.

Chapter Thirty-seven

I handed Vellum the book in silence. He examined the cover but he didn't open it to look inside. Instead, he pushed it into a pocket of his long black coat. To see him standing there in his fine rig – he wore a tall black hat and carried a silver-topped cane in his kid-gloved hand – you might have thought him a regular toff on the way home after an evening's entertainment.

A church bell sounded the hour. It was early in a new day. Soon the deserted street where our carriages had met would be full of traffic, people and noise.

We were on the edge of a park. I wasn't sure where exactly, but from the taste of soot and metal on my tongue I knew we were in London. The smell was a thousand times cleaner than the reek of Fetch's chamber. An owl called from the wooded darkness over to the left. To the right, gas lamps lit a row of pale, smart buildings with steps and railings. Gentlemen's residences. Lights in the attic windows and down at the lowest levels showed that servants were already up and about their business.

Dozens of people were needed to stoke a house for the day but their efforts from the earliest hours to last thing at night were invisible to their employers. A lot of things went on right under people's noses without attracting notice.

Vellum glanced at his man, the one who'd come into Fetch's house with me. His brows arched a question and the man nodded.

'Dead, sir. By his own hand.'

'The pistol?'

'Here, sir. Retrieved from the scene.' The man patted his coat.

'Good. I require a moment with Miss Peck. You will wait here.'

'As you wish, sir.' The man gave a sort of salute. Brackish eyes slid to my face and then to the ground.

At the sound of the pistol Vellum's man had hurled himself into the chamber. I was standing at the window, staring at the mess on the wall. I couldn't move or make a sound. The smell of blood and shot cut through everything else.

Once he'd assured himself that Fetch was dead – which was bleedin' obvious, I'd say – he'd taken the pistol from the corpse's hand, wrapped it in the green silk square and pocketed it. Then he'd herded me down the stairs and back to the carriage outside. If Golden Boy had heard the shot, he didn't bother about it. And neither did anyone else in the House of Requirement. We didn't see a single person in the passage, on the stairs or in the hall as we hurried back to the carriage and the men waiting outside.

Once we were on the move, Vellum's man had turned to me. In the dim light of the carriage's single candle lantern his face was bland as ever.

'Miss Peck?'

I knew what he was asking. I shifted my bag onto my lap. 'Here.'

If he had an opinion on that he didn't show it. And his face was blank as a sheet of paper now.

Vellum pointed the cane to the lamplit street.

'Walk with me, Kitty.'

427

I noted I was on first-name terms again. We passed Vellum's carriage, which was smaller and smarter than the one we'd arrived in. The horses danced on the cobbles and the muffled driver hauled at the reins to steady them. There was a chill in the air that my velvet jacket couldn't ward off. Again, I wished I had Nanny Peck's old shawl wrapped around me. For so many reasons.

We went a little way along the railings together. When we were twenty yards or so from the carriages, Vellum spoke.

'The book is an exceptional and valuable tool. Thank you.' He paused. 'And the other matter?'

A falling leaf caught in the feathers of my hat. I'd never wear it again. The sickly sweet scent of jasmine, in particular, would always turn my stomach now. I plucked the leaf free and rolled it between my fingers. The flesh of it wore apart.

'If you mean your question about . . . A. F., then yes.' I wasn't sure what more to say. I looked up at the stars. Through the net of the veil, they winked cold and sharp as the light in Fetch's eyes. It came to me that the best answer was in the pocket of Vellum's coat.

'I think . . .' I hesitated, trying to catch a way to frame it right. He strummed the metal tip of the cane over the railings and halted. I saw him flick a glance over my shoulder to the carriages to make sure we were still private.

'What do you think, Kitty?'

'I think you need to look in the book of names. Page one hundred and twenty-seven. Lady Sarah Carew.' I had an urge to pat his arm or offer some words of condolence, but he turned away from me, so I couldn't see his face. I crushed up the remains of the leaf and tossed it away.

'He was your friend, this A. F. . . . Alexander, wasn't it?'

Vellum nodded, but he didn't add no more. It was clear I'd have to put the spade work in. I took down a lungful of cold air.

'I'm not one to make a judgement. Where I come from we don't mind where a person finds comfort. Fetch told me that the Barons used him to test you, just like that time they took Danny Tewson. You don't need to tell me about it, not if you don't want to, but the rest – what happened next – is in the book in your coat pocket. I reckon you might want to be on your own when you read it.'

For a long moment he didn't answer. When he turned back to me, a tick was playing in the skin beneath his left eye.

'Your Madame Toth-Varda was right.'

'She wasn't mine.'

That tick pulsed again. 'Whoever she belonged to – and despite my rationality, I cannot think of her as anything other than a creature of Hades – what she said was correct. I betrayed him.'

'Like I betrayed Danny.'

'Is that what you did? What *we* did?' A new light glowed bright in a window over the street, carving shadows in half of Vellum's face beneath the brim of his hat. 'I thought I was clever, Kitty. I foolishly allowed myself to believe that I was pulling the strings when I sent Alexander Felstead to enquire into the business of the House of Requirement. Do you remember what I said about *The Art of War*?'

I nodded. 'Know your enemies and know yourself?'

The fidgeting muscle tightened the corner of Vellum's eye. 'In this case I did not know my friend, and poor Alexander did not know himself. He was weak. He became his own enemy. Fetch used him, but I used him too. Fortunately for me, before he fell completely into that foul company he confirmed the existence of the book of names. The night the Barons tested my loyalty, I concentrated on that knowledge and tried to convince myself that it was worth Alexander's sacrifice. I have often thought about what I did, and what I did not do. I imagine you have done the same, Kitty?'

Danny was always with me. Every time I looked at Peggy he was there in the shadows. I stared up at Vellum. That twitch under his eye put me in mind of an insect fluttering beneath the skin. I breathed deep. The beads on my shoulders clicked and glittered in the half-light.

'I'll never be free of the thought of what I did to Danny Tewson.'

He nodded. 'But thought is not atonement and it will not bring them back. I will punish myself with this . . .' Vellum's hand moved to the pocket of his coat. 'And I will visit the place where they buried him.'

I stared at the ground. 'I think . . . well, I don't think . . .' I couldn't carry that through. It wasn't my place to tell him. 'Like I said, you'd better read Fetch's book.'

Vellum's grey eyes caught the yellow of the street lamps. I was minded again of that panther, Russig. He looked back at the carriages where his men were waiting and raised a hand, spreading his gloved fingers wide. I imagined it was a sign that our conversation wouldn't last much longer.

'Do you remember that draught at the Sanctuary, Kitty?'

'The one that blew all the way to Kite's ears?'

'The very same. Thanks again to your information, I have

stopped that draught. I must also thank you for the book . . . and for your discretion. I have not been idle since we last met. You will, no doubt, read about it in due course or perhaps Mr Collins will inform you. I believe *The Pictorial* will carry a most lurid account. Only Kite and his brother now remain. Traitors were always brought to justice at the Tower. I wonder if he will recognise the irony when I confront him in the chapel.'

I peeled back the veil to see his face clear. 'You mean this meeting on the 27th in the peculiar place?'

Vellum almost smiled. 'At the Royal Peculiar, yes. I have made further enquiries, based on your intelligence. Next week in the Chapel of St Peter within the walls of the Tower of London there is to be a most unusual investiture. The Queen herself will be present at the creation of a new order of chivalry.'

A damp grey feather drooped between my eyes. I was almost grateful to it. He was talking about the Chapel of St Peter ad Vincula. The word was so close to Vinculum I could almost taste the metal of the chain tightening to a knot in my head. I wondered what to say. Maybe it was best to wait? After all, Vellum hadn't mentioned the Vinculum for a while. And he didn't seem to have made a connection.

Know your enemies, girl.

I batted the feather aside. 'What's that when it's at home? An order of . . . chivalry?'

He circled the tip of the cane on the paving stones between us. 'The ideal of a chivalric order is rooted in the past. The term applies to a group of men, usually of noble rank, gathered together to form a society or brotherhood dedicated to the service of the Crown. No doubt you have heard of the Garter?'

'I take it you don't mean the stand-up down Hind Street?'

He smiled properly now. He looked much younger when he allowed himself that liberty.

'You are quite correct in that supposition, Kitty. The Order of the Garter was established by King Edward the Third more than four hundred years ago. Even today, members of the Order are chosen by the sovereign. Next week, twelve senior members of the London Imperial Agency will be admitted to the new Imperial Order.'

I batted that bleedin' feather away again. 'I thought you were supposed to be officially connected to this London Imperial Agency. It's why you were at Windsor and how your face got into *The Pictorial* in the first place. Why weren't you invited to this meeting at the Tower?'

Vellum shook his head. 'I was appointed as clerk to the Agency, as you say, but the Order is another matter. The ceremony next week is a strange affair. Such an occasion should be a public celebration, not hidden in a dark chapel. You are right to call it peculiar, but I will be ready.'

At the sound of voices I swung about. Two mashers three sheets to the wind were swaying along the street towards us. Judging by the song they were singing and the uncertainty of their stride, they'd had a full night of it. One of them collapsed against the railing and had to be helped to his feet by his friend, who wasn't too steady himself. As they staggered past, they tipped their hats to me with a knowing leer and winked at Vellum.

Once they were clear of us and nearly level with the carriages they turned back, made gestures it wasn't possible to mistake and let off a stream of comments that ended with the suggestion that Vellum should find a room to '. . . dip his wick in that neat-tailed whore'.

Vellum's eyes narrowed. He raised his cane and called to his men. 'Take them.'

Immediately, two grey coats blocked the path of the mashers. They were bundled without pause or ceremony into the larger of the two carriages. A moment later it rolled towards us and juddered to a halt. The horses, two big bays, dipped their heads and snorted. A grey coat pushed down the window.

'Where to, sir?'

Vellum tapped the side of the carriage with his cane. 'Bow Street, I think. A week in the lower cells will improve their manners.'

'Very good, sir.' The man tipped his head and closed the window. Before the blind came down, I heard a commotion from inside the box and then something like a crack and a yelp of pain. I watched the carriage turn the corner and found myself thinking, once again, that I wouldn't want to make an enemy of the man I was standing next to. But was he a friend?

Now it was just me, Vellum, the smaller of the two carriages and the man who'd taken me into the House of Requirement. He hadn't gone with the mashers and the rest of them and was still idling by the railings thirty yards distant. He stared at his feet, careful not to look in the direction of his master.

Two bright stars glittered in the band of purple over the trees. Dawn wasn't far off. I turned up my collar close to keep out the chill and looked at Vellum, who was consulting a pocket watch. He glanced up at the last stars dandling over the park.

'"*And watching, with eternal lids apart,*"' he murmured to himself.

'Keats again, is it?'

He smiled and nodded, stashing the watch back into a pocket.

'You don't sleep much, do you?'

'Neither do you, Kitty. Am I right?'

'I did once.' I chewed my lip, trying to remember the girl who slept like a newborn. Over the way, another row of windows brightened in the terrace. The day was pulling itself together. A delivery cart clattered around the corner and pulled up outside the first house. A boy carrying a box jumped clear of the canopy and darted down the steps to the lowest quarters. I caught the tune he was whistling – a simple, carefree sound it was. The echo of an ordinary, uncomplicated life.

I shivered and wrapped my arms tight around me. 'The Agency is above board. It's legal, isn't it?'

He nodded. 'The London Imperial Agency will be an office of the government working hand in glove with the Foreign Office. Eventually, it will employ hundreds of people, thousands perhaps, once it is fully established. It is intended to be a commercial network for those whose interests – financial, legal, martial, administrative, even ancestral – give access to the furthest corners of the Empire.'

'And what's your position there, exactly? You don't strike me as the clerking type.'

Vellum sighed. 'Very well. I have been appointed to gather information and pass it on to those who might find it useful in the furtherance of the nation's interests. In time, the Agency will become a mechanism through which the affairs of distant nations can be . . . manipulated.'

'You're a spy, then?'

'I am a shadow, as I told you. But shadows are insubstantial.

They do not leave a trace.' Vellum frowned. 'When the picture of me appeared in *The Pictorial* – your own newspaper, I might add – I was exposed.'

I leaned back against the railings and stared at him. 'I heard something like that when I was under the bed at the Angevin Club. Kite's brother said they'd flushed you out, "like a rat from a drain".'

It came out before I had a chance to consider the insult. Vellum blinked. The twitch beneath his eye jittered like a moth beating against the glass of a candle lantern. I thought I might as well tell him the rest.

'It worked out well for Kite when your face was printed with the others. It moved things along nicely. What he actually said was . . . let me get this right: "He has helped to clear away the dead wood and prepare new ground."' I tapped the brim of my hat. 'That's exact. You've done him an accidental favour. Kite didn't reckon the Barons would have taken easily to retirement but you've put them out to pasture. Or under it, more like. And there was something else he said that evening. I've got that off pat too: "I will not mourn the passing of the brotherhood. Instead, I will celebrate a new beginning."'

Vellum stared over my head at the last faint star glinting in the low-slung ribbon of pink over the trees. In a minute more the star would be gone, dazzled by the sun.

'And what do you make of that "new beginning"?' he asked without taking his eyes off it.

Of an instant, it was like I was standing on a hill, looking down on a river greasy and dark as the Thames. I was so high up I could see where that river began and where it ended.

'It's the Imperial Order. All those letters we found in

Denderholm's room – it's them. Those men will be the members of the Order. You said something about the ones with the garters being 'specially chosen by the sovereign, but this lot meeting next week have been picked out by Kite. I know why; it's not just wealth and position. At the Club he said something about them all having secrets to exploit and binding them up in the law. So, whether they like it or not, he's caught them.' I glanced up at Vellum, who was watching me close. 'You're not the only one partial to blackmail. Now the Barons are gone – mainly thanks to you – Kite and his long-lost brother are finding a way to replace them. But this new lot, the ones in the Imperial Order, will be looking further than London. They'll have their hooks into the whole world.'

'You have it exactly.' Vellum struck his cane on the stones and let it leap into the air. He caught it deft on the bounce. 'Kite might be blind, but he saw that the world of the Barons was old and small. Now there is a new Empire for the taking. To be at the heart of that enterprise was a prize worth sacrificing the past for. He has made alternative plans. I believe his intention is that the members of the Imperial Order will seek to control the work of the Agency. But they will never get the chance. I will arrest them all in the presence of the Queen. There is a word uglier than blackmail and it is treason.'

I pushed the feather out of my eyeline. 'So, to be straight, the Barons live again – secrets and ceremony just like before. It's the same, except this time with a royal blessing. How come . . .' I paused as the carter's lad came bounding up the steps of the house opposite. At the top he caught the post, turned and blew a kiss. Somewhere below a girl laughed and called up to him.

'Bet you do that for all the girls, Alfie Perks.'

'Only the pretty ones.' He hopped back on the cart and it rumbled off. That kiss put me in mind of Sam. I wondered where he was now. I'd been checking the personals like he said, but his mother hadn't left a message.

'Your question, Kitty?' Vellum brought me back. I ripped that bleedin' feather from the hat and threw it to the gutter. It curled itself to a question mark.

'How come Kite managed to get the Queen involved in this? That's a rare prize, isn't it? A personal meeting at her own peculiarity.'

He nodded. 'It is difficult to examine the matter. The royal household is a fortress of silence.'

'Even to you?'

'Even to me. You and I know Kite's true nature, but he is highly placed. Good God! He is even trusted in the highest quarters. I understand that the chaplain of the royal household approved the ceremony last week. Like his brother Edmund before him, Kite has always been protected.'

'Why?'

Vellum didn't answer. The church bell sounded the half and he turned to sign at his man and the carriage. The driver flicked a whip and the horses trotted forward. Grey Coat peeled himself from the railings and walked behind it.

'It is very early or very late, Miss Peck. Either way I must return to the Sanctuary. My carriage is at your disposal, as is my officer. I promised Mr Fratelli that you would be safe. I always keep my word. My man will accompany you to The Palace. I will walk.'

When the neat black carriage was beside us, Vellum opened the door and gestured for me to enter. I stood my ground and thought about that view from the hill. The river was black. It looped and curled back on itself, but at the end it tumbled its filth into the sea. This was a chance to wash everything away.

At the club, Kite had called me an irritation and his brother had called me a drab. When I thought about all the things they'd done – it was little Abha who came strong to mind – the idea of a 'miserable chit from the halls' besting them, unravelling their world, was hard to resist. To see them brought low would be a fine prize.

Know your enemy.

I looked up at Vellum's face. He'd trusted me with a secret. Surely he was more of a friend than an enemy? God knows, I needed as many of them as I could get. It was time to play my card for better or worse.

'You don't see it, do you?'

Vellum quizzed at me, surprised. His man flicked me a look that told me he wasn't used to seeing his employer questioned.

'A while back, you asked me about the Vinculum.'

Vellum took my arm roughly and escorted me a dozen paces from the carriage.

'Now is not the time, Miss Peck.' I noted I wasn't Kitty now. 'When I have Kite where I want him, I will deal with the matter of the Vinculum. Kite will give me its location and you will give me the key. It is a simple matter of timing. It will be the last move in my game.'

I struggled to shake him off, but his fingers dug into my arm. I tried to prise them away.

'Let me free! You don't understand. *I* know where the Vinculum is. It's all come clear tonight. This place where they're holding the meeting next week has been chosen deliberately.

It's not just about cant and ceremony to them. There's more. Listen to me, the full name of this chapel at the Tower is St Peter ad *Vincula*, isn't it?'

Vellum's eyes skewered mine. I saw him test the worth of the information I'd just passed on. It must have rung true because he loosened his grip.

'Explain.'

'The Vinculum is in the Chapel of St Peter ad Vincula. It's why Kite and his brother are so keen to hold their ceremony there. It wasn't until just now that I understood it all. At the Club I heard them talking about getting access at last, but Denderholm – Rufus, whatever his name is – admitted that they don't know how to open it. That's why they need time in the chapel in secret. Kite reckons it might be possible to find a way to—'

'Of course.' Vellum held up a hand to ward off Grey Coat, who was moving closer. 'You will continue.'

I could tell I didn't need to persuade him now. 'When Joey gave me the key to the Vinculum, he told me that one Baron knew the exact place, the other knew the code. It's always been the way to keep it safe. Now, if Kite can—'

'Wait!' Vellum's grip tightened again. 'Are you saying your brother knew the code?'

I nodded.

'It wasn't Lady Ginger who gave it to you?'

'No. Joey had it locked here.' I tapped my head. 'We used to play memory games. The pair of us had a rare talent. When he was in the Bethlem he wrote it out between the lines in the pages of a Bible and gave it to me.'

'So, the code is in this Bible?' Vellum's face was difficult to read.

'Not now. I burned it, but not before I'd memorised the sequence too.'

Vellum stepped away. He glanced at the carriage and then at me again. He struck his cane on the ground with such a force that the silver tip broke off. It rolled away and into the gutter.

'Take the carriage, Miss Peck.' He pointed the way with the blunted cane.

I folded my arms. 'Is that it? Not even a thank you. You're just packing me off home? I've just given you something very helpful.'

'Oh, you've done that, Kitty. You have certainly done that.' Vellum turned from me and began to walk away fast. He raised the cane as a sort of farewell. I glanced at Grey Coat, whose face was bland as ever. I spun on my heels and ran after Vellum. Darting past, I blocked his path.

'What comes next?'

He tried to step aside and go on his way, but I caught his arm. 'You said that you were a man of your word. I've just given you a lot more than that bleedin' book of names. You said that if I went to Fetch for you, you'd give me something in return. I haven't even had that.'

Vellum halted. The twitch near his eye jumped like a flea. He seemed about to shake me off, but he changed his mind. 'You are quite right . . .' He slipped a gloved hand into a pocket and took out a small black book. He flicked through it until he came to the place he wanted and ripped out a page.

'Take this. Make of it what you will. I advise caution – do not go alone.' He paused. I saw him weigh some words on his tongue. 'I am sorry, Kitty.'

I looked at the paper. It was an address – just one line, nothing more.

'What's this?' I looked up at him.

'Your enemy.'

Chapter Thirty-eight

When I arrived back at The Palace the door swung open. As usual, Tan Seng was ready for me. His tunic billowed as he moved aside to let me into the hall. Mouse-black eyes skimmed the stump of the feather on my hat. I was aware of him scanning the rest of me. Satisfied that the feather was the only casualty from the evening, he went out onto the step to see Vellum's smart carriage drawn up at the end of the lane. Grey Coat was still standing watch. He said he had orders to see me safe to my door.

Two men whose faces never gave anything away studied each other from a distance with something near to mutual respect.

The pink sky of dawn was a false promise. The day had turned out grey as Vellum's man and an east wind had come with it. A scurry of dry leaves followed Tan Seng back into the hall. The leaves chased each other across the tiles and scuffled to a rest in the corner near the foot of the stairs. It took a couple of determined shoves before he managed to close up. Flattened against the door, he took the opportunity to study me again.

'The Lady is . . .?'

'In need of a drink. Tea – hot and strong as you can make it, please.' I pulled off my hat and tossed it to the hall table, grateful for the freedom. My short hair had prickled uncomfortably under the black straw. I turned to the mirror and ran a hand through the thatch. The girl in the glass looked like a bleached hedgehog. Purple shadows under my eyes told a tale.

Tan Seng stared at my reflection. He bowed.

'I will bring tea and bread, Lady. I will tell the others that you are home.'

Home? I watched his grey back disappear down to the basement and felt warm for the first time in hours.

*

As soon as Lucca came into the parlour I could tell he was still stewing about me going off alone. Quite the sermon he gave me, with asides about his lack of sleep on my account. I didn't have the heart to fight him, not when he was wearing his own so plain on his sleeve for my sake. Eventually, when he saw I was still in one piece, his mood improved enough for him to stop his scolding and show some interest.

Before Peggy joined us, I'd laid it all out for him, just as I had for Vellum as dawn crept up over the park. When I pointed out that I partly took the clue for the Vinculum from him, I could see he was pleased with himself.

I poured myself another cup of tea and then I passed Lucca the scrap from Vellum's notebook.

'What do you make of it?'

'All I know of Neptune Street is that a workhouse is nearby.' He frowned and handed the paper back to me. 'A family I knew went there when their business failed. The father, Samuele, came from Pisa originally. He was a tailor. When he lost his sight, they lost everything.' He shrugged. 'A poor place, a sad place.'

I looked at the paper.

11 Neptune Street

Vellum's tight, elegant hand didn't offer anything more.

'You going there, then?' Peggy took a bite out of a slice of bread and butter. Tan Seng had brought up a stack on a tray along with the tea. 'Didn't he tell you anything more, Kit?'

'Not unless you count a warning. He said it was my enemy and told me not to go alone. I couldn't get anything out of his man when we came back in the carriage. I might as well have been travelling with a stone, for all the help he was.'

Lucca reached for his cup. 'Do you recognise this address, Fannella?'

'Only that it's over the river in Rotherhithe near the timber ponds, I think.'

'*Sì.*' He nodded. 'And that is a bad place when ships from the Baltic come in.'

Peggy sucked butter from her fingers. 'Before my cousin went to Canada with her husband she lodged for six months in Swan Lane down near Grand Surrey. She couldn't go out alone after dark and sometimes not during the day neither. Not even to get a bit of fish. He's right about them Baltics.'

I noted that Peggy often mentioned her cousin these days. I wondered if it was the baby – the thought of not having a real family around her.

'*È vero.*' Lucca stared gloomily into his cup like a gypsy telling a fortune. 'A woman would need to take great care there. Perhaps that is why Vellum warned you not to go alone?'

'I'm not sure that's what he meant.' I rolled the scrap of paper into a ball. 'He promised me something in return for what I did for him. He said it was something I needed. And this was it.' I flicked the ball to the hearth.

'What if it is a trap?' Lucca shifted on the couch to see where the paper had lodged. He pushed the hair back from his face, exposing the crimped raw patch on the side of his scalp where it never grew. He was usually so careful to keep it covered, even with me, that I was caught off guard. He saw me looking and shook his hair forward again.

'This man is using you.' There was an edge to his voice. 'He knows you cannot resist. *I* know you cannot resist. That –' he pointed at the hearth – 'is an invitation, not a warning.'

I was on the point of a sharp reply, but I buttoned it. I took a sip of smoky tea instead. Anyway, he was right. About me not being able to resist, leastways. Peggy reached out for another slice of bread. 'Will you go, Kit?'

I nodded. 'But not alone.' The bread hovered in mid-air. 'Before you say anything, Peg, you're staying here. I can't have you traipsing over the river to Christ knows what in your condition.' I set down my tea. 'You'll come with me, Lucca, won't you?'

He sighed. 'You did not even have to ask, Fannella. I am simply saying that we don't know what we will find in Neptune Street. We must be *diffidente*. Vellum is . . . dangerous. I do not trust him, and . . . and I am wary of being summoned so easily.'

Ah! I saw it now. Lucca was still scarred by what had happened when he was caught out by Kite's man, Schalk. No wonder he was cautious. I didn't blame him. I moved closer on the couch.

'For what it's worth, I don't think it's a trap. For a start, Vellum warned me. If you're sending someone on a fool's errand, you don't tell them, do you? Besides, he's had chances enough to . . . *send me to Leeds*, but I'm still here.'

Lucca quizzed at me. We both looked up as the door opened and Lok came into the room. He handed me a copy of *The Pictorial* and bowed.

'As The Lady wished. Bought this morning. First thing.'

I slipped from the couch to the floor and flattened the newspaper out on the rug. It was a shadow of its former self, not that *The Pictorial* was ever much to write home about, mind. It didn't take long to flick through to the personals at the back. I ran a finger down the column . . .

Samgreave . . . Semmings . . . Shelton . . . *Simpson*

**Simpson, Esther: The Mitre, Old Gravel Lane.
Five o'clock sharp.**

*

The Mitre was in my ledgers – my grandmother's ledgers, that is. Even amid that low company it was scraping its arse on the floor. The cracked ceiling was the colour of a rotten tooth. In places it bulged down, making the place seem smaller and more crowded than it truly was.

I peered through the smoke. The customers were mostly men who hadn't managed to get a day shift over the way at London Docks. They'd spent the day drowning their sorrows in gin bought with brass they hadn't earned. Most of them were so far gone they wouldn't know the sun from the moon.

There were a few women there too. Types. Not the sort a wife would take to, if you get my meaning. And not the sort a man would look once at unless he was blind drunk, which was why they were here.

The sawdust on the boards was so thick with spilt gin and ale it was more like mud. The Mitre was an odd place to pick for a meeting.

I'd washed the night away and slept for couple of hours, but I couldn't do a thing about the shadows beneath my eyes. As I got ready to go out again, I'd looked at myself in the little mirror on my bedroom cabinet and wondered what Sam would make of me.

I turned to make sure Lucca was still close behind and pushed through the press in The Mitre. If Sam was here, he was keeping himself hidden. We went to the end of the fug-filled bar and ducked under a screen that led to a series of wooden stalls lit by cheap tallow candles that reeked of rancid fat.

He was alone in the last of them, smoke in hand.

I paused, head bent low, one hand on the side of a sticky panel. Sam was sitting on a bench against the wall, studying the notebook open on the table before him. That battered silver strike box was at his elbow. His smokes were rough, but I'd take them over Vellum's anytime.

Sam flicked to a new page and looked up for a moment to tap away the ash from his smoke. I didn't call out. I wanted to look at him sitting there, lost in his own thoughts. I found I could look at him like that for quite a while.

The moment didn't last long.

'Kitty!' He shifted on the bench and caught me watching. He stood up abrupt and came round the table. From the way he reached out, I thought he was going to take me in his arms, but as Lucca came through the low square entrance he stepped back and fiddled with his frayed cuffs. 'You saw it, then?'

'Of course I bleedin' did.' I sat down opposite him.

'Otherwise I wouldn't be here, would I?' I glanced up at the stains on the wall. 'Nice place you've chosen, Sam.'

Sam nodded at Lucca and reached for a pewter jug and three mugs set on a shelf. 'This is a grim place, but it's off the usual track and very convenient for our purposes this evening. I've used it before. These booths are private. And, surprisingly, the porter is fine. Here.' He poured a stream of dark liquid into the mugs and pushed two of them across the table. You'll need this where we're going.'

'Where's that then?'

'The lion's den, Kitty. It's time to confront the bad Reverend with what we know about his past. Look at this.'

He took a large folded sheet from the back of his notebook and handed it to me. I spread it across the table.

CHILDREN OF PURITY, YOUR HOUR HAS COME

The MENACE of the MUSIC HALLS is an INFECTION.

Would you stand idle if your child, mother, father, sister or brother was CAUGHT in the GHASTLY embrace of TYPHUS FEVER? NO! You would do all in your POWER to FIGHT that HIDEOUS DISEASE. Now you are CALLED to do BATTLE. A SERPENT raises her head in Limehouse. WE MUST STRIKE the head from that MONSTER before her VENOM infects all that you HOLD DEAR AND TRUE. IF YOU WOULD STAND AT THE SIDE OF THE REVEREND AUCHLYNE-DOUNE, come hear his COMMAND.

The ARMY of the RIGHTEOUS will CLEANSE.

Billy Downie sprinkled his capitals like salt on a hot potato. I noted he was making it personal now. With The Comet due to open in less than a fortnight, I had no doubt about who that serpent raising her head was.

The bill was clipped straight at the bottom. The paper was stiff and clean. It hadn't come off a wall. If these were going up around Limehouse again, it was strange that Ramesh Das hadn't sent word. I looked up.

'Where did you get this?'

'From an old . . . contact. I was trying to find cheaper labour for *The Pictorial*. Peters tells me that half the boys in the basement have gone and the other half are planning to. Yesterday I made a visit to Dunk Street, Whitechapel, where I happen to know a printer with some very . . . particular clients.'

'You mean dirty stuff?'

Sam grinned. 'I think Mr Horniman regards it as art, Kitty. The main thing is that he's very inexpensive and he wouldn't want details of his more obscure publications to appear in a newspaper. Even *The Pictorial*.'

I leaned forward. 'You mean you went there to blackmail him into helping you?'

'Not at all. I offered him money as well. I simply wanted to persuade him to help *you*.' He tried to look aggrieved, but from the way he was fidgeting about and tapping his fingers, I could tell he was pleased with himself.

'The point is that I saw this on his desk.' Sam pointed at the bill poster. 'When I asked him about it, he told me he'd printed this one and others like it for a young woman who was rather careful with her purse. This was a draft set for approval. She wanted two hundred like it ready for collection this morning.'

Lucca rose from the bench. He rested a hand on my shoulder. 'These will be going up now. Bell Wharf is not far, Fannella. We can go to Ramesh Das and get him to send out his people to stop them.'

Sam lifted his mug. 'Don't worry. They've been burned. All of them. Mr Horniman was very amenable. He's a sensible man and a pleasure to do business with. I got him to shut up shop for the day too. When the Reverend's daughter went to Dunk Street this morning there was no one there.'

I took a sip of porter and was surprised to find it was good, just as Sam had said.

'This meeting.' I tapped the sheet. 'When *was* it set for and where?'

'Tomorrow evening, six o'clock, same place as before. I take it you went to the Cotton Street Seamen's Rest Hall last time the Children of Purity were summoned, Kitty?'

I nodded. 'Lucca came with me. I thought we might see you there.'

Sam lit a new smoke. 'I intended to go, but something happened. In the afternoon before the meeting I'd arranged to see Peters at a quiet pub in Holborn to go over some items for *The Pictorial.* I've tried to provide him with leads and copy where I can. He's doing his best without me, but it's hard going. The paper's thinner every day. We'll be printing it on Rizlas soon. I was in Star Yard when I realised I was being followed. I doubled back on myself to make sure I wasn't mistaken, but wherever I went the same man was still there thirty yards behind. I must have walked five miles around London before I shook him off in the maze of St Giles, but by then it was too late for Peters or the Seamen's Rest.'

I ran a fingertip round the rim of the mug. 'This man, do you think it was Matthias Schalk?'

Sam took a drag. 'I'd know him anywhere. No, it was a man in a long grey coat.'

'One of Vellum's men!'

He sat back on the bench and quizzed at me. I told him, briefly, as much as he needed to know about my last meeting with Vellum and the grey-coated men who worked for him.

'Thing is, Sam, why would one of them be following you?'

'Ah.' He spun his strike case on the table. It skittered around until the end flicked free and all the Lucifers tumbled out. 'That *might* be because I made some . . . enquiries about your friend, Mr Endymion. I thought I should try to find out more about him. Don't worry, I was very careful.'

'Well, you weren't careful enough!' I thumped the table so hard the Lucifers jumped. 'No wonder he set someone on your tail. Don't you realise what you're getting yourself into when you poke him?'

'Do *you*?' Sam stared at me. He tapped the ash from his smoke on the side of the table.

Lucca cleared his throat. 'We took someone to the meeting in Cotton Street who recognised the Reverend for what he is. You were right about his past.'

Sam was still watching me. It came to me he suspected I might have a softness for Vellum. I didn't know what to do with that, except tuck it away for reference. I held his eye.

'Dismal Jimmy came with us when we went to the Seamen's Rest. He played the halls in Edinburgh and Glasgow with Billy Downie before he went to the Bridewell. He knew him straight off.' I paused. Poor Dismal, he didn't know about Marnie. On balance, I reckoned it was better for him to think she'd left him rather than to know the truth. If Fitzy had kept his word, Marnie was likely at the bottom of the river now, trussed up in a canvas sheet and weighted down by rocks.

'We'll confront him with the truth and threaten to print it.' Sam brought me back. 'If the facts appear in *The London Evening News*, I'm sure the police will be interested too. I don't imagine the Children of Purity will take it well either. He deceived them and pocketed their money. If they catch him, they'll flay him alive.'

Thinking of the people I'd seen at the meetings, I couldn't argue with him on that, but there was something else I wanted to question.

'Why not use *The Pictorial*, Sam? It's a good story.'

'It is.' He shrugged sadly. 'I'm loyal to *The Pictorial*, Kitty, but I'm not a fool. The *News* has twenty times more readers. I intend to threaten Billy Downie with the exposure of his crimes to the largest possible audience. We'll go to his lodgings and threaten to reveal him as a criminal and a charlatan unless he desists.'

Sam finished the last of his porter and scraped the Lucifers back into the strike box. He dipped to fetch up a leather bag from under the bench and pushed it across the table.

'You need to change into these things. It's no place for a woman after dark. Don't worry, we'll guard the entrance to the booth while you change.'

I opened the bag and considered the rumpled clothes inside – breeches, a shirt, a woollen jerkin and a coat.

'Pantomime again, is it, Sam?'

'You make a very good boy, Kitty.' He grinned and lifted a badly patched, moth-eaten coat from the back of the bench.

'Come on, Lucca. We'll stand outside while she changes.'

Lucca frowned. '*Che follia!* We do not know where his lodgings are.'

'Yes we do.' Sam bent double to go out through the gap in the wooden screen to the next booth along.

'Mr Horniman gave me the name and address of his Scottish lady client. Miss Ishbel Doune lodges at 11 Neptune Street, Rotherhithe.'

Chapter Thirty-nine

I could hardly see a hand in front of my face. The alley leading down to the river was thick with a yellow-tinged fog that clung to my skin and to my hair. The murk swirling about us was matched by the fug in my head.

11 Neptune Street.

It seemed all ways led there tonight. Billy Downie *was* my enemy, that was clear enough. Sam reckoned Vellum had slipped me his address by way of payment for services rendered. That seemed a reasonable suggestion, didn't it? All the same, as we made our way to King Henry's Stairs I couldn't shake the thought that the itch on the back of my neck came from something more than the scratch of Sam's woollen jerkin under the coat.

A single gas lantern lit the entrance to the river passage along from The Mitre, but the further we went the darker it got. We linked hands to form a chain; Sam went first, I was in the middle and Lucca brought up the rear.

I liked the feel of Sam's hand in mine.

When the cobbles slanted downward to a flight of dripping stone steps, Sam halted and struck a couple of Lucifers to show the way. I could hear the river now, waves slapping on stone. The steps turned back on themselves sharp and we came out to a wooden platform.

There was a wall at our backs. Water swirled and sucked beneath the jetty and the smell came fierce. London's filth tumbled from drains into the Thames and bobbed about, waiting for the tide to carry it away. From the rattling and screeching I knew there were ships close by. The wind made the rigging of the invisible boats moored on the river sing. Not in a tuneful way.

Sam whistled loud and clear. A moment later a long, low whistle came back, followed by the splashing of oars and the bump and creak of wood. Gradually, a dim glow in the fog brightened to show a row boat pulling up alongside. A man swaddled in a mound of blankets took a lantern from the front of the boat and swung it up to see us clear.

'Where to, sirs?'

Sam crouched down at the edge of the jetty. 'Elephant Stairs.'

The man sucked his teeth and whistled. 'Thickest it's been for months. Not easy, even for Wilkes.'

Sam jingled some coins in a pocket. 'It's a five-minute journey. Straight across.'

'And it's a rising tide, sir. In the dark as well as the fog. That takes the knowing, it does.' The man tapped the side of his nose. 'I'm not saying I won't, but I am saying it'll cost.'

'How much do you want, Mr Wilkes?'

'Not more than a sovereign. I won't take a penny more than that. Wouldn't be fair.'

'No, it certainly wouldn't.' Sam stood up. 'I'll call again. This time an honest lighterman will hear me.'

Wilkes sat back in his row boat and regarded us all from the depths of the blankets huddled around his body. 'As you like, sirs. But I don't reckon you'll get much in the way of a bite. There's not many of us abroad looking for trade this evening. Not on a night like this. You was lucky I was passing.'

The man was carving us down to the bone, but I didn't have time for haggling. I went to Sam's side and peered down at the boat. Trails of fog moved like waterweed in the glow of Wilkes's lantern. 'A sovereign it is then, but only if you wait at Elephant Stairs to bring us back. There might not be many lightermen about, but I don't hear anyone else calling for a passage across tonight.'

Wilkes sniffed loudly and ran the back of a hand under his nose. 'How long will you be?' I noted he was keen enough to ask the question.

'As long as it takes. We've got business in Rotherhithe. I'll give you half when we get there and half when you bring us back. I reckon that's a very fair night's takings for two trips?'

He grumbled and plucked at the blankets. Muttering some more, he stowed the lantern in the front of the boat and then he ploughed an oar into the river. The little boat swung about.

'What was that?' I caught the edge of a wooden post and leaned further out over the water. 'I didn't hear what you said.'

'I said you'd better get yourselves down here.' He moved the lantern so the beam slicked at the struts of a weed-draped ladder leading down to the river. Wilkes kept the boat steady as we clambered down to the slatted benches. Lucca and me sat up front near the lantern and Sam took a place at the back end. Once we were in position, the old lighterman, who hummed like a dog left out in the rain, pushed free of the jetty and began to row.

The journey across took nearer to fifteen minutes on account of the tide and the fact that we had to navigate around rows of ships moored in the Lower Pool. They loomed up sudden in the fog, black sides towering above the little wooden boat. Most of them were lit at the prow and the stern, but on a night like this the lights couldn't cut far. Wilkes was right about the fog. It was like floating through suet.

When we'd been out for ten minutes, the horns for the London Pools began to sound. I clapped my hands over my ears against the mournful noise, but each time they wailed over the river, I felt the long, low shiver of warning in every bone.

*

We paused under a bent lamp at the end of Church Street. The glass was shattered and the blue-tinged flame guttered in the wind. It made our shadows flicker on the black bricks of the stand-up on the corner of Neptune Street. Music came from inside, a squeezebox wheezing out a broken tune. A single window leaked dim light onto the cobbles.

Away from the river, the fog was thinner, but I reckoned it had done us a favour. Since we'd left Mr Wilkes, still sniffing and muttering, in his row boat at Elephant Stairs we'd passed no more than a score of people, most of them scurrying to their homes.

And mean homes they were too. I knew my grandmother's ledgers included some interests over this side of the river, but I'd never bothered to visit them. I'd let Telferman deal with all that. I should have taken better note.

This was a poor place. Some of the windows of the hovels we passed were boarded over or covered with rags. There were people inside, mind. You could tell by the light creeping out through a hole in the fabric or around the edge of the planks. It stank too. Gutters led out from the alleys, tumbling a foaming stream into the open sewer that ran down the middle of the wider passages. The stench lodged in my nose and at the back of my throat.

Lucca held back the brim of his hat to get a view of the dingy street running off to the right of the stand-up. The light from the broken lamp didn't show more than a couple of houses along the terrace. He turned to Sam.

'The man you blackmailed. Mr Horniman. Did you ask him anything more about Ishbel? Is there more we need to know, or put to use?'

Sam shook his head. 'I thought the address was enough. I didn't know at the time that Kitty's friend in high places would send us here too.' He sidled at me. 'Did *he* say anything more?'

I scratched my neck. 'Like I told you at The Mitre, he just handed me that paper and then he took off like a devil was on his tail, leaving me with his man and his carriage.'

I glanced up at the street name painted on the wall above Lucca's head. 'Neptune was the god of the sea, wasn't he?'

Lucca nodded. 'He was the brother of Jupiter, the King of the gods, and also brother to Hades, King of the Underworld.'

The mist coiling around our ankles seemed to soak through my breeches to the skin. It was bleedin' cold for September. I pulled up the collar of Sam's coat. No one had cast a second look at me in his gear. Not even Wilkes, and I didn't reckon much got past him.

'Actually, there was one thing Horniman said.' Sam's face flared up bright as he struck a Lucifer against the wall. 'Ishbel came to Dunk Street with her brother a couple of times.'

'Donal – that's his name.' I nodded at Lucca. 'We saw him at the Seamen's Rest. He's a big lad – well, a big *man*, really, but

458

he seems more like a child. He tried to run out at the end, but Ishbel caught him.'

Sam took a pull to get his smoke going. The tip glowed red in his cupped hand. 'Horniman mentioned the brother, but nothing more.'

I thought about the conversation we'd heard going on behind the brown curtain at the Seamen's Rest. 'Billy Downie is a cruel bastard. I reckon he knocked his boy about in the past. He damaged him, and Ishbel's still trying to protect him.'

'Perhaps she too is a victim?' Lucca nodded. 'The way she cradled her brother on the steps, Fannella? I thought she cared for him very deeply.'

'That's true enough. Then again, I don't . . .' I held that. The door to the stand-up swung open and the reedy music came louder. Two men blundered out, one of them clutching a bottle in his fist. He turned to look at us and the lamp shone up the gold of his cropped blond hair. He said something to his companion in a language I couldn't understand. Both of them were dressed the same – dark coats with brass buttons, banded caps with trailing ribbons. Baltics, perhaps, or navy men from somewhere a long way east of Limehouse?

The man with the bottle stumbled closer and jabbed a dirty finger at me, breathing a fug of cheap liquor into my face. He grunted out something that sounded like a question and the finger crept to my cheek.

'No!' Sam stepped between us. The man grinned. He looked back at his friend and barked something more. The pair of them laughed. It must have been quite a joke because they bent double, slapping their thighs and honking like geese.

The friend pissed himself; steam rose from the stream trickling over his foot to the gutter.

'Fannella . . .' Lucca whispered. I felt his hand on my arm.

Sam held up his smoke. The man's eyes swam towards it.

Digging his brass case from a pocket, Sam flicked open the end and held it out. It was a gesture of friendship. The man with the bottle sidled at me and then he shrugged and took a couple of smokes for himself and more for his friend. He offered Sam the bottle, but he shook his head and stepped back, forcing me to stand further off too.

The man collapsed against the wall of the stand-up, made a sort of salute and clipped out something to his damp-legged friend. Then he gathered himself together again and the pair of them staggered into the mist.

Sam raised his smoke to his lips and took down a lungful. 'If I'm not mistaken, Kitty, they just made Lucca and me an offer for our boy.'

Lucca spat on the cobbles. An unlikely gesture for him. He moved his hand to my shoulder. 'If they thought you were a woman, Fannella, I'm not sure that . . .'

When he didn't finish that I squeezed his hand. 'Thanks to Sam and his scissors, I make a very convincing young man these days.'

Sam made me a mock bow. 'Before we were interrupted, Kitty, you were saying something about Ishbel and her brother?'

'Lucca thought she might be a victim, but she don't seem like that to me. Not the way she runs those meetings for her father. They're partners. It's a going concern.'

Sam nodded. 'That's true enough. The Reverend has left an unsavoury trail wherever he's been. I've not been idle these

460

past days. I've managed to track him with help from some colleagues in the press. Before Auchlyne-Doune came to London he was in Southampton. It was the same there. He whipped the locals into a frenzy of righteous anger directed at The Royal York. After three public meetings he disappeared. By then, of course, with the help of Ishbel, he'd pocketed a considerable sum of money.'

He flicked ash from the smoke to the gutter and scrutinised Neptune Street. 'He won't hold another meeting in Limehouse, not after tonight.'

Taking a last drag, he ground the stub underfoot. 'Odd numbers are on the right.'

*

'Do we just knock?'

I stared up at the squat, shabby house. It was difficult to imagine someone like Billy Downie crammed inside. There was a faint light in one of the two windows on the first floor.

Lucca wrapped the trailing ends of his scarf around his shoulders. 'What else can we do?'

Tell truth, now we were standing here on the street outside number 11, the thought of giving Billy a sermon on the error of his ways and seeing him take it down meek as a child sipping Winslow's Syrup from a spoon seemed unlikely.

Sam stepped back and looked up at the lighted windows. 'Someone's home. That's something.' He rubbed his hands together. 'Lucca's right.'

Without another word he sprang forward and rapped on the door three times. When nothing happened, he tried again, louder. The sound made the rags twitch at the windows of the house next door. I couldn't see anyone through the chink, but I felt eyes on us as he knocked a third time.

Now the light upstairs brightened. I saw a shape at the window. Someone was looking down at us. They held a lamp to the glass and the glow of it fell across my upturned face.

A moment later there was a thumping sound from inside the house. Someone was running down the stairs. Bolts were drawn and the door was flung open.

Ishbel Downie flew into the street, wrapping me in her arms. She buried her head in the gap between my shoulder and neck and clung tight.

'Thank God!' She breathed the words into my ear and I felt her tears on my skin. 'Oh, thank God!' I wasn't sure what to do. I patted her shoulder and glanced at Sam and Lucca, who were watching with equal surprise.

Ishbel burrowed deeper and stroked my hair. 'You're back. You've come back to me. Now we can go anywhere we please, Joseph.'

Chapter Forty

I stiffened in her arms. Ishbel looked up. One of her eyes was swollen and circled with a purple shadow. She reached out to trace a finger down my cheek, the tip moving gently from the side of my mouth to my ear. Her pale eyes filled with confusion.

That was when I knew, of a certainty, that it was my brother she'd thought to be standing beneath her window. When I'd seen Joey that last time in the Bethlem, his handsome face had been torn by Swami Jonah's blade. Ishbel was trying to find a scar that wasn't there.

Just for a moment, the woman clasping me tight in her arms still seemed to believe that it was my brother she was holding. 'Joseph?' She whispered the name and searched my face for confirmation. Her eyes told me she didn't want to believe what she saw.

'But, you're . . . you're not . . .'

She let me go and brought a hand to her mouth.

'I know who you are!' Ishbel pushed me away. She took a step back to the open door behind her. Over her shoulder I saw Sam and Lucca move to block her way. She caught me looking and spun about, but it was too late, she was cornered. Eyes blazing, she came back at me spitting like a cat, desperate to push me aside and run from us down the street. She was tall and wiry with it, but I caught her arms as she flailed and clawed at my face.

All that time I'd spent dandling from a bar in a cage had made me strong. I twisted one arm up behind her back and

463

thrust her forward to Sam. He clamped round her and held tight.

'You unnatural bitch!' Ishbel struggled and spat into my face. 'He told me about you. How you'd taken his place. How you'd wheedled your way into your grandmother's affections. What have you done with him?'

I wiped the spittle from my chin. Now *I* was confused.

Ishbel thrashed like an eel. 'Where is he?'

I stepped closer. 'If you mean my brother Joey, and I reckon you do, then that's a question I'd like the answer to as much as you.'

'Liar!' She tried to kick out, but Sam held her tight. Lights were showing at several windows along the street now. Lucca pointed at the open door to number 11. 'We should go inside.'

'No!' Ishbel fought as Sam dragged her back to the doorway. He hauled her over the threshold, feet drumming on the boards, and I followed. Lucca shut the door and we were swallowed by darkness. The hallway smelt of mouse and mould.

She started to weep. Her breath came in great ragged sobs. 'Leave us be. You've got him now, isn't that enough?'

I put a hand to the wall to steady myself. The paper was damp to the touch.

'I don't know what you mean. I swear it. Until a minute ago I thought my brother was a thousand miles away, not here in London.'

'But you sent for him this morning. He always said you were dangerous.' Her voice was choked with grief. 'Your grey-coated men dragged Joseph from my bed and they took him to you.'

*

464

The lodgings upstairs were spare as a cuckoo's nest. Just four chairs, a table and a shelf of mismatched crockery. Over by the narrow grate a tin box spilled paper and tiny nuggets of coal to the boards. There was a door at the back of the room opening onto another staircase. After we'd made sure Ishbel couldn't go far, we took the lamp and checked the two rooms upstairs. In the first of them we found a narrow brass bedstead piled with a tangle of sheets. An assortment of clothes hung limp from hooks on the wall. In the second, a broad wooden box bed, straw poking free from the stained striped ticking, slanted across the boards. The room had been stripped bare, and by someone in a hurry if the marks on the boards and the angle of the bed told a tale.

Back downstairs, I set the lantern Ishbel had brought to the window on the table. It was the only light in the room. Seated at the table, hands tied behind her back with Lucca's scarf, she watched him poke rolls of paper into the tiny grate to start a fire from the scanty coals. Her bruised face was pinched with fury, but she couldn't stop the tears from sliding down her cheeks.

'I knew you both when you came to the meeting in Cotton Street. That scar . . .' She flicked a look of contempt at Lucca's back. 'Joseph told me his perfidious sister went about with a maimed dog.' Her soft Scots accent sat at odds with the venom in her voice. I didn't know what 'perfidious' meant, but I imagined it described my brother rather than me.

Ishbel hadn't finished. 'You tricked me. Just look at you with your clipped hair and breeches. Joseph said you were unnatural.'

I resisted the urge to slap her. Instead, I leaned against the wall and tried to imagine Joey in this room. He'd been here in

London all this time and I never knew.

And now he was gone again. Vellum's grey coats had come for him first thing.

Jesus! What a fool I'd been. I saw the view from another hill now. Vellum had known all along that Joey was involved with Ishbel Downie and her father – that's what he was always going to give me as reward for helping him out. But he didn't know that Joey had the key to the Vinculum in his head until I'd told him in the early hours today.

Sam pulled out a chair and sat down at the table opposite Ishbel. 'We don't mean you any harm.' His voice was calm and low. I reckoned it was a trick he used when he was trying to milk a story.

'We came here to . . . persuade your father to stop this campaign against the halls. We know who you are . . .' He rubbed at an ink smut on his thumb. 'Well, that's to say we know who your father is. He's not a man of God. We know his real name is Billy Downie. Where is he, Ishbel?'

'Gone.' She turned her face to the wall.

'Gone where?' I straightened up. She didn't answer. Lucca shifted back from the hearth. A tidy little blaze was going there now. Christ knows that room needed some warmth.

He sat on his heels and spoke softly. I noted that the pair of them were treating her like a frightened animal.

'Who hurt you, Ishbel? Did the men who came this morning do that to your eye?'

She didn't answer. Lucca tried again. 'Was it Joseph?'

'No!' She turned sharp to look at him. 'Joseph would never hurt me. My father did this. When your men came here –' she slid pale eyes full of hatred to me – 'he said it was time to move

466

on. He said we'd had a good run of it. But I wouldn't go, not without him.'

'Not without Joey, you mean?'

She ignored me and studied the top of the table.

Lucca stood and brushed his hands. 'Your brother – Donal, was it? Where is he now?'

Ishbel's head shot up. 'How do you know about Donal?'

'We saw him at the Seamen's Rest.' Lucca smiled. 'He is a musician, *si*? The music at the meetings was played by your brother – I think that must be true? Your father was performing. You were at the door, but the music was played by someone else.'

Lucca was right about that. I hadn't given it a thought, but he clearly had. He had an ear for music and a softness for talent. I knew the orchestra boys respected him.

She gave the ghost of a nod as he came slowly to the table. 'Your brother is very gifted. You must be proud of him.'

Another tear slipped down her face. 'Donny always loved music. Our mother taught him to play. It was all he had left after . . . after . . .'

'After your father beat him so badly that he destroyed his mind?' Lucca sat at the table next to her.

It came to me that it was a good thing Lucca and Sam were here with me. I wasn't sure I could be so polite.

Sam glanced at me and tried another tack. 'Where is Donal . . . Donny now? Is he with your father? Did they go together? Is that it?'

Ishbel gulped back a sob. 'He didn't understand. It was like the old man and the dolls. He thought he was hurting them.'

Old man and the dolls?

I went to the table. Sam shot me a warning look, but I planted my hands on the wood and bent towards her.

'When you say dolls, do you mean puppets?'

She didn't answer.

'These puppets, were they in a theatre? One of *my* theatres?'

She looked at me now, her good eye still brimming with spite. 'Joseph's theatre, you mean. He took us there to show us his rightful inheritance.'

I stood back to take her in. I spoke slow so there was no danger of her mistaking the question. 'Are you saying my brother was there at The Carnival the night Signor Marcelli died?'

Of an instant, the room was so silent you could have heard a spider spinning a web in the furthest corner.

Ishbel started to cry.

Chapter Forty-one

It all came out then. Once she started talking about Joey she didn't want to stop. She minded me of a schoolgirl mooning for a first love. At first, she needed gentle prompts to get her going. Lucca and Sam were good at that. I sat back and let them get on with it. I watched her as she told her story. I knew her type from the halls. Ishbel Downie was the kind of woman who enjoyed the attention of men. She lapped it up like a starved kitten.

The facts of the matter were simple enough. She and her father had met my brother on the train from Southampton to London. Billy Downie and his children were moving on to find a new patch for their trade. Southampton was turning a bit too hot for Billy's liking, and besides, now they'd got the routine so neat that silver was coming thick as a shoal of pilchards, there were better places to cast their net. London was very appealing.

Joey had heard them discussing likely venues on the platform at Southampton and he crept into their company. He'd told them he was just back from a journey overseas, which in a way was true, although he hadn't come very far.

It was plain that the *Helena Mena*, where Ramesh Das had left Joey in a cabin, had made at least one stop in England before heading out to Australia. Joey had jumped ship at Southampton.

I remembered what the grave-faced old man had said as he sipped his chai. *He would be a greater fool than I imagine him to be if he did not take this opportunity.*

469

Ramesh Das was wrong. Joey was a great fool, but he was something more too. I chewed on my lip as I listened to Ishbel worship his name.

My brother hadn't lost his charm, I'll give him that. It didn't take long for him to sinuate himself with the three of them. Just a two-hour train ride, in fact. He and Billy discovered a shared passion for the halls. The pair of them were burning with hate. Billy was all for paying them back for his years in the Bridewell, and Joey? According to Ishbel he was a wronged man, a saint unfairly robbed of his birthright. It didn't surprise me to hear it was my own brother who suggested that Limehouse might be a good place for the Reverend Auchlyne-Doune to turn his hellfire cant to gold.

By the time they pulled into Waterloo Station, Joey was part of the family business. It was him who found the halls for the meetings and told them where to plaster their bills for the best effect. He was very useful to Billy.

Ishbel didn't say as much but putting it all together it was obvious that Joey had made himself useful to her too. I got the impression that men hadn't paid her much attention before he took a lively interest. I studied her skinny frame, sharp face and mousy hair. No wonder she was easy to deceive.

'And he was always so good to Donny.' Ishbel shook her head. 'The night of the . . . accident, it was Joseph who cleared everything up. He made everything right again.'

I sidled at Lucca. It didn't look like an accident when we found Signor Marcelli.

Sam leaned across the table. 'What happened that night? What do you mean by accident, Ishbel?' The way those two spoke so gentle, coaxing her with the use of her name, made me want to take her by the throat and throttle the story from her thin lips.

She swallowed and bent back her head to stare at the ceiling. The knot on the top of her head had come loose and now a thin trail of dull brown hair hung down her back.

'Donny often came out with us. It was better that way. Father was cruel to him, but Joseph, now, he loved him like a brother.'

I almost laughed out loud. I managed to button it as she carried on.

'We had some bill posters to set around the area. Donny liked helping with that. It was late, but afterwards Joseph said he wanted to show me his birthright – the places you stole from him.' She glared at me.

'He took us to The Carnival. The door wasn't locked so Joseph led us inside. It was dark, but there were lights showing under the curtain. Someone was on stage. We heard . . .' She paused. '*Thought* we heard the voices of children, laughter. Donny ran forward. He was just a child himself. I called out to stop him, but it was too late. He followed the sounds, found a way up the steps and went behind the curtain. Then I heard him cry out. A great howl it was. We heard an old man's voice and a crash. Joseph ran to the stage and there he found . . .' Ishbel shuddered. 'It was too late. Donny had killed that man. It was an accident. He thought he was hurting them. The puppets, I mean. He couldn't tell they weren't real. Joseph told us to go home. He said he would deal with it.'

'You didn't see him clear up, then?' I glanced at Lucca. He frowned and circled the tip of a finger on the table top.

'I think I understand, Ishbel.' Lucca spoke very gently.

471

'Donal thought he was protecting them, *sì*?'

She nodded. 'The old man had fallen back on the boards and his head was bleeding. I tried to help, but he was . . . dead. Donny had killed him. I didn't know what to do.'

'But Joey did?' I thought of the mess we'd found on stage. The nails driven into the old man's body. The cat's cradle of lines stringing him up like one of his own puppets. And I remembered the savage way those puppets had been maimed. If Joey did that, he was . . .

'So good to us. He sent us home in a cab.' Ishbel gulped back another sob. 'And we never heard another thing about it.'

I stood and went over to the dying fire. Some of the papers Lucca had used to get it going were curled and scorched at the edges, but they hadn't caught. I stared at a gaudy picture of a bearded, blue-eyed man clamping a couple of lambs under his arm. It was a page ripped from a big old Bible – one of Billy's props, I reckoned.

What did you do that night, Joey? I stared at the shepherd's mild eyes. *Why?*

I knelt to gather up a few more coals and threw them into the hearth. A small flame spread from the coals and licked at the edges of the Bible page. In a count of five, the shepherd was alight. The purple flame soon turned him and his lambs to ash.

'What about the dog?' I stood up. 'The one we found nailed to the door at The Comet? Little Spark, that was her name. And Marnie too, what about her? The woman strung up over the stage at The Carnival?'

'Dog?' Ishbel stared at me. Her bad eye was ripe as a plum. 'I don't know what you mean, and I don't know anyone called Marnie.' She shook her head. 'Joseph never took us to The

Comet. Donny was very sensitive. We didn't want to upset him again . . . or remind him of what happened.'

I didn't think she was lying. There was something in that answer that caught me, mind, but I didn't have time to follow it home. Now that Ishbel was actually speaking to me there was more I needed to know.

'Were you ever down by the river in a place called The Hope?'

Her eyes slid from mine. She shifted on the chair and wriggled.

'It's too tight. I can't feel my hands.'

I went back to the table and sat down. 'There was a fight at The Hope on the night I was there. It spilled out onto the street. A real Punch and Judy show it was.' I looked at Lucca who nodded. '*A tuth for a tuth.*' I mimicked her. 'I think I saw you there with your father.'

She turned to me sharp. 'I was not with him. I was with Joseph.'

I sat back. 'So you *were* there?'

She considered the question. After a moment or two she nodded. 'I was showing Joseph how to . . . was teaching him the way of control, just as my father taught me. He has the knack for it. Joseph is very talented. When we go—' She stopped herself and dropped her gaze to the table top.

Sam dug into a pocket for his smokes. 'Where is your father now, Ishbel?'

'Where is Joseph?' Her head snapped up.

I thumped the table. 'I don't know. I didn't even know my brother was here in London until half an hour ago. But I'll tell you this for nothing: he's not to be trusted.'

She raised her chin. 'Joseph loves me.'

'Does he?' I snorted. 'I very much doubt that, Miss Downie.' I couldn't bear listening to her lovestruck claptrap for a moment more. 'Tell me this, has he ever been away for the night of occasion and come back the next day full of excuses as to where he's been?'

Ishbel sat very still as I carried on. 'You're of a size with him. Have you ever found any of your clothes missing or something – a dress, a coat maybe – put back in the wrong place? Or damaged. Perhaps you didn't know how it came to be so?'

She blinked and I saw it. A flicker of doubt in her eyes told me all I needed to know. I pushed the point home.

'If you've been reckoning on setting up house with my brother, I think you'll be very disappointed. You're not his type. Sam over there is more to his taste, or Lucca. Did you not realise that? No, I don't think you did. There's a lot about my brother that you don't know. I'll be kind – let's say there's a lot he doesn't *want* you to know. He's used you, Ishbel, like he's used everyone else, me included. This is the truth of it – and may God strike me down if I'm speaking false – the only person Joey Peck truly loves is himself.'

The crackle of the fire was the only sound in the room.

'You're lying,'

The break in Ishbel's voice was a small, sour victory.

I felt Sam's eyes on me. I cleared my throat. 'I wouldn't say no to a smoke, Sam, if you're offering.'

'Of course.' He handed me the box and struck a Lucifer. I let him light the smoke and his hand cupped mine. She watched me. Watched us both. Of an instant, I felt for her. All that love wasted on a man not worth the effort.

474

I took a drag. Sam's tobacco was rough, but it calmed me.

'Listen. I'd like to know where Joey is as much as you, Ishbel. What happened this morning when he was taken?'

All the fight had gone from her now. She slumped in the chair and answered in a voice as flat and drab as her hair. 'It was early. There was a knock at the door and I went down. I was expecting to go over to Whitechapel to collect some . . .' She paused. 'I'd ordered a dress and I thought it was being delivered early.'

Sam drummed his fingers on the table. 'That's not quite true. You were expecting some printed bills, weren't you? For another meeting. You thought they were being delivered to your door.'

She was about to deny it, but then she sighed. 'Yes. But it wasn't the boy from the printers. There were five men outside, all dressed alike. They pushed past me into the hall. Two of them held me against the wall. The others went upstairs and pulled Joseph from my bed. He wasn't even dressed. They . . . they put a sack over his head and they dragged him down to the street where a carriage was waiting. I gave them clothes. I begged them to take them. That was the last I saw of him.' She looked up. 'Do you know who they were?'

Now it was me who avoided her eyes.

'What of Donal and your father?' Lucca frowned. 'They must have heard the noise?'

Ishbel nodded. Another tear tracked down her face. 'Father was angry. He said that we had run out of luck. It was time to move on. He didn't like it here anyway.'

Sam waved his smoke at the room. 'Why were you here at all? This is low, even for a man like Billy Downie.'

She almost smiled. 'Oh, we've stayed in worse places than this. It's cheap. Father always likes it that way.'

'But is it not dangerous?' Lucca shook his head. 'A woman here . . .'

'Would be quite safe if she had a brother built like a mountain at her side, and . . .' Ishbel swallowed.

I took a cup from the shelf above the table and flicked ash from my smoke onto the blue flowers curling in the china at the bottom.

'What happened, Ishbel?'

'Please. It hurts. Untie me.'

Lucca quizzed at me. I nodded. There didn't seem to be much point in keeping her bound any more. When he freed the scarf from her arms, she shrugged and gave a little gasp as the blood flowed back. She laid her hands flat on the table before her. The nails were bitten to the quick.

'Father went this morning. I don't know where and I don't care. He tried to force us to leave with him, but I wouldn't go. Not without Joseph. There was a fight.' She ran the tips of her fingers over her bruised cheek and swollen eye. 'He did this to me.'

'What about Donal? Is he with your father now?' I set the cup on the table and studied the roses looping around the rim. I had a bad feeling about what was coming next. I knew what had pricked at me now. All the time we'd been sitting here, Ishbel had been talking about her brother like he was gone. Gone permanently.

She clasped her hands together. 'Donny loved me, very much. After our mother died I was all he had for the longest time. When Father came at me this morning he tried to

476

stop him. Donny was very strong, but so was our father. His hands . . . hands . . .' Ishbel paused and shook her head. A tear fell on the wood. Billy had fists like a brawler, I remembered that from the meetings. She swiped at her cheek. 'There was a fight and then our father left us. He took everything we had with him. Every penny.'

Poor mare. I reached for her hand, but she pulled away.

'Where is he? Donal, I mean?'

She raised her eyes to the ceiling.

'He's not there, Ishbel.' Lucca spoke like he was soothing a baby. 'We went upstairs, remember.'

She shook her head. 'There is another room above the one Joseph and I shared . . . sometimes.' She darted a look at me. The damaged eye was nearly closed now, but there was no fire or light in the other. 'Father dragged him up there and then he left.'

'We must help him!' Lucca sprang up from the table. He snatched a candle from the shelf, lit it with one of Sam's strikes and went to the door. Sam stubbed out his smoke and followed. I heard the pair of them on the stairs. Ishbel bent forward and held her head in her hands. Her shoulders shivered through the thin material of her dress. She looked up and stared at the wall opposite. Her pale blue eyes moved over the plaster like she was seeing something there.

I sat with her for a minute, but when she didn't move or say another word, I followed Lucca and Sam.

In the room with the brass bedstead a ladder had been folded from a hatch in the ceiling. I climbed up the rungs and came out into an attic space. Lucca's little candle flickered wildly on the walls. In one corner an old mattress was pulled up under

477

the skylight. In the other, Sam and Lucca were kneeling beside a long, dark mound. It looked like a roll of fabric stashed against the wall. I crouched down next to them.

Donal was lying on his side. In the dim light you might have taken him to be sleeping. He was a man, but his pale skin was smooth as a child's. His big jaw didn't carry the shadow of a beard, not even a single bristle. Thick black hair fell over his eyes. I pushed it away. He was cold.

Now, when I looked properly, I saw the way his head was angled. It rested askew as if it didn't connect to his shoulders. Billy Downie had broken his own son's neck.

Lucca whispered beside me. Again, I recognised the patter of a prayer. Sam reached for my hand and held it tight. 'Poor man.' He shook his head. 'Poor Donal. And look . . .' He turned and pointed to the far side of the room. At first, I couldn't see what he meant, but as my eyes adjusted to the light it came clear. What had once been a pretty, portable organ, the wooden casing decorated with roses and bows, was smashed against the wall. Its innards – all the pipes and workings – lay scattered around it on the floor. Someone had trampled them underfoot. It was almost more shocking to see the violence of it. Donal looked peaceful, but his treasure had been savaged by a beast.

When we went back down again, Ishbel Downie had gone. I didn't think of her as my enemy now.

Chapter Forty-two

The tea slipped to my belly. The heat of it reminded me I was lucky to be alive, unlike poor Donal. I wasn't sure that Ishbel had much life left in her either, wherever she was. The woman I'd left at the table had been staring at an empty wall and an empty future.

Wilkes was good as his word. After we shut the door to number 11 and walked in silence back to the river, he was still bobbing about in the scum at Elephant Stairs, waiting for the rest of his sovereign. I said I'd double it if he took us east to Kidney Stairs and he didn't argue.

The tide had turned and the going was easier. As we pushed upriver in the fog, I listened to the wind whistling through the ropes of the ships and I thought of that broken, mangled organ.

I had to knock on the door of The Palace, which was unusual. When Tan Seng opened up, he was breathless as if he'd come running. A dusty hat sat on the hall table and an old-style coat with caped shoulders hung from a hook near the door. The hall reeked of naphtha.

'Dr Pardieu's here?' I stared at the hat. 'Is it the baby?'

Tan Seng closed the door and bowed. 'There was a fall, Lady. We sent for him. All will be well. Mrs Tewson will be well.'

'And the baby?' I ran to the foot of the stairs, intending to go up to her, but Tan Seng stopped me.

'She sleeps. The child she carries is safe. Lok is with her also.'

'What happened?' Lucca took off his hat and scarf. Strands

of damp black hair clung to his forehead. 'How did she fall?'

Tan Seng's eyes slid regretfully to the polished stairs. Lok had been busy with a pot of beeswax. I could smell it over the naphtha. 'The doctor has examined her. All is well, Lady. Now she needs rest and silence. Come, it is warmer below and the hour is late. I will make tea.'

It was odd to be invited down to the brothers' domain, but as Peggy's room was over the parlour, I suspected Tan Seng had herded us down here to give her peace. The copper pans strung along the walls reflected the light from the brass candle lanterns on the table. The cheerful glow and the familiar scent of spices and herbs was a comfort. Laundry swung from bars under the ceiling. If a person was to tell me there were a thousand miles between here and Neptune Street, I wouldn't have thought it far enough.

After setting a fresh-brewed pot and three cups on the table, Tan Seng took a tray up to Dr Pardieu and Lok, who were with Peggy. The three of us sat in a silence of weary confusion. There were smuts of black on Sam's face. I wanted to lick my fingers, lean across and wipe them clean, just as Nanny Peck would have done. Lucca stared into his tea. Donal had cut him deep.

I was still numb from the cold. I hadn't been aware of it until the heat from the china drew the blood back. My hands were white as a sheet of tripe, but now the tips of my fingers were on fire. I put the cup down and splayed my palms on the wood.

Sam pushed the fringe from his good eye. He cleared his throat. 'Kitty, it . . . it must have been a shock to find that your own brother was working against you. I'm sorry. So very sorry.' He laid a hand on mine. I glanced up. Just for a moment

480

I saw through the quick, clever front he showed the world. That tumble of words was a shield. He looked away sharp and carried on.

'And now Vellum has taken him. It can only be because of the Vinculum.'

I shook my head. 'Gave it to him on a plate, didn't I? Practically the last thing I said to Vellum was that Joey had the key in his head like me. He seemed surprised at that.'

I badly needed to rub my hands to stop the tingling, but I didn't want to lose the feeling of Sam's skin on mine. Tell truth, I wondered if the rush of heat I was feeling now was entirely caused by the cold.

It was Sam who pulled away first. He drummed his fingers on the table. 'And then, as soon as he knew, he sent someone to take him? It can only be because he intends to use Joey to open the damned thing.'

'But I could do that, and he knew it.' I took up my cup.

'It is like chess. We must look at the pieces on the board.' Lucca took three china bowls from the shelf behind him. He placed one upside down in the middle of the table between us.

'Vellum knew where *Joseph* was.'

He lined up another next to it.

'And all the time, Joseph was working with . . . with *that man*.' He couldn't bear to say Billy's name.

The third bowl went down.

'*Vellum* gave you the address himself.'

'And when he handed it to me, he said it was my enemy.'

I studied the row of pretty china domes. The pattern was the same as the one on the bowl that Tan Seng had given me before. A pair of moths fluttered over a beetle rolling a tiny ball. Night creatures, that's what he'd called them. A crescent moon curved over the scene and beside it there was a small blue star. I thought of the stars that glinted over the park when Vellum gave me the scrap of paper from his book.

Watching, with eternal lids apart.

Vellum had been doing a lot of watching. He had that address ready for me long before I told him about Joey knowing the code.

Sam tapped out a tune on the wood. 'He gave you the address because he was offering you the chance to bring an end to the Children of Purity. It was your reward.'

I reached out to swap the upended bowls around in the way of a sharper. Find the Lady was the game. I was good at it.

'That's true, I suppose, in a way.' I moved a bowl to a new place with the tip of a finger. 'I can't help thinking there was more to it.'

'He said he would give you something you needed, Fannella.' Lucca watched me slide the bowls on the wood. 'I was there, remember? Vellum told you it would be something of value to you and to those close to you.'

'He said he was offering me my *enemy*.'

'And he sent you to the Reverend Auchlyne-Doune.' Sam agreed with Lucca. 'He was good as his word.'

'No.' I shook my head and switched the bowls round again. 'I don't think he really meant Billy and Ishbel when he said that. *Joey* was the enemy he meant, I'm certain. That's why he said he was sorry.' I looked up. 'Like you did just now, Sam. My own brother hated me enough to help them. That's bad enough, but what if Joey struck out for himself too?' I turned to Lucca. 'Do you think it's possible that the night he found

Signor Marcelli at The Carnival gave him ideas?'

'*Che male.*' Lucca shuddered. 'It must have been Joseph who . . . arranged the old man and the puppets. I do not believe Ishbel or Donal had anything to do with it.'

'Neither do I.' I shifted the bowls around for a last time and then I lifted the middle one. There was a silver sixpence from my pocket there now. 'All this time I've thought it was Schalk stalking the halls, but what if it was Joey? Spark and poor Marnie – what if they were both down to him too? "Something of value to you and to those close to you." Vellum was right, I care about the halls. Joey knows that. He's full of anger and spite, and it's twisted him into someone I don't recognise any more. As far as he's concerned, *I* am his enemy.'

'*È pazzo.*' Lucca thumped the table. The sixpence bounced and slipped over the edge. 'I am sorry, Fannella. I have always thought that he . . . Joseph is not . . . There is something in him that . . .' He paused, unwilling to cause offence.

He needn't have worried. There was a time when I would have jumped to defend my brother, but that was long past. Joey had squandered any scrap of feeling I'd had left for him.

'If you're saying he's run mad, Lucca, I won't argue. In fact, you might be right in more ways than you know. When I last saw Joey at the Bethlem, he said he'd been knocked so hard he lost his senses for days. That can't have done his mind much good. I think it's likely Vellum knew about *all* the things Joey was doing. The man's got eyes in his arse after all.'

'Which brings us neatly to the prime question again.' Sam rubbed at the stubble on his jaw. I resisted the urge to reach across and run my own hand against his reddish bristles. '*Why* did Vellum take your brother this morning? We need to think

483

this through.' He stopped scraping. 'Actually, I think I have it.'

'It's something to do with Kite and the Barons, isn't it? Something else you've found out?'

'No, not this time.' Sam shook his head. 'Although that reminds me, there was a rather good story in *The Evening News* the day before yesterday about several prominent figures – army and navy men – who died, most horribly, at the inaugural launch of a submarine craft in a Scottish loch. It's so deep they'll never be able to bring it up again. I believe I detected your friend's dark hand in that. Peters has . . . borrowed the story for *The Pictorial*. It should run tomorrow.'

I shrugged. 'Vellum said I'd see something of the sort. So, the Barons are out of the way then and I never had to lift a finger. That's something to thank him for.'

'But there's still Kite and his new venture.' Sam frowned. 'And in a way that takes us back to Joey. Have you heard of Occam's Razor?'

I folded my arms. 'Another story is it, Sam? It's late and I'm not in the mood for a fairy tale.'

'It's not a fairy tale. Brother William of Occam was quite real. He was a monk.'

'I don't care if he was a monkey's uncle, Mr Collins.'

He grinned. 'It won't take long, Kitty – and that's rather the point. The basic principle of Occam's Razor is that the simplest solution to a given problem is likely to be the correct one. In the case of Vellum and your brother, I believe the matter is straightforward.' He paused to adjust the strap of his eye patch. I knew he was waiting for a prompt.

'Well? What's the answer?'

Sam flicked the sixpence into the air, caught it deft and

pushed it towards me. 'Vellum needed your brother as a guar-antee. If, for some reason, you can't open the Vinculum, at least he now has a second chance to fall back on. Or vice versa. Two for the price of one! He must want whatever is inside very badly. It must be something of great value.'

There was a clatter on the steps outside. Tan Seng came into the kitchen followed by Dr Pardieu.

'Lady!' The old boy sucked on his big front teeth. If he was surprised by my hair and my gear, he didn't show it. He bowed his head low. 'A pleasure to be called at any time.' When he straightened up, his curtain of limp grey hair left a scatter of scurf on his shoulders.

'And Mr Fratelli and also Mr . . . Collins, is it? I had the pleasure of . . . of . . .'

The last time Sam and Lucca had been tended by Pardieu, it hadn't been a pleasure for either of them. I stood up abrupt to stop him rambling down that road.

'How's Peggy?'

'She will be quite well. Thanks be.' Pardieu raised his hands like a clergy. As he moved, a waft of old moth and old man cut with something medicinal filled my nose. He attempted a smile, but the graveyard of his teeth robbed it of cheer.

'Yes indeed.' He nodded again. More of that dry white stuff from his scalp fell to his black shoulders. 'She needs rest, but the child is comfortable. No harm was caused by the fall.'

Pardieu's rheumy eyes wandered to the pot on the table. He sucked at his teeth again and widened his nostrils to take in the smoky scent of the tea. Most people think of men in the medical line as crows, but old Pardieu – whose services I'd inherited from my grandmother – always minded me of a rabbit, or perhaps, given his height, sparseness and the stoop of his crusted shoulders, a hare.

He cleared his throat. 'After I examined Mrs Tewson, I administered a tincture of laudanum to promote rest. I have been at her bedside for several hours to be certain. Mr Lok is with her still, but I do not envisage any problems.' His eyes sidled to the pot. 'It has been a very long night. I am quite . . . yes, quite . . .'

I pointed to a chair. 'Would you like tea before you go, Dr Pardieu?'

'Oh! I could not trouble you so.' He sprang back, affecting surprise. 'But that would be most welcome.'

*

Pardieu might have looked like a rabbit, but he snored like a hog. Slumped at the end of the table, his head resting back against a shelf, he twitched and mumbled in his sleep between great clotted snorts.

He'd gone off almost as soon as Tan Seng set down a fresh-brewed pot. As I watched the caverns of his nostrils quivering, I wondered how old he was. He'd served my grandmother for years and had been at Fraines Abbey with her at the end. Now he was mine.

Listening to him saw like a woodsman, I found I had an affection for him. I was fond of all the men I'd inherited from Lady Ginger, tell truth, especially the Beetle.

The Beetle.

Guilt jabbed again. I hadn't seen him for a long time. Even Ramesh Das had chided me for ignoring him. And there was The Comet too. Soon it would be opening its doors again, but apart from new paint and freshly gilded cherubs, it was a stale offer. I wouldn't say I was fond of Fitzy and Jesmond, but I owed them and everyone else who worked for me in the halls. The Comet needed a draw. I searched for answers that didn't come in the knots in the wood of the table.

Sam stubbed out a smoke and gathered his things together. We'd talked a little more while Pardieu slept, but now we were turning in circles. Five minutes back, Lucca and Tan Seng had gone upstairs to look in on Peggy and Lok.

He reached out across the table and brushed my hand with his. 'I should go, Kitty.'

'Don't.' It came out before I had a chance to stop myself. His eye caught the gleam of the candle lantern.

'Is that an invitation?'

I was careful to look away. 'An invitation to stay here tonight, yes. It's very late.' I hurried on. 'I'll make up a bed in the office for you. Besides, we haven't finished. Let's talk again tomorrow when we're all fresh to it. As I see it, everything turns on the Vinculum. Kite wants whatever's inside it. Vellum's taken my brother because of it.'

I slapped my hands on the table. 'My own grandmother took the trouble on her deathbed to make me aware of it. Why? All the time that bleedin' thing has been hanging over everything like the stench from a tanner's pit.'

I looked up. 'We need to plan our next move, Sam, whatever that is.'

'I've done that, Kitty.' He sat down again. 'I just need to work out how.'

He caught my hands in his. I looked down at our fingers linked together across the knotted wood. It came to me that

487

Sam might have been working out something other than what I had in mind.

He stroked the back of my thumb. 'We need to find the Vinculum and open it before Vellum gets a chance.'

'Oh!' I snatched my hands from his. 'Yes. Yes, that's right.' I stood, collected the cups and went to the basin under the window. I took a deep breath as he spoke to my back.

'If we assume that Vellum is hoping Kite will lead him to the Vinculum at this meeting, we need to move first. We'll go to the Tower, Kitty, and we'll scour the chapel for anything that might point the way.'

I spun around. 'That's a fool's game, Sam. We don't even know what we're looking for.' I heard my voice rising. 'A fine plan that is. How are we going to poke around without anyone noticing?' I folded my arms. 'Excuse me, Mr Beefeater, sir, do you mind looking over there for an hour or so while I have a good rummage about?'

Pardieu cleared his throat. He shuffled upright in his chair and drew out a grubby 'kerchief to blow his nose. He stared at me above the expanse of stained cotton. His eyes seemed sharper than usual. 'Forgive me, Lady. I fear I may have fallen asleep for a few moments.' He dabbed at the drool by the side of his mouth. 'Forgive me also for intruding, but I could not help but hear the end of your conversation.'

I sidled at Sam, who was spinning his strike box on the table.

Pardieu coughed and dabbed again. 'You mentioned Beef-eaters?'

I rolled my eyes. 'And what of it?'

'I have an elderly client. She is the widowed mother of a Yeoman Warder.'

'A what?'

Pardieu smiled. 'I believe the Yeomen Warders are more commonly referred to as Beefeaters, Lady. My client lodges with her only son inside the walls of the Tower of London.'

Chapter Forty-three

Mrs Gurney was old as the Tower itself and deaf as the stones it was built from. The lodgings she shared with her son, a man of fearsome whiskers and a bark like a bloodhound, was at the centre of a row of identical cottages overlooking a patch of greenery. The back of the cottage was formed by the Tower's walls. The jagged whitewashed stones jutting into the room where we sat seemed at odds with the widow's rocking chair and the canary chirping in a cage at the window.

Through the small latticed panes, I could see the edge of the great square fortress that Sam called the White Tower, even though it was black as sin on account of the soot. He said it was where the Crown Jewels were kept and guarded night and day.

We'd come in as day visitors, paying our shillings at the gate, but we'd soon found our way to the address Pardieu had given us. Once you were inside the walls it was easy enough to navigate. Other visitors were promenading about the green, consulting the penny guides sold at the gate. I'd never been here before, but it struck me that the Tower of London was like a village once you got your bearings, albeit a village with a bloody past.

As we'd walked past a young couple, I heard the man reading aloud to his girl.

"*And it was on this very spot on the fifteenth day of May in 1536 that Queen Anne Boleyn was executed, beheaded by an expert swordsman summoned from France, a final mercy from her husband the king.*"

'Ooh!' The girl had shivered with pleasure and turned about to get a full view of the place, which was, in truth, a patch of grass. 'He must have loved her very much.'

Christ! If that was love, I wouldn't have wanted to get on his bad side. I sidled at Sam, who was swallowing a laugh.

The young man continued. '"*Queen Anne's body was placed in an arrow case and buried without ceremony in the Chapel of St Peter ad Vincula near the place of execution.*"' He looked up and pointed. 'That's it over there.'

Across the green stood a long stone box of a building with a square bell tower. So, that was a Royal Peculiar? It didn't look much. I squeezed Lucca's arm and we carried on to the warders' quarters where we were all sitting now.

'The doctor's been very good to us. I can't say otherwise.' Yeoman Warder Gurney adjusted his red skirt and handed the letter back to Sam. 'Medical students, you say?'

Sam nodded. 'Mr Fratelli and I attend St George's where Dr Pardieu, an alumnus, lectures occasionally. Anatomy is his speciality. He asked us to visit your mother, the delightful Mrs Gurney.' Sam smiled in his most charming way at the widow, who was eyeing the basket of fruit on my lap.

He was wearing his glass eye today. We decided the four of us looked peculiar enough as it was without offering another notable distraction. I was dressed in a plain dark dress with a collar buttoned up to my chin. My bonnet was small, grey and dressed with starched striped ribbons. 'Prim' was the word that came to mind as I examined my reflection in the mirror. A good thing in a doctor's sister.

Lucca had given Sam the loan of a sober suit that fitted him well. As for himself, he sat next to me now on the widow's couch, quiet, smart, and careful to keep the scarred side of his face hidden as much as possible.

'As you can see from the doctor's letter of introduction,' Sam continued, 'your mother's case is most intriguing. He thought it might be helpful if he were to send us here to examine her foot free of all charge and exchange opinions. Mr Fratelli is a gifted physician and Mr Chan –' he gestured at Tan Seng – 'is an expert in the field of Oriental medicine. He too is a colleague of Dr Pardieu's – as you have just read.'

Gurney slid a look of distrust at Tan Seng, who was dressed in regular breeches and a black coat. His hair was bound up tight to his head and hidden beneath a round cloth cap he wore under a tall black hat. A pair of golden specs balanced on the end of his nose and the hat was now resting in his lap. I almost hadn't recognised him when he'd come up to the parlour two hours earlier.

He smiled and dipped his head at the man in the red dress. 'I am honoured.'

'And my dear sister –' Sam turned to me – 'thought that it would be seemly for your mother to have a woman in attendance. She insisted on bringing this gift. Fruit is so helpful to the constitution.'

'Indeed it is.' Yeoman Warder Gurney reached across Lucca and took an apple from my basket.

'My sister has a great interest in church architecture.' Sam glanced at me. 'I wonder, after we have tended to Mrs Gurney, if we might visit the Chapel of St Peter? It will be open, will it not?'

'You're in luck.' Gurney spoke through a mouthful of half-chewed apple. 'If you'd come any later this week, the place would be locked.' He tapped the side of his nose. 'We're expecting a visit from a personage, a royal personage. Place has to be got ready. It's all very private. Even the Constable doesn't know what's going on.' He grunted. 'Great rigmarole, if you ask me.'

We sat in silence for a moment then Gurney slapped a knee. 'Well, this is unexpected, but Mother and I have known the good doctor for many years. I see no reason to refuse your offer.' He crammed the last of the apple into his mouth. 'As long as it's free and Mother has no objections.'

He swung to face her. 'They've come to see your foot.' She put a hand to her ear. He tried again using the full force of his warder's bark. By the time he got the message home, I reckoned there were lascars on the clippers at St Katharine Dock who knew about his mother's bunion.

He burped loudly and squinted out of the window.

'Terrible weather we've been having. Can't remember a September like it for the wind.' I sidled at Sam. Surely the man wasn't going to sit here making small talk for the rest of the afternoon? Didn't he have things to attend to?

Sam moved to the edge of his chair. He rubbed his hands together. 'Right, Mrs Gurney, let's take a look at that foot then.'

The Yeoman Warder leapt from his stool. 'Duty calls. I'm on rounds this evening until midnight so I dare say I won't see you again.' He made a little bow to me, and, after helping himself to another apple and a couple of pears, he collected a black hat the size of a cushion from a hook on the back of the door.

Gurney stashed the pears into a pocket of his skirt and consulted a large gold fob stored in the same place. 'It's four o'clock now. That should give you plenty of time with Mother.'

'More than sufficient.' Sam nodded. 'What time does the

493

Tower close to visitors?' He made a great show of opening the black leather bag at his feet. It was borrowed from Pardieu, and smelt the part. The stench of mothballs and medicine filled the little room.

The warder wrinkled his nose. 'Visitors leave at sunset, but the gates are locked at ten.' He scratched the pie-crust frill at his neck. 'Another rigmarole, that is. Make sure you're out by then or you'll be locked inside the walls all night. And you wouldn't want that.'

*

Mrs Gurney had been sleeping soundly for at least three hours by the time we crept from the cottage. Once her son had tramped off to his duties I offered her a couple of carefully selected plums from the bottom of the basket and she sucked away at them, quite unaware that I'd coated them with a tincture of laudanum mixed special for the purpose by Pardieu.

Now the visitors were gone the Tower was quiet. The green was lit by a large gas lamp and the glow from the windows of the warders' lodgings. Occasionally, doors opened and shut, men called out to each other and booted feet crunched past on the gravel path. After a clock struck seven, the place became notably empty. I reckoned most of the warders were indoors. I imagined them warming their feet at the fire, a tankard of ale and a plate of cold beef to hand.

The ones who weren't so lucky were making rounds. They were easy to keep track of in their bright uniforms. We watched the green from the latticed windows and it wasn't difficult to work out the time between their comings and goings. Five minutes was enough for us to slip over to the chapel without being noticed.

I closed the door gently behind me and stepped into the shadows. Tan Seng and Lucca were already near the chapel. Sam gathered Pardieu's leather bag in his arms and I heard the rattle of tools. There was a hammer, a chisel and a pair of pliers inside, along with candles and a box of Lucifers.

'Do you really think this might work, Sam?' I whispered to his back as we made our way along the row towards the chapel. He turned to look back at me. He was wearing the patch again, having swapped it for the glass eye in the privacy of Mrs Gurney's room.

'When we were hiding at the Angevin Club, Kite said you were very resourceful. I'm relying on that, Kitty. That and a huge dose of luck.'

A door opened and a man, another warder, came out to the path. He was smoking and his red dress was unfastened. We flattened ourselves into the shade of a bush growing against the wall. The man took a drag and then made his way past us. I held my breath until he turned a corner and disappeared.

'Now. Quickly.' Sam loped along the row, careful to keep to the wall. I followed close. At the last cottage, we jagged out across the path and joined Lucca and Tan Seng in the shadow of the bell tower. The door to the chapel, square in the stones beneath an arched window, was standing ajar.

I was surprised. 'Don't they lock it at night?'

'*Sì*. Lucca nodded. 'But our friend Dr Chan is very . . . talented.'

Tan Seng held up a thin metal spike with a hook at one end. He bowed. 'It has been a long time, Lady. Long time.'

The brothers had surprised me before with their skills. I found myself thinking again that my grandmother had chosen well when she put her trust in them.

We went into the chapel and pulled the door to a close behind us. Sam rummaged in the bag, lit a small candle and passed it to me. I shielded the light with a hand. Over to the right, four large windows were set high in the wall. I reckoned it would be difficult to make out the glow from the outside, but I was careful just the same.

Our feet echoed on the stones. I untied my boots, pulled them off and stashed them at the end of an old box pew drawn up against the wall. The others did the same. It was colder inside the chapel than out on the green. I could feel the chill of the stones through my stockings. I held the candle lower. I was standing on the grave of a knight and his lady. As far as I could see, most of the floor was littered with dead people.

I heard the strike of another Lucifer and straightened up to see Sam passing candles to Lucca and Tan Seng. He stuffed a handful into a pocket and set the bag down next to our boots. We stood there like a row of choir boys, candlelight gilding our faces.

I motioned for us to go into the shadows and away from the windows. We went under a row of columns into a second smaller aisle. St Peter's might have royal connections, but I was surprised by how small and plain it was inside. It didn't feel old and dark as I'd expected; quite the opposite in fact. It smelt of polish, new-carved wood and fresh-cut flowers.

I lifted the candle and stared up at the beams overhead. The flat ceiling wasn't high.

'What are we looking for, Fannella?' Lucca peered up at

a black marble memorial above my head. Richard Fareham, Constable, had died in 1742.

I studied the tablets jostling for space on the walls. The worthy, the loyal, the righteous and the just – all of them dead and forgotten. 'The Vinculum has to be here somewhere. It's why Kite and his brother have gone to such trouble.'

'Gurney didn't seem very happy about that. Still, at least he confirmed that the ceremony is going ahead.' Sam held his candle higher to read another inscription. '"In memory of Samson Kelly, Yeoman Warder 1789–1802. *Sapientia et Virtus*."'

'Wisdom and strength.' Lucca translated the last words on the memorial stone.

Sam nodded. 'Very apt. We could use both of those qualities now.'

'We need to split up and search the chapel.' I swung about sharp as my candle caught something flying overhead. The shadow flitted over the plaster and the monuments at our back.

'*Un pipistrello.*' Lucca smiled. 'A flying mouse.'

I picked up again. 'We'll start in the corners and move in until we've covered every last inch of the place. Look out for anything unusual or unlikely. The Vinculum could be marked by a stone in the ground, on the wall, under a bench. It could be . . . could be . . .' I stumbled to a halt. I didn't know what it could be. I slammed my hand on the wall. Plaster pattered to the stones. 'This is ridiculous. Why are we even here?'

'Because we are looking for a needle in a haystack, Kitty. And that's all we can do. We're alone, undisturbed and we have plenty of time.' Sam's voice was calm and reassuring. 'I'll take the top right near the altar and work across.'

I watched his tiny candle move away from us into the dark.

'I'll go to the west, Fannella.' Lucca headed back to where we'd come in.

'Lady?' Tan Seng raised his candle to quiz at me.

'I'll go up there.' I pointed to the far end of the aisle.

*

The candle was burning so low the flame was almost licking my fingers. I backed away from the large tomb in front of me. On the top a man and woman lay side by side, their hands clasped together in prayer. As far as I could tell, the inscription was more Latin. There was a lot of Latin in the chapel. Written on plaques on the walls and on the stones in the floor. For all I knew, the Vinculum might have been right under my nose without me seeing it.

I heard a bump. A moment later a glow flickered across polished tiles from behind a column.

'Sam? Is that you? I'm over here.'

He came to stand beside me and held his own candle high. The pious couple shone up clearer now. The pair of them gazed at the ceiling. The woman's mouth was set into a grim little pout. I didn't blame her. I reckoned I'd look like that if an eternity of praying and staring was all I had to look forward to.

'It's hopeless, Sam.' I felt his hand slip into mine.

'We don't know that yet.' He squeezed tight. Outside, a bell started to ring. Crisp, quick chimes echoed in the chapel. From somewhere else another deeper bell joined in. I counted.

'Ten. That means we're locked in the Tower for the night.' Hot wax dripped to my skin. I dropped the candle and it skittered across the stones into the dark. The smell of singed hair rose between us as I rubbed the back of my hand.

'Here.' Sam took another candle from his pocket and lit it. The light deepened the shadows under his cheeks as he concentrated on the flame. 'That gives us plenty of time to keep looking.'

'But we don't even know what we're looking for.' I stared at the woman on the tomb. If only those lips could talk.

Sam tugged at my hand. 'Kitty, look!'

I spun round. In a corner a few feet off, a blue-green flame danced against the plaster.

I darted over the stones. 'It was the candle stub. We have to put it out before all the red skirts come running.'

Despite my stockings, I held up my skirt and stamped on the little blaze. Every time I thought I'd put it out, the flames fluttered back against the wall. There was something soft underfoot and the fire was feeding off it. A glow like golden lace spread from the corner to the end of a small wooden pew.

'No!' I pulled off a stocking, wound it round my hand and chased the sparks along the wall, patting and dabbing and willing them to die.

A sudden rush of water did the trick. I stood there, soaked to the skin, and watched Sam gather up flowers strewn over the floor. He forced them back into a large glass vase. 'I'd better put this back on the altar.'

I dripped and nodded. 'And when you've done that, come back here with the candle so we can see the damage. We might be able to hide it.'

'Lady?' Tan Seng came through an archway followed by Lucca.

'Something is burning, Fannella,' he whispered.

'It's not now. Bring your light over here.' They moved closer.

'How is it?' Sam knelt beside me, candle in hand. Our shadows shot up the wall.

I saw what had caught now. A green felt runner had been tacked to the floor. It went under the pew and into the corner. The scorched edges curled away from the smoke-stained wall.

I bit the side of my thumb. 'We can move the pew. If we shunt it along a couple of feet to sit over the marks, no one will notice. This corner doesn't look like it gets much attention.'

Sam and Lucca set down their candles. They took an end each and lifted. The pew came away easy enough, but so did half the felt underneath. There was an ugly ripping sound as it tore away from the stones beneath the pew.

'Stop.' I crouched low to see what we'd done now. No wonder they'd covered the floor over here. Most of the stones under the felt were cracked and uneven. I brushed away the strips of torn material, wondering what to do. As I dabbed away at the dust and shreds, a word, beautifully carved in curling script, appeared in a patch of smooth black stone beneath my fingers.

chains

I cleared some more of the damage away.

house of chains

A tinder sparked in my belly. I could feel it tracking its way up my spine to the top of my head. I scraped away at the stone.

free at last from the mortal house of chains

'Fannella?' Above me, Lucca and Sam strained at the bench ends. The ripping came again as it took more felt from the stones.

'Hold still, please. I need to see this clear.'

I lay out flat and tugged. The rest of the felt came away in my hands, revealing a long dark stone covered in more of that curling script framed within an elegant scrolling design.

I sat up. 'Can you move the pew along and set it down over there?' I pointed to the wall six foot off.

'But the floor,' Lucca hissed. 'We'll never be able to—'

'Don't worry about that now. We'll think of something later.'

I carried on scrubbing and clearing as they hefted the pew aside. Tan Seng knelt beside me and watched in silence. In a minute the inscription was clear.

Lucius Magg, Clocksmith, appointed to serve the Crown.
True to the last as brother and master, he rests in great renown.
A pious life, a grieving wife, these he has left on earth.
Beneath this stone, along with bone, is the total of his worth.
A rose, a lion, a crown, a star, compass his remains.
For Lucius Magg is free at last from the mortal house of chains.

I rocked back on my heels. Sam bent down beside me as I ran the tips of my fingers along the last line of the inscription. 'I know these words – all of them. If you asked me to repeat it without looking, I could.'

'How?' He brushed away the dust on a flower carved into the corner of the stone and our hands touched. I turned to him, half amazed and half relieved.

'Jacobin, that's how.'

'The parrot?'

I nodded. 'Jacobin belonged to the Carstone brothers for a long time before my grandmother had him. He sang out these words to the tune Lok uses to calm him. That's right, isn't it, Tan Seng? About the tune, I mean?'

When he didn't answer I sidled at him. He was still as a funeral monument. As he stared at the stone, a furrow appeared between his eyes. I looked again. Lucius Magg's memorial was the length of a small man and perhaps a yard wide. And it pointed the way to the Vinculum. I was sure of it.

Chapter Forty-four

'It's no good.' I handed the chisel back to Sam. 'If we keep hammering away, someone will come.'

'I'll try the other end again.' He shifted along from me and tried to force the tool into a hair-thin crack between the black memorial slab and the crumbling flagstone butted up next to it. He pushed hard, but only succeeded in scattering chips off the weaker stone.

'Do you want to try again, Lucca?' He passed over the chisel.

Tan Seng slipped into the end of the pew we'd moved an hour back and watched Lucca work at the stone. I'd asked him to lock up from the inside, using his hook, by way of insurance in case anyone disturbed us. I went to fetch a hammer from Pardieu's bag. The battered thing was sitting on a bench end alongside my hat. I picked that up too. Perhaps if I muffled the hammer in my stockings and the ribbons, I could try smashing the stone?

'This is strange.' Lucca tapped the end of the chisel on the floor beside him. 'Nothing we do can loosen it. It is as if it has been locked into place.'

I let the hat go. Something he said there made sense.

'Locked, you say?'

He nodded. 'Despite everything we have tried, the stone has not moved at all. We cannot force it.'

I put the hammer down too. 'Perhaps that's the point. We don't need to *force* it, we just need the key.'

Sam stared glumly at the stone. 'You might have memorised

the code, Kitty, but I can't see how you'd use it anywhere here.'
The candle on the floor next to him sputtered and died. 'And
now I can't see much at all.'

I collected the last candles from the bag and handed one to
him.

'There are just four left now.' I studied the inscription for the
hundredth time.

Beneath this stone, along with bone, is the total of his
worth.

If that wasn't a suggestion of buried treasure, I was the
Queen of Sheba.

A rose, a lion, a crown, a star, compass his remains

I frowned. 'What does that mean?' I pointed at the word
that rang false. '"Compass."'

Sam shrugged. 'It's an old inscription. I assume it's a mistake
or perhaps an archaic version of *en*compass.'

'What if it's not? A compass points the way, doesn't it? Look
at the words again – "A rose, a lion, a crown, a star, *compass*
his remains". And now, see the pattern around the edge of the
stone? There's a rose in that corner, a lion there, a crown bottom left and that's a star.'

I knelt and reached to the rose. The centre of the carved
bloom was round and raised and very smooth to the touch. I
pushed down hard. There was a loud click.

'Fannella!' Lucca moved his candle to give me more light.

I went to the lion, running my fingers along his back to

504

the raised tip of his tail. Again, it was smooth to the touch. I pressed. Another click.

Sam dropped to his knees as I moved to the crown, finding the smooth raised place amid the carved jewels. Same again. And finally, when I pressed on the mounded middle of the star, a whirring, ticking noise thrummed from somewhere deep below. The black stone trembled, rose and then, very slowly, it opened like a trap on a stage to reveal a set of narrow stone steps.

*

Light from my candle flickered on the glassy black walls of a square-cut passage. They pressed so close that two people couldn't walk abreast. My reflection quivered in the stones as I went a little way forward. The walls were cold and dry to the touch and there was a faint trace of something dead and long-buried in the air. Judging from the dust underfoot, no one had visited the place for years.

Sam and Lucca had argued the toss about who went first, but while they were wrangling, I took a light and went down before they could stop me. I turned now to see Lucca step down into the passage, candle in hand.

'Fannella?'

'I'm here. It goes on a way.' I held up my own candle to show him. 'You can't get past.' Sam was just behind him and I saw the glow of Tan Seng's candle at the foot of the steps.

'Keep close.' I turned and carried on down the passage. After a dozen yards or so, it sloped down and veered right. The way broadened out, but now the roof was so low I had to duck.

I followed the curve of the wall and came out into a circular chamber shaped like a bell. It was a dead end, but on the curved wall opposite there seemed to be the shadow of a doorway.

I raised the candle to get a better view and I took a gulp of musty air as I recognised what I was looking at.

'*Cosa diamine?*' Lucca was at my shoulder. Wavering light from his candle picked out the rows of tiny stone tiles that covered a door set into the wall in front of us. There were hundreds of them, each one carefully engraved with a number, letter or symbol.

Sam let out a low whistle. 'Is that what I think it is?'

'Lady?' I turned to see Tan Seng emerge from the passage into the chamber. The skin of his face was pulled tight as a drum.

I ground the end of my candle into the dust on the floor so it stood free and I sat down cross-legged to study the door. The patterns, numbers and symbols on the tiles were a lock. I was looking at a great, complicated mechanism that would, if I managed to remember the order, open the Vinculum. Until that moment it hadn't occurred to me what the bleedin' thing would actually look like.

This is it then, girl, I thought. *Everything leads here.* I heard my grandmother's voice:

The contents of the Vinculum can destroy them, Katharine.

What was behind that door? She said it was where the Barons hid treasure, but they were men of wealth and power without need of a cellar-full of jewels. I fished for her exact words.

Your brother is the only person alive who can complete the sequence to open the Vinculum – the vault where the Barons have stored their wealth and, more pertinently, their secrets for centuries.

Well, she was wrong about one thing at least. Another person could complete the sequence to open the vault, and just now she was sitting right in front of it.

Sam put a hand on my shoulder. 'Can you do it, Kitty?'

I looked up at him and nodded. 'I need quiet just for a minute to be sure.'

I closed my eyes and concentrated. Then I began to write in the dust on the stones. When I reached the last of the forty-five symbols I stood up.

'That's it. Let's see if it works.'

*

'It's like a letter S with a line through the middle.'

We scanned the wall.

'There!' Sam pointed to a row near the bottom. I reached down and pushed. The ticking, whirring sound – much like a clock getting ready to strike – came again. I didn't know if that was a good or a bad thing.

'Just one more, Fannella.' Lucca held his hands together as if he was praying. 'What if . . . if . . .'

'Trust me. The last is like an upside-down U with curls to the sides.' Sam glanced back at the symbols I'd written in the dust. 'Omega – the last letter of the Greek alphabet. How appropriate.' He looked at the wall again, but I'd already found it. I jabbed at the final tile.

Nothing happened. Not even the sound this time. I stared at the door, thinking it might take a moment or two to come to life.

'Kitty?' I heard the question in Sam's voice and swung to him sharp.

507

'It was right. I swear it. Not a single one of them keys was false.'

He sidled at the wall. 'What if—'

'No! I'm telling you, it was right.' I took up my candle and held it to the rows and rows of engraved tiles. The more I looked at them all, the less certain I felt. The patterns started to swim in my eyes. After coming through all this, I'd failed. I looked back at the code I'd scrawled in the dust. It *was* right.

Joey? What if it was down to him? What if the sequence he'd given me was false all along? What if my brother had strung me again?

I went to the letters and symbols on the floor and I kicked at the lines in the dust until there wasn't a trace of them left.

'You bastard, Joey Peck.' I swirled about and thumped a fist on the curved wall next to the door.

It swung inward, silent and easy as a newly oiled gate.

'Kitty! You did it!' Sam leapt to my side and folded me in his arms. I dropped the candle as he huddled me tight and planted a kiss on my forehead. 'Oh, my brilliant, brilliant . . .' He held my face in his hands and tilted it upwards as if he was thinking about planting another kiss lower down.

Instead he released me and stepped back. He glanced at Lucca, who was peering into the darkness, unlike Tan Seng, who was examining his feet. Sam picked up my candle, relit it with a Lucifer from his strike box and handed it to me.

'Right.' He cleared his throat. 'We'd better take a look inside, then.'

*

The Vinculum was a square space, no bigger than my office, lined with shelves running from top to bottom. Candlelight brought a glow to the jumble of objects stacked around us. I turned about slowly, taking it all in – the golden platters, the teetering piles of gilded plates, the goblets studded with rubies the size of pigeon eggs, the ropes of pearls dandling free, the chains threaded with diamonds, the cracked leather boxes leaking jewels.

I won't lie, I was disappointed.

The treasure of the Barons was plain to see. It was good stuff, I had no doubts on the matter, but it wasn't like Ali Baba's cave in there. There was something mean about it. Point of fact, I could have cleared the place in ten minutes if I'd thought to bring four wheelbarrows with us.

'Is this it, then?'

I watched Lucca stretch an arm to the back of a shelf near the open door. He pulled out a small portrait of a young woman in a pretty oval frame and held it to his light. He shrugged and put it back.

'There are paintings here too, Kitty.' He took out a larger canvas without a frame and examined it.

Tan Seng held back near the entrance. His eyes skipped warily over the shelves.

'Lady, I do not think . . .'

'You're right.' I nodded. 'This has hardly been worth the effort.'

Sam scooped up an old-style necklace from the floor. 'Why would Vellum want this? It's not exactly the Crown Jewels.' He snorted. 'Considering the White Tower is practically a stone's throw away, the thought of the Barons keeping their own tawdry haul close by is shabby . . . almost pathetic.'

I held the candle high to light the furthest corners. The lower shelves on the back wall were covered with dark cloth. I went over and pulled at the fabric. A musty smell came rolling out from untidy stacks of papers and documents.

'Now, this might be something.' Sam squatted beside me and pulled out an ancient leather-bound file. A cloud of dust rose into the air as he opened it.

'Latin on parchment. Not my strong suit. It's legal stuff as far as I can tell. There's a seal here.' He moved a large red wax disc attached with ribbon. 'It's very old. I can see that.'

'My grandmother said something about secrets.' I frowned. 'She kept a safe in a London bank that was full of information that might prove useful – letters, notes, scribbled things that might incriminate a person or persuade them to a point of view. What if this is much the same? Secrets going back centuries, I mean? That's a powder worth keeping dry, isn't it?'

'Blackmail again?' Sam grinned and took another sheaf of papers from the shelf.

There was a clatter from the door. I turned to see Lucca gathering a pile of small paintings together. They'd tumbled from a shelf.

I angled my candle to the stacks of papers again. The light slicked up a glint of gold back against the wall. I reached out and felt silk beneath my fingers. The silk was wrapped around something hard and square. I drew out the package and looked at the curling golden pattern worked into the dark red Oriental fabric.

A familiar smell came to me. The package reeked of opium, but to be more specific, it was the sickly blend my grandmother had favoured. As I weighed the parcel in my hands, I knew, of a certainty, that the fabric was hers too. It was the same as the silk bound about the damaged book that Telferman had given me. The one I'd locked in a drawer at The Palace.

'Lady!'

I looked up. Tan Seng was struggling with the door, trying to push it back. The bleedin' thing was quietly shutting itself and closing fast. As it swung into view, I saw that the back was alive with spinning cogs and twitching levers.

Lucca dropped the painting he was trying to stash back into the shelf and threw himself into the fast-narrowing gap. He put his back against the door and pushed a foot to the wall, but it didn't help. Tan Seng was outside in the bell-shaped chamber now. I could just see his face in the space between the door and the wall. His fingers scrabbled round the edge of the door as he struggled to force it back.

We ran across the room, but it was already too late. The gap wasn't wide enough to get through and it didn't matter how hard we gripped or pulled, the thing wouldn't stop. Lucca gave up the fight. Before he was crushed, he just managed to lurch away from us and into the chamber beyond. Sam swept a couple of platters from the nearest shelf and tried to wedge the thing open, but the door chewed them up like they were made of butter. Through a chink as wide as a pencil, I heard Lucca call out and then, as the door settled back into place, I heard nothing.

Nothing at all.

The glinting cogs spun silently. The levers ratcheted back and forth, and then the clockwork mechanism stopped. A tune began to play. It jangled and tinkled, the mocking notes falling around us like raindrops made from brass.

The door was still working! It gave me a hope. I hurled myself at it, shouting and yelling for Lucca and Tan Seng over and over. Sam joined in and we beat against the metal and hollered until our fists were raw and our voices were hoarse.

The jingling stopped abrupt. I fell to my knees and listened for the smallest sound from outside. I didn't hear nothing, and I knew without a doubt that Lucca and Tan Seng hadn't heard us neither.

I looked up at the back of the door. The Vinculum wasn't meant to be opened from the inside.

Lucius Magg, Clocksmith, appointed to serve the Crown.
True to the last as brother and master, he rests in great renown.

Lucius Magg had been a most skilful clockmaker. The mechanical maze he'd created for the Barons glowed in the light of the single candle Lucca had set on the stones beside the shelf of paintings. As I ran my eyes over the workings, searching for a key that wasn't there, I had a bad feeling about *brother* Lucius. I remembered what Kite had told me about the pit at Great Bartholomew's after I'd sealed poor Danny inside it.

In the last century, one of our more practically minded brothers made some refinements. By closing it you have reset the device. It cannot be opened again for one hundred days.

'One hundred days'? The words sounded in my head like hammer blows.

I swallowed. 'I don't know what to do.'

'Neither do I, Kitty.' Sam ran a hand lightly over a row of cogs at the centre of the door. He shook his head and sank down beside me as I went on. 'Do you think Lucca and Tan

Seng . . .' I let that hang there. What could they do for us now? I looked at the crowded shelves, but I already knew. There wasn't another way out of this place.

'I . . . I don't think we . . .' I tried again. 'It's all been for nothing. Everything . . . Everything I've done – and not done – has led here, and now look. Look at us. I thought I was so clever, but as it turns out we're going to d . . .'

I couldn't finish that. A great sob stopped me. Tears rolled down my cheeks as I tried to get out the words I wanted to say.

'I'm sorry, Sam. So very sorry. Sorry that I ever . . .' I looked direct at him now. He was staring at me, his eye very dark. The single candle flame danced in the heart of the darkness. He leaned in towards me so close our noses almost touched and then he raised a hand and smudged away my tears. That made it worse. I gulped and took his hand.

'Sam, I want you to know . . .'

And I didn't finish that neither on account of the fact that his lips stopped me. I felt the scratch of the stubble on his jaw and tasted smoke in his kiss. There was fire in it too – a fire that caught me like kindling.

'Kitty?' He drew back, but I took his face in my hands and gave him my answer. I was so lost in him, that kiss might as well have lasted a hundred days.

It actually ended when the light from Lucca's candle sputtered and died.

Sam's voice came in the dark. 'Do you have any more candles in your pockets?'

I shook my head, not that he could see. 'Just the one I dropped when we ran to the door. You?'

'I've got two left and my strike case is half full of Lucifers.'

There was a scrape and a brilliant flash as he struck a light. He reached out and traced the tip of a finger down the side of my face. 'Perhaps, if it comes to it, we can make torches from the papers?' He raised the candle to light the space. 'There are plenty of them.'

At the far end of the Vinculum, the fallen candle poked out from beneath the red silk bundle I'd taken from the back of the shelf. I'd dropped that too as we ran to the door. Papers had come free and lay scattered across the stone floor. I hauled myself up and went to collect the candle.

As I bent down, I saw a name written large and very bold on one of the fallen papers.

Elizabeth Redmayne

I snatched up the sheet and took it back to Sam, along with the candle. He must have thought me mad as I smoothed the paper out over the stones between us and bent to examine the close-packed lines.

And perhaps I was. But I tell you this for nothing, as I sat there reading my own mother's marriage licence, signed and dated in the presence of four witnesses, two of them men of professional rank, I came to an understanding of why Kite was untouched by the law and why Vellum and everyone he stood for wanted the key to the Vinculum.

Chapter Forty-five

Cold, harsh notes jangled in my head. I huddled against Sam's body, tucking my hands into his jacket. I was chilled to the marrow and my back ached from lying on the stone floor.

The nightmare had come several times now. Every time, I'd lain there somewhere between sleeping and waking, and the only thing I really knew in that clouded moment was that the jingling was something bad. Something very bad.

This time the tune didn't stop. I listened to the notes tumbling from the door.

'Sam!' I fumbled for his shoulder in the dark and shook him. 'Sam, wake up!' My voice was dry and cracked. My tongue felt like a fat-bodied moth in my mouth.

He muttered and rolled onto his back. I sat up and shook him harder. 'Listen. It's the door.'

I stood and felt my way along the shelf towards the sound. The last of our candles had burned itself out a long time ago. Beneath the music came the whisper and tick of a thousand cogs spinning in the dark. A flash of light told the truth. We didn't have many Lucifers left now, but the one Sam held to a twist of paper showed that the back of the door was moving.

'Thank God!' His voice was rough and cracked as mine. He came over with the taper, wrapped an arm around my shoulder and held me close. We stared at the ticking, twitching mechanism.

'But who is it out there, Sam?'

'I don't care if it's the Devil himself, as long as we get out of this damned place.' He passed the burning roll of paper to me and used it to light the end of another from the pile we'd prepared.

I gripped tight as I stood beside him. The tune jingled away as the levers jerked and the cogs whirled. Tiny jewels set into the workings sparked in the light of the little flames that guttered from the end of our makeshift torches.

Of an instant, the music stopped, along with the movement of the wheels and gears. I tried to swallow but my tongue stuck to the roof of my mouth. Sam reached for my hand. We stepped back as the door opened slowly, revealing shadows moving in the chamber beyond.

'Good morning, Miss Peck.'

Vellum's voice was crisp and light as if he was hosting a charity breakfast and welcoming a guest to his table. A blast of clean air swept into the vault as he stepped through the entrance and swung a lantern around. Our shadows danced on the shelves and up to the ceiling.

'And Mr Collins.' Vellum nodded at Sam. 'I trust you are both well. This must have been something of an ordeal.'

'How . . .' I choked on dust and tried again. 'How long have we been here?'

'Nearly three days.' Vellum's grey eyes scanned the vault. His gaze rested for a moment on the mound of paper screws we'd made for tapers and then, true as an arrow, they went to the shelves at the back where the musty papers were stored.

He held the lantern higher. 'You have your friends to thank for your release. Mr Fratelli sent an urgent message to *Endymion* through the personal columns of *The London Evening News*. It came to my attention. Now –' he held the lantern to the door – 'I am sure you must be eager to leave this place.'

'How did you open it?' I thought I might know the answer, but I asked anyway.

Vellum moved aside as four of his grey coats came through the door. He passed the lantern to the nearest of his men and pointed to the furthest wall.

'Take everything. Do not leave a single scrap of paper.'

He turned to me. 'Outside, please. You too, Mr Collins.' I glanced at the grim-set faces of the men standing around us and realised it was an order. I went to the door and out into the bell-shaped chamber. Even though it was crowded with a dozen more of Vellum's grey coats, packed in tight as herrings in a barrel, my eyes went straight to my brother.

Joey was leaning against the wall, swirling patterns in the dust with the toe of a shoe.

'Kitty.' He straightened up and gave a small bow. 'Queen of all she surveys.' He laughed. The sound echoed from the stone walls. There was a shrill strangeness to it.

'Aren't you going to thank me, little sister?' He shuffled towards me.

Joey was still a looker, despite the scar that ran from his ear to the side of his mouth. I could see how a young woman like Ishbel Downie might have fallen for him. The marks of a struggle were on his gear, but his clothes – presumably the things Ishbel had begged Vellum's men to take for him – were fine and chosen with care. Joey was always proud of his rig.

As he came close, I saw that his hands and ankles were chained. He angled his head and smiled lopsided.

'If it wasn't for me, you and your . . . *friend*, is it?' He looked at Sam. '. . . would have been trapped in there until you died. It would have been a slow, dry, lingering death. Rather like

Australia, I imagine?'

'Why, Joey?' I looked into his blue eyes. They glittered like diamond chips in the lantern light, but deep inside there was a darkness that didn't come from the shadows.

'Old Marcelli. Why?'

He shrugged. 'He was dead. It was intended as a . . . *tableau vivant*. Well, a *tableau mort* to be more accurate. It was theatre. You always liked that cautionary tale. It was for you, Kitty.'

Turns out I should have left my brother in the Bethlem after all. I swallowed dust.

'The dog, little Spark? That was you too, wasn't it?' A twitch in Joey's jaw told the truth.

'And Marnie? Why her?'

Now he looked away. 'That was unfortunate. I was in Emmett Street . . . helping a friend. She recognised me.'

'You mean Marnie saw you posting flyers for the Reverend?'

Joey didn't answer. The chains at his wrists rattled as he brought a thumb to his mouth and brushed his pouting lips. The man standing in front of me was a stranger. I found I didn't have anything more to say to him.

I appealed to the grey coats.

'Water, please.'

One of them looked over my shoulder. I turned to see Vellum at the entrance to the Vinculum. He nodded. The man handed me a large glass bottle. I pushed at the marble stopper and drank deep. The finest champagne wouldn't have tasted so good. I passed the bottle to Sam. He tipped it back, wiped his lips and gave it to me again. In the light of the lanterns set around the floor, I saw that the stubble on his jaw was almost knitting itself to an auburn beard.

Two of Vellum's men, bulging canvas sacks slung over their shoulders, came back through the entrance to the Vinculum. One of them paused.

'It won't take long to clear, sir. Six more of these I'd say.'

'Good.' Vellum sidled at the door. 'I understand that the mechanism is very precise. It must be closed again before the visit later this evening.'

I set the bottle down on the stones. 'Do you mean Kite?'

Vellum nodded. 'Who else?'

'So, this rigmarole is going ahead then?'

I reckoned Gurney's description was about right on that score. I carried on.

'The London Imperial Order will still be created by the Queen this evening in the chapel up top?'

Vellum nodded again. 'And when the investiture is over and the Queen has returned to Windsor, Kite and his brother will take the opportunity to examine the site of the Vinculum. But I will be waiting. I am confident that I will have in my possession something that will destroy them. For nearly twenty-five years, Anthony Carstone has been a malignity at the heart of the State. The only reason the Barons were able to operate as they did was due to his . . . *influence* at the very highest levels. I recall you once used the word "blackmail" to me.'

He let that hang there.

'And now?' I brushed at the bodice of my dress. It must have looked like I was swiping at the dust from lying on the floor.

'Aren't you going to tell her?' Joey came very close to me. He flicked a look of contempt at Vellum and grinned. 'You don't understand, do you, little sister?' He ducked and hissed in my ear. '*We are the treasure.*'

One of the grey coats yanked him away. Vellum stared at us both. His eyes went from Joey to me and then back again. With my hair cropped close we looked very alike. But I wondered who else he was searching for in our features. That was the heart of this. My hand went to my bodice again. Joey was wrong. I understood all right.

Two more grey coats came out into the chamber, hauling sacks behind them.

'We've cleared all the papers, sir.'

'Excellent.' Vellum peered into the Vinculum. 'Take everything to the Sanctuary. We can deal with the rest of the gimcracks later.'

The man dipped his head and crossed to the passageway leading to the steps and the chapel.

Vellum brushed his gloved hands. Very tidy he was. There wasn't a speck of dust on his black coat, and his sleek hair shone in the lamplight. 'It seems your adventure is over, Miss Peck. Allow my men to take you back to The Palace.'

I didn't think that was an offer, exactly.

'This has been a most unexpected twist to our . . . association –' Vellum's grey eyes bored into mine – 'but I imagine no harm has been done.'

'Is that right?' I took Sam's hand in mine. He squeezed tight. He knew what I was keeping hidden.

'Not like the harm done to a girl twenty-two years back?' Vellum quizzed at me.

'A girl who married high and married legal?'

Now he understood. He raised a hand to stop me, but I carried on.

'A girl who had two children, a boy first and a girl in her

belly when her husband tired of her? He was a ripe piece of shit, wasn't he, to do that to *my mother*?'

'That is quite enough, Miss Peck.'

A voice, cut like the finest crystal, came from the passage. Tell truth, I had a lot more to say on the matter, but I stopped as a long shadow fell across the chamber. A tall man came slowly towards me. As he moved into the light, I recognised him. It was the hawk-nosed gent who'd given me a ride in his carriage to the Sanctuary the first time I went looking for Vellum.

He spoke again. 'I do not imagine that anyone present needs to hear this tawdry tale. It is an old, old story.'

'It's something more than that and you know it.' I pulled away from Sam and took a step towards him. 'Look at me. And at my brother there. Who do you see in our faces? I reckon you should take a care. And perhaps you might think about kneeling?'

The man's eyes were hooded beneath the hedge of his brows, but I could feel the force of them. He turned from me and then to Joey.

'It is true then.' He nodded. 'You have them both.'

Vellum caught my eye. He flicked a hand of warning. The quick, slight movement was intended for me. I frowned and sidled at Sam, but his attention was locked on the gent.

'Sir.' Vellum dipped his head in a curt bow. 'Everything is quite in order. We had almost completed our business when you arrived.'

'I heard.' The man gestured at the remaining grey coats ranged around the chamber and drawled again, 'Was it really necessary to bring so many?' I smelt cloves and good cigars. I remembered that from before.

'No matter.' He opened his coat and reached into a pocket. I caught a flash of gold and thought he was taking out a smoke box, but then I realised it was a small pistol. He pointed it direct at me.

Sam stepped sharp between us. He looked at Vellum. 'What the hell is this?'

Vellum swept his hair back from his forehead. 'I do not know. I swear it, Mr Collins.'

'Oh, I believe you do, Jonathan.' The old gent sounded like he was talking to a pet. 'The Ministers of the Shadow Parliament have been watching and waiting. I am sanctioned by the Crown to clear the mess away.'

'You cannot do this.' Vellum's voice was tight and low. 'It is not the protocol agreed.'

'They are insects.' The old man waved the gun at Sam. 'Stand aside.'

Sam didn't budge, but I did. From my bodice I pulled the document that proved my mother's marriage was legal and prior to anything that came after. Her husband was a bigamist, and that was the least of his troubles if the truth came out. I handed the licence to Vellum.

'This is what you need. If he kills me and my brother, you'll still have this. He'll have to shoot you and every person here to keep the secret on that paper hidden away. I don't think your men will allow that.'

I held Vellum's eyes, hoping I was right and willing him to be the man I thought he was. I pointed at the paper. 'Love that cannot be told is not a crime. My mother did no wrong. Her husband, my *father*, he's the villain.'

'Give it to me.' The man swung his pistol towards Vellum.

'That is an order.'

I was gratified to see the grey coats rouse themselves for their master. They likely didn't have an idea of what was happening in front of their eyes, but even they could tell a turd from a muffin.

Vellum stared at the document in his hands. There were smuts of dust on his fine kid gloves now. He shook his head.

'She was to be unharmed. It was agreed.'

'But she *knows*, Jonathan. That is her death warrant. His too.' The man nodded at Sam.

'And what of me?' Joey spoke very softly from the wall.

The old gent snorted. 'You were always doomed. A thief, a murderer, an invert? Any one of those could hang you. The world will not blink at your passing.' He didn't even bother to turn and look at my brother, which was a mistake.

Joey leapt at him. He threw his chained hands over the old man's head and yanked at his neck. I heard the sound of choking as my brother pulled tighter. The man clawed at his collar, trying to free himself from the chains. Then he raised the pistol and levelled it at me.

'No!' Joey's voice echoed off the walls of the chamber. As the gent cocked the trigger, my brother swung him round so the pistol was clamped upright between them. The sound of the shot was muffled by their bodies wrapped tight as lovers.

The pair of them stood there for a moment, eyes wide with horror and surprise. Then they collapsed, a tangle of limbs and blood. The bullet had passed through the side of the old gent's head and into my brother's neck.

'Joey!' I darted across the stones and knelt beside him, taking his hand in mine. He choked as a dark pool formed around him on the floor. He writhed in the dust and stared up at me. I thought there were tears in his wide blue eyes now.

'Ki . . .'

He tried again, but my name died on his lips.

Chapter Forty-six

He is your brother. At the end remember that.

I heard my grandmother's voice tripping from the lips of Madame Toth-Varda as I knelt by Joey's body, holding his hand. And in all the days that followed, I heard it again every time I thought of him and tried to work out whether he died for me, or for himself.

The words came to mind now as I sat at my desk and blotted the sheet in front of me. I signed the letter and tried to muffle the sound of her. Was it a reminder or an accusation?

We'd been a tight pair, my brother and me, for a long time after Nanny Peck and then Ma went away. On the day of our mother's funeral, it was Joey who'd broken the ice in the basin to wash my face. He'd combed my hair, buttoned me into my one good dress, tied the laces on my boots and forced my rigid fingers into Nanny Peck's old woollen gloves. I was barely twelve years old and he was fifteen.

Now he was dead at twenty-one. Joey Peck could have been something special, but it all went sour on him. Or perhaps the truth of it was that *he* went sour?

I don't know whose fault it was. Not really. All I knew was that it was no use crying over something I'd never known. If I thought about family it was Ma, Nanny Peck and Joey, God rest him, who came to mind. Not the woman whose rubbed face was on every coin in my purse. And not Lady Ginger neither.

The past was a treacherous place. Walking there was dangerous. Vellum had made that very clear after we left the

Vinculum with Joey's body sealed inside it. Surrounded by the Barons' treasure deep beneath the Tower of London, you could see it as a fitting place to bury him. I'd never open it again, not for anyone.

We came to what you might call an accommodation two days back, Vellum and me. The gist of it was that I was *never* to speak of the man I now knew to be my father. Not if I valued the lives of everyone I knew.

Besides, Vellum had the proof he needed. It was me who'd given him the marriage licence. I'd put the truth into his hands. In the space for profession, my father had written '*Gentleman*'. Which was a lie.

Wind rattled the panes of my office window. I thought about Vellum, Endymion, Jonathan – whatever he was calling himself today – and his draughty rooms. I folded the paper, sealed it tight and then I went down to the hall.

'Lok?' I called to the basement. A door opened below. I heard the slap of slippers on the stairs.

'Lady?'

Lok bowed. It came to me again, most forceful, that all this Lady business had gone stale a long time back. We were equals in The Palace, a strange new family tied together by the darkness of the past and the promise of the future.

There wasn't time for that chat now, but there would be.

'Can you take this to Fitzy and Jesmond at The Comet, please?' I handed him the note. 'Either of them'll do, but Fitzy would be best. He'll know straight off. I'd go myself, but I'm expecting visitors.'

Lok bowed again and took the note from me.

'And when you come back, join us. We'll be in the parlour.'

We went to the door together. I gathered Nanny Peck's shawl around my shoulders as I watched him make his way to the end of the row. Did she know the truth of it, I wondered? The old girl had always treated Joey like he was precious, but I always thought it was because she was partial to him. She was good to me too, mind. But Joey now, he was always her little prince.

I gripped the shawl tight around me as the wind came strong. It whipped Lok's plait into the air and his tunic fluttered about him. The pattern broidered in the dark silk of his gown glinted in the sunlight like the sheen of feathers.

At the corner he stopped as a man turned into the passage. The Beetle dipped his head in greeting and the two of them spoke. I knew he'd be the first. You could set a fob by Marcus Telferman. He looked up and, just for a second, the sun turned his specs to golden coins.

I raised a hand to welcome him and went back into the hallway. Sam, Lucca and Peggy were waiting for me on the stairs.

'They're coming.' I held the door for the Beetle and turned back to the hall as Tan Seng reached the top step from the basement. I wondered when was the last time nearly all the witnesses to my mother's marriage had gathered together in one room.

*

'It was dangerous, Lady. For you . . . and for your mother and brother as well as for us.'

The Beetle sidled at Pardieu, who was pulling at the knees of his breeches, plucking the dusty fabric into little tents and letting them fall again. I opened the window to let the fug of naphtha escape from the room.

'Silence was our defence.' Telferman stared at the rug. Tan Seng studied his hands folded in his lap. His mark, a beautiful Chinese figure of dashed and sloping lines, was on that document too. Along with the looping signature of Ramesh Das.

'*Silenzio.*' Lucca nodded. 'It is not a secret I would want to keep.'

I went to the couch and sat down. 'After today we will never talk of it again. That's a promise.'

'But how did the marriage happen at all?' Sam, who was resting his elbow on the mantel, took up a china shepherdess, another of my grandmother's unexpected dainties, and studied the girl's pretty painted face. 'Lady Ginger was a lot of things, but she was not a fool. I cannot imagine her agreeing.'

'Ah, but she did not.' Pardieu sat back. 'Your mother was quite . . . quite determined, Lady.'

It was hard to imagine that. 'Determined' was never a word that came to mind when I thought of Ma. 'Melancholy', that was one for a start; 'fey', that was another, along with 'lost'. Now I knew why.

Pardieu sucked at his front teeth. 'She tricked us, all of us, into attending the ceremony at St Anne's. She also invited Mr Seng here and Mr Das to ensure that there were more witnesses than is usual. As I remember they also signed the document, as insurance.'

I glanced at Tan Seng and thought about the story on the bowl.

Anyone who knew of the marriage was turned into a night creature, to remind them of the darkness of the grave.

It came to me that Pardieu was the hare, the butterflies were Lok and Tan Seng, and Marcus Telferman really was the Beetle.

The only one missing from the china was Ramesh Das. And he wasn't here now.

It was deliberate. I had a meeting near Bell Wharf Stairs later in the day and I had it in mind to stop by and tell him in person and in private about Rufus Carstone. Vellum had given me his word that Kite and his brother would hang, and I didn't doubt him, but I felt I owed Ramesh the truth and perhaps something more – *justice*.

'It's romantic.' Peggy shifted in her chair and smoothed the loose folds of her wrapper. She was too big now for any of her dresses. 'Just imagine. He must have loved her very much.'

I was minded of the girl with her beau on Tower Green and of King Henry's mercy with the swordsman.

'I don't think that lot go much for romance, Peg.' I tapped Pardieu's arm. 'This ceremony. It was real, wasn't it?'

He nodded. 'Indeed it was. The young curate who offici- ated was about to take up a missionary posting. I believe he died shortly afterwards in Africa. But that is of little conse- quence; by the time we realised why we had been called to the church, it was too late. Your . . . *father* was most insistent too.'

The Beetle cleared his throat. 'He even signed his Christian names in full, Albert Edward, if not his titles. He thought it was a charade. He called us "exotics". I believe he thought us all to be people from the halls, actors. It was a great jest to him, Lady, an adventure in the gutters, until he found out that two of the witnesses summoned by your mother were men of pro- fessions. By then it was too late.'

'*Too late, too late. Late, late, late* . . .' Jacobin started up in his corner. I went to the cage and took up the broidered cover, think- ing to silence him. He tilted his head to one side and peered at me.

'*Pretty girl.*' He bobbed on the perch and repeated the unusual compliment. I paused, surprised to hear a civil tongue in his beak. He studied me with a beady eye and blinked. What would have happened if it hadn't been for Jacobin and what he'd heard over the years? I draped the cover over my arm and went back to the couch.

'How come the licence ended up in the Vinculum?' I folded the cover to a square and looked at Sam. The pair of us had tried to find an answer to that as we sat in the dust, the document spread out on the floor in front of us.

'I cannot tell.' The Beetle frowned. 'I always thought it was in the final package your grandmother asked me to give you.'

'You didn't look then?'

'Certainly not.' He seemed stung by the accusation. 'Those papers were private and were always meant for J— *You*, Lady.' I knew he was about to say Joey. Before she learned the truth about him, my grandmother had meant to pass everything to my brother, not me. I was a second choice.

'Besides,' the Beetle went on, his voice a whisper, 'such knowledge would have been dangerous.'

Sam came to sit beside me. 'Remember Occam's Razor, Kitty?' He rested a hand on my knee. 'Perhaps the answer is simple. The Vinculum was the one place where that licence could be hidden from those who wanted it most.'

From the corner of my eye I caught Peggy arching her back. I turned to her sharp.

'Peg?'

She gasped. 'It hurts.' A puddle flowed from beneath the hem of her wrapper.

Dr Pardieu rose. 'It seems that I am here at a most opportune moment. We must take Mrs Tewson upstairs immediately. I will need hot water and clean towels.'

'But it's too soon.' Peggy was breathless with pain.

'Nonsense,' Pardieu smiled. 'When I examined you a few days ago, I knew your time was very close.'

I sidled at Lucca and then I went to Peggy's side. 'He's coming then?'

'Looks like it.' She smiled weakly and winced as I helped her from the chair. Just as we reached the door, Lok appeared on the landing. He ran forward, clucking over his friend like a tiny hen. I had a feeling that he'd be more useful in a birthing room than me.

The Beetle sniffed and polished his glasses. 'Perhaps I should . . . Well, that is to say, I still have many affairs to attend to on your behalf, Lady. Matters pertaining to the disbursement of your grandmother's estate. I really should . . .'

Peggy gave a low moan and clutched at the door frame with one hand. The fingers of the other dug into my arm.

'You'll be fine, Peg.' I whipped about. 'That's right, isn't it?'

Pardieu opened his black bag and delved inside. 'Mrs Tewson is a healthy young woman. I have no doubt that she will be delivered of a strong and healthy child.'

*

'For the time being he's being held at the Angevin Club along with his brother, although no one apart from a select few know they're related. It's being given out that the pair of them have contracted an unusual and highly infectious disease. Vellum tells me that Schalk's gone missing. He's got people watching the ports.'

Ramesh Das folded his hands together and I caught a glimpse of the snake at his wrist. I sat forward.

'There's going to be a trial of some sort, eventually, nothing public. In the meantime, the brothers are being watched round the clock, but not by doctors.'

He nodded slowly. He didn't say a word. A fire blazed in his deep-set amber eyes.

'I thought you should know.' I set my tea glass down on the tray. 'Rufus Carstone is in room twelve. On the third floor.'

I'd lost track of the time at Bell Wharf Stairs. I'd had a lot to tell Ramesh Das about the man who'd killed his sister and questions of my own that he didn't quite answer. As I'd sat with him in his beautiful, sweet-smelling room overlooking the Thames, I thought I understood it all. I was back on that hill, seeing the river from beginning to end. Watching all the filth tumbling out into the sea.

Before I left, I told him that Peggy had delivered a fine baby girl, just as the clock in the parlour back at The Palace tumbled out its pretty tune and struck five times. I'd left her cradling her child, lost in amazement and a fierce joy that would likely never leave her. Lok and Lucca were at her bedside. I won't deny it, the pair of them were a deal more competent around a newborn than I was. When I slipped away none of them noticed.

Ramesh Das gave me a parcel of herbs and chai and words of good will for Peggy, then as I went to the door he called me back and pressed something small and hard into my hands.

'The obstacles are no longer in your path, Lady.' He smiled. 'The way is clear for you, whichever path you choose.'

Now, as I stood outside a familiar door, I took out the little metal figure of the dancing elephant. Mocking green eyes slanted up at me; the jewels glinted in the moonlight, slicing down between the tall, close-packed houses.

Whichever path you choose.

I turned Ganesha between my fingers and wondered what Ramesh Das had meant.

It was late by the time I got to Schoolhouse Lane. I wondered if she'd be too far gone to help me. It was a long time since I'd been here last. A bell chimed and I counted. It was nine o'clock. She probably wasn't even awake, let alone sober.

The moon floating in a puddle by the peeling door looked like a bowl of milk set out for a cat. I knocked loud and waited. When no one came I tried again, even though I didn't have much hope that she'd be in a state to answer.

I was wrong. The door opened to a crack and a fug of gin billowed into the lane. A cat slipped out through the narrow gap and wound itself around my ankles.

'Who's out there, now?'

Pouched eyes squinted at me through the slit.

'Ah, it's yourself, is it? Fitzpatrick told me you'd come knocking. I've had the trapeze set ready all day.'

Madame Celeste opened the door wider and half a dozen of her scrawny cats escaped into the lane. She watched them dart into the shadows and sighed. 'They'll come back. They always do.'

She stood aside to let me in. It was a struggle to pass her corpulence in the shabby passage. My eyes went to the faded circus bills plastering the stairwell leading up to the cavern of an attic where a swing hung twenty foot from the floor.

There was a time when Madame Celeste had been a dazzling aerial artiste, but that was at least half a century ago. The girl on the bills was lithe and young and soared through the air like a painted angel; the woman puffing away behind me resembled a walrus draped in a curtain. As I turned the corner at the first landing, the stink of cat piss came strong and familiar.

'I'll tell you this, Kitty Peck.' I felt a sharp prod in the buttock. 'You still have my body. You're a natural, so you are.'

Finale

The London Evening News: 5th October 1881
TAKEN TOO SOON

It is with deep regret that this newspaper must report the sudden death of General Arthur George Denderholm, Bt., lately returned from distinguished service in India.

It was intended that the General would continue to serve Her Majesty's Government in the newly created post, Director of the Imperial London Agency, but without the benefit of General Denderholm's guiding hand, this venture has been postponed until such time as a figure of similar wisdom, experience and reputation can be found to take his place.

I smoothed out the blue page on the table in front of the mirror, careful to keep it clear from the pots of paint and wax I'd been daubing on my face. There was a deal more about the General's fine character and notable military prowess, although the detail was thinner than you might expect for someone who'd been distinguishing himself in India for more than forty years. It was the end that interested me most.

. . . came to be in the General's room is a mystery. The London Zoological Society has confirmed to this correspondent that none of its venomous

specimens has escaped. However, Dr Cornelius Pardieu, expert in tropical maladies, who attended the scene, confirmed that the General's body bore the unmistakable marks of snake bites. The possibility that a deadly cobra is loose on the streets of St James's cannot be discounted.

And I never knew his name was Cornelius. I smiled and looked up. The girl watching me in the glass seemed like a regular bangtail with her rouged cheeks, arched brows and pouting red lips. But if you was to be standing fifty foot beneath her, the limes firing like a furnace, she'd look like an angel.

It wouldn't be long now. Any moment Fitzy would come knocking. I breathed in and pulled the satin ribbons of the golden corset as tight as I could. I wished Peggy was with me, but she had more important things to do these days.

The clipping from *The Evening News* had come in a package with a letter from Vellum but he didn't mention it. I reckoned it was included just to let me *know* he *knew*. On the face of it, he was writing to wish me success tonight, but there was more. An offer.

I read the last page again. Vellum's script was neat and elegant as his person.

. . . I understand that the bulk of your grandmother's estate has been disbursed by your man of law, Marcus Telferman, and that your full attention will be focused on the three music halls, known as The Carnival, The Comet and The Gaudy, these being the only part of your

grandmother's legacy with which you wish to continue an interest. In addition, I have been informed of your plans to expand and improve The London Pictorial News, with Mr Collins newly installed as Editor.

While I must applaud your loyalty, I would ask you to consider the unusual position in which you find yourself. You are now a person of interest to the Crown and, as such, may experience unwelcome attention. Indeed, anyone associated with you will be regarded with <u>curiosity</u>. I cannot imagine that your friends Mr Collins and Mr Fratelli will be easy in such circumstances.

In short, your life will never be simple again, no matter how much you might wish that to be so. In the package accompanying this letter, I have provided documentation to enable you and your friends to travel to Canada and to new lives under new names. I would not be surprised or disappointed if you decided to take this opportunity.

However, there is another offer I wish to put to you. You are a uniquely gifted woman, Miss Peck. A person with your talents would be <u>rewarded and protected</u> by the Crown if those abilities were to be utilised for the purposes of Empire. I asked you once if you would be willing to work with me. I ask that question again and offer you a wider stage for your gifts.

If you wish to discuss my proposal, I will await your communication in the personal announcements column of <u>The London Pictorial News</u>.

J

I was about to rub chalk into the palms of my hands but instead I took up that little metal statue of the dancing elephant and quizzed at him.

Whichever path you choose.

Was that what Ramesh Das had meant when he gave me his great-grandfather's token?

I reached for my purse and took out a coin. I flipped it and caught it in my palm. I didn't look for a moment, but when I did, my grandmother's copper face glowed in the lamplight.

There was a light tap on the door. Lucca stepped into the flower-filled dressing room. Truly, it was like Covent Garden in here tonight. He handed me a large cloth-bound parcel and watched as I unwrapped a pair of gorgeous wings – real feathers painted silver and gold and mounted on a delicate network of arcing wires.

'Do you remember, Fannella?'

'Of course I do! They're beautiful! Thank you!'

I leapt from the dressing table, flung my arms around him and kissed him on both cheeks. In the Italian manner.

'Any other man might be jealous!' Sam leaned against the door. I winked at him over Lucca's shoulder and blew him a kiss.

'You're not any other man, Sam Collins.' I stepped away from Lucca and twirled before the pair of them.

'What do you say?'

Sam smiled. 'I'd say *The Pictorial* has a scoop on its hands, Kitty. After tonight The Comet will be the talk of London.'

He bowed low and caught sight of Vellum's letter, which had slipped from the dressing table when I'd unwrapped the wings. I hadn't had a chance to talk to him about it. He took it up and scanned the elegant script. He frowned and began to read it properly.

'Sam, I—'

The door swung open. The fug of liquor and tobacco rolled into the room. I heard the crowd thumping and calling out in the hall. Even here in the dressing room, I could feel their stamping thrum through the boards.

Fitzy raised a cigar and nodded. 'You'll do, Ma'am. Very nice, so you are.' He sucked, puffed out his cheeks and blew out a ring of smoke that lingered over his head like a filthy halo.

'The cage is set ready. The hands are at the sides with the chains and the ropes. You could go up there every night until the end of the century and they wouldn't tire of you. Jesmond reckons there are five hundred punters out there tonight. We had to bar the doors in the end. Never done that before, not even at The Gaudy.'

He sucked on that cigar again. 'Hot for it, they are, all of them burning themselves to a cinder for the return of The Limehouse Linnet.'

Epilogue

The bright ribbon on Peggy's hat danced in the wind. She was easy to spot in the crowd pressing at the rail. That red-and-white silk was like a bleedin' flag fluttering over her head. Maybe that's why she wore it. All that time we spent in the halls together sewing sequins on shit taught us a few things about getting yourself noticed.

She cradled little Kitty in one arm and raised her free hand to wave so frantic I thought she might do herself a mischief. I waved back and blinked down hard to stop tears from glassing the view.

Folding back the veil on her straw, Peggy pushed forward. I saw the nod of her head and the movement of her lips, but I couldn't make out a word she said above the thudding chug of the tender as it moved away from the quay. It wasn't just the engine – all around us people were calling out to their family and their friends. The further the tender went out the more they had to say. They couldn't touch their loved ones now; the only thing they could reach them with was their voices.

You'd think that setting off for a new life was a cause for celebration, but most of us were crying. Along with hope there was a deal of misery stirring the air. An old girl standing next to me was running a rosary through her fingers. The way she counted through the black glass beads, her head bobbing up and down like a sparrow feeding on spilt grain, put me in mind of Nanny Peck.

The luggage had gone across first. A life packed away in four leather trunks – good ones from Zedelman's on Burdett Road – had bobbed across the harbour to the RMS *Terpsichore* three hours back and now it was the turn of the passengers. I was glad of Peggy's hat. As the frothing gap between the tender and the oily stones of Liverpool quay opened wider than the Thames at Wapping, I could still see the flapping of that red-and-white ribbon marking her place.

Marking an end and a beginning.

'Are you sure you've made the right choice, Kitty?'

I nodded and squeezed the hand caught fast in mine as a pillar of smoke bloomed from the ship's funnel.

'I just hope *she* has, Sam.'

I bit down hard on my lower lip. It was only now Peggy was going that I realised how much I'd miss her. It had seemed such an easy thing to do to offer her Vellum's tickets. Easy for my conscience anyway. When I looked into her daughter's eyes it was Dan I saw looking back at me. That was a very good thing and a very bad thing.

I waved so hard my hand nearly flew off my wrist.

'She'll come back, Kitty.'

I nodded, not taking my eyes off the ribbon. 'She might, Sam, but I reckon once she's safely in Canada with her cousin, Peggy'll build herself a new life and new family.' I tugged at Lucca's sleeve. He was still craning and waving at the tender.

'Come on, we can't stand here all day. We need to catch the midday train back to London. You've got a newspaper to edit, Sam. I've got a cage to fill, two theatres to run and one to build again. And Lucca, you've got an appointment with Mr Wild at the museum to keep. An offer like that don't come around often.'

The three of us linked arms as we turned and pushed through the crowd. I swiped at the soot in my eyes. Liverpool was a filthy place, worse than London if you asked my opinion on the matter.

'Kitty, this meeting with . . . Jonathan tomorrow . . .' Sam quizzed at me, his brown eye sharp beneath an arched brow.

'I'll deal with it.' Of an instant, I pushed back my bonnet, twisted about and planted a kiss on his lips. 'Besides, it does a girl good to keep her options open.'

Acknowledgements

Warning: contains spoilers!

. . . And so we draw the curtain.

Thanks to everyone who has followed Kitty's adventures and exploits though all four books. I have loved your messages of support and your passionate investment in the lives of these characters. I hope the ending has left you satisfied and perhaps wondering what comes next.

If this is the first time you've ventured into deepest, darkest Limehouse and you are intrigued, do read the previous books to find out how *everything* led to a locked chamber beneath the Tower of London.

In order, they are Kitty Peck and . . .

The Music Hall Murders
The Child of Ill Fortune
The Daughter of Sorrow

This year marks the 200th anniversary of the birth of Queen Victoria. I have greatly enjoyed playing with the fact that Kitty's progress has always been shadowed by two powerful women, Lady Ginger and the 'Widow of Windsor'.

Family, in all its guises, has always been at the heart of this saga.

My mother's family were tenants in Limehouse in the second half of the nineteenth century. They lived in St Ann Street, which appears in dark blue on social reformer Charles Booth's famous *Maps Descriptive of London Poverty* (1898–99). This colour classification reveals that my family were poor. Dark blue denotes: 'Very poor. Casual. Chronic want.'

This was not quite the bottom of the ant heap but I take little comfort from the fact the street immediately next to theirs is shown in black: 'Lowest class. Vicious. Semi Criminal.'

Like so many who lived in the East End in the Victorian era, many of my antecedents were immigrants, mostly from Ireland. They lived alongside people who came to London, during the era of Empire, from all parts of the world. In the books I have tried to reflect that rich cultural stew.

Beyond my own family story, I looked to the fascinating and often troubling world of music hall to create a second family for Kitty. Anyone who fondly imagines that *The Good Old Days* – a creaky TV variety show running from the 1950s to the early 1980s – bore even a fleeting resemblance to the real thing would be shocked by reality. I have to say that my nan,* Hannah Kelly, absolutely adored this programme, which is odd, considering that as a child (she was born in Limehouse in 1895) she often visited the real thing!

Writing this series has been a joy. I have taken gleeful pleasure in snatching at the tropes of Victorian melodrama, throwing them into the pot and stirring vigorously until they are turned inside out and upside down. This is a heightened world of artifice, theatricality and the penny dreadful – but just occasionally I hope I've dropped in a scene or a phrase that breaks through the fourth wall to halt a reader in their tracks.

* Where have all the 'nans' gone?

As usual, my thanks go to many people, the 'family' that made it possible for me to write and encouraged me at every step.

I'm so grateful to my editor, the wonderfully perceptive Libby Marshall, and to all the team at Faber and Faber. Huge thanks also to Tamsin Shelton for her willingness to suspend scholarly belief and to throw herself so wholeheartedly into Kitty's topsy-turvy world.

A special mention for my agent, Eugenie Furniss, for her enthusiasm, support and wise counsel.

A shout out to friends, Lisa Rodger, Frances Parsons, Leah Wells and Daisy Coulam; to my dad, John Cain, who gamely reads every book even though he'd much rather be reading something by Bernard Cornwell. And to Alison McClary, Felicity Martin, Pippa Evans, Sophie Martin and *everyone* at The Society for the Protection of Ancient Buildings who put up with me.

As ever, my greatest thanks go to my husband, Stephen, whose belief in me is *infinitesimally* more precious than Queen Victoria's Koh-i-noor diamond.

Kate Griffin
May 2019